LILY

Captive to the Dark
Special Edition 1
Alaska Angelini

LILY

Captive to the Dark
Special Edition 1
Alaska Angelini
Copyright © 2014 by Alaska Angelini

ISBN: 9781508546504

All Rights Reserved

Dedication

To amazing author, Allyson Young. Your insight and critique means more to me than you will ever know. I can never truly express how much it means to have your support. Thank you so much for everything you do.

Also, to my girls. My Sexy Subs (AKA: Boss Ass Bitches). You girls rock my world! Nadia, thank you for all of the amazing graphics, and Dee, for your ability to create videos that bring me to tears. To see my stories come to life in your eyes moves me so much.

And to all of you who are constantly sharing my teasers, voting in contests, and promoting me in any way you can…THANK YOU! Seriously, you have my heart. I can't thank you enough.

Last, but definitely not least. MJ. Miranda Sue, lol. I love you, girl. You have my back when I need it the most and you're always there for me. Your friendship is something I know will last a lifetime. I look forward to many, *many* more years of having you by my side. Not just as my PA, but as the dear friend you are. You're an amazingly beautiful person and I'm lucky to have you in my life.

Prologue
Lily

I never had an enemy quite like nostalgia. The comforting blanket that cloaked around me, trying to change my mind, had me battling myself more than I ever had to physically fight anything in my past. I could so easily look back and let myself believe that everything happened for a reason. That fate had caused me to be taken and forever changed so the result would help me grow as a person. But in reality, I'd been a captive — a sex slave who had been through hell and yet thought herself in love with her Master.

Even now, my heart ached for the man I thought I'd been meant for. It was a lie. A twisted, coping mechanism I'd forced myself to accept in order to survive. At least, that's how my shrink described it. Nostalgia…that bitch continued to trick me into believing the four months I spent in Afghanistan wasn't so bad. It made me want to return. Want…*him.*

I refused. I'd forever deny these feelings that destroy me.

The things I witnessed, undergone…lived. They would be seared into my memory just as deep as the scars that cover my body from the girls his family tortured. So many, and nothing either of us could do unless we wanted to die. Yes…there were times I had wanted death as a way to erase what I'd seen from helping those girls. If it weren't for the strength I'd been forced to portray from the beginning, I might have been able to disappear from this world. But it wasn't meant to be. Once my Master got ahold of me, he refused to let me be weak. He'd made me fight from the beginning, and showed me how much I could love it. How we could disappear from the lives we'd been trapped in and lose ourselves in each other. I longed for those moments the most. Especially now, as I stared out the dark windows of my lonely penthouse. My brother, Slade's old penthouse.

Flashes of memories blinded me like they always did when I finally left the office and came home. So clearly, I could still see the details of my abduction, as if I'd watched a movie of myself being lured out of the nightclub by a woman insisting on my help. The lights of downtown San Francisco blurred in my mind while I helped the staggering blonde from Vixen's main entrance toward the parking garage across the street. The pop-playing, upscale establishment sat atop a luxurious building, the last few floors covered by fog as I glanced up to where my friends were.

I should have never left Samantha's side. If it weren't for the woman nearly passed out on the bathroom floor, insisting I take her to her car so she could get her phone to call her dad, I probably wouldn't have been taken. But someone else would have. I couldn't bear the thought of another girl going through what I had.

Back then, I'd been too nice. All I wanted was to please people. That had been my biggest mistake.

Not anymore.

The sound of the brakes squealing from the road behind us barely registered as my sole focus was on not letting the older girl fall. She was heavier than I imagined and I knew it had to do with her height. She looked like a model —blonde, tall, amazing green eyes. She was beautiful and shitfaced drunk, crying over her boyfriend cheating. All the while, I told her everything would be alright. How stupid I had been.

Those had been my last moments as an innocent girl. An arm locked around my waist and a leather bound hand slammed over my mouth. A scream didn't even register until the SUV's door slammed shut and the force of the acceleration jerked me back. When the woman began laughing and spouting off orders to the man holding me down, I knew I'd been played.

I fought against the man with everything I was capable of, but it hadn't been enough. Back then, I'd been weak in that way of life, too. They'd taken me, put me in a room full of other girls and sold me, but not before the real damage was done.

Tears collected in my eyes as my fingers pushed against the glass. I momentarily came back to the present, but the past wouldn't be stopped tonight. There would be no more escaping what I'd spent weeks trying to push away.

Master.

The moment our stares met, my whole world stopped. I'd never seen a more handsome man. Dark hair, lightly tanned skin. His eyes...they were so close to the color of the sun. Orange mixed with gold, yet surrounded by a dark green. The shade mesmerized me. Even considering the distance that separated us, they seemed to glow. I stood there with my hands clutched together, trying to stop shaking. Nothing was working. I was scared. Nervous as to why these people in this fancy house would want me. Nothing made sense.

Whack!

The brute force of the back of a hand connecting with my cheek left me almost positive that my eye had somehow exploded. Colors flickered and mixed with bright lights. My body crumbled to the floor from pain and shock. I couldn't even comprehend what had happened until the voice of

the older man standing beside me came though, an unrecognizable accent confusing me even more. I could barely make out his words due to exhaustion.
"Did I tell you to look at my son?"
Before I could answer, multiple kicks to my stomach had me curling up on the marble floor. I didn't miss the stranger walking forward in my peripheral vision, or how he had his fists balled up at his side.
"I asked you a question, slave. Did I give you permission to look at my son?"
All I could do was shake my head as I fought not to get sick. Pain seared my scalp as I was jerked to stand. Although my stare wanted to return to the man watching at the far side of the room, I kept my focus on the floor. Raped by multiple men, surviving off stale bread and water for the last few days, I knew when not to be stupid.
"Look at her, Zain. She already learns. She will do you well."
My gazed snapped up in time to see his blurry, shocked expression, but I quickly let it fall back to the marble. Throbbing pulsed in my head and my heart ached with the weird twist of terror and desperation. All I wanted was to wake up from this nightmare.
"Me? What am I supposed to do with a slave? I have responsibilities. The last thing I need

to do is care for a...girl. Fuck, how old is she, Father?"

"Not of consequence. You'll take her. She's yours. A gift for all of your hard work."

American. The son sure sounded like it. So, how was this man his father? Although they shared a slight resemblance, I would have never pinned them for relatives if they hadn't spoken of the connection. And the son wasn't young. Maybe thirty, from what I could tell. Possibly younger, by a year or two.

"Come." The growled command had me fleeing from the father as fast as I could with a throbbing side. As we swept through the large home, I tried to take in everything. And not the expensive vases or golden statues off in the distance. Escape was my main focus. The reality of fleeing disappeared as I took in the guards that stood post throughout the large space. They looked out of place, dirty in the sparkling interior.

Stairs showed in the distance, but we turned down a dark hall until we reached the end.

"You'll stay here. If you leave this room, they'll kill you." His distinct eyes rooted me to the floor as he pushed the wooden barrier open. "They'll cut off your head where you stand. Don't disobey me or do anything stupid. Leaving here is impossible. Trust me," he said, lowly.

With that, he ushered me inside and locked us in. The palace we'd just been in almost seemed a dream in contrast to the room that surrounded us. A bed sat on the cement floor in the far corner. The walls were bare except for some chains mounted to the top of one. It looked like a cell.

Was this what my life had come to?

Involuntarily, I edged back to the door. "Is this my room?" The strength I'd displayed was disappearing as my new life was became apparent.

"Our room now. This was mine."

My head shook at his words. Our...no...

"Send me home. My brother is rich. He'll pay you whatever you want. Please." My knees nearly gave out at my surge forward. I stopped a few feet away, half tempted to sink to the ground and beg.

He laughed. "Did you not see where you are? Do you really think I need money?"

"I see this," I gestured, cautiously. "Your father has the money. Not you. I'll make you a millionaire if that's what you want. Just help me get out of here. Please?"

Again, he laughed. "You think because of this," he said, waving his hand around, "that I don't have money? You have a lot to learn. Bribery will get you nowhere but killed here. I suggest you not do it again. Especially not with anyone else, slave."

"Lily," I snapped, growing angry. "I'm no one's slave." The word disgusted me. Slavery was over. Everyone was equal. At least, in my eyes.

"Lily," he repeated, cocking his head, a smile edging his lips. I took a step back at his narrowed expression. There was something there I didn't like. Something...scarier than the man who'd just used me as a punching bag. "Such a pretty flower. But you're not pretty."

My mind all but stopped at his rudeness and I temporarily forgot what my intuition had been warning me of. "I don't give a shit what you think of me. As long as you help me get out of here, that's all that matters. Besides, you're not very attractive yourself. You're probably nothing but a spoiled, rich, pansy ass...son of a criminal."

His eyebrow rose in what looked to be surprise, but faded as rage took the prominent role. "Who do you think you're talking to? You think you know me?"

The stranger was on me so fast, I didn't have time to prepare myself. Panic and visions of the attack from my rapists surged to the forefront and my arms were already swinging.

"Get off!" I screamed, planting my palm against his cheek to push his face further from mine. My feet kicked as I was picked up and spun toward the bed. It only had me struggling even harder.

"Fight all you want. It's not going to change your situation. You're mine now, Lily, and you're going to learn my rules real fast." I was rotated and put across his lap, stomach down, like a child. The *robe was lifted and I tried to twist in his grasp. Pressure from his forearm pushed into the middle of my back, leaving me rooted to his thighs. My toes searched for some sort of leverage, but I was too short to reach the floor.*

"You'll learn these rules and obey my commands or else you're not going to like what happens when you fuck up. I can't have you disobeying here. I may have a hell of a lot of pull, but I won't be around at all times. If you don't want something worse happening to you, you'll do as I say."

Whack! Heat scorched my ass and my head flew up, both from the pain and his words. "Rule one. Simplest rule of them all. Obey every single command I give you. I don't care what it is. Your life depends on it. Understood?"

My life...was it really my life anymore?

Whack! Whack! Whack!

The last had me sobbing.

"I said, understood? You better hope this time you answer."

I nodded, a cry breaking through as fatigue kicked in full force. "I'll only obey your commands on how to act. Anything else..." It was almost impossible to swallow past the lump in my throat.

"You'll obey everything," he stressed. "No matter what that is." Whack! "Rule two. I'll provide a wrap. You are to cover your face outside of this

room from here on out. Within these walls is a world you can't even imagine. No one is to know what you look like. If they've already seen you, I want the memory to fade. Rape, Lily. Use that as your reason to conceal. You're too beautiful, not pretty, but beautiful," he emphasized, "and I don't want you catching anyone's attention. Do you hear me? This is for your safety. Agree."

Whack!

Rape. I was nodding before he even finished.

"Last rule and just as important as the first." I was spun over, the robe pooling in my lap as he settled me to sit on my throbbing ass. "Never lie to me. Ever. About anything. Fear of admission will fail in comparison to the punishment of a lie." His fingers gripped my cheek, his thumb pushing in to angle my face toward him. "Now, answer my questions honestly. How old are you?"

I sniffled past the tears that involuntarily came. "Nineteen."

"Young," he breathed out. "But not as young as I thought. Did they rape you before you were brought over?"

My body stiffened and I couldn't stop the caving of my shoulders as the tears grew heavier. He didn't appear to need my answer to know the truth.

"Were you a virgin? Did they use protection?"

All I could do was fight to catch my breath.
I wasn't sure why he cared or where the sudden
softness of his tone had come from, but I clung to it
in hopes that I could change his mind on helping me
escape. "Yes, to both."
"How many men hurt you?"
The tick in his jaw tightening off and on had
my brain kicking back to attention. The memory
made me shudder. "Four. They...took turns."
Slowly, his head nodded and he licked his
lips as he kept his stare fixed on mine. "You may not
want this, but it's done. We are each other's and the
only way around that is death on one of our parts.
To give you away is an insult to my father. As much
as I hate him, you're safer with me." His hand
hesitantly came forward, tucking my hair behind my
ear. "I've never had anything belong to me before.
Or anyone," he said, moving in closer. "For you, my
gift, I'll find out who your rapists were and I will kill
them. You're mine now. Nobody hurts what's mine.
You're going to learn that very fast. Unfortunately,
you're going to learn a lot of other things you're not
going to like."

And I had. My master was both kind and
cruel. A lethal combination for the girl looking for a
hero and the woman I'd been forced to become.

16

Chapter 1
Zain

"Did you think I'd let you get away with what you've done? All those girls, dead, broken."

The smell of sweat, sex, and expensive liquor assaulted my senses, making the hate I had for my uncle come to a boiling point in my veins. My fist tightened in his hair and I pushed the tip of the angled blade deeper into the top of his neck. He was silent, but I didn't expect him to beg for his life. He had too much pride for that. Instead, a grunt followed as he turned his body to try to break my hold.

"Your father will know it was you. You won't get away with this. He'll kill you like he did your whore mother."

Blood soaked into the collar of his robe and I pushed in deeper. He spoke Arabic. I refused to in the moment. English had always been my primary and although I could speak four different languages, I stuck to what spoke of home. Of America. A land that had been stolen from me at the tender age of eight. Stolen, kidnapped to live with my real father. Not the one my mother had married and tried to pass off as my dad. Maybe I'd always known Jeff wasn't my blood, but I loved him as if he had been. Their deaths had broken my childhood. Turned me from an innocent little boy into an angry kid who longed for revenge. My rebirth landed me in years of beatings and training. I took everything, embraced the evil man I'd been made into, letting the horrors I saw become ammunition for the day I could put an end to it all.

Amir saw me as his successor and I allowed it.

"My mother was smart to hide from that bastard. If you think I'm going to let him get away with what he did, what he's *done*, you're stupider than I thought. Taking me and turning me in to his own personal killer was the biggest mistake he ever made."

"Wrong." Another sound came from his mouth as he tried to pull his head further away from my knife. "He wanted what was best for you. You're blood, Zain. You're an Amari. You can't escape that."

"Watch me." His blood poured over my hand as I drove the blade home and let his lifeless body fall to the floor, not far from the slave he'd raped and beaten to death. Shuffling outside his room didn't give me time to contemplate what I should do. The flight back to the US would allow me to process my next move. Right now, I had to get back to San Francisco. Back to Lily and the life I'd created outside of the one I was trying to cut ties with. If...I ever could. Even if I killed my other two uncles and my father, there were still people who knew who I was. I might never be safe. Not without some sort of inside help.

Knocking on the door had my head snapping in that direction. I eased through the window, onto the roof, being sure to keep my steps light. The security was lacking and I knew I could take care of myself when it came to any of his four guards, but I didn't want to waste the time on having to.

More knocking faded into the background as I kept low and eased from the roof. The mile run back to my car didn't take long when all I had was my slave in my thoughts. Lily consumed me, made me ache to be by her side. It was almost impossible to focus on driving when all I could see were flashes of her eyes. Of her lips. I missed her more than I could even begin to describe and I was here for her. For the promise I'd made so long ago. Had I been able to, I would have taken care of my past months prior. Years, even. But death didn't sit well with my family and the first caused more problems than I could handle on my own. Now that my time had come, I was left with little choice. Safety was key, and I was trying like hell to make it back alive.

Ringing filled the interior just as I pulled into the parking area of the airport. My mouth twisted as I looked down at my phone. I was so close. My father's name on the Caller ID had me reaching for it. It was crucial that I answered, regardless of whether I wanted to.

"Hello, Father." I kept my tone bored, neutral like I always did concerning Amir.

"You haven't left yet."

I took in the clunker I was sitting in. I knew the car wasn't being tracked. "Not yet. I'm waiting for my plane now. Why, what's going on?"

"Tel called. Your uncle is dead."

"Dead? How?"

Silence. I cringed at not asking which uncle. Had he caught that?

"They're going to get back to me." He let out a deep breath. "First your uncle Samir, now…this. I don't like it. After you finish the finalization of the next shipment, you're coming home. That's an order." I wanted so badly to ask if Adul or Saul would be there when I returned. Adul was a given, but Saul wasn't. He came and went as he pleased. I'd half expected to see him when I'd arrived at my father's to go over the details of the new shipment, but he evaded me. Knew, whether or I gave any indication or not, that I wanted him dead. Had Adul not been at my father's side the entire time, I would have killed him today, too.

I let his last words filter back through. *You're coming home. That's an order.* Home. Because he knew I could figure this mystery out, or so he could kill me himself?

"Absolutely. It shouldn't take long. Maybe a week. Two, tops."

"A week. Make it happen."

The line disconnected and I closed my eyes. If I were smart, I'd go back now and finish them all off. But it wasn't that easy. My father's house was locked down tighter than Fort Knox. Even if I did make it in, Saul wasn't there. I'd only get to kill my father and Adul. Plus, I'd never make it out alive.

And I had to if I ever wanted to get back the only thing that had ever been mine. Lily.

God, I was so fucking close. All I needed was the right moment to slip in and she'd be mine again. Then I could finish my father and uncles off for good. We'd be safe, set in the new life I had planned for us. It had to work. The guards that protected her were getting too comfortable. Last month it dropped from three to two. At her insistence, so said her brother, Slade. Although he didn't know I overheard that piece of information.

A smile pulled at my lips as I grabbed my bag from the back seat and walked toward the entrance of the airport at a fast pace.

Slade. He had no idea who I was. Not really. To him, I was some guy he'd met at one of his fancy parties. Someone whose face he'd recognize and maybe make small talk with, but not one he'd invite over for dinner. At least, not yet. I made sure to pop back into his life at random moments. Let him know enough about me to sate his curiosity and gain his trust. To him, I was Zane Collins, unlike the Zain Cook I had been born into. Unlike the Zain Amari my Arabic family knew me as. Slade was my only link to Lily. The key would be getting past all the blockades he set in my path.

I'd spent the first year hating him, wanting nothing more than to spill his blood and that of his men for taking my gift away from me. Then reality sunk in and I let the facts play out. The world I lived in was different than everyone else's. Concerning the sex trafficking, I was a criminal by association. My knowledge damned me, regardless of whether I was a part of it. I hated it with a passion. My dealings consisted of money transactions and being the muscle when things went wrong. Until last month, when I needed an excuse to continue to stay in the states. Now, it was up to me to handle the next shipment of girls, and little did my father know, there wouldn't be any. Not anymore.

Voices echoed throughout the airport from so many people. I kept my head down as I made my way to the gate. I boarded without incident and the flight was uneventful. I had a first class row to myself, but I didn't let myself relax until I was arriving in San Francisco. The cool air had me taking in a deep breath. Even though I was only gone a short amount of time, I missed the place I now considered home. Three years of worming my way into Lily and Slade's life and I'd embraced San Francisco. But it was almost time to say goodbye.

The long term parking sign hung ahead. As I approached, I slowed, glancing at my BMW in the exact same spot I left it in. Although I kept a steady pace, I observed everything. A woman in an older SUV was pulling out of a space at the end. A man was waiting for the elevator on the far side of the garage. I grabbed my keys, unlocking the car. The lights flashed and I hit the button for the trunk, throwing my bag in at my approach. The feel of being watched was real. I knew it. Lived it. Had been on the other side. Someone definitely had their eye on me. Question was, who?

Again, I scanned the area, searching for some sign that would trigger me. Nothing. "Son of a bitch." I climbed in, starting the car and heading out of the garage, watching the rear view mirror almost the entire time. Everything seemed as normal as it could be. Maybe I was overreacting. My slip up with my father could have been playing a role, but I wasn't sure.

The sun was beginning to rise and I contemplated whether I should go forward with my routine. I couldn't have timed my arrival any more perfectly. I'd have just enough time to stop by my place, shower, change, and pick up some coffee before I headed to Lily's building. She'd be at the office early. She was always the first one there and the last to leave. Knowing her personality like I did, I wouldn't expect anything less. But should I?

My hands tightened around the steering wheel as I surveyed behind me one last time — nothing. I let thoughts of her overwhelm me. It took a good year after the trial for her to emerge, but she'd done it so bravely. Just like she'd stayed strong before and after she was taken from my arms. Facing her rapists without me, when I promised her I'd kill them myself…it destroyed me. The murder, the trial, the mental facility, all the appointments and treatments she'd gone to afterward…I had so much fixing to do within my poor Lily. But would she let me? From what I'd seen, glimpsing her from afar, she'd all but forgotten about what we shared. Forgotten *me*.

Fuck, I couldn't think about it. If I did, I'd say to hell with my plan and take her now. Kill anyone who got in my way. That was dangerous, not only for her, but me. So why was I fingering the button to the console where my gun was hidden?

Time. It was driving me crazy. Years, I'd waited. I couldn't do it anymore. My slave had shown me a world I never thought existed. Shown me what love could do to a man who'd all but cursed the emotion. Now I was desperate to get both back. What would she do if she saw me? Got the briefest glimpse? Would she come looking for me or would it scare her off? Would the security get tighter and ruin any chance I had of taking her?

I sighed as I battled with traffic. So many scenarios, yet none of them were putting me at ease. I just wanted her back in my arms. To run my fingers down the side of her face until I reached her throat, letting her pulse reassure me that what we shared was real. But who was I kidding? My gift would run. Fight me just as hard as she ever had. Probably even harder.

I was going to have to put her back in her place and convince her that what we shared was right and meant to be. We'd be able to connect all over again. Just the way it was before, but away from the rest of the trouble that had surrounded us.

My heart raced as I turned onto our road. *Our* road, because I made sure to get a place not far from hers. Diagonally across the street and directly above her floor so I could see through her glass windows perfectly, to be precise. Penthouse for penthouse. It had worked out better than I could have dreamed. But it came with a price. Her sadness turned mine into fury. The tears she shed while she looked off into the distance were equivalent to razorblades over my skin. She needed me, and fuck if I didn't need her, too. Soon, I'd stop all the pain and replace it with the kind I knew she enjoyed. Lily would be crying, but only for release.

Chapter 2
Lily

If there was one thing I'd learned on my journey, it was to shut myself off. The numbness left me cold. Distant from everyone around me. It worked with the position I held at Slade Industries. People were scared of me, and for the first time, it wasn't because of who my brother was. They truly feared the killer that walked their halls. Their silence may have prevented the truth from being said, but panic couldn't stay hidden from the depths of their eyes when they had to face me —especially alone. Both men and women fled when I appeared. When they were called into my office, they cowered. That sort of power corrupted the weak, made them hungry for more. With me, it left me feeling dirtier than I already was. But I didn't balk from my job and I didn't show weakness. I couldn't afford to if I was going to stay in control of this new stranger lurking inside my body.

Who was I?

"Ms. Roberts, you have more flowers. Would you like me to bring them into your office?"

My eyes flickered to the clock on the wall. Eleven thirty-two. They always appeared around the same time. Who they were from, I had no idea.

I hit the button on the phone to answer. "Bring them in."

On instinct, my stare went back my inbox. Still, no news from Slade on whether he wanted me to go after Kingston Corp. Not having anything to do left me jittery. Boredom brought dangerous thoughts. Ones I couldn't let linger for too long.

The door opened and I glanced up, expecting more white roses in a light pink vase. The red petals had my eyes flashing wide and me easing to stand.

"What is this?"

Patrice shrugged, a smile coming to her face. "I was surprised, too. Seems your secret admirer wanted to change things up. Three weeks, Monday through Friday, and only now he decides to send flowers with some color to them. About time."

I frowned, walking over. "There's a card." The surprise was etched deep in my words and I regretted it almost instantly. I didn't want to sound like I was intrigued by the daily ritual. I'd always pretended to be annoyed by their presence. Somehow, I'd come to depend on them, even if the gesture was something as simple as flowers. Their arrival was becoming my one bit of happiness for the day. Stability of the comforting kind.

"Look at that. You're right." Her hand reached forward before she seemed to catch herself. "I'm sorry, Ms. Roberts, I'll leave you."

I nodded, already walking closer to the large bouquet of roses mixed with lilies. The card was perched at the top in a plastic stand and for the life of me, I couldn't reach forward with Patrice still in the room. As the door closed behind her, my fingers moved. Would it say who it was from? Would it be empty? Or would a signature be present so I could finally discover who this mystery person was?

The door eased shut only to swing back open. The space was almost completely filled with my brother's towering frame as he barged through. My hand drew into a fist and I stepped away from the flowers.

"Slade. I was just waiting for your email. I didn't know you were back in San Francisco. What has it been, over a year?"

The dark suit clung to his wide shoulders as his eyes cut over to mine, but he continued toward the desk.

"Couldn't be helped. Mary needed off the yacht."

"Off?" My arms crossed over my chest. The suit jacket I wore hugged to my back and I shifted at the exposure to my wrists. Even now, I couldn't take my scars showing in public. Behind closed doors, the crescents and claw marks didn't bother me in the least, but they were mine to see, no one else. They told my story. My gruesome life of witnessing the horrors of beaten and broken slaves. Ones who died in my arms and others who suffered from fractured bones and internal injuries. I was there for them through the worst. The only one who was there for them. Of course, I couldn't have been if it weren't for the permission of my Master.

I sighed as Slade pulled out the chair and began messing with the computer.

"Mary's pregnant. She can't take the motion anymore. She's sick and I can't stand it. I feel so damn helpless."

"Pregnant?" The excitement sounded so alien that I wasn't even aware it was me who had spoken the word. Confusion had my brow drawing in before I could stop it.

"That's right. Eight weeks." His gray eyes rose to mine. "What do you think about being an aunt?"

I could see my brother's smile wanting to surface and it pulled mine out, until I could feel my teeth become exposed. "I couldn't be happier. Congratulations." Slade stood as I rushed over, throwing my arms around him. I couldn't remember the last time I had any sort of contact with another person. My skin prickled and I tried not to flinch at the discomfort. How had we drifted so far apart? Slade practically raised me. Sure, we weren't super close as we grew older, but I couldn't remember being this withdrawn.

"Is Mary excited?" I pulled back, distancing myself.

"Elated," he breathed out, sitting back down. "We weren't trying, but we weren't opposed to it either. Months went by and it just...happened. Amazing, really. I've never been able to picture myself as a father." He smiled, again. "I think I like it."

"You're going to be great. You'll see, it'll come natural."

Typing sounds filled the air and he paused to look up. "Listen to you. You sound so grown up. Full of wisdom. What do you know about babies?" My smile melted. "Nothing. I just..." What I knew, he'd never know. There was no way I could tell him that one of the slaves who'd been there long before me went through a birth not weeks before I had been physically removed. How she thought she'd hate the baby because of who it was from, but loved it at first sight. Or how I almost...

"It's just what I hear. Your fatherly instincts will kick in and things will play out just as they're supposed to."

"Didn't work out for ours so much." His eyebrow cocked and I rolled my eyes.

"He's the exception. You're nothing like our father."

More typing. "No, I'm not. I'll love my children. They'll always be protected."

"I believe that." And I did. Slade was as ruthless as he was possessive. But he cherished what was his. Mary was loved by him more than I could put into words. It made me miss that feeling. I once felt protected. Cared for.

"Shit," Slade said, under his breath. "Where in the hell did I put those documents?"

My head shook as I neared. "Probably in *your* computer. My folders are set up differently than yours and it's not like we share the same ones, anyway."

"My computer?" Slade looked around, as if seeing the room he was in for the first time. "This is my *old* office."

"Yes," I breathed out. "I took it over last year before you left. You," I said, pointing toward the door, "are three rooms over, corner office. You said you liked the view better, remember?"

He stood. "I'm sorry, Lily. I'm not in my right mind today. Things have been…crazy lately."

"You never even came back after you passed over the reins here. I'm the one in complete control. What is it you're looking for? Maybe I can help."

A twitch in his cheek flashed only a second before he rounded the desk. My heart exploded as I followed him to the roses.

"You have a boyfriend?" The glance he threw me had me nearly stumbling. I knew the rules. Or, the *rule*. Slade made me promise when he left me his penthouse and set me up with a job that I'd inform him when I decided to date. I knew he wanted to run a full check. Make sure I wasn't dating a psycho or some deadbeat.

"I'm not seeing anyone. I don't even know who those are from."

The look he threw me was full of uncertainty. "Let's see, then." He grabbed the card, inspecting the envelope before he handed it over. "Open it. Let's see who has an interest in my little sister."

There was a playfulness there, but I knew better than to buy into the act he was projecting. In his eyes, my abduction and everything that had come along with it was his fault. He was still trying to make up for the damage he believed he caused by his absence—the penthouse, the job, a bank account with a small fortune in it. I knew he believed I wouldn't have been taken if he had been keeping a better eye on me, but that's where our opinions differed. We were both stubborn. I would have helped the girl who I now knew as Mary's sister, Bethany, regardless. Being sold into sex slavery was no one's fault but mine and the ones responsible for my abduction. All of them were dead, but two. Bethany and her husband. As for the ones who bought me, I knew I was powerless to put an end to their lives. I wasn't even sure where to begin looking, aside from the country itself.

"Go on," he said, leaning forward.

"I'm going, jeez." My hand shook as I broke the seal. Anxiety surged and I wasn't sure why I was so nervous. It's not like I knew the person. I never went out anywhere. Not even shopping for groceries. They were delivered like everything else I wanted or needed.

I pressed my lips together as I pulled out the small card. The one word had me crumbling it in my hand before my brother could see.

"Well?" Slade's head cocked to the side. "What did it say?"

"Nothing." I forced a smile and stepped back, clenching my fist even tighter. At his step forward, I could so easily see the brother in front of me and not the boss. He'd try to get that card any way he could and I had every intention of trying my best not to let that happen.

"Lily, let me see it."

My head shook and I felt the pins holding my hair up, loosen. "No. It's gibberish, really."

"Lily." The way his tone deepened, I knew this was my last chance before he'd physically remove it from my hand. Fuck, I hated how overbearing he was at times. But I couldn't deny how much he'd helped me. Hell, continued to help. I was safe because of my brother. Back here…because of him. Would he understand what the card said?

No. Even as I watched him take another step, I knew my guilt was making me overreact. Besides, maybe *I* was misunderstanding the meaning.

"Fine. Here." The small ball of paper that sat in my palm was picked up and unfolded. As I watched my brother concentrate, I knew he was trying like hell to decipher the same message I had.

Red. It could be the color of the flowers. Passion. *The code word for when I wanted the pain to cease.* No. That was ridiculous. Zain was history. He didn't exist anymore. What we had died in Afghanistan and all the memories I carried over were forbidden to resurface here. He was the enemy. He'd brainwashed me into thinking I loved him. And I had allowed it.

"You want to explain?" Slade asked the question, but his attention was focused on the card.

"Color of the flowers? It would make sense. They're usually white."

That got his attention. His head snapped up. "Usually? I wasn't told you were getting flowers."

I shrugged, trying to brush it off. "Maybe they're from Brace. Maybe that's why he neglected to mention it."

He tilted his head, even angrier, and I forced a laugh to cover my unease.

"Calm, Slade, they're not from your guard. He probably doesn't even know they're for me, if he's seen them delivered at all. Your men stay downstairs now, at my request. The flowers could have been for anyone on this floor. Besides, they've been coming every work day for three weeks or so. They're not a big deal. Today was the first day they were red or held any sort of card. They're harmless, I'm sure."

"They're flowers. They arrive *every* work day. They are not harmless."

I rolled my eyes. "Let's drop it. Tell me more about Mary. Where is she? Is she at the penthouse?"

"Hotel. And we're not just going to push this to the side, Lilian." He tossed the card to the shelf the flowers were sitting on and pulled out his phone. "The insignia is from a shop not two blocks away. I want to know who sent these." At his back turning to me and the phone rising to his ear, I made my way back to the desk. Still, I couldn't stop the shaking.

"Marcio, I need some information. Lily has been getting flowers for the last few weeks. They're coming from Betty's Flowers. Figure out who they're from. I want an address of where this person lives and a telephone number." He hung up, but I didn't miss the anger behind his stare before he softened. Slade might try to hide who he really was, but I'd seen that look before. I knew what he was capable of.

The chair squeaked as I sat down. "So, what do you plan to do once you find out who my secret admirer is? Gouge his eyes out for being interested in me? Remove his brain so he can never think of me again?"

My patience was gone. Something about my brother mixing in anything possibly having to do with Zain left me in a weird place. I knew my guess was probably way off. I doubted my Master even remembered my name, but I couldn't help but get defensive on his behalf. And that only had my temper spiking even more. I shouldn't try to protect the worst kind of criminal known to man.

"Removing his brain or eyes because he has an interest in you is a little extreme. Even for me. What I will do is make it a point to meet this man and see what his intentions are. Why hasn't he contacted you? You said it's been three weeks. That's plenty of time."

I shrugged. "Probably because he can't get close enough to ask."

"Bullshit. All he would need is ten feet and he could try to get your attention from there. Or, he could call. He obviously has the address and phone number of where you work." Slade came to stand before the desk. "Or maybe, he could have done the gentlemanly thing and called me. Asked my permission to date my sister. I would have respected that and possibly set something up."

A laugh burst from my mouth. "Call *you*? Slade, you can't be serious. You're…intimidating."

His full lips twisted into a smile. "All the more respect I would have had for him. Either he doesn't have the balls to step up or his intentions aren't good."

Zain wouldn't have been afraid to face my brother.

"I'm sure his intentions are fine. He's probably just shy. Anyway, I'm not looking to date until I'm at least thirty. I need to focus on my career first and I seriously don't see when I'd have the time."

"Career is good. Stick with that. I like the idea of not having to worry for at least another seven years. It works out for both of us. Now, if you'll excuse me, I'm going to go hunt through my computer for those documents for Mary. Call me later and we'll set up dinner." He began to walk toward the door when my hand outstretched before me. Panic was resurfacing and I didn't like that my brother would know who this admirer was before me.

"You'll let me know, right?"

"Know what?" Slade pulled the door open and I frowned at his blank expression.

"Who sent the flowers. I want to know who it is." I paused. "You'll tell me, won't you?"

Silence reigned between us, but he eventually shrugged and nodded. "I'll call you when I get a name."

The door clicked as he shut it behind him and I let myself lean back in the chair. *Red.* Could it be?

Zain did say he wouldn't let me go. Well, more yelled it as they were pulling us apart. And I always had taken him for his word. But...

"No," I whispered, shaking my head. I only knew him for four months. That amount was short enough where someone could hide their true colors. He wouldn't keep his word on this. It had been too long. Where I expected him to come at the beginning, he hadn't. It was over. I needed to just focus on what my shrink said and let this go. Let *him* go. He was my enemy. I had to remember that.

Chapter 3
Zain

Tests. Life was full of them. You either failed or they had the opportunity to change the path you were on. I pushed through the large glass double doors of Slade Industries, about to face the biggest one of my life.

Metal detectors rested ahead and I noticed three guards in black uniforms standing beside them. Two of the men were on the younger side and another was a tad bit overweight. They were the least of my problems. The other four in civilian clothes, talking beside the elevators, were my challenge. Two were Lily's. One had a shaved head and was almost seven feet tall. *Brace.* The other was a few inches over six feet and just as muscular as his partner. *Terrance.* The other two were Slade's. *Marcio and Caleb.* They all seemed deep in conversation, but their eyes never stopped scanning the room. I'd done my research on those four and they were a force to be reckoned with. Together, they surpassed deadly. They were the finger of God and if they knew who I was, I was as good as dead.

The hum of footsteps echoed through the large entrance, but I tuned myself out to everything as I strode through the detector as if I didn't have a care in the world. My attention stayed straight ahead as I made a beeline for the elevator closest to them. If I was going to go through this test, I wanted to make it as hard as possible. To do that, I'd have to face my obstructions head on. For Lily, I'd do it with honor. She deserved that after my failure to protect her.

"Hey, where do you think you're going?"

I looked at the dark skinned man known as Marcio. He worried me the most. There was something not right with that one.

"I'm getting on the elevator," I said, nonchalantly.

"You have an ID card? You're not wearing one."

Fuck. This was exactly what I wanted to test out. Time to go with plan B and I didn't necessarily like it. It would put me too close to Lily, too soon. But, it was either that, or these men were going to pry more into who I was. That could be dangerous.

"No, I'm sorry. I just came here to visit a friend. I wasn't aware I needed a card to do that."

Marcio's eyes narrowed. "Who's your friend? Do you usually socialize with them while they're working?"

I kept my face devoid of any nervousness. "Well, my friend happens to own this company and I was in town so I thought I'd stop by."

"Who would that be?" Marcio looked to Brace and relaxed his right hand for better access to his weapon. I knew he was carrying beneath his expensive suit.

"Slade Roberts, of course. Should I call him so you can talk to him personally?"

Tightening erupted down Marcio's jawline and I knew he was starting to doubt himself.

Before he could think too much, I continued. "I don't mind, really. I can call Slade if you'd like to talk to him. Or, why don't you call him? Let him know Zane Collins is downstairs. He'll tell you to send me up." My hands pushed into the pockets of my slacks as sweat broke out under my suit's shirt. The damn red tie I wore was giving off the impression that it was choking me. Shit, I didn't like showing up on Slade like this. Our run-in wasn't coincidental like the others had appeared. Now, I would be here for a purpose and I'd have to make it believable.

"Hold on."

My heart leapt as he pulled out his phone and hit a button. A few seconds went by before he spoke. "Boss, I have a Zane Collins down here. He says you know him." Marcio's eyes narrowed even more and he hung up the phone. Fuck, I didn't like this. If Slade had forgotten who I was...if he had found out who I *really* was.

"Go on up. Top floor. Head straight back and make a left. It'll be at the end of the hallway."

"Thanks," I mumbled as I walked into the already opened doors. My pulse exploded in rhythm and I couldn't shake off how bad this was. If Lily saw me, it was all over. Damn, I should have come up with something better for plan B.

The door shut and I took a deep breath, letting myself calm. Nothing ever got to me. I was a dead soul walking in a shell of a body unless it concerned my slave. Everything about her brought me to life. The new feelings were something I wasn't used to, but I'd be damned if I was going to run from what I knew was too good to be true. I loved Lily with everything I had. Fuck, she was *all* I had.

Ding.

A light hum of voices all but seemed to stop as I exited. A man peered over the top of his cubicle, but lowered as he seemed to deem me unimportant. Or a threat. I wasn't sure yet. My jaw was aching at how hard I was clenching my teeth together. I kept my head down as I walked toward the back at a torturous pace. My instincts told me to rush, to get out of sight before I was spotted, while the killer in me said if I did, it would draw attention.

"Excuse me, may I help you?"

I turned at the woman's voice. She was a redhead, standing from her cubicle. The side of my mouth lifted into a charming smile, one I'd practiced repeatedly to mold into society. "I'm just here to see Mr. Roberts. His office is that way, right?" I pointed toward the left.

"Yes, sir."

I didn't miss the wariness on her features as she lowered and fixed her eyes back on the screen. Did people fear him so much? I didn't. I'd yet to see anything threatening about him. Sure, there was that underlying dominance behind his mask, but I could see through it. He was someone to watch, yes, but be afraid of? I wasn't so sure. Of course, I'd yet to spend any significant amount of time with him.

A door opened toward the right and my chest caved in at the sight of my Lily. Her quick turn took her away from me and had me heading in her direction before I could stop myself.

"Sir," the redhead whispered, loudly. "That way."

A battle like none I'd ever known played out in my head and body. My legs didn't want to move in the direction they needed to. It took pure willpower to turn myself and walk the other way. Angrily, I headed toward Slade's office. The hall opened up at the end and another woman sat behind a large desk.

"Zane Collins to see Mr. Roberts."

I didn't even give her time to ask who I was. If I didn't make it in there quick, there was no going back. I'd blast my way out of this motherfucker with Lily in tow. The beast inside of me was dying to claw its way back to her.

"Go right in. Mr. Roberts is waiting for you."

The knock I gave came off louder than I intended, but I didn't give it further thought as I opened the door and made my way into my *once* enemy's office. Still seeing him, the temptation was there to spill his blood. He'd taken what was mine. Sure, she'd been abducted first, and she was his sister, but once she was owned by me, there was no going back.

"Mr. Collins. Great to see you again. What can I help you with?"

Slade stood, walking around his desk. He leaned back against the large mahogany structure to stare in my direction. Flashes of Lily hit me hard. I could see her in him. The lips, the color of their eyes. And then…nothing. My mind blanked for the first time in my life as I thought his question over. There were plenty of things that wanted to come, but rational answers wouldn't break through. I licked my lips, lowering my head, but never taking my eyes off him. I could see his curiosity and something else. Regret? Uncertainty for letting me in his space?

"I'm here to collect what's mine." And just like that, my eyes closed, only to wrench back open. I cursed in my mind.

"I beg your pardon?" He pushed from the desk, tilting his head. There it was. Anger. But more than that. It was threatening rage, as if he only hoped I'd say something to set him off. Now I could see what put people at unease. Luckily, it didn't faze me like it would most.

"I have money and I want to partner with you. Name your price."

A deep laugh echoed through the room and I felt myself relax.

"You want to partner? That's hilarious. Sorry, I'm not looking for anyone to buddy up with. Is there anything else I can help you with?"

My mouth jerked, playfully. "Maybe." I switched to French. "I'm in a predicament. You can say this is a turning point in my life. I need to start a legitimate career. Work on some form of stability." I switched to Russian. "I have plenty of skills, but no work history. None that I can put down on paper anyway. Not unless it's written in blood, that is." Arabic. "I'm a killer. It's something I love to do, but I can't continue if I want to settle down and have a real life. A life with your sister. Fuck, I love her with every fiber of who I am. Soon, I'm taking her and keeping her for the rest of my life and there's nothing you're going to be able to do about it. Do you hear me?"

"Whoa, whoa, whoa." Slade raised his hand. "You lost me halfway through the Russian. I don't speak the language very well. So, let me get this straight. You need a job, but you don't have work history? Am I getting that right?"

I shrugged. "Close enough."

"Sit." He walked over, pouring two glasses of Scotch. I took the offered glass and watched him return to his chair. The man people feared was back. He looked ready to eat me alive. I almost wished he would try. A fight would do me good, although I wasn't sure how much of one it'd be. I knew of ways to kill someone in two seconds flat. He didn't appear to be an actual fighter.

"I'm a little confused as to who you are. You attended the Paxton Banquete. I've seen you a few places after that. But you don't belong in the business world. I see that now. So, who the fuck are you?"

My Scotch disappeared in one swallow and I rotated the glass back and forth in my hand. "I'm a man with a dark past, but I'm hoping to improve my future. My skills are varied and I don't accept failure. I speak four languages fluently. I know a lot about money. How to earn it, and how to spend it. If it's persuasion of a client, I can do that, too. Name it and I'm your man."

"You didn't answer my question. Who's the real you?" He took a gun out from inside his jacket, pointing it at me, but I never broke my stare.

"I just told you." I stood, walking a little closer to him. "If you don't mind, I can demonstrate."

"You come any closer and your brains will decorate my floor. Who. The. Fuck. Are. You?"

A sigh left my mouth. This was backfiring in my face. What the hell was I doing? "My name is Zane Collins. You know that. I'm a jack of all trades. *All*. Although, I'd like to put that part of my life behind me and look for something a little more…respectable." A step closer brought me within perfect range. My hand lunged forward, removing the gun from his grasp. I had it disassembled in seconds flat. "I'm asking for your help. Something I never do," I said, placing the pieces on the desk next to him.

"Quite the party trick," he said, raising his eyebrow, "but I'm not impressed. I've seen it before. And I'm not sure I can help you. You're hiding something pretty big. I can feel it."

I laughed. "Aren't we all?" The darkness in me swirled and I brought up my hand, shaking my head. "Listen, I'm going to be frank. You and I have the opportunity to get along great or we can be worst enemies. I really don't need any more of those."

The ring of his phone had his hand coming up. "Marcio." He pushed off the desk and headed back for the Scotch. Shit, was he going to have me thrown out? Killed for showing up and running my mouth, not to mention threatening him?

He paused in pouring. "Are you fucking kidding me?" Hesitation. "No, not yet. I'll get back to you."

A growl tore from his throat as he hung up the cell and pushed it back into his pocket. My lips parted at the new man I was staring at. A caged animal surfaced from the depths of the mask I was so sure I'd seen through. Glass shattered against the wall, sending liquor all over the surface.

"Fuck! I'll destroy him. Sending flowers to my sister. I'll—"

Slade's glare melted as he turned to look at me, the composed imposter sliding back into place. "You want my help, you'll do something for me to earn it. How does that sound?"

Flowers? To Lily? He…another man trying to take what was mine? "Name it," I gritted out.

"If you've done your homework on me, and I have no doubt that you have, you know I have people I don't get along with. First, I want you to tell me who those might be. Let's see how good you really are."

The internal list I had made would have been pages long. Slade was far from popular. He had more enemies than anyone I'd met outside the trafficking world. "Well, there's Taylor Williams from Putlzer, David Lang from Weston, and if you want to go way back, there's your ex-best friend and right hand man, Christopher. He didn't take to being fired very well, if what I heard was right. Forcefully removed from the building, so I hear."

Anger returned. "He hit on my wife. Showed up at my yacht while I was out of town. Mary thought she could trust him. He crossed the fucking line. He's luckier than he knows."

"I have no doubts."

He shook his head. "Besides, I'm not worried about any of those people. This goes past that. This is about my sister."

Heat rushed through my limbs. "The Brightons, then?"

A tick pulled at Slade's eye for the briefest moment. "The flowers I mentioned came from none other than Alec Brighton, younger brother to Jordan. If you recall, which I'm sure you do, my sister killed Jordan, his father, Julian, and my wife's father for her kidnapping. Now, why would Alec be sending my sister flowers for the last three weeks? White roses and suddenly today, red. It doesn't make sense. She got a card, too. It said, *red.* Tell me why."

My hands gripped around the glass hard. I was surprised it didn't shatter in my grasp. "He's going to try to kill her. Red equals blood in my book." I was standing before I could even finish. Pressure on my suit jacket pushed me back down.

"If that's the case, I'll finish him off myself. You stay," he snapped.

It took everything I had not to drive my fist into his face over and over again. Lily needed *me*, but I was smart enough to know that now wasn't the time. Let Slade check on her. I had to get the fuck out of here and put my plan into action early. It was time.

Chapter 4
Lily

"Alec, it's nice of you to come. Please, take a seat." I gestured across from my desk and watched the tall, dark haired man drop his hand and nervously sit down.

"Thank you for having me. I know how hard it must be for you each time we meet, given our pasts. Please know I hold nothing against you for how things played out. What my father was mixed up in was wrong."

My hands wouldn't stop shaking as I pretended to relax in my chair. Alec and I had met on several occasions due to the world we both worked in, but we'd never actually talked about what I had done. I wasn't so sure it was a good idea now. "I'm glad there are no hard feelings. What happened…it had to be that way. I'm sorry, but it's the truth. Your father was a very evil man. And so was your brother. He hurt my sister-in-law very badly that night. I think that may have been what triggered my reaction."

"I saw the pictures. They…" he cringed. "I was shocked to realize my brother and father lived their lives that way. I never truly knew them. You see, my father wasn't happy to have kids. I grew up in boarding schools and after that, college. I only ever came home on the holidays, so you can say I really didn't know them too well. That's something I've wanted to tell you for a while now. There are no hard feelings on my part."

I sat straighter in my chair, feeling a little relief take over, but still remaining wary. "Thank you for that. I'm not sure how things would be if it were the opposite. We see each other quite often."

"Yes." He nodded, scooting further down the chair, closer toward me. "That's another reason I'm here. We've seen a lot of each other off and on for the last few months and I've been doing some thinking. Perhaps…" he paused and my brow drew in as I watched him shift uncomfortably. "Would you like to go on a date with me?"

"What?" I blinked at him stupidly. Had I just heard that right?

"A date. You know, mend this bad blood for good. We can start something fresh between our families. A new chapter. Something pure." He stood, walking back to the roses. I felt myself stand. Pure...white. "You."

A smile greeted me as he turned around. "I like you, Lily. You come off as a hard ass, but I don't think everything is as it appears. How about dinner? If you don't like the real me outside of work, we walk away and pretend it never happened. I really think you'll enjoy yourself if you just try. This is could be a good thing. Healing, for both of us. Maybe even our families, too."

The door flew open and I jumped at Slade barging in. His heavy breaths were combined with a look that made my blood cold. It reminded me of the day I returned. He had pulled my terror stricken body over to face my rapists. While he had his gun on them, he'd made me point them out. That was shortly before I killed them.

"Out. Now." His voice boomed through my office and I rushed forward, putting myself between them. Alec's hands rose and I couldn't ignore how sincere he'd been.

"I'm not here for any trouble, Slade."

"Explain the roses. Why send them? Why go from white to red? Are you planning on hurting my sister?"

One minute, Alec was a few feet away, the next, Slade was jerking him forward and patting him down.

"Hurt her? Why the hell would I do that? I like your sister. Hell, I just asked her out on a date."

Slade pushed him back hard, causing him to stumble.

"Enough," I yelled. "Slade, you have to stop. Alec and I work together. He wanted to meet so we could talk about the past and I agreed it was time. What you're doing is uncalled for."

The angry stare was thrown at me. "Uncalled for? You killed his father and brother. You don't think he wants revenge for that? I do."

"I *don't*. He explained he didn't even grow up with them. If that's the case, maybe he doesn't blame me. His family was sick. Surely he can see that. Besides, we've never had any negativity toward each other, even when we were battling over accounts. Quite the opposite." I couldn't stop the smile from coming. "Getting Wes Corp was actually

his doing. He pretty much handed me that one.
Didn't you." It wasn't a question.

Alec shrugged and returned my smile. "You
worked hard. You deserved it. Plus, I think you
would have gotten it anyway. I just eased back
some."

"Jesus fucking Christ," my brother cursed.
"You both can't be serious. This is so not happening
right now. Alec Brighton?" he said, turning to me.
"Seriously?"

I looked nervously between both of them. Alec
wasn't my Master, but he was nice in his own way.
And I liked him. Besides, I couldn't have Zain like I
wanted. It wasn't right. Not in the eyes of society,
and Slade surely wouldn't accept that scenario.

"Slade, can you leave now? Everything is
okay, really."

He shook his head. "Not until you tell me
whether you're planning on dating him. I want to
know right now. Are you going on this date or can I
happily toss him out of my building?"

I rolled my eyes and took a deep breath.

"Slade." Alec took a step forward. "I
understand Lily is your sister, but she *is* old enough
to make up her own mind. You're looking out for

her, I see that, but I hope you can look past who I am and give me a chance, if that's what she wants."

My brother kept quiet as he continued to stare at me.

Did I want to do this? Date Alec? I'd just told Slade I didn't have any interest until I turned thirty. Now, here I was, seriously contemplating having a life again. The appeal was there. The guilt over my Master was, too. It felt wrong to say yes. To turn my back on someone I loved and expressed as much.

He's your enemy, Lilian. He associates with people who deal in selling girls and boys for a living. That is not acceptable.

"I think I would like to go on one date with him. Just to see."

"Shit." Slade ran his fingers through his hair and turned to Alec. "Her guards will be there the entire time. You are not to make it past the lobby of her building and she sure as fuck isn't going to your place. Dinner, movie, whatever. Nothing else. You understand me?"

"Slade!" My hand gripped his jacket. "That's enough. I'm old enough to make my own decisions concerning that. Now, out," I snapped.

"I'm serious," he said, turning back to Alec. "You touch her, you won't have a hand left when I get done with you. That *is* a threat. Feel free to take it with a grain of salt if you don't treasure your body parts."

"Out," I growled, pushing him toward the door. The moment he was past the barrier, I slammed it shut.

Alec had a smile on his face when I turned back around to face him. "I'm so sorry," I rushed out. "He's not serious."

"Oh, yes he is," he said, laughing. "I know your brother and I don't put it past him. He's dead serious."

I nodded, knowing what he spoke was the truth. "You still want to go on that date? I don't blame you if you're ready to run out of here."

Three steps and he was before me. "I've been dying to ask for months. Threats of missing limbs aren't going to keep me away now. How about tonight at seven? There's a restaurant not a block from here called Lucien's."

"That's one of my favorite places to order out from," I cut in.

"Great. Then you'll like the food. So, seven?"

All I could do was stare up into his light brown eyes. They weren't anywhere near as captivating as my Master's, but they had a certain draw to them. Slowly, I nodded. "Seven."

"See you then." He picked up my hand, brushing his lips across my knuckles. The tingling was automatic and I inhaled deeply, unable to stop myself at the shock of contact. Fuck, it had been too long.

"See you," I breathed out.

As he walked away, I couldn't stop myself from taking in his wide shoulders and slim waist. Now *that* was appealing. He looked like he was in good shape. His build was definitely just as attractive as his face. Why hadn't I noticed before?

The door shut and I reached back for my desk. My legs felt like they were going to give out at any moment. Was I ready for this? Suddenly, I wasn't so sure. Too many questions were going through my head and I couldn't think straight. A knock had me pushing myself to stand straight.

"Come in."

Slade strode back through, his arms coming to rest across his chest. "I'm sorry about losing my temper. I realize you're old enough to make your own decisions and I smother you at times. You understand it's because I love you, right? I'm just trying to keep you safe. No one will hurt you again. I won't let them."

"I love you, too." I forced myself to hug him again. "Everything is going to be alright. You'll see."

"No, you'll see," he said, squeezing. "I'll make it so."

There was no point in saying anything else. Slade was determined and at this stage, it was pointless to continue. Instead, I stepped away and grabbed my purse. "I'm heading out early. There are some things I need to do before tonight." I clutched the strap tighter. "I need you to back off some with Alec. You know I wouldn't ask if I didn't need this. And I do," I stressed. "More than you know."

A groan filled the room as he pushed his hands into his pant pockets. "I don't like this, Lilian. I don't. Just...be careful around him. Don't trust anything he says, and God forbid, if he pushes you too hard on anything you're uncomfortable with, walk away. Your guards will take care of the rest. You owe this man nothing. You don't."

His words hit home and my gaze lowered. Maybe a part of me did feel that way. Even though I'd killed his family because of what they did, I still felt bad that he had to go through that pain. Regardless of whether he denied their closeness or not. And I truly hadn't killed Jordan. Slade had, but I'd never tell a soul the truth. To the courts, it happened during my mental break, and that was the story I was sticking to.

"I won't do anything I don't want to do. You have my word."

"Good. You have fun shopping or doing whatever it is you're going to do. I'm about to head out, too. Damn guy in my office already left. He doesn't listen for shit, but a part of me likes him and I have no idea why."

"What guy?" I stepped over, walking to the door with Slade.

His eyebrows drew in. "Zane Collins. I've met him a few times, but today was different."

My heart all but stopped at the first name.

"Different how?" I managed.

"He…reminds me a lot of myself. He has balls. Drive. I'm intrigued by the mystery that he is."

I paused as he turned the handle, pulling open the door. "Mystery?"

Slade laughed. "You wouldn't understand. It's a guy thing. Anyway, it doesn't matter. Maybe I'll never see him again. I kind of blew him off."

"Oh."

"Yeah, no big deal. You better get going. It's almost four. Your date is in three hours."

I stopped mid-step and faced him. "How do you know that? Were you listening or something?

The smile I knew Slade by, appeared. "I didn't miss the kiss across your knuckles, either. Tell him he owes me a hand."

"You were watching me?" The gasp couldn't be contained. "Dammit. That's crossing the line and you know it." My eyes searched around for a camera, but I didn't see any.

"Safety first." He nudged me toward the elevator and I threw him a look as I headed to it. *Damn him.* Nothing I did was private. Well, home technically was, but I had guards outside my door at all times. I knew why, but I thought I'd be on my own by now. It wasn't as if I didn't have a security system. Slade installed the best of everything. He'd made that apartment impenetrable from when he lived there. No one was getting in if I didn't want them to. So, why, after three years, were they still following me everywhere? What did I have to fear anymore? Nothing.

It was time to get rid of my guards and I knew just how to convince my brother.

Chapter 5
Zain

"What...the fuck?" The binoculars slipped from my hand, hitting my chest. I scrambled to bring them back up. "What are you doing, Lily? What...the fuck are you doing?"

Did I really need to be asking? My slave had her leg propped up on the bed, sliding a black stocking up her thigh. Lingerie was something I'd never seen her in and I wasn't sure what the hell was suddenly going on now, but I knew it wasn't good. I'd watched her lay a clear plastic bag with what looked to be a black dress down on the bed before she'd taken a shower. The rollers in her long black hair surprised me a bit. When the robe dropped, I was floored. My cock got so hard, I had to reach down to adjust myself.

Black strapless bra. Black thong. Now, stockings.

My hand traveled over the slight growth on my face as I narrowed my eyes even more to take her in. Red lipstick. Pearls.

"Where you going all dressed up, slave? You looking to get fucked?" The last came out through gritted teeth and I pulled the strap from the binoculars over my head, sending pieces sliding across the tile floor at my throw. My gun was suddenly in my hand and I walked closer to the window. The view wasn't as good, but I could still see her clear enough. And I didn't like it at all. Curves. By God, those fucking curves hidden under that tight black dress were going to kill me. Or someone else, if that was her plan.

"Calm, Zain. Get a fucking grip. Just wait and watch." I closed my eyes as I realized I was talking to myself. They didn't stay shut for long. I surged forward turning on the dim lamp and came to stand right next to the glass. "Look at me, Lily. Look over here." And just like that…she did. The squint and part of her lips was followed by a slow walk toward me. "That's right, baby. Get a good look. Take me in. I'm right here." A smile came to my face at her hand flying to chest, but I quickly stepped out of view, moving over to the next room. Easing the curtains back, I could still see her staring at where I'd been. And crying. I wasn't sure if that was a good thing or not.

Minutes went by. Still, she stared. Aching had my chest cramping and breath coming in shallow spells. I knew she was questioning what she'd seen. Hell, she'd probably already talked herself out of the truth.

Slowly, she stepped back, only to return. Nausea threatened at seeing her so upset, but I couldn't let her forget what we shared. Did she see that, though, or did she see something entirely different? It had been a long time. Had she erased the love we had and replaced it with the fear over her entire situation? It was possible. Damn possible. Shit.

"Soon, baby girl, I'll remind you why we're meant to be together. I won't stop until you see. You *have* to see."

There it was again — anger. And it only increased as I watched her disappear from the window. I didn't wait. I grabbed my phone and keys, rushing to the elevator. There was no way I was going to miss where she was going.

Ringing had me blindly answering my cell as I waited for the elevator car. "Yeah?" My finger pushed steadily on the button.

"You're almost impossible to track down. Almost."

My body became still as I focused on the voice. "Slade."

"Surprised? I think you underestimate me."

I laughed under my breath. "I think you may be right. You shouldn't have been able to find out my number. Let me guess. Marcio?"

"Brace. He's a fucking genius when it comes to electronics. That's beside the point. I told you to fucking stay put. You left."

I stepped from the elevator, hitting the parking garage. "You said you didn't need me and I'm not looking to be one of your hired killers or bodyguards. I want a respectable job. I thought I made that clear."

"You have no experience in an office. What you do have is experience in is getting your hands dirty. Why the sudden change now?"

I let out a deep breath. "I found the woman I want to spend my life with. I'd like that life to last more than a few months or years. Plus, I want to be home every night, not gone for who knows how long."

"I see. Tell me what you can do. You said something about money."

The door opened and I unlocked my car, rushing over. "What I know is muscle when it comes to money. I took care of transactions. Deliveries. Picked up payments. That's not what I'm interested in, though. I know numbers. Put me in accounts."

"So you can steal my money out from under my nose?"

The groan was automatic. "Believe it or not, I don't need your money, nor do I technically need a job. I want this because it's the right thing to do."

"The right thing? As in, appearances?"

What, did he want my life story? Tough shit, he couldn't have it. "Yeah. I want to live a normal life. That consists of having a job."

"You must love her a lot to want to settle down and walk away from a life that has provided a good living."

The engine purred to life and I headed for the exit. Pausing, I waited for the black Town Car she rode in to exit her own garage.

"My life was nothing until she was in it. Love doesn't even begin to describe the way I feel for her."

"I can respect that. So, tell me, if I got you in and tested you out in a few departments, what am I supposed to do with you if you can't handle the everyday hustle and bustle of being a normal person?"

Technically, I wasn't going to be working for him, but a part of me almost wished this conversation was real. If he could get to know me before he found out...no. I was taking Lily tonight. There wasn't time to try to be buddy-buddy with Slade. He'd hate me before this was over with. Lily was my main concern. She needed to love me again, become my slave, like before. Then we could settle into a routine and figure out what we were going to do. After I took care of my past, of course. What I needed to do right now was break ties with Slade.

"You're probably right. I won't like it. Maybe I just need to suck it up and realize what I am. Couples sometimes need time apart. It's for the best. Thanks for the offer, though. I won't forget it."

I disconnected just as Lily's guards drove past with her in the back seat. Her head was lowered, twisting my stomach into a million knots. I let a car pass before I pulled out. Just seeing her so sad made me regret putting her in that place. If only I knew exactly what it was that had her so upset. Didn't she know I would come? I told her I would. It wasn't like I could knock on her front door and take my place in her life where I belonged.

Ring. Ring.

Slade, you're killing me. I picked up the phone, looking at Unknown Caller on the screen. "Didn't I make myself clear?"

"No one hangs up on me. I wasn't finished."

"What more is there left to say?"

Footsteps sounded and I strained to hear.

"You know more than I'm comfortable with. Work for me, behind the scenes. Show my men what you know so they can place you accordingly. I won't take you away from your girl more than I have to."

How tempting his offer was.

"I...can't. You wouldn't understand."

"Try me. I'm more understanding than you think."

Not *that* understanding. I'd bank on it. But if I did fill him in a little, would it help in the future?

After he found out about Lily and me? And he
would find out. It was only a matter of time.

"My family is very powerful and corrupt.
They're bad people. I want out. To do that,
well…you know what that entails. Right now isn't a
good time. When I came to talk to you, I meant to
tell you I would need a few months before I could
start. That's probably longer than you're comfortable
with waiting."

Silence and then the faint sound of more
footsteps. Was he pacing?

"Doesn't that put your girl in danger?"

I swallowed hard, taking a right turn, leaving
enough space between Lily and me.

"Yeah, but she'll be safe until I can get
everything to fall into place."

"Sounds really risky to me. Don't you think
she'd be better protected if you had people that had
your back? My men would."

Fuck, he was making this impossible. No
wonder he was good at what he did.

"Let me think on it."

"You have three weeks to contact me with the
status of where you're at in your head. If I have to

track you down again, so help me, I'm going to be pissed. That's never a good thing, Zane Collins."

"Three weeks. Fine."

"Good. Oh…and Zane. Good luck with your family. I hope you're around to make things work, for your girl's sake."

The line cut out and I pushed the phone back in my pocket. I sure hoped for her sake it worked out, too. If I could remind her of what we shared, open her eyes to the fact that I was still the Master who loved her, she'd wait for me to come back from Afghanistan. And she'd be safe doing that back here with Slade. But then what? Would I be able to convince her brother that we were meant to be? Would he try to keep me away for good? No.

Lily was the one for me, regardless of how we met. I'd fight for her. Kill for her. And I'd be damned if her brother was going to take her away from me again. I'd like to see him try. Slade may have been powerful, but it wouldn't compare to the wrath I'd bring if he tried to separate us for good. With Lily on my side, I found it hard to believe he would. It all came down to me convincing her.

Chapter 6
Lily

What was I doing? The restaurant doors loomed before me, but for the life of me, I couldn't get myself to walk through them. Had that been my Master? From the small distance between the buildings, I was sure it was. But, then…I couldn't be certain. He wasn't standing there for long. It had to be someone who resembled him. Zain never wore suits. He had always been dressed in dark clothing when he returned from his missions. It was nerves that were causing me to see things. It had to be.

"You okay?"

Brace's voice had my heart rate slowing. I turned, giving him the fake smile I'd become used to. "Great. I was just thinking."

"You sure? We can take you home if you're not feeling up for this."

I took a step backwards toward the door. "No, I'm fine, really. I shouldn't be too long."

At his nod, I turned and forced myself to continue. My skin tingled and I couldn't get over the fact that I was being watched by more than my guards. The hair on the back of my neck stood on end and I shivered as I headed through the entrance.

"Lily Roberts here for Alec Brighton."

The hostess threw me a wide smile. "Right this way, Ms. Roberts."

My fists clenched repeatedly as I glided past the tables to one in the very back. It sat right next to a window and I couldn't help but think my brother had something to do with that. No doubt he wanted my guards to see every little move made toward me.

"Lily." Alec stood, walking over behind my chair as I approached.

"Alec." This time, the smile was genuine. I let him take my hand as he helped me to sit down. As he rounded back to the chair directly across from me, I tried my best to keep calm. This was just a date. That was it. I didn't have to go on another if I didn't want to. And it was only dinner. It wasn't like we'd be heading back to his place or mine afterward. There'd be no stolen kiss outside my door. My bodyguards would destroy him if he even tried.

The hostess was replaced by a waiter taking our drink orders. I stuck to what I knew, what had rubbed off on me from my brother. "Scotch, please."

Alec's eyes flashed to mine, but he smiled. "I'll have the same."

At the departure, he turned, giving me his full attention.

"You really surprise me. I expected something different. Maybe a martini. But, no, Scotch. I like that."

"I'm glad. I won't pretend to be something I'm not."

He smiled. "Which is why you've kept my attention for so long. I won't lie, at first, I was cautious to be around you. I had to see what type of person you were. The more I learned, the more I began to respect you. You're an honest woman. Tough, but someone a person can trust."

Well, that wasn't what I was expecting to hear, but a compliment, which I appreciated. "Thank you. Honesty is important." *And I'm full of blood soaked lies.* "I try to tell the truth as much as possible."

"A rarity in this field. You amaze me. You're going to go far. Well, you already have and it had nothing to do with Slade. You're a natural leader,

Lily. At your age, you've surpassed men who have spent the last decade or more trying to accomplish as much. Your future is set. Now, all you have to do is enjoy the ride."

The waiter returned with our drinks and I lifted my glass, lowering my voice. "To the ride. May it be rough, with mind-blowing rewards. I don't think I'd like it any other way."

A shocked expression turned into a smile. It pulled at his mouth and it was one I knew all too well. I pushed away the shyness at the blatant flirting. The voice inside was screaming to run from embarrassment. The taker I'd become said to keep her game face on until she was ready to allow anyone in. After all, this blunt person was who Alec knew. Not the sweet, insecure girl who still lurked around on occasion.

"You like it rough?"

I turned, smiling at the waiter. Alec's back straightened. He hadn't been aware the man was still there.

"Are you ready to order or do you need a few more minutes?"

"I'm ready." I faced my date, who nodded he was ready, too. The menu flipped open and his hand scanned down the page, reading over the contents of what he wanted. While he looked between the waiter and the choices, I couldn't help but notice how truly attractive he was. How had I missed it all this time? Had I been so under my Master's spell that I'd been blinded to everything but my memories of him? What had changed?

"Ma'am?"

My eyes stayed on Alec as I spouted my order from memory. The spark was there. I could feel the lust thickening between us. An odd sense of dominance reigned supreme on my behalf. For the first time, I wanted to be the one in charge. With Master, it was so natural to submit. It came from my soul. Here…I wanted control. To be the one with authority if anything happened between us.

"Your eyes are so beautiful," he said, continuing to hold my stare. "I'm sure you've heard that a million times, though."

"Maybe a few, but I think I like the sound of it from your mouth. Tell me again," I said, lowering my voice and leaning more toward him.

Alec's eyes flashed down to my cleavage, pulling my own devilish smile. When our gazes met again, there was no embarrassment on either of our behalf.

"You're more than beautiful. Fuck, Lily. I've wanted to tell you that for so long now. I've wanted *this* for so long." He swallowed, taking a deep breath. "Your brother is going to kill me before it's over with. I'm not sure I can keep my hands to myself."

"You will if I tell you to."

"Yeah?" He rested his arms on the table, moving closer. We were less than a foot apart and I couldn't help but suddenly want to close the distance. What in the hell was happening to me? How had I gone from prude to promiscuous in the matter of a few short hours? Guilt over my Master had my arousal extinguishing.

"Yes. He can't kill you if you're not the one initiating, now can he?" I leaned back, grabbing my glass again and taking a sip. Still, Alec stayed transfixed on me. *Slow down, Lily. You're obviously not in your right mind. It had to be seeing someone who reminded you of Master. You're jumping the gun to block him out. This isn't the way.*

"No, I guess he can't. Are you going to tie me up so I have an excuse?"

I laughed, while at the same time, my stomach turned. "Tie you up, bind you, maybe break out my handcuffs. Whatever I feel in the moment." My eyes took in the surroundings. Everyone seemed to be in their own little world. An inexplicable warning bell rang in my mind even as my mouth opened to speak.

"Go to the restroom. Wait for me outside of the stall of your choice. Don't ask questions. Don't say a word. Just...obey."

My heart thudded hard against my thickened throat. I wasn't sure what reigned supreme, the thrill, or the sick feeling from the unstableness inside of me. Fuck, I was cracking inside. I could feel myself becoming someone I didn't know. Someone I didn't want to be. Still, I continued to follow through with my spontaneity.

"Lily..." Alec shifted and looked around. My hand rose and I closed my eyes.

"Go, if you're inclined. If you're not," my eyes opened, "then I bid you goodnight."

Something passed over his face. An emotion I couldn't understand. Slowly, he rose and didn't once turn back to me as he headed for the restrooms at the far end. I picked up my glass, downing the rest of the Scotch. My face turned toward the window and I could almost feel the broken pieces inside of me racing throughout my body. How much longer could I go on before I shattered? Why did I want to find out?

Master. The internal sob nearly brought tears pooling in my eyes. What was I waiting for? Someone to rush in and save me before I possibly made the biggest mistake of my life? No…wait, I'd already done that when I followed Bethany out of the nightclub. So, mistake number two? This one I could prevent, yet I didn't want to. I wanted to be rescued. Proof that I wasn't as alone as I felt. But I knew the hero I wanted wasn't going to show up to kiss me back into submission. I was on my own.

I stood, pushing my palms against the table. The dimness of the restaurant drove me to the back. It was so close to the lighting of Master's room. It was always dark in there, just like we were. But the best parts came when the sun went down. Pleasure was always found in the shadows of night. It was my favorite time. I could walk around in the pitch black as calm as if it were day. Maybe I was craving danger like I'd once been exposed to. The level of adrenaline always pumping through my body didn't compare anymore. *Master.* Was it possible my transition had to do with me holding on to the only piece of him I could bring to life? Dominance. Power. Control. Yes, I'd been grasping at anything that could make me strong or remind me of him this whole time. Here I was, about to commit the ultimate betrayal and sin, and it was all due to the god I saw him as in my mind. Desperation could make the strongest souls weak. What a web of guilty pleasures I craved tonight. And it all boiled down to one thing — if I couldn't have him, I'd *be* him.

I pushed the bathroom door open, not stopping as I spotted Alec pulling nervously at his tie. His weakness was my fuel. I let it soak deep within as I swayed my hips with each step closer.

"Take it off."

His hand paused at adjusting the knot and in one swift pull, he removed the silk around his neck. A slight trembling left his hand shaking as he passed it over to me.

How would he react when I unleashed what I wanted? What I yearned for in a depth so deep, it was endless?

My nails raked over his palms at a leisurely pace, removing the black material. With my other hand, I grasped the lapel of his jacket, bringing him toward me.

"Consent to give yourself to me fully." I pushed to my toes so our lips were but inches from each other. The fog in my head grew thicker. Master was the only one before me. Those full lips. Eyes the color of the sun. But *his* words were coming out of my mouth, not mine. "Let me have you how I want. Put your trust in whatever I do and I'll bring you the best pleasure you've ever experienced. I'll leave you something you'll never forget. A gift," I whispered. "Let me be your gift, Alec."

The smell of Scotch had me closing my eyes and pulling him closer. "Say yes," I said against his lips. "Anything I want."

"Yes."

My tongue swept over his lips, tasting what had now just become mine.

"Enjoy the loss of control. Surrender to it. To me."

Smooth silk eased down my palm and I brought both hands up. I had the tie around his throat before he could break from the spell I had sucked him under. Panic had his hands jerking. At my eye contact, he stilled.

"Very good." My lips pressed into his hungrily and I increased the pressure around his neck as our tongues slid against each other. The smoothness from his cheeks left me in a weird place. Master always had stubble. Maybe I'd make Alec stop shaving but for every other day. I didn't like not feeling the roughness.

"Now, take me into the stall."

There wasn't a moment of hesitation as he pulled my dress up so I could straddle him. Pressure from his shoulder pushed into the door and it slammed against the wall of the small enclosed space. We practically fell in at the frantic need of our lips.

"Fuck, Lily." Fingers gripped my ass as he spun to push me against the wall, locking the door. My pussy grinded against his stomach and I jerked my hands tighter.

"I didn't tell you to take control. That's mine. Now, put me down, sit, and unbuckle your pants." My grip relaxed and I pulled the tie loose. Alec obeyed, easing me to the ground. He was still shaking as he undid his pants and sat down. Fuck, what was I doing? Dirty. Yes, it seemed like I kept finding myself in these situations.

"Put your hands behind your back and lean forward."

"Kiss me again," he said, getting in position. I leaned in, securing his hands to the metal pipe.

"I'll kiss you when I'm ready. Now, lean back." I lifted my foot to rest on his thigh, making sure to press the stiletto in just enough to make him groan. His dark hair drew me in and I weaved my fingers through, gripping tight. *So close to the color of Master's.*

"Kiss this." In a slow stroke, I made a path over my bare skin, just above the stocking.

As he eased forward, my hand allowed him to go at his own pace. But I never let up the pressure at which I held to him.

"You're driving me fucking crazy. Fuck, I've never had it like this before. I'm always the one making the moves."

"Not anymore. Not with me."

Teeth sank lightly into my skin and I moaned, feeling myself grow so much wetter. Before, what we were doing was nice, but the pain sparked who I truly was. What I needed, regardless of my sudden switch in personality.

"Harder." The word was so full of need, I barely recalled how my voice dropped to that seductive tone. "Ooh." I sucked in air at the increase in pressure, closer to my pussy. "Like that. Yes." Still, his lips grew closer to the one place I wanted them the most.

Bang!

The door slamming open had us both jumping. Slowly, I moved my leg down, fixing my dress. My saviors were here, but not in the form I wanted.

"Lilian, open the door before I break it down."

My brother's voice had me cringing and Alec pulling at the tie. With the knot I fastened, he was getting nowhere fast. I reached to the lock, pushing it back and swinging the door open. At the surprise on Slade's face, I tilted my head.

"He didn't touch me. As you can see, I didn't allow him to."

Still, Slade stared in disbelief. "Out." He waved, not breaking his bewildered expression.

"If you don't mind, I'd like to ask that you not hold Alec accountable. He didn't know what I had planned."

Slade pulled me out of the way, but didn't get any closer. "What is that...?" He moved even more to the side. "Did you choke him with something? The tie before you secured him? His neck is red all the way around."

My head lowered, but I didn't drop my act. "That's between Alec and me."

A furious glare was turned on me. "Lilian, answer my question."

"It was consensual. I didn't choke him because I was trying to seriously hurt him." My own anger was pushing in and I tried to stay calm. For some reason, it wasn't easing like it usually did. Tonight was just too much. "Are we done? I really don't think this part of my life is any of your business. I'm a grown woman, whether you want to see that or not. And this," I said, pointing toward Alec, "is only the beginning. I'm finished with all of the security I'm stuck with. Guards," my head shook, "no more. Not a single one. I want my freedom."

Shattering...fuck, it was happening. I was breaking. That word...

"Do you hear me!" I yelled. "I'm done being a slave. I want *freedom*! I want to be on my own. No more," I said, slicing through the air. "I'm finished. Brace and Terrance can take me home, but then they leave. If they don't, I will, and if you try to stop me, I'll never forgive you. Never!" I yelled again.

The hurt on Slade face disappeared as fast as it had appeared. "This is all my fault." The way he ran his hand over his mouth had me fighting not to explode.

"This is *my* fault. Not yours. Do you hear me, Brother? I did this. All of it. And you know what? I'm the only one who can fix it. Not you. Not your detail. *Me.* Now, back the fuck off and let me figure out my life for myself."

I didn't wait for his reaction. I wheeled around, heading toward the door so I could leave. The temptation to take off and disappear was there. What would happen if I just got in the car and started driving to wherever I wanted? To leave and never look back?

Brace and Terrance almost collided with me as I broke past the door, but I didn't stop. I glanced back. They seemed too fixated by what was before them that they didn't even notice my increase in pace. My quick walk turned into a jog and I turned up the speed as much as I could in heels. The sidewalk pounded beneath my feet and I felt myself becoming free for the first time since I'd come back home.

Traffic blurred by and I kept going. People moved out of my way and thinned out the further I disappeared from downtown. My lungs were on fire with each intake of breath, but I pushed myself harder. Before I knew it, I'd somehow kicked my shoes off and was blocks away. My building was only fifty yards ahead when I stopped, gasping for air. Shit, had I just done that? I laughed, huddling over as I breathed in the cool San Francisco breeze. A hole in the nylon fabric had one of my big toes showing and it made me laugh even harder.

"You always were a rebel, disobeying at every opportunity."

My eyes widened and I jerked to stand. Breathing became impossible as I connected with a pair of eyes I only saw in my dreams.

"Well, hello, slave. Did you miss me?"

Rage was present on my Master's face and I barely heard my cry escape past the roaring of my pulse.

"Answer me," he said, dragging me to an inlet on the side of the building.

Darkness cloaked around us as we became concealed from the main road. "You have to let me go," I said, weakly. God, my voice hadn't sounded convincing in the least. How could it? My wildest dreams flirted with my worst nightmares. Every desire tugged and pulled at my core, making me wet.

"Let you go?" Shadows played across his face as he shook his head. "But, slave, you knew once you became mine there was no going back. You belong to me. For life. You even said so yourself."

It was my turn to shake my head. All the therapy told me to run. To call the police and report the dangerous man before me. The submissive who loved her Master begged to drop to her knees and take hold of his legs so we would never be separated again.

"What's the matter, my gift? Did you forget who you are?" The caring person I'd fallen in love with shone through and I grabbed his wrist. This couldn't be real.

"You never came to get me. You weren't supposed to come." The two statements clashed about as much as the conflict going on inside my brain. Cold brick bit into my back while he pushed into me, pinning me to the wall.

"You doubted my vow? I killed for you. I'll *still* kill for you."

"Please…"

Zain covered me with his body even more, grinding his hard cock against my lower stomach. "Please, nothing. Forgetful slaves have to face consequences. Bad ones hurt even more." His hand dove into the top of my dress, forcing its way under my strapless bra. A moan poured from me at him squeezing my nipple and rolling it between his fingers. "If you asked me, I'd say you've been a very, very naughty girl tonight, Lily. I think it's time you partook in your punishment."

Chapter 7
Zain

Feeling Lily under my hands again, smelling her sweet skin as she breathed against my cheek…it didn't get any better than that. The scent of her perfume made me lightheaded with lust. I wanted my cock in her so desperately, I knew there was no stopping the events that had been set into motion. Our time had finally come, and it was all thanks to my slave's temper.

When I saw her stand and follow Alec Brighton into the men's room, blood red jealousy had me easing from my car, gun in hand. I'd been lucky to get a view of them at all. The flirting I saw from the beginning had been a time bomb waiting to go off. Every smile, every inviting expression…Lily had hit the detonator when she stood and joined him. If Slade hadn't pulled up at the same time, I'd probably be in handcuffs. Whatever happened in that restroom had been bad enough to leave all of her protectors dropping the ball on her safety. What had they seen? Were they killing Alec this very moment? Had they already left his lifeless body on the floor, a mystery to anyone who happened upon him?

"Tell me what played out when you joined Alec." My finger pinched her nipple harder, while my other hand pulled her dress up past her hips. The garter belt stretched as I twisted it in my fist, still angry that she'd worn it for him when she never had the chance with me.

"You saw that?" Her voice cracked and she sobbed as she moved against me.

"I've seen almost *everything* you've done since you were taken from me." I jerked at the belt, turning it even more, bringing her impossibly closer. "I fucking said you were mine. I said I loved you a million times. How could you turn your back on that?"

Another sob. "You never came," she said, pushing against me angrily. "You left me here. Let them take me. You fucking—" A sound laced with pain had her crying harder while she thrashed beneath me. "No, you're in part responsible. You ruined my life. Get off of me."

"Never." With a yank, I broke the belt, moving my hand down to the side of the thong. "Did he see this? Did he touch what's mine? Hmm?" Fabric ripped under my hand and I jerked the other side just as hard, removing the barrier completely. The sway of her body bumping into mine sent a growl pushing past my throat. "Fucking speak, slave. Did you let that motherfucker touch what I own?"

"You have to stop. Please."

"Answer." My hand let go of her hip and I held her face level with mine. "What happened in that restroom, Lily?" My tongue licked over her lips, needing to taste her again. I nearly moaned as I pulled at her lower lip with my teeth. "Do you know how much that hurt watching what I've tried to get back give herself away so freely? You didn't have to go back there, but you did. Now…tell me," I gritted out.

A sniffle left her and her eyes cut up as she tried to straighten. There was that strength I knew in her.

"It's all your fault. You turned me into this."

"Into what?"

Silence. My shake had her weeping. "Don't you see? I became you. Every single part. I tied him up. Told him what to do. Then, my brother walked in. End of story."

The world could have stopped and I wouldn't have known it past the pain that slammed into my chest.

"You told him what to do?" I gripped her face tighter. "And what was that?"

"Let me go," she said, angrily. "This ends now. I'm not yours. I never was."

The building of pressure against my heart was damn near breaking it. This wasn't my Lily. I knew to expect this sort of reaction, but experiencing it firsthand was far from easy.

"You're going to tell me every single detail. I want to know what you just lived. What you let him experience."

"No. If you don't let me go, I'm calling the police. I'll have you arrested for assault."

"Assault? On what's mine?"

She tried to move her face out of my hand but I gripped tighter, not allowing her to break our stare. "You can't do this here. The law won't even let you touch me if I don't want it."

I kissed her, cutting off what she was about to say. "But you do want it," I said, rubbing my cock against her again. "I feel how your body gravitates toward mine. Your hips are moving into me as we speak." She stilled, but I kept going. "Don't close your eyes, slave. Look at me." Tears streamed over my fingers as she obeyed. "Good girl. Now, tell me you don't love me. I know you can't. God, Lily, you're *everything* to me. Do you know how long I've been waiting to get to you? How hard this has been for me, too? I love you," I stressed. "Do you think I would be here right now if I didn't?" Again, my lips pressed into hers. "Fuck, I've missed you so much."

The crying only got harder. "We can't. This isn't right. You're the enemy. You're the bad one I'm supposed to stay away from."

"Your enemies are dying off one by one. I've killed two of my uncles so I can cut ties. Two more and my father, and we're home free. No more worrying about them ever hurting anyone again. I promised you I would make them pay for what they've done. I'm keeping my word. Just like I kept my word on coming for you. I'm here. Right fucking here. Don't stop loving me now. We're so close."

The squeal of brakes had her eyes breaking from mine. I thought she had been taking my words sincerely, but she began to struggle in earnest. Fuck, I didn't want it to be like this.

Her mouth opened and my hand slammed over it, muffling her scream. "Don't you dare. You know in your heart I'm the one for you. I don't give a fuck about the conditions that surrounded us when we first met. Something happened when it was just you and me. We fell in love. Now you're trying to find any excuse you can to deny what you know is true." My head shook. "I'm not going to let you. I refuse to stop until you're the Lily who was forcefully removed from my room. She fought with every ounce of strength she had to try to stay with me. I want her back and you're going to give her to me."

I removed my hand, taking her mouth with all the brutality I felt she deserved for her betrayal. I couldn't get enough. For the briefest moment, I felt her kiss me back. "That's it. Let yourself go. Come back to me." My arms wrapped around her as I deepened the kiss. At my hand tugging at her hair, she broke the connection, taking in a deep breath.

"This is so wrong."

"No, this is right. We belong together and I'm going to show you why."

I fixed her dress as I let her feet search for the ground. Slade's fancy sports car was parked in front of Lily's building, but the Town Car was nowhere to be seen. They had to be out looking for her or dealing with Alec.

"One night to try to convince you," I said in her ear. "You give me that and if you want to go home in the morning, you can. If you refuse to stay with me tonight, we leave the country immediately. Your choice." Before she could answer, I continued. "One night or Afghanistan. Either way, I get my chance. Think my proposition through. There, you'll never escape and you know it. I'm willing to be miserable under my father's roof if it means I get to keep you, so I'm fine with it either way."

A frustrated sob left her. "This isn't fair. You have to see how complicated things would be. My brother would kill you if he knew how we met. We have to go our separate ways. You have to leave while you still can."

"Slade doesn't scare me. Besides, do you really think he can best me at my own game? Death is nothing more than a delivery service in which I excel. He doesn't stand a chance."

The fighting grew stronger. "Zain, tell me you're not going to hurt my brother."

Killing was something I never joked about and I wasn't going to lie to convince her either. "Your brother is safe...for now. Unless he gives me reason. Now, choose. One night, or do you want to go back?"

Lily closed her eyes and a shiver had them reopening. Was it from the cool air or her imagining what the night would hold? I knew she didn't want to verbally admit her true feelings. She was trying to view me as the enemy now — as if I had been the one who ripped her off the street and sold her. But I was determined to pull out her need for me, no matter what.

"Do you give your word you're truthfully going to let me walk away?"

"Yes."

The tension left her body and I loosened my arms as she found her footing. "Fine. One night. That's it. I'm warning you now, you're not going to change my mind. We can talk all night and try to figure out this mess, but it's a waste of time. You should just go home. Things can't go back to the way they were between us."

Oh, they wouldn't. They'd be better. We'd be here, away from my family and the danger that surrounded them. There was nothing that could force my hand in taking her back to that hell. I'd never broken my word before, but tonight I would. Desperate times came with desperate measures. Lily would be mine again. She'd come to overlook our past and focus on our future.

"I love you and I'm not going anywhere." I cupped her face, giving her one last kiss. She remained quiet as I eased us around the side and led her quickly into the building. "No talking until we get to my place. If you speak to anyone, I'll shoot them. You know I'm not lying. If you say I'm going to lose you, what's left for me? Don't do something stupid."

"It was you I saw earlier?"

"Yes. I told you, I've been here all along. When you stand at your window crying, I feel it. When you sleep, I'm there when you wake from the nightmares. You didn't have those when you were in my arms, did you?"

She kept her head down as I pushed the button to the elevator. "You didn't, because you felt safe with me. I can give you that back. All you have to do is embrace this new chance we have."

The sound of the elevator arriving had her dragging her feet as I tried to push her forward.

"I don't know if I can do this."

My hand tightened and I gave a tug that sent her stumbling my way. "You have no choice anymore. It's time you remember your place."

Chapter 8
Lily

More times than I could remember, I'd lie in my bed and fantasize about Zain rushing in and sweeping me away. We'd go to some exotic island and live out the rest of our days making love under the stars. Nothing else would exist but us.

In reality, a life like that could never happen. His family would come looking for him. Slade, for me. The two wouldn't stop until they hunted us down. When they did, the repercussions would be unthinkable. And even if we could bypass that, even *if* somehow my Master was able to put an end to the evil tied to him, we still had my brother to deal with. Sure, I could do the unthinkable and disown him, but I loved Slade. He'd done more for me out of love and devotion than anyone ever had. He raised me.

For me and Zain to work, Slade would have to give his blessing and allow us to be together. I knew my brother. There was no way in hell he'd even allow Zain to continue to breathe air if he knew who he was, let alone become something as close as a boyfriend or husband. It would never work. The best I could do was make my Master hate me. Make him change his mind and release me. That way he could move on with his life.

Why did that break my heart? Because I loved him more than what was comprehensible. A person shouldn't be allowed to feel so much emotion for another. It had the capability to destroy. To make one dead inside. Love was nothing more than a gun and Zain was the trigger. Bang, bang, baby, blow me away.

Even now, as I stared at him from across the elevator, I could feel that all too familiar feeling of home. Nostalgia. It had sure as fuck done its job of convincing me how great our lives had been. What a crock of shit. We'd spent our days in a constant state of anxiety and the nights disappearing from it. That was, unless the cries dragged me from our room, right into the hands of a broken or dying slave.

"Zain."

His eyes flickered before narrowing, making my pulse jump.

"Try again, slave."

All I could do was shake my head. If I called him Master, I would be accepting he owned me. He couldn't believe that, regardless of what I knew.

"This really isn't necessary. Talking isn't going to accomplish anything."

He stayed quiet until the doors opened. At the wave of his hand, I eased into the entrance, just outside of his door. It didn't look much different than my own. A mirror stood off to the side, a table underneath. Flower arrangements rested on other surfaces and pictures randomly hung on the surrounding space.

"You weren't one for flashing money. Why the penthouse?"

"Let me show you." Pressure pushed against the small of my back and I trembled from the mix of fear and how close he was. Those hands, they'd shown me both pleasure and the most delicious pain imaginable. I'd spent hours kissing his fingers — my silent appreciation for the power he could wield over me.

The door unlocked and he pushed it open, locking it behind us. Heaviness settled in my legs the deeper we walked into his dark home. When we stopped at the large glass windows, I could clearly see Slade rummaging through my room.

"I was never truly away from you. Let that sink in for just a moment. Although there was only a street separating us, it could have been a million miles away for all the longing I felt while watching what I couldn't have."

The brush of his finger down my neck only had me shaking even more. My lids lowered and I could feel my lips part. All I wanted to do was turn and face him. To sink to my knees and give myself to him completely. Oh, what a beautiful torturous dream that would be.

"You still can't have me," I barely managed.

His touch left and I'd never felt colder. It took every ounce of strength I possessed not to wheel around and pull him into me.

"Before we start, I want you to call your brother. Tell him you need time to cool off and you'll be home as soon as you calm down."

I blinked, battling over whether I should alert my brother or truly spend the last night I'd ever get with my Master. I didn't want to leave him even though I knew I had to. One night...what could happen in such a short span of time?

"You know the consequence if you even hint that something isn't right. I'll take you for good and we'll disappear. I promise you that."

I spun around to see him walking back toward me, a phone in hand.

"He'll be able to trace that. Probably even be able to pick up my location."

Zain laughed, shaking his head. "No, he won't. He was able to get through on my last phone, but this is my spare. Our location will be impossible to track. The most he'll be able to do is call it back. I don't think even he can do that with this one."

"Before?"

"That's not something you need to worry about right now. Call him."

My stomach twisted. "Won't it look suspicious, me calling from a phone that's not traceable?"

"No, it'll read that you're calling from a random address somewhere in the city. Mostly motels and businesses. By the time he gets there, he'll have no idea if you were there or not."

I blindly nodded, still staring at the phone. Hesitantly, I reached for it and punched in my brother's number. As I turned and the ring sounded,

I watched Slade scramble for his cell, clearly panicked. My heart sank.

"Hello? Lily?"

Swallowing was almost impossible at the lie I was about to tell. "I just wanted to let you know I'm okay and I'm not coming home until I cool off."

In a swift motion, he ran his fingers through his hair. "Let me come get you. We can talk about this. I'll back off some. Just…come home."

Tears filled my eyes. "I can't. It has to be this way. I'll be home soon. I love you." I disconnected, watching his phone bounce on the bed and then over the other side as he lost his temper with frustration. Zain's arms wrapped around me from behind as my brother collapsed to the mattress, putting his head down, and supporting it with his hands. I'd never seen Slade so upset. Was this how he'd been when I'd been taken the first time? It had to be, but worse. He'd kidnapped Mary to get me back. To hurt him now…

"You did very well. Now, we begin."

I tried to shrug off his embrace but it only tightened. "Uh-uh, baby. Shh. Just let me hold you. Take it in while you can."

"No." I knew what he was implying and I wasn't sure how to feel about it. "We're not going to be doing much talking, are we?"

One of his arms moved to cover my breasts while the other settled over my cheek, bringing my face to rest against his.

"We'll be doing a lot of talking. For instance, do you remember the first day we met?" He laughed under his breath. "You were so scared, yet you didn't back down from me. I spanked your ass and what did you do not two hours later?"

My lids lowered while his fingers caressed down my neck, right over my pulse. "I disobeyed you." The past came barreling back and I let it. Darkness encompassed me. In Zain's arms, standing here, in his dark penthouse, I could almost believe we were back in his room.

"You need to take a bath, Lily. Follow me."

I pushed deeper into the corner of the wall, pulling the blankets up to my chin. All I could do was shake my head. A sigh left his mouth as his hand darted out and pulled me from the safety I had only just begun to feel. A cloth was wrapped around my head and half of my face. I almost pulled it off, but didn't at his look.

"What did I tell you about listening? Let's go."

"No," I said, pulling back. "I want to stay here."

"Too bad. You're filthy. You need to get clean. When was the last time you bathed? I'm guessing it was before you were taken. Am I right?"

He was, but I couldn't imagine taking my clothes off in such a scary place. I didn't trust him or anyone else here.

"No, please." I tried wiggling to break his grasp. With a jerk, he sent me stumbling toward the door. I instantly turned, trying to race back around him to the bed. I knew it was pointless, but I had no other options. To go outside of the room led to horrors I couldn't even consider. They'd chop off my head. I wasn't ready to die.

Zain grabbed me around the waist, flinging his door open. As it shut behind him, he placed me back down and gave me a shove back toward the way we came.

"Start walking, slave. If they see you misbehaving, I might not be able to save you. Obey, remember?"

Slow steps carried me to the stairway area and he turned me, pointing to a door beneath them. My legs gave out and silent sobs wracked my body. I was past the point of exhaustion. At his arms sweeping me up, I couldn't stop myself from turning into his large chest. He'd left me alone up to this point. He hadn't tried to touch me or hurt me. Would he rape me now?

"Shh. No crying. I'll stand watch at the door. You'll have as much privacy as possible." And he'd stayed true to his word. For a while.

"Yes, you never did listen too well. I can still remember it all so clearly. It took you almost half an hour to undress. When you finally did, it was only because I threatened I was going to do it myself. I was very patient with you. More so than I thought myself capable of. Just the tease of your naked shoulders that night made me realize how much I truly wanted you."

Light kisses traveled over the expanse leading to my neck. My eyes reopened and I tried to step away, but he held on tighter.

"Don't." The word came out more as a moan and I could have cursed myself. It was so obvious that I didn't want him to stop. Even now, I was leaning back against him. It was as if I had no control over it.

Suction against the side of my throat had my fingers digging into his thighs.

"And the first time I touched you. Do you remember that?"

My ninth day there and what felt like an eternity later. A sound escaped at the memory combined with the increase in his sucking.

"I was sleeping. I woke up to your fingers tracing over my palm. I…hit your hand away."

"Yes, you did," he whispered, running his tongue over the mark I knew he'd just placed. "But you didn't fight for long, did you? Once I pulled you to me and kissed you softly, leisurely…by the third attempt, you were kissing me back. Still, I took it slow with you." His fingers buried into my hair, pulling back slowly until the pressure was nice and tight. "Have I ever hurt you to where you didn't enjoy it?"

The need to answer, while addressing him as Master, begged to pour from my mouth. I forced the term back as I tried to hold onto my resolve. "No."

The jerk against my hair had me gasping
and growing even wetter. "Say it, slave. You know
you want to."

"No," I repeated. "I will not. Never again.
I...don't love you anymore. I'm ready to move on
with someone else. Let me go."

"Wrong," he growled. "You *do* love me. As for
moving on, that's the biggest lie I think I've ever
heard come out of your mouth. And the most hurtful.
You know the consequences for that, don't you."
Not a question. My legs pressed together at the
tingling it evoked.

The straps from my dress broke as he tugged
the silk down under my strapless bra.

"Your body is going to look beautiful covered
in my marks. It's been so long. I've dreamed of this
so many times. Now, reach forward and put your
hands flat on the glass while I unzip your dress. I'm
going to start by spanking you until you tell me
about Alec. In detail. Then, you'll be cropped for
lying to me."

"Cropped?" I asked, in disbelief. He'd never
gone that far. "No way," I snapped. "I came here to
talk, nothing more. And I'm telling you, this ends

now. I don't love you anymore. We're finished.
Go back home and never come around me again."

"Oh, slave, such work we have ahead of us.
I'm not going anywhere and neither are you. You'll
stay right here with me until I make you see what I
so clearly do. Even if that takes forever."

I was spun around with my back pushed
against the glass. Zain's hand locked on to my throat
and my own flew up to grasp his wrist. He didn't
apply pressure or choke me, he just held.

"You're breaking your word?" The last of my
sentence was silent. My voice had given out at the
clash of emotion. Was I happy that he wasn't letting
me leave in the morning? Afraid? Both? What were
his plans for me? Would we return to his father's?

"I'd never break my word, but this isn't just
anything, Lily. This is our lives, our love, I'm trying
to save. You can deny it as much as you want, but I
feel what we share." He stepped in closer, pulling
me forward with the hand that was around my throat.
"Your heart beats for me. *Thump. Thump.* Right
here, under my fingers." He increased the pressure
until I could experience what he spoke. It pulsed
throughout my body, slamming prominently in my
lips at the lack of oxygen. "You feel that? Every

thud that is happening right now is for me. Each beat that is giving you life is a reminder of who it's making you live for. *Me*, Lilian. Your heart beats only for me."

All I could do was stare into his eyes. How did he know? Was I so readable that he could see a gone slave when he looked at one? Was his name written in the depths of my connection with him? The one place people spoke of when it concerned the soul? Perhaps, if we were one, like I had always believed, it was obvious to my other half. Too bad what we both wanted couldn't happen.

"My heart beats for me and if what you say is true about you not allowing me to leave, I have no other choice."

"Other choice? What are you planning to—?"

Before he could finish, I used the element of surprise to bring my fist flying down as hard as I could at the bend of his elbow. The sudden loosening on my neck gave me the opportunity to lunge to the side, but he had me pinned against the window before I could get any further.

"Ah, your training was good, but not good enough, baby. Now, face forward and take your punishment. You'll have extra because of this stunt."

My zipper was ripped down. The dress yanked and fell to my ankles. *Whack!* The first spanking sent fire flaring over my ass. A cry escaped and I pushed my palms into the glass. Another quickly followed and I tried to turn — anything to not submit to him like I truly wanted.

"Forward," he bit out.

A quick succession of two more had tears rolling down my cheeks.

"You have to stop," I breathed out, pushing against him. Stop? No, I didn't want this moment to ever end. It would be all I had left when I returned home. *If* I got to go home.

"I will not. Such pretty lingerie," he said, changing the subject. "How much did he get to see of it?"

"That's none of your business," I sobbed, a moan slipping out as his teeth grazed my neck.

Zain's hand fitted over my bra, giving my breast a good squeeze. "Answer. Did you take off your dress for him? Show him what I spent months worshipping? Years, even." The warmth of his fingertips pushed past the black lace and teased over my nipple. At the pinch, I couldn't stop my gasp.

My legs crossed while my pussy begged for attention.

"I didn't take off my dress. Now, please."

Fighting the lust was unbearable when all I wanted to do was throw myself at him.

"So, he just touched you. Briefly."

A groan mixed with an internal cry, so full of pain, released and I couldn't stop it. "Yes, briefly."

Zain's face buried further into my neck and moved up into the hair just above my ear. "I'm so disappointed in you, slave. I can't blame you for wanting to begin to live again, but fuck, it hurts so badly. Can you feel what I do? The pain, here," he said, moving his hand to rest over my heart. "From the whimpering, I know you can. It hurts you just as much as it hurts me. Let's stop this agony we're both in. Submit to me. Love me even more than you used to. We could be so happy together."

Oh, how I wanted it. It was the words surrounding almost every dream I'd had of him. We'd make love and he'd whisper his devotion to only me.

"Lilian," he said, lowly.

At my silence, his fingertips lowered, tracing down my stomach and not stopping until the light touch brushed over my slit. Need had me instantly moving forward to apply more pressure against my clit. Stinging on my lip told me I'd bit it too hard, but I couldn't control myself anymore.

My fingers bent, wanting to claw into the glass. Realization washed over me at seeing I'd kept them there this whole time. God, I was his slave. Even, subconsciously. Where was my fight? My control?

"Spread your legs wider for me, baby."

And here I was, obeying. Shame made my cheeks burn, yet I opened wider for him.

"Now....breathe."

Two fingers surged into my pussy and my guttural moan echoed through the large space. Deep they thrust, spreading me wide, sending a slight sting to the one place I'd all but forbidden myself to touch since I'd left him.

"This pussy is mine and gets treated how I deem appropriate, correct?"

I bit my lip even harder to hold in the continuous sounds of pleasure he was evoking.

"Answer. Am I correct?"

"Yes," I said, rushing, only to correct myself. "No. We can't keep doing this."

"Wrong. And for your refusal to acknowledge the truth, I believe my pussy will have to face the consequences."

A slap over my clit left me lurching forward toward the glass. My bedroom light was off now. Almost all the lights were, but I barely cared to look as his fingers rubbed circles over the top of my slit. Fast. Rough. *Slap!*

"Fuck." That one word was all I could get out in my attempt to hold in a million other things that wanted to be said. Begging, for one. I was so close to pleading for him to fuck me faster with his fingers. To drive them deep and mercilessly into my pussy. Each swift thrust had me literally clawing at the window and I was already so close to coming. At the hand that wrapped around my waist, arching my hips, I nearly did.

"You not saying your pussy is mine in this moment doesn't matter to me, slave. You *will* be saying it before the night is over with. You watch and see. For now…you're mine, regardless."

The sound of his belt coming undone gave me a moment to pull my thoughts together. I shouldn't be doing this. Not because I knew it was wrong or that he wasn't going to wear protection. I was safe from pregnancy and would bet my life he hadn't been unfaithful to me once, but what we were doing was only going to make things worse. Was going to—

The head of his cock pushed against my opening, wiping all thoughts from my mind. My eyes closed, and I pushed back, savoring his thickness while it inched inside, stretching me wide.

"God…dammit. You feel so good."

His fingers wove into my hair, pulling back, and making me arch even more. The city lights were but a fog as the side of my face was pushed against the glass before he drove all the way in.

"Zain. I…"

"Don't. You want this." He plunged into me again. "You've missed me just as much as I've missed you. Admit it."

For the life of me, I couldn't answer with words. Instead, I moved my hips, trying to make him go faster. The slap to my ass was a warning to be still. I knew my Master, just like I knew my sudden lack of movement was going to get me what I wanted. Eight torturous thrusts built me up when all of a sudden, he slammed into me. The pace turned frantic, desperate, just like we were for each other.

"Say you missed me. I have to hear you say it." His fingers pressed over my clit, rubbing back and forth as I fought to breathe through his pounding.

"I...can't. We shouldn't—"

Whack! "Say that again and I'm going to tear your ass up, Lilian."

A scream broke past my throat, but not at the spanking. The return of his hand over the top of my slit moved faster, beginning a combination I knew all too well. *Slap! Rub for a few seconds. Slap! Rub again.*

"Oh...God!" I pushed to my toes as my orgasm built to the point of not being sure I'd contain it.

"Almost, baby." Harder he pushed me into the thick glass, until the top of my chest was flattened to the surface. *Slap!*

Tightening pulled at my insides and I shifted to try to bring him to the spot that would push me over the edge. I had waited too long. I didn't want to wait anymore.

Slap! "I said no. Stop moving."

The sting had me sucking in and I let out a cry as he slowed and grinded into me. "Mine," he said, lowering against my back and continuing his torture over my clit. Combined with the slow thrusts, my whole body trembled.

"Please…"

"Do you think I'd allow just anyone to call me Master, slave?"

"No," I rushed out.

His fingers pushed back to where we were joined, collecting my wetness, only to move back up and use it to slide easier over my clit.

"Then ask and address me correctly. Remember what we've been through and how far we've come."

Flashes of memory blinded me, visions of just before and after we'd made love barreling through. To kneel before him came natural. To call him Master, was a gift. He'd taught me that. I had been separated from other women. Put on his pedestal and cherished. Hadn't he said worshipped? Yes, he had worshipped me just as much as I had him. We were yin and yang. We were one…and we couldn't be.

"I won't disrespect you by lying."

A growl was followed by another slap. I bit my lip as the slow movements turned rough. "You're lying now, slave. Aren't you?"

His hand pulled back on my hair as the other slapped my ass. I inhaled deeply as he increased the thrust until all I could do was make continuous sounds.

"You know how I feel about liars, Lilian. If you don't want to respect the title I so easily grant you, I'll just remind you of how we got there."

Pressure from his palm fitted over my nose and mouth while he slapped my ass harder than all the other spankings combined. Tears filled my eyes and spilled over almost instantly. Although my mind reeled from the shock, it was as though my soul sighed in relief. There was my pain — my missing link that only Master could satiate.

"Do you feel how you've relaxed? You're lowering. You're getting very heavy." *Whack!* *Whack!* "Submission is calling, baby girl. It's time to answer. Now, let go and submit."

Air filled my lungs and the new movement over the top of my slit left heat rolling from my body. Especially, my ass. Combined with the pleasure, I was lost.

"Oh…"

"Say it," he snapped.

My head shook as my orgasm beckoned.

"Now, God dammit. Say it, slave."

The sobs still came, but I couldn't think of anything past my love for the man behind me. When we were faced with each other, how could I so easily slip back into the state of mind that he was good? Was he? What was right and wrong, anymore? I couldn't think. Didn't want to. All I knew was what my inner-most self told me, and that was that Zain was the one for me. That I was being stupid for denying what I so clearly knew.

"No!" I screamed, as the spasms shook my body.

His hand cupped back over my nose and mouth while I cried through the waves of what only he could bring me. Warmth shot over my ass and I barely noticed as he used something behind me to clean me up. The smooth feel was so wrong from what I knew should have been touching my ass. The paddle. His hand. Something that would punish me for the stubbornness I was showing.

"You break my heart, Lily. You really do."

I wiped the tears from my eyes, refusing to turn around to face him. Shame for what I had done led me to dip lower and pull up my dress.

"They call me the ice queen at work. I guess that's just who I am now. I'm sorry, Zain, but you have to see, I'm not the girl I once was. She's dead now. She's been dead since she left you."

"You're not the same. I see that. But your love for me is still alive."

Slowly, I turned, meeting his eyes.

"I'll always love you. It doesn't mean that we can be together. I'm serious when I say we're over. A relationship between us, a future, is impossible. We both know why."

I didn't wait to seek his permission as I headed for the door. That wasn't who I was anymore. Lily, the girl, the submissive, was gone. The new woman who had taken her place didn't take orders from anyone.

"Slave." A threat laced his tone, but I didn't so much as slow. Instead, I quickened my pace, the door almost within grasp.

"You're not leaving."

My heart was pounding as I reached for the lock and turned it. I couldn't believe I'd made it so far. Was he really going to let me leave? The thought left an uneasiness, but I didn't stop. I flung the door open and stepped through. Never once had I heard

Zain approach. Fingers gripped my arm and I didn't think as I jerked and raced for the elevator, pushing the button frantically.

"No, baby. Don't do this." He spun me around to face him and I brought my fist down on the back of his elbow again. I watched the arm drop and then pain race over his features, but he didn't let up. His other arm wrapped around my waist. "Look at me. You love me. Now, stop this. Running away and ignoring what we both know isn't going to make things easier. Whatever you're afraid of, we can get past it. Is it Slade? Is that the reason why you're denying what we both know?"

"You have to let go." Even though I flailed, I wished what he spoke could happen. That we could get past it. But he didn't know my brother. Didn't understand or see what I did. He was bad. I couldn't bring that sort of trouble back into my life.

Ding!

The sound of the doors opened while I tried to wrestle free.

"Zain, let—"

Stinging pain flared at my scalp from behind. One second, I was trying to fight Zain off, the next, I was trying to hold onto him as someone from behind fought to pull me free. I could see the panic and confusion so clearly written on my Master's face. He wasn't sure what was going on any more than I was, but we were both trying to disconnect me from the force that was hell bent on separating us.

"Let go!" I screamed. "You're hurting me!" I grabbed Zain tighter.

"Baby, reach inside my jacket pocket and get my gun, I can't let go of you." Zain's low voice had me obeying immediately. The moment I moved my hand from the grip on his jacket, an arm locked around my throat and jerked me free. The deafening explosion next to my ear had sound ceasing to exist. My heart…stopped. As if to tell me the love of my life no longer was inside of me. Or alive. Zain's hand reached to his chest, blood oozing through his fingers as he crumbled to the floor.

Chapter 9
Slade

"Tell me you've got something. What the fuck is going on here?" My voice boomed through the street as I half stared at my men, half watched the ambulance drive away with who I now knew to be Zane Collins. Had it not been for my men alerting me to the gunshot and suspicious activity they picked up on the police scanner, I might have missed the whole episode of the police arriving.

Marcio glanced at Brace, who took over.

"They got him in the chest. Doesn't look good. There were no witnesses to the attack, but it appears it happened just outside the elevator on the top floor. Witnesses reported a man forcing a screaming woman into a dark SUV in the parking garage."

"His girlfriend? Shit, his family must have gotten to him." My hand came up to my mouth while I shook my head. Why the fuck hadn't he taken me up on my offer? Maybe he would have been safe. Now this, on top of my sister having some kind of break down and running off. I couldn't stand

her not being looked after. I supposed it was time
I backed off, but I didn't like her being so
unprotected. Too much shit surrounded us. Bad
blood came a dime a dozen in my circle and now she
was part of it.

"Boss, there's more."

Brace glanced back at Marcio. I knew that
look. They were hiding something.

"Well, what the fuck is it?"

What looked to be black lace was pulled from
his pocket. The stocking attachments were the first
thing to catch my attention.

"Speak, Brace. I'm not a fucking psychic. And
stop looking at Marcio. He's not going to help you.
Just tell me."

I reached for the garter belt and what I soon
realized were ripped panties.

"I found these around the side of the building,"
he said, pointing off to the distance. "I went
shopping with Lily earlier. She bought the replica of
those. The call we tried to track…it was a buffer
call. It had to be. Holland's Hotel is on the far side
of the city. With traffic like it is, it would have taken
her at least a half hour to make it there by car. She
was walking. I think your man who just got shot

might have something to do with Lily calling. The number you had me track down earlier had similar characteristics. And the description of the woman…it's Lily to a tee. The hair, the dark dress, the black stockings…"

My head shook, refusing to believe what sounded so certain. "Coincidence. It has to be. Women wear black undergarments all the time. And Lily didn't sound scared when she called. Angry, a little, but afraid for her life? No. Besides, how would she know Zane Collins? It doesn't make sense. You've seen everyone Lily's came in contact with. Have you ever seen them together?"

"No," he said, shaking his head. "But we both know Zane Collins isn't his real name."

Of course I knew that. Why hadn't I been tempted to find out what it was earlier? There was just something about that guy that made me a little soft and I had no idea what it was.

The more I let everything play out, the faster my heart raced. One by one, the possibilities hit me and I could feel myself freaking the fuck out. Not again. *Lily.* "Well, what have you been waiting for? Get it for me! If my sister had an association with him and she was the one taken, I want to know everything." I took a few steps closer to the street, not sure of where I was going. "Son of bitch. Marcio, get the car, we're going to the hospital. If he wakes up, maybe we can learn something."

Please don't fucking die. And please tell me they're wrong. Lily can't be the one taken. Not again. Fuck...I couldn't do this again!

I nearly groaned as I let everything sink in. Whether I wanted to admit or not, I already knew in the pit of my stomach. Zane and my sister had been together. How, I had no clue. But it made sense why he kept showing up at random places. And then, asking me for help, and wanting to get his life straight because of the woman he loved. He'd stressed that part, as if he were trying to tell me why it were so important. The woman....it had to be my sister. Fuck! I could kill him for the danger he put her in. Yet, I knew the cost of love. Had lived out my own hell with Mary before we found peace.

The car pulled up next to me as I still stared at the flashing lights. I had to force myself to slide in the back seat. I felt rocked inside, right back in the same spot I'd been when I learned my sister had been taken the first time. I grabbed my phone from my pocket, hating to have to call Mary so late. She'd been so tired lately. It was only just before nine, but she was probably already asleep.

Ringing sent my hand to the door grip and I squeezed tightly.

"Hey, I was wondering where you were." She yawned. "How'd Lily's date go?"

My head leaned back against the headrest. The last thing I wanted to do was upset my wife, but we shared everything. If I couldn't be open with her, she'd know I was hiding something. That would stress her out even more. "She's gone, baby. I think she's been taken again."

"What!" Breathing heavily, her words tumbled over each other as they came out. "How? I thought you were there? How could someone have taken her?"

My head shook. "We were caught off guard. Lily…she fucking tied up Alec in the restroom. Sexually," I emphasized. "I was shocked, to say the least. She ran out, angrily, while we were getting him untied. She called a little while afterward and said she was okay, that she'd be home when she cooled off, but something has happened." My hand rubbed at my eyes as I tried to think of how to shorten the story. "You remember the guy I was telling you about earlier? The one who needed a job?"

"Zane," Mary rushed out.

"Yes. Well, he got shot tonight, right across the street from Lily's penthouse. A girl was taken."

"The girlfriend you told me about?"

My head shook. "I don't know. I think Lily *might* be that girlfriend. It's really confusing right now. We found some…clothes that she might have been wearing, next to the building. It could be hers, or maybe it belongs to someone else. We might be way off and maybe she is just away for the night. I don't want to take any chances, though. We're headed to the hospital now. Maybe we can get in to see Zane somehow."

"I'm coming." What sounded like blankets ruffled in the background and I flew forward.

"You leave that room, so help me God."

"Slade, you can't just expect me to stay here when—"

"Oh yes, you will stay. Do not leave that room. I want every single door locked. I'm sending Marcio over there to stand guard. We have no idea what the fuck is happening right now. Think of the baby, Mary. If something happened to either one of you…" I trailed off, running my hand through my hair —a habit that had suddenly come back due to all this stress. "Stay. Promise me."

A few seconds went by before I heard her sigh. "You're right. I'll stay."

"Good girl. Now, lay back and relax as best as you can. You don't need to worry. I shouldn't have said anything to begin with, but I knew you'd want to know."

"Thank you. Be careful, please."

"Always. I love you."

"I love you, too."

I hung up, sliding the phone back in my pocket. "You're dropping me off and going to stand guard outside of my room with Caleb. Send Brace and Tor up here. I'm not sure what the fuck is going on with Zane and his family, but I have a feeling it's not going to be good. If Lily *was* taken, we have to figure out if it had to do with them or something completely different. He knew about my past as far back as Lily returning. He knew about the Brightons. I can't shake the impression that saying their name set him off. Shit, what the fuck is happening? I can't think. If she was taken, was this on my and her side, or his?"

My fingers rubbed circles over my temple.

"Boss, can I make a suggestion?"

I looked up, meeting his eyes in the rearview mirror. "Have I ever told you no?"

"No." He turned, bringing the ambulance in view as it pulled into the hospital entrance. "I think we should call the FBI. Have them check the clothing we found to see if it matches with Lily's DNA. I'm sorry, but I have a really bad feeling about this and I'd like to bring them in as fast as we can. If you don't want to take that route just yet, at least allow me to make a few calls. I know someone who has a connection with a man at the FBI office here in the city. His name is Agent Gaige Sullivan. I think he could help us out. It'll strictly be under the radar. No news crews. No big scene. We can just call him and tell him the story, accompanied with Lily's history. Although," he paused, "I'm betting he's heard all about it."

"FBI." I nearly cringed at the bad taste it left in my mouth. But, Marcio was right. Maybe they could help. "Call your connection. Tell him to meet us here."

Marcio nodded and pulled out his phone as he drove in and parked. I didn't wait. I threw the door open and raced toward the ER entrance. The ambulance was still parked with the back doors opened, in the process of taking him out. I slowed at the roar that echoed from inside the space.

"Lily! Lily!"

My legs turned weak as I tried to keep them moving. The stretcher was pulled out and a pale body fought against the restraints strapping him in. Zane turned to me as they lowered him out all the way. Blood splatter stood out against his ghostly appearance, dotting his face and staining his neck. My whole world tilted as our eyes met.

"Slade, find Lily. Slade," he yelled, beginning to cough. "Find her, please." The last word were weak. I could see how hard he was fighting to stay conscious.

As they began wheeling him in, my body kicked into gear and I rushed to catch up. "Who took her? Who took my sister?"

All he could do was shake his head as his eyes began rolling off to the side.

"Zane! Dammit, you fucking tell me right now. Who has Lily?" I reached forward in desperation when I was cut off by a team of nurses. The paramedics began going over their report as the nurses began taking his vitals.

"Sir, you have to stay here." Someone was pushing against my chest, but I saw nothing except the last man to see my sister before she was abducted. They were taking him further away, and with it, any information that could help.

"Fuck." My hand blindly reached out to the wall. "Tell me this isn't happening." I turned, catching Marcio coming through the main doors. I rushed forward, grasping his shirt and dragging him outside. "It's Lily. Someone *has* my sister. God dammit!" My shoe connected with the trashcan mounted to the cement. I punched against the metal next and I didn't stop swinging until Marcio pulled me back. Blood ran from my numb knuckles, but I barely noticed. Flashes of Lily raging in front of me appeared and it only made me swing again. Hadn't she seen why I'd been so protective?

"Enough. Gaige is on his way. He already called. Did Zane say anything?"

My head shook as I stared toward the entrance. "I'm going to kill whoever took her. They'll be in pieces before it's over with. Nobody fucks with what's mine. No one."

"Let's go get your hand looked at while we wait."

"It's fine," I ground out.

"It'll give us something to do. Come on, boss."

Like a zombie, I let Marcio lead me inside. My mind went over every possibility of who could be responsible. Even through the paper work and admitting, I never stopped plotting revenge. Someone was going to pay and I wasn't going to stop until they did.

Chapter 10
Zain

A blur of colors swirled above me and somewhere within, I knew doctors were working to keep me alive, but all I could focus on was my slave's face. Her smile beamed above as she leaned down, running her fingers over the stubble on my cheek. It was the moment I knew my heart was hers. We'd just finished making love and I was surprised she was still awake from the punishment I'd put her through. Marks from the spanking and where I'd sucked against her skin marred random places, and exhaustion showed on her face, but that smile and affection…I soaked it in like the starving man I was.

"What was your life like before you got taken?" I tucked a lock of hair behind her ear while she twisted her mouth.

"Lots of school, shopping, the typical college girl stuff."

"School." My attention piqued. At twenty-seven, I'd never attended a real college. All my

education was done by private teachers that came to my father's home. "What were you studying?"

She laughed and shrugged. "Nothing too exciting. Just business stuff. My brother owns a really big company. I'm going to work for him when I finish school." A frown took over her smile. "I was." Tears appeared and I pulled her to lay down on my chest while I stroked her hair.

"I'm sorry your life has taken a different path. I've come to see they often veer from what we expect."

"No." She pushed off of me to sit. "I'm going back. I won't be here forever. Slade will find me. He will. You don't know my brother."

"I don't, but I know my father and his connections. You won't be going home, Lily. Your life is here now."

Dark hair spun around her nude body as she turned to get off the bed. My arm wrapped around her waist and I pulled her back, making her lie down again.

"Is it so very bad here with me?" I used the pad of my thumb to wipe the tears from her cheek. "I take care of you, don't I?"

"Well, yes, but…"

"Stop," I said, lowly. "The more you think about what can never be, the worse it'll become. I know this from experience, slave. I was every bit the captive you were. Sometimes we just have to accept what is and continue living with what we're given."

Her head lifted while she cupped my cheek. The soft press of her lips had my eyes searching hers.

"Let's leave together. We can go back to San Francisco and you can get a job while I go to school. You can have a new start. Once my brother knows everything, he'll destroy this place. We can do it, Master. We can escape."

The happiness on her face had my hand fitting over her mouth—hard. "No more. You're living in a fantasy world." In truth, the temptation rocked me. I wanted to leave with her. Wanted to work a normal job while she went to school. We could get a little place and spend every minute of our free time in each other's arms. What I liked even more was how she saw us together outside of this place. For some reason, I hadn't expected that—hadn't even let myself think of the possibility.

"No," she said, managing to turn her head away from my palm. "You are the one living in a fantasy. You're brainwashed into believing your father is more powerful than he is. You watch. My brother is going to kill him when he finds out where I am and what he's done to all those girls."

My fingers buried into her hair and I tightened my fist. "The only one killing that bastard is me. Enough of this talk. I want your pussy on me again. Kiss me and let me taste what's mine." I spun her underneath me, still holding her head steady and under my control. "You want me?"

Moans poured from her mouth as I let the underside of my cock glide over her wet slit. Her hips pumped, urging me to go faster.

"Yes, Master."

"You said you wanted to be with me in your little fantasy world. That really true?"

Lily paused and the pink that tinted her cheeks had my mouth crushing into hers. I didn't need an answer from what I'd just seen.

"I want to be with you, too. There's no one else for me, Lily. You're the one." My hips shifted as I reached down, sliding one of my fingers deep into

*her pussy. Nails dug into the back of my biceps
and I eased another in, thrusting at a slow pace.*

*No matter what was going through my mind, I
couldn't break my stare from the pleasure on her
face. Her sounds grew louder, hypnotizing me.
Warmth filled my chest until it resembled nothing
short of liquid lava. How had she done it? Come into
my life and turned a cold, ruthless killer into a man
full of tenderness and love? True, it wasn't to
anyone but her and an outsider would see it
differently with the punishment I inflicted on her, but
I never thought myself capable to care for someone.
To...*

*"I love you," I breathed against her lips,
telling her for the first time. "God, I do. And nothing
will ever break us apart."*

"No matter what?"

*Such raw hope on her face. "You have my
word, baby girl. No matter what."*

Bright lights shone through the darkness taking
Lily away from me. There was something over my
mouth and nose that kept rocking my head the
slightest amount. For the life of me, I couldn't react
to try to remove whatever was suffocating me...or
was it giving me air? I couldn't think to decide. Fire

covered my chest and my body swayed at someone pushing down. *Chest compressions?* Opening my eyes took every ounce of strength I had, but my surroundings didn't become visible before darkness blanketed me once again. A multitude of voices grabbed my attention and I fought to make out the words.

"Let's do a Dopamine drip to titrate the patient's blood pressure. Systolic blood pressure of one-forty." A voice further away, broke through. "We're going to have to get him into surgery fast. He's losing too much blood."

"You're bleeding." My voice was cold as I walked forward, pulling Lily from the corner of the room she was huddled in. Nausea and rage mixed, sending my adrenaline through the roof. "What happened? Who hurt you?" I angled her face to the side, taking in the fresh bruise and laceration on her cheek.

"It's nothing, really. It was my fault."

It took everything I had not to shake her. *"What. Happened?"*

Tears rolled down her cheeks, feeding my anger even more.

"There was a slave. She was hurt. I tried to help."

My head shook and I lifted her hand to kiss her palm. The long sleeve of the robe fell away and my eyes widened at the claw marks embedded deep in her arm.

"Oh...baby. Did they do this to you, too?"

She jerked her hand back. *"No, that was the girl. She's..."* A sob broke from her and she threw herself into my chest, crying harder than I'd ever seen her. *"She's dead. She died in my arms while I was trying to comfort her. Then, Saul found me and—"* A deep groan vibrated my insides as she broke.

"No more. I'm here now. I won't let anyone hurt you again." I covered her face, leaving her eyes showing as I led her to the shower. The moment the robe dropped to the floor, I knew what I had to do. The bruise on her face was enough to convince me, but the damage I saw covering my slave's body went past simple murder. I was going to carve my uncle up every way I could for putting his hands on what belonged to me.

Lights broke through the darkness again. I blinked, feeling my eyes roll as what looked to be shadows hovered over me.

"He's waking up."

The voice sounded distant and my head turned to the side as I tried to figure out which direction it had come from. More talking and movement swirled and I knew I should have been scared, but the only thing on my mind was Lily. Someone had taken her. A man, wearing dark clothes and a ski mask. Was she okay? Was she getting hurt this very moment?

I heard myself groan as pressure pushed into my chest.

Was it my family who'd orchestrated it? Someone she knew and wanted to hurt her because of the murders she committed? How did they know to look on my floor? Did they witness us going inside?

So many question began flooding my mind, but nothing would come in the form of an answer. I was drowning in both theories and what I assumed was my own blood. I was dying, and from my guess, it wasn't the first time tonight. Was I going to make it out of this room alive and be able to search for my slave, or would she be lost forever?

Chapter 11
Lily

"Rise, baby, and give your Master a kiss."

I stood, racing for Zain and throwing myself in his arms. My legs ached and my knees were numb from kneeling for the last hour, waiting for him to arrive from one of his missions. The details had been vague when he left, but I knew it was going to be dangerous, just like everything surrounding him.

My arms locked around his neck and I pulled myself as close as I could possibly get. Not two hours before, I'd been covered in blood. Saul had a new slave, one he was breaking, one night at a time. This time, it had been a broken nose and one that seemed to take me forever to get to stop bleeding. And, I'd bled, too. But not from his uncle. Not that night.

The blowout that had happened after the first incident could be heard all the way in our room. Even Zain's father got in on the yelling, but when it was said and done, I was granted permission to help those who were wounded. I was off limits to every

*male in the house and as long as it was to give
my service, I was able to go as I pleased, but I paid
dearly for it.*

*Rachel's crescent shaped nail marks were
embedded all down the length of my forearms. When
Zain reached up to remove my locked wrists from
behind his neck and I winced, he knew.*

"How bad was it?"

*I stepped back, letting him take off the bullet
proof vest and belt he wore that carried his
weapons.*

"Broken nose. Bruises to the face."

*He shook his head and his jaw clenched
repeatedly.*

*"How was your night?" Fatigue was settling
in, but I was far from ready for bed.*

*"Went pretty smoothly. Transaction made.
Easy deal."*

*My frown was instantaneous. He was never so
vague.*

"Oh. That's it?"

*His eyes darted to me, but went down to the
button of his pants as he began taking them off.*

Silence.

"Are you seeing anyone else when you leave? Like...a woman?"

I swallowed hard, hating that my insecurities had me speaking my fears. Zain's eyebrows drew in as he turned his attention to me.

"What in the world would make you think that?"

All I could do was shrug.

He sighed and cocked his head to the side. "Does it look like I need another woman? I obviously want you."

His cock was thick and long. So hard and ready for me. Embarrassed, I turned to the side and lowered my head. "We've had sex multiple times in one night. You could easily fuck someone else and come back here to me."

Slowly, he moved forward. I could feel his dominance pushing against my skin like a living thing.

"I'm disappointed in your doubt of me. Have I ever given you reason to believe I'd be unfaithful to you? Have I not catered to you? Cherished and protected you to the best of my ability?"

"You have."

"Wall."

The deepness of his voice had me dropping the robe to the floor. I kept my head high as I walked over and stood to face him. My arms rose, waiting.

"Trust. Have I not taught you anything? You trust me more with your body than you do with your heart. I want it equally. I want it to capacity. You will learn to believe in me."

The cuffs locked around my wrists and I watched as he lifted his hand, raking his nails down the center of my chest. The delicious heat had me licking my lips. A tap to my feet and I spread my legs even wider.

"Look at that," he breathed out. "You have no idea what I feel when I see you give yourself to me like this. Why would I want to risk losing your submission, slave? You may see it as a pleasure for you, but it's a gift to me. I treasure what we share. Nothing could make me ruin that."

He grabbed his belt and used the end to slap the outside of my leg, harder than he normally began.

"Tonight will be the last time you question my devotion to you. I'll make sure of it."

A steady connection began on my hip and moved toward my knee, working the outside. When it changed to the inside, I sucked in air at the sting.

"*Who loves you?*"

"*You do, Master.*"

"*And do people who love on each other cheat?*"

A cry escaped at the slap over my clit. "*Sometimes.*"

He moved to the opposite inner thigh with a force that had my jaw dropping and tears filling my eyes.

"*Then that's not love. If I called my brother in here, would you let him fuck you?*"

My head shook frantically. Amir's namesake was someone I tried to stay as far away from as I could. The hate he had for Zain was clear. Zain was the bastard child. The one his father always doted on, if one could say the man doted on anything. It was clear to anyone who saw the three together which one his father favored.

"*Answer,*" *he growled.* "*I want to hear the words come from your mouth.*"

"*No, Master. I don't want anyone but you.*"

Whack! Whack! Whack! Whack!

The tears streamed down my cheeks as I searched for my breath.

"It better stay that way. We belong together. You and I. No one else." He walked forward, slightly brushing down my slit with his fingers. At him separating my folds, I bit my lip, moving against the almost nonexistent touch "Be still. You haven't earned enjoyment yet."

"I'm sorry. I was wrong to think you were seeing someone else."

His eyebrow rose. "You have no idea."

Four hard spankings to my ass ended with him gripping into my flesh and pulling me into his body. My legs wrapped around his waist while I tried to bring him closer.

"You want my cock?" He rubbed the length along my pussy. I tried rotating my hips to allow him entrance, but he denied me.

"Yes, Master. Give it to me. Show me I'm the only one for you. That you love me."

One arm wrapped around my waist while the other twisted in my long hair. Zain nipped at my lip, tracing over the bottom one with his tongue before he leaned back to look into my eyes. "I'm going to do more than show you that I love you, baby girl.

*I'm going to fuck it so hard into your memory
that you'll know no one but me. I may be your
Master in this new life of yours, but I'll become your
everything before it's over with."*

The head of his cock pushed into my opening
and I gripped to the chains as he eased in an inch at
a time, letting me adjust. His withdrawal left me
wanting more and I wasn't disappointed. In one
swift motion, he buried himself inside of me. My
scream filled the room and our lips connected at the
same time.

"Remember this, slave. Always remember who
you belong to. No one is going to love you more than
I will. I won't let them."

The thrusts came savagely, leaving me fighting
to catch my breath. Cold cement stunned my heated
skin as he pressed into me, removing the hand in my
hair to cover my throat.

"Your life is mine. I feel the proof of it right
here," he said, applying the smallest amount of
pressure and slamming into me even faster. "And
I'm yours. Put your hand over my heart. Tell me who
it beats for." He let one of my hands free while the
other was left above my head.

I took a deep breath, pushing my palm into his chest. "For me. We are each other's."

"Yes. Forever. And I mean that. Every day until our last."

My sob woke me from my dream. From the memories of my Master. Pitch black surrounded me and I flew to a sitting position, only making it inches up before my head connected with something hard. I froze for the briefest moment before confusion set in. Then...panic.

Frantically, my hands flew up, patting around me, realizing I was surrounded by what felt to be wood. Fear had my legs drawing up, only to be stopped from lack of space. The strangled cry that left me couldn't be stopped. Was I in a wooden coffin? Some sort of crate?

"Oh, God. Help! Somebody, help me!" My fist beat against the hard surface as my body went crazy inside the confined space. Louder, I became, each plea for help making my throat burn even more from the force of my yells.

But no one came. There wasn't a sound I could detect, except my own.

Sobbing, I forced myself to calm and replay the events of how I'd gotten here. Nothing was really registering. My brain felt fuzzy and my tongue was thick and swollen in my mouth. Where was I? My ears ached and I wasn't sure if it was from the dead silence or—

A blood curling scream left me as I saw my Master crumpling to the ground in my mind. Dark crimson poured from his chest. Pain was clearly etched on his features as his knees buckled and he fell to the ground. Was he dead? He'd been rushing forward. Right in the direction of me and my kidnapper.

My head shook and I couldn't bear to think of the possibilities. Not yet. I moved forward in in what I could remember. Leather. The whole time it had remained, sliding over my face at our rushing through the parking garage. It didn't lift until the door opened and a cloth pushed against my face. Then...nothing.

Now, here I was, trapped in a prison of my own making. Again. Why had I fought Zain? He loved me and wanted to protect me. Hadn't he proved that time and time again? Yet, I'd probably broken his arm, if not hyperextended it, and more than likely, he was dead. All due to my stubbornness. Of my lack of indecisiveness. I'd lost the only man I ever loved and it was all my fault.

No, I refused to believe that. He was a fighter. He'd survive.

Sobs returned and with each one, I could feel how hard it was to breathe. The air supply wasn't good, and would probably continue to get worse until I was dead. Especially if I was underground.

But if I wasn't...if I was in the air...on a plane...

Was that even possible? Wouldn't I hear engines? Could I have not boarded yet? Already be off a plane? How long had I been unconscious? There were too many questions and none of which I had an answer for.

Enough of this, Lily. Focus. Feel. Search every inch of this box as best as you can and try to figure out a way to escape. Master wouldn't want you lying here completely helpless. He'd want you to be strong. To exhaust every option. Do it. Think like him. Become him.

I closed my eyes and let my hands rise to the very top, all the way to the far left. Slowly, my fingers explored, taking their time as they worked their way to the right and then down. Back and forth, I went until I got to chest level, and even lower to my hips.

I refused to give up. Nothing was impossible. My Master had taught me that. And if he wasn't dead, I'd make my way back to him, no matter what I had to do.

Chapter 12
Slade

"Let's go over this again. Zane Collins introduced himself to you back in May, six months ago. From there, you both had run-ins, but nothing except small talk. Then, out of the blue, five days ago, he comes to you asking for a job."

My fingers weaved through my hair as I stared at Gaige's narrowed eyes.

"That's right. It was the day he was shot. He came to the building asking if I had a department I could put him in. Accounts, I believe he asked. He stated he had a background with handling money."

"Legally or illegally, Mr. Roberts?"

I sat up, matching Gaige's suspicious expression.

"What the fuck is that supposed to mean? If it was illegally, why would he supply that information to a complete stranger? Unless you're implying something else. Something that I really don't think I like the sound of."

Gaige's finger flicked over the folder he held, while his gaze stayed fixed to mine.

"You called me in because of your sister's abduction. It was supposedly linked to Mr. Collins. Thing is, Mr. Roberts, I have no evidence aside from your word that your sister has been taken. No ransom call. No video surveillance whatsoever due to faulty footage from the building the supposed abduction took place. And, you're having me investigate a fucking ghost."

"A what?" I sat up straighter, confused.

"Zane Collins is not Zane Collins. He's Zain Cook. His mother, Amelia Cook, and his step father, Jeffrey Cook, were killed when he was eight years old. He disappeared that night, never to be seen again. It was speculated he died in the fire that was set to destroy the evidence, but a body was never recovered. I guess we now know why."

My head shook. The family he mentioned, were they linked to the ones that had died, or was this the new family who took him? "He *has* family. He told me they were dangerous."

Gaige's head tilted to the side. "Why didn't you mention that before?"

My jaw clenched. "I did. I told you there were people he had bad blood with. I can't help it if I forgot to say they were family. I'm a little fucking unstable right now." I scooted to the edge of my chair, feeling so much rage that it was almost impossible to stay sitting. "You won't even acknowledge that my sister is missing. Zain was screaming her name and telling me to find her for fuck's sake. Why are you not looking?" I exploded.

"I have been looking," he said, just as forcefully. "But if you gave me the correct information the first time, maybe I wouldn't be on some witch hunt about a situation I know nothing about."

The door creaked and I stood from the desk in Lily's penthouse. My old desk, in my old office, to be precise.

Mary gave an apologetic look as she eased her head in.

"It's okay. Come here, sweetheart. What's the matter, you okay?" I held out my hand. As she swept in, I noticed she was carrying a tray.

"You haven't eaten anything today and it's already after lunch. I thought maybe Agent Sullivan would like something, too. I'm sorry if I'm interrupting."

She placed the tray on the desk and I wrapped both arms around her shoulders, pulling her close. The scent of her hair had me breathing in deeply. For a moment, I was at peace.

"I can't believe you're worried about me when you're the one who's been so sick. I do love you. And thank you. I'll eat, if it makes you feel any better."

"It would." She turned, smiling sadly down at Gaige. "I just wanted to thank you for helping us. I know you think Lily may have just run away, but I know my sister-in-law. She loves Slade too much to hurt him. She just wouldn't do that, not for this long. If you could find any way to continue with her search, I'd be very thankful. I..." Her head lowered and she furiously wiped a tear away before it could stain her face. "I know how this may sound, but I'd like you to check out my sister and her husband. Bethany changed for the worse after our father was killed. Charles lost his job. They lost their house...everything. She blames me, Lily, and Slade."

Gaige grabbed a sandwich, taking a bite. "And that's who Lily accused of taking her the first time, am I correct?"

"Oh, they took her," Mary rushed in. "If it wasn't for lack of evidence, they'd be in jail right now."

"And your sister told you this?"

"Yes," Mary said, weakly. I knew when her eyes darted to mine that she wanted to tell the entire truth about what happened during her own abduction —an abduction I was responsible for. But the secrets we carried couldn't be told. Luckily, I knew the incident she was about to speak of and was glad Bethany had stuck her foot in her mouth when she did.

"After the trial was over. We've only seen each other once since then and purely by accident, but she went off on some rampage about how we'd all pay. Said she should have killed Lily the first time."

The agent took another bite, nodding seriously as he stared into the distance. There was a darkness that festered within him. I could see it, so close to the surface. "Well, I've already talked to Bethany and she even let me inside to check around their house. Nothing looked suspicious. She was very polite. If it'll make you feel at ease, I'll go by and check with her again. Maybe her husband will be home this time."

"Thank you. That would be great. Now, if you'll excuse me, I'll let you two get back to talking."

I bent down and kissed Mary's forehead before watching her walk to the door. As she stood there and stared at me, one of her eyebrows rose. My gaze lowered to the sandwiches and I picked one up, showing her, before bringing it to my mouth to take a bite. Only then did she turn to leave.

"Sweet wife you have there. Reminds me a lot of my own. She'd have done something like that. Although, my Elle can't cook. Sandwiches, soup, and freezer meals she can do."

I laughed, unable to help it. "Sounds like Mary. It's the thought that counts, right?"

"Absolutely," Gaige agreed. "So…she's sick?"

I finished up the little triangular shaped sandwich and picked up another. "Pregnant. Right at nine weeks. The morning sickness is really taking its toll."

"I'm sorry to hear that. But, congratulations. I have a son. My wife had morning sickness pretty badly, too. What are you wanting, boy or girl?"

"Boy," I rushed out, a little too quickly. I frowned. "Don't get me wrong, I'd be just as excited for a girl, but a boy would be so much easier. These women will make me gray before my time. I feel so damn old already."

A loud chuckle echoed throughout the space. "I know what you mean. More than you know." Gaige leaned forward, taking another, and stood. "Listen, Mr. Roberts. I'm going to be blunt because I feel there's really no other way."

As he stood there, waiting for me to approve, I grabbed for my glass of Scotch. "Please do."

"I'm supposed to keep an open mind and look at the evidence, but I believe your sister was taken. There's no proof and Mr. Cook isn't speaking yet. Sure, I can continue to look into what we have, but due to my position with the department, there are boundaries I can't cross. No one legally can. However, you don't mark me as a man who really cares for the law."

Slowly, I shifted, wondering if this was some sort of setup. But, could it be? Marcio told me he trusted his sources, therefore trusted this man. Could I?

"I'll do anything to get my sister back." I left it at that, letting him decide if he wanted to continue or not. To say I wasn't interested would be a lie. All I wanted to do was beg and tell him I was willing to do anything to get Lily back. *Anything.*

Gaige finished off his sandwich and walked over, picking up his glass and downing it in one drink. "There's talk amongst the agents I work with. There's a man who specializes in your sort of situation. I've never met him personally, but I know people who have. He's not one to mess with. He takes his job very seriously and from what I've heard, I believe he's probably the only one who can save your sister."

My head shook. "What does that have to do with laws?"

Gaige looked around the room and lowered his voice. "To say we've turned a blind eye is an understatement. Within the last year, we've specifically been told to. We could have easily nailed his ass any time we wanted. We don't, nor will we ever. He's protected and I have no idea by who, and seriously, I don't care. This man used to be a detective. Now, he's one of us. He saves the missing, but his methods aren't for the faint of heart. Not if you're looking to get your sister out in a clean sweep. Blake Morgan will not leave with Lily until everyone associated with her disappearance is dead. That could be a scary thing. A lot of bad shit can go wrong while he's doing that."

"My sister is trained. If she had to, she could take care of herself. I'm guessing the only reason she didn't before was because she got caught off guard. You haven't seen her, she can...fight. As for Blake Morgan, why do I know that name?"

"Probably because he's been all over the news. He's the one that found, and then married, that supermodel, Kaitlyn Summers."

My lips parted and all I could do was nod. I'd seen their story. It caught my attention because of the woman. She'd been trafficked and it reminded me a little too much of Lily. The story had stayed with me for a while.

"I want him. Price doesn't matter. How fast can I get him here?"

Gaige pulled out his phone and scribbled a number down on a piece of paper from his notepad. "You'll have to figure that out yourself. I have to get going. If I'm ever asked whether I gave you the contact information or not, I'll deny it, Mr. Roberts. This never happened. It's just the way it has to be. Blake Morgan is a loose cannon. He's a killer, through and through, and I will not be liable for anything wrong that might go down. Now, working with both of you, I can do. But, being the one to actually bring him in?" He shook his head.

My hands lifted, as if in surrender. "Your name will never be mentioned. I promise you that."

The cautiousness behind his stare faded and his hand came out, displaying the number. "Program this into your phone."

He waited while I saved it to my contacts and then stuffed the paper in his pocket. "If he decides to help you, give me a call. We'll go from there."

"Thank you, I will."

Fuck. Could this guy, Blake, really find my sister before it was too late and we lost her for good? Was she already hurt? Dead? My whole body shook as I watched Gaige leave my office. I waited for the door to shut before I hit the button to call. It was answered after the first ring.

"Blake Morgan."

Something about the deep voice put me at ease. It was cold. Detached. Yet, I couldn't help but feel it was determined. Lily needed someone like him looking for her. We all did. "Mr. Morgan. My name is Slade Roberts. I need your help."

Chapter 13
Zain

Beeping had my eyes fluttering open, only to close again. Something wasn't right. I could feel it, but I couldn't put my finger on what it might be. I was too tired. Hurting too bad to roll over to see what time it was. No. I had to get up. I had to see what Lily was doing. Had she left for work yet? Did I sleep through her morning routines?

Like a cannon blast, the memories exploded into my brain. My hand flew to my chest at the memory of the gunshot wound and my eyes jerked open. I'd been awake before. A couple of times already, but every time I went to sleep, it was as though my mind shut down and refused to remember that Lily had been taken. It was too heartbreaking. Too much of a reminder on how I failed her.

"Good morning, Mr. Cook."

An unknown voice had my head turning to the far side of the room. Three men, and they were all staring at me as if I were the enemy. They were all tall and wide. The hatred behind their stares was all I needed to know that these men were not my friends.

My attention went to Slade. "Where's Lily?" My throat was scratchy. Raw and burning from whatever the nurses and doctors had done while I was dying.

"Maybe you can tell us," said the man in the middle. "If you don't mind, I have a few questions for you. I'm Special Agent Gaige Sullivan. This is Blake Morgan, and you know Mr. Roberts."

"Questions?" I went to move my arm and winced at the pain. *Lily...she'd gotten me good.*

Gaige walked forward while Blake and Slade followed closely behind. "Let's start off with the obvious. How do you know Ms. Roberts? What was the relationship between the two of you?"

Realizing they hadn't found her yet, my heart ached even more. I looked between the three men, unsure as to what I should say. Lily needed my help. My family could possibly have her. But did I risk exposing our past to these men? What would happen if I confessed? Would the police cart me off to jail for who I was?

No. They had no evidence that I'd done anything wrong.

Cook. Fuck, they know who I am. I pushed the button to make the bed rise a good few inches. There seemed no way around what I knew I had to do.

"I met Lily three years ago. She's my...girlfriend."

"As in, she's your girlfriend now?"

Slade's eyes were narrowed as he stared. I'd worry about him later. I needed to work with this agent. Maybe he could tell me what they knew so far.

"I was trying to get her to be. She was worried about her brother not approving."

"Ah." Gaige raised the notepad, jotting down something on the paper. "So, when you dated, was it before or after she was taken the first time?"

There it was. I'd known this moment was coming. Again, I looked at Slade. This time, I didn't break away. "During. Lily was brought to my father's house as a slave. I took care of her. Protected her while she was there. I fell in love with her."

All three men seemed to lock up in shock. Their bodies stiffened and not a single eyelid blinked.

"I came here to escape the life I, myself, had been kidnapped into. My father killed my mom and stepfather when I was eight and raised me from there on out. The life I've led has been far from glamourous. It was downright hell until Lily. She changed things. Changed me."

"I'll fucking kill you." Slade took a step forward, his arm reaching toward me. Blake caught him just before he reached the bed. "Mark my words," he said, pointing his finger, "you'll never get near my sister again for what you've done."

"Try to stop me." My voice was weak, but the threat was clear. "I love Lily and she loves me. No one will keep her away from me. Not even you, Slade."

The tightening of his jaw was joined with the clenching of his fist as he shrugged Blake off with a hard jerk. "We'll see about that."

"We will. Have you noticed how unhappy she is? Have you been there to see? No, but I have. She wants me. She loves me, but refuses to try to make it work because of how much she loves *you*. She's afraid to find happiness, Slade, all because she's too focused on yours. How we met...I can't change that. I don't have any part in the trafficking, but yes, I was surrounded by people who did. Death wasn't something I wanted, sorry. And death wasn't something I was willing to let find your sister. That's the only reason I've held off for so long. Do you not think I could have killed your men to get to her? It would have been so easy. Yet, I waited, bided my time. Me," I growled. "I risked *our* happiness to give her time to adjust to life and make her safe. Now this? It's nothing more than a slap in the face for the precautions I tried to lay out."

The last words faded as my voice gave out from the rawness. I closed my eyes, only able to open them when Slade began talking again.

"You don't have to worry about finding her anymore. Mr. Morgan will take care of that. I'm sure you can thank him later for taking care of your other problems, too."

"I will not sit back and do nothing. Lily belongs to me," I forced out. "And I'll be damned if any of you are going to stop me from searching for her."

A loud knock was followed by the door opening. The nurse paused, glancing at the three men. "I'm sorry, are you family?"

Gaige smiled and shook his head. "Police business," he said, quickly flashing a badge. "We're almost finished."

"No, you're finished now. Get out of my son's room."

I heard my father before I saw him. My stomach turned and my eyes jerked to Slade. All I could do was shake my head, a silent plea that I didn't want it to play out like it was.

He grabbed Gaige's jacket, but still stared at me. Something flashed behind his eyes and I knew he didn't have the rage he'd projected toward me. He was scared about Lily, but he didn't hate me entirely.

"Sir, I'm going to have to ask you to step out of the room until we're finished." Gaige's anger was visible in his words and the other man, Blake, was staring at my father like meal. All three eyed every movement he made, but my father appeared not to notice as he shook his head.

"It's okay. I've got this." I threw off my hardass look — the one that said I didn't let anyone push me around. For seconds, he looked between all of us. Surprisingly, he stepped out. Gaige wheeled around, leaning close to Slade.

"This isn't a real investigation, Mr. Roberts. Do you know the trouble I can get into if he reports this to my superiors?"

Slade kept his focus on me. "If it comes down to it, I'll say I came to you to file a real report. Right now," he said, walking toward me, "I want to know what's going to happen."

It was the perfect question. One I already had the answer to. "I go home," I said, looking into his eyes. "If they have Lily, I get her and we escape. It'll knock out my biggest suspicion of them taking her. But, if she isn't there and I can't find proof..."

Blake came closer to the bed. "That's where I'll come into play. I'll start searching here. You'll look there. In one week, I will show up at your residence. Let's say…at two in the morning. You're going to be outside waiting for me. From there, we will discuss what we know."

My head shook. "You don't even know where I live."

His eyes grew cold while he crossed his arms over his chest. The long-sleeve black shirt hugged his wide shoulders tightly as he tried to stare me down. "Well, you can spit it out real quick, or you can waste an hour of my time while I search for it. Regardless, I *will* find it."

"No, you wouldn't. Pen," I breathed out. Fuck, my eyes were so damn heavy. Why the hell was I sleeping so much? I needed to get out of here fast. I needed to get back home so I could see if my family had Lily. Or maybe, I'd luck out and learn the truth before...

"I'm ready when you are." I read out the address from memory, keeping my voice low in case my father was somehow listening. If he knew I was working with these men, he'd kill me on the spot. Maybe that was his plan anyway. Did he know I was the one responsible for two of my uncle's deaths?

Blake pushed the notepad into his pocket, stepping back deeper into the room. Gaige followed and I couldn't make out what they were saying. Slade, coming even closer, wiped away any care I may have had toward the tracker.

"You say you protected my sister while she was there. How so? By fucking her? By using her as your own personal sex slave?"

Slowly, I rose to sit up straighter, ready to crush his throat in my good hand. Pain flared, making my jaw clench, but I refused to back down. "If you ever say anything like that about her again, brother or not, I'll fucking kill you."

"Answer the question, Zain."

Why should I give him the satisfaction of knowing? I hated it, but I knew why. *Because you love her and she loves him.* "Lily was a gift from my father. A gift I couldn't refuse. One I'm glad I didn't. If I hadn't taken her, she would have gone to someone else in my household. Have you seen the scars she carries from the girls there? That," I emphasized, "could have been her if she hadn't been mine. Girls died in her arms. So beat up and broken, there was nothing either she or I could do. I never once hurt your sister, but I sure as hell have killed a lot of men who've tried. Lily is my life and I love her, whether you accept that or not."

"Slade, let's go."

Gaige and Blake were already by the door. Slade stepped back, not turning away from me. "If they have my sister, you better find a way to get ahold of me."

"You have my word."

His attention stayed on my face for a few more seconds before he nodded and turned his back. And like that, they were gone. My eyes closed and heaviness settled in my bones as I rested back against the pillow. Lily engulfed my mind and I let her take me over.

"What the hell is going on here?"

I never heard my father come in, but he was good at that. There was no one I feared more than the soulless man only feet away. I knew it was because of the impact he'd made when I was a boy. Lily had been right in one aspect—in my mind, I'd made him into something he really wasn't.

My eyes opened. "Hello to you, too, Father."

"Don't hello, me. I just flew halfway around the world. What have you gotten yourself into, Zain?"

A groan left me as I turned more toward him. Fuck, how was I going to explain this without it sounding completely fabricated?

"I got mixed up with the wrong girl. I think she had a boyfriend. Let's just say he wasn't too happy when he showed up at my place and found us leaving."

"A girl? That doesn't sound like you."

I twisted my mouth. "What, am I not supposed to date?"

Still, he stared, reading me. "It just wasn't what I suspected."

"What did you think I did to get shot?"

My father's hand rose, his signal for he didn't want to talk about it. He trusted nowhere but his home to speak openly. He was smart. Too smart.

"How did you know I was here?"

He exhaled deeply while reaching into his suit's pocket and pulling out a piece of paper. "I called and you never answered. There was something I needed to discuss with you and when you dropped off of the radar, I had my people search. It didn't take long for them to find you here." He thrust the paper in my direction and I took it, reading the Arabic words before me. *Amir is taking your place. You're coming home.*

A deep breath left me as I fought to think. The medication they had me on was fucking with my head. I couldn't focus enough to decipher what I should do. If Amir was staying, more girls were going to be sold. If I went back, it very well might be because my father knew what I'd done to my uncles; possibly knew I'd been here for Lily the whole time.

"I'm okay, really. I can still continue."

"No. It's decided." He kept it short and from his tone, I knew pushing the issue was pointless.

"Alright." My eyes closed and I let them stay shut. It was time to come up with a plan. I couldn't let my brother continue in my place. And my father wasn't taking me anywhere. This was my chance to finally end things with him, once and for all. Away from his home full of guards. The three men ready to bring me to the ground were my only answer, but could I get to them before it was too late?

Chapter 14
Lily

Silence. The cocoon of safety my mind had slipped into left me in a weird state of being. I didn't speak. Didn't cry. My only solitude and peace of mind was seeing my Master play out as I slipped into a dream state. Awake or asleep, I stayed there, blinding myself to what surrounded me.

My crate was long gone, now replaced by four wooden walls and a white ceiling with peeling paint. The windows were boarded up. The smell of my new home, thick with mold. A mattress sat on the floor in the far corner and although it wasn't an exact replica, there was something about this place that reminded me of where Zain and I had spent the majority of our time.

I'd been sleeping when footsteps woke me from my Master's arms. I hadn't wanted to return to the pitch black of my coffin, but the reality of what I was hearing had my hands flying up, ready to beat against my prison. Desperation begged me to scream for help. Instinct told me to keep quiet and wait. If I was dealing with traffickers or Zain's family, again, I knew better than to react frantically. They'd feed from my fear—bask in it and beat me to shut me up. A task they loved to do.

At the splinting of wood, I kept my eyes closed, pretending I was asleep. My heart rate had my whole body trembling and I knew there was no point in pretending I was either asleep or dead. I couldn't stop the jerks that left my limbs twitching.

Light filtered through and I squinted at the brightness, praying my eyes would adjust so I could defend myself against an attack if need be. It was pointless. Tears streamed down my face from the sensitivity and I was ripped out before I could see where I was being taken. My feet stumbled and I fell three times, but I never hit the ground. The hand held tight and didn't leave until one of my abductors opened a door and threw me inside.

That was days ago.

My eyes traveled over the small space to take in the stash of food and water that rested on the floor by the door. No bowls or dishes. Two large milk gallons had been filled with water and a store bought loaf of bread sat beside it. Now, they were

practically gone. How long had I been here?
Been missing?

Days blurred together and I couldn't get a good
frame of time. Surely my brother knew something
was wrong when I hadn't come home. He had to be
looking for me. And if Zain was alive, maybe he told
the police and they were looking for me, too.

My legs drew up closer to my chest while I
pressed my back deeper into the corner I was huddle
in. A spring pushed through the mattress and I
shifted to get it further away from my bare thigh.
The black dress I wore was torn and broken in more
places than I cared to think about, but I couldn't
stomach removing it. Not only because it would
leave me exposed, but it held the memories of the
passion my Master had before our lives changed
forever. Fuck, I missed him. Guilt ate away at me
and I pushed the side of my face harder into the wall.
The need to scream almost made it uncontrollable to
sit still. I wanted to explode. To destroy everything
in my path for the predicament I was now in. For
what I'd done to him. What if I hadn't hurt his arm?
What if I had stayed in his home instead of leaving?
He would have killed them. I knew he would have.
And we would have been together—safe.

Knots met my fingers as I buried them in the front of my hair, lowering my head to rest on my knees. What was I doing just sitting here? I may have checked this place repeatedly, but I shouldn't be giving up now. What if I had missed something?

The moment I stood, the door flew open, making me jerk back defensively. I hated showing fear. Hated even more that I was back to the point of being afraid. I'd spent years living with my nightmares. Now, here I was, living another one.

A finger pointed back to the corner where I'd been sitting, as if to say, "Sit back down". Slowly, I rounded to the far side, further away. There was no way I was obeying their order. The wall stayed at my shoulder and I crept lightly toward the corner straight ahead. The figure took a step forward, but didn't come after me. I could see their hesitation, almost as if fear shone in their eyes. The dark depths made jerky movements between me and the bed, but seemed to give up on making me obey. They grabbed the nearly empty jugs of water and disappeared. I listened, waiting to hear the bolt slip into place.

Still, the man wore a dark ski mask, only revealing his eyes. And he'd be back soon. I knew there was someone with him. He'd been the one to knock me out. It was just like last time. Just like...

My eyes narrowed and a snarl left my lips.

"Bethany!" I rushed toward the door, slamming my closed fists against the wood. "Bethany! Charles! Open this fucking door, you psycho motherfuckers."

Harder, I hit, until my hand went numb. I was determined not to stop until they opened. It didn't take long. The door swung, slamming into the wall. I scattered back at the gun pointed directly at my chest.

"Do we have a problem?"

Different man. And this one didn't seem afraid of me. Had it been the other one, I'd have snapped that gun right out of his hand and shot him with it. I'd learned enough self-defense to kick any normal person's ass. With these men, I wasn't going to risk it until I learned more about them.

"I know Bethany and Charles are behind this. They took me, didn't they? You're just, what? Watching me so they're not exposed?"

I could see the guy's eyes squint and suddenly, I wasn't so sure.

Green eyes. I'd have to remember that.

I kept the questions quick, to buy me some time.

"What are you planning to do with me? Are you going to kill me? Hurt me? Sell me? Is this connected to me? My brother? Zain? Speak!" I yelled.

The man stalked forward, moving the gun to my head as he forced me back against the wall. Metal from the barrel pushed into my forehead and I could feel myself shaking. But not from fear—pure adrenaline.

At this point, I had nothing to lose.

"Shut…the fuck up," he said through clenched teeth.

My left hand shot out, grabbing his wrist, while at the same time, my right hand grasped the gun, bringing it down out and turning it back on him. The action was so fast and natural, I was still holding my breath. It was a move I never thought I'd have to use, but I'd never been more thankful to have learned the one thing that helped with my fears. Martial arts had become my life and although I hadn't had my instructor come over for the last few months, it was like riding a bike. Natural, like the air I breathed.

The shock had him frozen and I knew I wasn't dealing with professionals. Had I done that to Zain, he would have taken that gun from me just as fast, if not faster. Maybe I wouldn't have even got it away from him.

"Move." My thumb slipped down to check the safety. It was off. Another blessing I'd made sure I'd learned after my return. I was one hell of a shot. Once a victim, always a survivor. And I'd live through this. No one took my control away anymore. No one but my Master.

"Move!"

The guy scrambled back toward the door just as another man came rushing through. I didn't think. Didn't want to after seeing the gun resting by the man's thigh. He was carrying and I wasn't going to chance it. My finger pulled back the trigger, once, twice, three times…four. Two in each man. One in the chest for my master, one in the head for me.

I didn't wait. I rushed past the door and was met with an empty, rustic looking living room. I didn't lower the gun until I spotted my saving grace.

A cell phone rested on the coffee table and I grabbed it, gripping it like a lifeline.

Boarded windows also covered these walls. I went to the front door, easing it open as I peeked outside. Trees. Lots of them. As if I were in a forest.

A gust of went sent a shiver down my spine. I glanced down at the black dress and cursed. Would anyone else come back? Regardless, I couldn't go out there dressed as I was. I'd freeze to death. It felt like it was about to snow.

My fingers dialed Slade's number as I quietly moved through the house to a bedroom in the back.

"Slade Roberts." There was a certain breathlessness that filled his tone and I nearly smiled and burst out crying at hearing his voice.

"I'm alive," I rushed out, fighting back the tears. Burning scorched my throat as I held them at bay. I tried to see the closet before me, but I was starting to break down and I knew it wasn't a good thing. I'd done so well.

"Oh shit. Lily! Lily? Brace! Get that shit tracking. Sweetie, talk to me. Where are you? What happened?"

I sniffled, grabbing a long-sleeved shirt. "Some men took me. They weren't very good at being kidnappers, though. I killed them, but I'm not sure if more will show up. There's lot of trees outside and it's cold. I don't know where I am."

"I'm on it, honey. Hold on and keep talking."

"There's a man." My throat nearly closed and I sobbed. "His name is Zain. He was shot. Do you know if he's alive?"

Slade got quiet and I took the time to grab a pair of men's jeans and slide them on.

"Do you know?" I asked, impatiently. "He was shot when I was taken. Surely, you've heard about it. It was across the street from the penthouse."

"He lives."

My legs grew weak and I fisted a jacket I'd reached for. "Thank God. You have to tell him I'm okay. Tell him I'm sorry for everything. You—"

The sound of the front door opened and I froze. "Slade, someone's here. Oh my God, hurry."

"Don't hang up, Lily. Just…fuck," he growled. "Brace, tell me you have something."

The deep voice of my guard only sent my heart racing even more. "Not yet, boss."

My voice lowered. "Tell him…tell Zain I love him, Slade. In case…" I wiped my nose, lowering to see if I could fit under the bed.

"Bullshit. In case, nothing. You're coming home. We're going to find you Lily. Don't doubt that. I have a man in the FBI and a tracker hunting you down now. You *will* come home. I promise."

Voices got louder and I had to force myself to fit in the tight space under the frame.

"What the fuck?" A surprised tone had my eyes closing. I knew they'd found the bodies and it only made me tremble even more. The amount of fear I felt was indescribable. Either I was going to get caught and suffer greatly, or these men might very well kill me.

"Get the room, I'll check outside."

My eyes opened just in time to see black boots rush through the doorway. At their approach to the closet, I felt myself automatically lean away the slightest amount. Danger was all too real and it didn't take seeing it before me to know how much trouble I was in.

Heavy breathing filled my ear from Slade and although it put me into a deeper panic that they'd hear him, having my brother by my side comforted me. Even if he wasn't physically there.

"Fuck," the guy whispered under his breath. Bangs filled the room and I tensed at the crash of something heavy.

Please don't let him find me. Please.

The box spring above me squeaked and I tried not to make a sound as I waited.

"Brace, anything yet?" Slade's whisper had my lips pressing together. I knew they probably couldn't have heard with as silent as he'd been, but my senses felt heightened and everything was more intense.

"Oh…well, of course," a man said. One minute, I was safe, the next, the mattress and box spring was pushed up and thrown clear off the frame. A scream left my mouth as I rolled to my back and raised the gun, just as he reached for it.

Bang!

The jerk to keep it within my grasp caused me to miss. His fingers pushed at the barrel, but not before I pulled the trigger again. And again.

"Bitch!"

What felt like a sledgehammer caught the side of my face. Bright lights filled my vision and I blinked hard to focus. Blood on the side of the man's arm came into view just before I was slammed over to my stomach.

"You're going to fucking pay for that, cunt." Tugging against my pants had me throwing all my weight to rock him off. Still, I screamed, but I hardly noticed. Flashbacks of my multiple rapes left my sanity shattering into a million pieces.

"You like it rough, huh? So do I. Keep this up and we should have a good ol' time."

"No. God. Fuck!' Muscles tore in my stomach as I repeatedly tried to jerk to my side so I could squeeze out from under him. I knew moves to help defend myself while lying down, but none for being on my stomach. I felt helpless and I couldn't stand it.

Stomping grew closer, but I was too focused to look up.

"What the hell are you doing? Get up!"

The heavy sounds grew closer and the resistance against my back eased. Cool air brushed my thighs and I sobbed at realizing how close I was to getting raped all over again. Would he continue?

"The bitch shot my arm. She deserves to pay."

"Is that a fucking phone?" I looked up for the first time, right into a face that looked extremely familiar. My mind spun as I tried to place him.

"What?" The guy covering me shifted just as the other reached down to my side, grabbing the cell.

Slade's yells broke through for the first time, but they didn't last. The phone was shut and the evil shining through the man's eyes nearly took my breath away. I knew those eyes. I knew that face.

"Bind and gag her. We're out of here."

Chapter 15
Slade

"Fuck! No." I shook my head, refusing to believe it. "How could we have not picked up her location, Brace? Five minutes and thirty-four seconds," I said, shoving my phone toward him. That was damn near ten minutes ago. "How?"

"I don't know, boss. I've never had problems like this before." The sadness mixed into his features had me calming. I knew how upset Brace was at not following Lily when she left the restaurant. He'd apologized a million times.

My hand rose. "We'll find her. We'll just have to—"

The phone ringing had me scrambling to turn it the right way so I could accept the call. "Blake." A deep breath left me as I hit the button, bringing it to my ear.

"I just talked to my sister. Tell me you found something while you were out."

"Well, I have a location, if that's what you want to know."

Time stopped as I stared at Brace. "You know where Lily is?"

"Unfortunately, for you, when I accepted your proposal to help your sister, I also secretly stole access to all your devices. I hear and see every conversation that plays out on your cell, your wife's, not to mention, your laptops and computers. I say unfortunately, because you probably didn't want me overhearing your private conversations with Mary, but, the good news is, it paid off."

Anger was there, but only a speck to the excitement I felt at the breach of my privacy. It couldn't have happened at a better time.

"I don't care what you heard or saw. Where's my sister?"

"Oregon. I'm about to head out there now."

"I'll meet you somewhere. I'm coming."

A soft laugh came over the line. "That's not how it works, Mr. Roberts. I work alone when it comes to this part. I just thought I'd let you know. Besides, they're already gone."

My heart sank. "Gone? How do you know?"

"I know how these men work. They'll run. The question that bothers me is why she's still alive. If she hasn't been sold, she's not dead, and they're not asking for ransom…what do they want from her?"

I got quiet, letting everything sink in.

"Revenge."

"Bingo. I think so, too. But against who, Mr. Roberts? Maybe that's the question we should focus on. Who gains to lose the most by Lily being hurt? You? The one who loves her, Zain? Or are they hurting her because of what she did so long ago?"

I grabbed the back of the desk chair and gripped tightly. "If they were looking to hurt me, they'd have taken Mary. Or at least attempted. It has to be either her or Zain."

"I guess we'll see before it's over with. What we truthfully need is more information from Zain. You might not like him, Mr. Roberts, but I think he's a victim in all of this just as much as your sister is. I've gone over his information with Agent Sullivan. The world he was forced into might be a mystery, but I know that side of life. His upbringing had to have been hell, especially for a child who had no say. He was forced to become something he obviously didn't want. I mean, he's trying his best to get out now. That says something. Besides, if you ask me, Lily loves him."

God, she did. What the hell was I supposed to do about that? Zain…I hated him, yet I couldn't stop part of myself for liking him for some reason. It had been like that from the moment we met.

"I'll get more information. It'll give me something to do. I'm losing my mind just waiting." *Plus, Lily would want me to inform him she was alive.* "Call me when you learn something. I'm headed to the hospital."

"Will do, Mr. Roberts."

"Slade," I corrected. "Mr. Roberts was my father and I couldn't stand the bastard. Talk to you later."

I hung up and headed to the living room. Mary was lying on the couch, asleep. My head shook as I knelt down, pressing my lips to her cheek. Her eyelids fluttered opened and I brushed back the blonde strands that fell over her eyes.

"I have to go to the hospital. You okay? You need me to get you anything while I'm out?"

A groan came from her as she rolled to her back. "More crackers. I'm almost out."

The frown couldn't be hidden. Who knew pregnancy was so hard? My Mary used to be so full of life. Now, all she wanted to do was sleep. If she wasn't sleeping, she was sick.

"Crackers. Got it. Anything else?" My fingers continued to brush back her hair, content to just touch her. Green eyes radiated as a smile came to her face.

"I could think of a few things I wouldn't mind having. Maybe tonight you can give them to me?"

Dammit. Fuck tonight, I wanted her now, but I knew she didn't feel better until later in the evening. "I'll give you whatever it is you want." My touch traced down until I had my hand grasping her face, gently. "But you're going to beg for it, aren't you?"

She moaned and separated her lips.
"Yes…Master."

My lips pushed into hers. I couldn't control myself when she called me that.
Tonight," I breathed out. "Right now, I have to go check on Zain. I won't forget your crackers."

With one last kiss, I stood and made my way to the door. Brace was quickly behind me. The other men were standing by the front door when I shut it behind me.

"Caleb and Terrance, guard my wife. She's not to go anywhere and neither are you. I want you here at all times. Marcio, Brace, you're with me.

The elevator dinged and I turned, confused. Gaige stepped out, looking just as surprised as me.

"Perfect timing," he said, placing his hand out to stop the door from closing.

"I'd say. Excellent, you showing up like this. We're headed to the hospital. You can get us in again. My sister called and I need to check on Zain."

He nodded. "Thought you might be going there. Blake called me when he first got a trace and I was only a few blocks over. I thought I'd come check on things. Let's head out. You can ride with me."

We crowded into the elevator and my eyes widened as Gaige pulled out his gun and put a bullet in the chamber. My men instantly reached for their own weapons. I could feel their confusion as if it were my own.

"You planning on using that?"

Gaige's eyes cut up to mine. "Not on you. I don't trust our boy's father. He came into the country with five men. One being his other son, and four who I assume are his guards, two of which are flagged in our system. They're bad news. I don't trust that he'll let us get Zain alone again. I'll push my weight around, but without direct orders, I can't make him allow us in. Not this time."

"You don't expect a shootout in the hospital, do you? I mean, that's just...stupid," I said, watching the light in the elevator travel down the numbers.

"Inside? No. Before we get up there or after...you never know. I've seen some pretty crazy shit in my time. I wasn't always FBI, Mr. Roberts. I've been undercover really deep before. You couldn't imagine the lengths some people will go to keep their deepest, darkest secrets buried. And Amir Amari's go about as deep as you could possibly comprehend. He makes Governor Hagen and Julian Brighton's operation look like child's play."

Sweat began to coat my skin as I tried not to think about my sister possibly being in their hands. If the father had been behind her disappearance, was he planning on killing her? Fuck, it was a scary thought, but I couldn't stop feeling like something was off.

"Lily said the men she killed were amateurs. That doesn't sound like a risk Mr. Amari would take."

Gaige looked over, his eyes narrowing. "You might be right, but he's not from here. Maybe he had unknown sources take Lily until he could get his hands on her. It happens."

"Yeah, I guess."

It made sense. Maybe I just didn't want to imagine her in that sort of danger. If Amir got his hands on my sister, I was almost certain we'd never get her back. Not alive, anyway.

The doors opened and we walked through the parking garage, getting into Gaige's SUV. The ride to the hospital consisted of small talk between the men. Mostly about weapons and military experiences. I stayed in my own little world, wondering what Blake would find when he arrived at the place where Lily had stayed. Would she still be there or was he right about them leaving? If they did, where did they go? Out of the country?

The SUV came to a stop and I blinked past the fears.

"Okay." Gaige unbuckled. "Let's do this. Men, keep your eyes peeled for anything suspicious."

The walk into the hospital was a blur as my thoughts were consumed by Zain and trying to stay alert. What in the hell was I supposed to do? Take him under my wing? Protect him, all the while plotting out his family's demise? Kill him, myself? I almost groaned out loud. I couldn't do that to Lily. Fuck, she loved him. How had I missed all of this these last three years?

The elevator dinged and I stayed quiet as Gaige talked his way in. I could see their hesitation, but one flash of the badge and they allowed us through. As we approached the room, a man was standing outside. His watchful eyes were narrowed and he stepped in our path as Gaige took the front.

"Agent Sullivan to see Mr. Cook. You need to step out of the way."

"Zain isn't seeing anyone." The Arabic accent was thick as he stood his ground.

Gaige shot me a glance. "I'm sorry, are you family?"

"Cousin," he said, proudly.

"Ah, well, move before I arrest you for tampering with an investigation."

Barely existent words broke through and I narrowed my eyes, listening.

"Give me your word," Zain ground out.

"You swear you didn't have anything to do with it?"

A phrase in Arabic sounded. I didn't have to speak the language to assume it was some sort of curse.

"Would I lie to you about something like that? I know nothing of a girl. If you were told she was taken, it wasn't by me."

The young man shifted and stayed grounded for a few seconds before reaching back and knocking hard. Gaige pushed past and slung open the door. Mr. Amari stood from the chair as we all walked inside. Zain looked at us nervously, but it wasn't from fear, more like anticipation.

"We're going to have to ask you to leave us for a few minutes. We have more questions for your son."

He stood, putting himself between us and Gaige. "May I see your badge?"

Gaige flashed it and moved in closer so he could see. I held my breath, waiting for him to ask for ours. "This shouldn't take long. We're wrapping things up and should be gone shortly," Gaige continued.

The lack of threat had the man's stiff shoulder's relaxing. I could tell he was slightly distracted. His eyes kept darting to the door, as if he either wanted to leave or was waiting for someone. "I'll be outside," he mumbled.

A nod was all Gaige gave as he stepped even closer to the bed. The moment the door shut, I walked over.

"Have you found Lily?" he rushed out.

I swallowed hard, feeling the anger surge. "No, but she called."

Zain pushed to sit, wincing a little. "What did she say? Is she alright?"

My head shook. "I'm not sure. She killed two of the men who had her. I listened while at least two more showed up. She was fighting with one, but then the phone went dead."

"Fuck," he said, catching his breath. "No. Fuck." The growl was followed by him throwing back the covers. "I'm out of here. I have to find her." He pulled out the IV, using the blanket to apply pressure.

"She had a message for you."

His distinct eyes shot to mine and he stilled. "What did she say?"

While I studied him, I couldn't denying how much raw pain he held. I could see it. Feel it. I looked over to Brace. "We may not have been able to track her, but we did record the conversation. I think you should hear for yourself."

I nodded at Brace, who took out a recorder and hit play.

"I'm alive," she said, rushed.

Zain leaned in closer to the recorder as he listened. Every expression on his face, I caught. To deny what I knew would be a mistake, but letting this go was harder than I thought. His brow furrowed and something flashed behind his eyes at Lily being attacked. As I stared deep within his glare, I knew there wasn't anything he wouldn't do for her. Mostly…kill. That's what worried me the most. This man was dangerous.

"You're going to fucking pay for that, cunt."

Zain's fist clenched, the rage ramping up through the posture of his body. But within all of that, I spotted control. His breaths were steady. He wasn't acting out or doing something rash. He was studying, deciphering every single sound he heard. And just like with Blake, I felt a confidence toward Zain. God, he did love her. A lot. And even if there was a killer within him, there was also a protector. He'd tried that night. Enough to almost die for it.

The room remained silent as the yelling came to a stop. My arms crossed over my chest as I watched Zain continue to stare at the recorder. Whatever he was thinking, I knew it wasn't good for whoever took her.

"How well are you? It's been, what, thirteen days? What have the doctors said?"

His eyes broke away and moved over to mine. "I'm not critical anymore. They were putting me in a regular room this afternoon. I'm good. I want to leave. Will you take me with you?"

"What about your father?"

His stare left mine and went to Gaige's, only to return. Words were useless when the murder was so clearly behind his gaze. "I'll deal with him," he said, lowly.

Gaige reached inside his jacket, pulled out a pair of handcuffs, and handed them to me. "I'm going to go outside the room and take care of the discharge. Put him in cuffs and help him out. Have your men guard your sides at all time. I'll have your back and explain everything to his family."

Zain pulled all of the wires free from his chest and stood. He was a little wobbly, but held the bed for support.

"Is that your clothing over there?" I pointed toward the small table across the room.

"Yeah, Amir had them brought over. Can you get them for me?"

I grabbed the bag and pulled out a pair of what looked like black jogging pants, a black T-shirt, and a pair of running shoes. My eyebrows drew in. Every time I saw the guy, he was wearing all black, whether it was a suit or regular clothes.

Gaige waited until Zain was dressed and eased out of the door. I opened the handcuffs. "Hands in front."

A look of uneasiness came over him. "You fucking try to kill me when we get out of here," he said, looking up at me, "I swear, you'll pay. I don't trust anyone and to let you do this—"

"Enough," I growled, locking one side on his wrist. "If I wanted you dead, you'd already be six feet in the ground. Now, lift your other arm and let's get the hell out of here."

Click.

My arm linked through his and I took on some of his weight as we headed for the door. It opened just as Brace reached for the knob.

"What the hell is going on here?" Amir stepped back as we kept walking. "Hey, I asked a question." He hurried to Gaige, who was scribbling across a piece of paper at the nurse's station. "Why are you taking my son?"

Gaige turned to face him, towering over the man. "Protective custody, sir. Surely you can understand that. Now, if you'll excuse me."

"But…" Amir followed. "I'm taking him home," he said, his voice booming.

We all stopped and Zain kept his voice low. "Calm. I'll see you soon."

"No." Amir and the cousin walked forward. "There's something you're not telling me. FBI? I may not be an American citizen, but I know a simple shooting doesn't bring in a department like theirs. What's going on, Zain?"

"Nothing you need to concern yourself over, Father."

As they kept eye contact, the tension between them grew so thick, I couldn't begin to process what was going through either of their minds. Secrets always had a way of getting out. Was Amir afraid his were going to become exposed with Zain out of his reach?

"If you say so." Amir gestured his head to the cousin and they took off walking at a fast pace. As we followed behind, I took my time letting my mind run. Amir was trouble and I knew Zain planned to put a stop to it. But he wasn't in any condition to do that yet. At least, not alone.

I promised Mary long ago that I would stay out of trouble, but Zain coming into our lives changed things. My sister loved him. I may not have been able to protect her, but I'd be damned if I was going to drop the ball concerning him.

Chapter 16
Zain

Seeing the inside of Lily's penthouse from her point of view left me anxious with impatience. Here I was, in a room I'd seen her walk through a million times, and she wasn't here. And she wouldn't be again until I did something to get her back.

The black leather sofa I rested on did nothing to put me at ease. I needed to get to my father. Put a stop to him before the next shipment of girls went out. If he lied about not having Lily, she'd be there. Another slave ready to ship out. I couldn't let that happen. I wouldn't have even brought up Lily's name to my father if I didn't have to rule him out and learn more about the deal. I had to see his reaction to her name. His expression. Like usual, nothing. Was it him? Someone else?

"God dammit. Who could it be?"

Slade continued to pace the living room with his phone gripped tightly in his fist. He'd had to have gone back and forth at least a hundred times. It left me even more determined to get my strength back. I felt weak next to him and I hated it.

"I don't know, but I'm almost positive it isn't my family."

My words did little to comfort him. They did absolutely nothing to comfort me.

A sniffle was followed by the bedroom door closing. My head lifted just in time to see a blonde woman stop in her tracks. Her eyes were red rimmed and she looked a bit on the pale side.

"Oh great, you're back. Did you get the crackers?"

Slade froze and his mouth parted the slightest amount. "I, ah…" His phone was to his ear before he finished. "Brace. Get the crackers out of the car. *Fast.*" He smiled apologetically and she groaned.

"Oh, Slade. You forgot, didn't you?"

"Of course not. Come here." His mouth twisted as he looked at me. I knew he was lying. We'd come straight here after driving around for a good half hour to make sure we weren't being followed.

The woman came forward, stopping as her eyes connected with mine. "Oh…I didn't know we had company."

Slade's arm wrapped around her shoulders, pulling her close. "Honey, I want you to meet Zain. Zain, this is my wife, Mary."

I pushed myself forward, starting to rise when she rushed forward.

"Oh, no, please, stay lying down." Her hand connected with mine. "It's a pleasure to meet you, Zain."

"Pleasure's mine." I looked back to Slade, only to return to Mary. "Are you feeling alright?"

She grinned, but I could see her fatigue. "I'm okay. Just a little under the weather. Morning sickness will do that to you."

Pain settled in my chest, but it had nothing to do with the wound from the gunshot. I knew the effects of morning sickness all too well. Lily had been sick pretty badly. Not for long, though. She hadn't been granted that opportunity. It tore me to pieces. I knew the hardships she would have had to face being young and pregnant, living at my father's, but the pregnancy had happened and we were a little excited at the thought. Until my uncle. Saul was going to pay for causing Lily to miscarry. I had yet to be able to get my hands on him. He disappeared while I was off on one of my missions. But the time was coming, and he was going wish he'd never put his hands on what was mine.

"Congratulations," I said, forcing myself to look at them and seem genuine. It really was great that they were having a child. I knew Slade was the type of man to take care of what was his. He'd made that clear concerning his sister. It still made my loss all too real.

"Thank you," she said, smiling even bigger. "Say, are you hungry? Thirsty? If I know my husband, he probably overlooked asking. Slade expects people he's close to to help themselves."

I tried not to smile at the jab. She was joking, I could see that not only in her expression, but on Slade's as he leaned down and kissed her head.

"My wife is right. Where are my manners? Would you like something to eat or drink?"

Food. Fuck, I *was* starving. I couldn't remember the last meal I'd really eaten. The hospital didn't count. I barely touched what they gave me, more as a precaution than anything. Poisoning my food was something I didn't put past my father. He knew I killed my uncles. I could feel it from the cold shoulder I'd been given over the last few days.

"Actually, there's a deli on the corner. I think I might try to walk over there and get a sandwich or something. I wouldn't want the smell of anything to affect your wife."

"Sounds like you've been through this before," Slade said, laughing, only to sober almost instantly. His shoulders got wider as he stood taller. Something passed behind his eyes, but he shook his head, as if to dismiss it. "I'll get one of my men to grab you something. I don't want you out there just yet. A few more days and you'll be good on your feet."

I pushed to stand. "I'm good now. I should really be moving around. That'll help more than anything. Been through this before. Not in the chest, but other places."

Mary's eyes widened. "You've been shot before?"

How she knew that's what had happened was beyond me. My guess was Slade.

"Three times, not including this one. One in the arm, the shoulder, and leg."

"At the same time or on three different occasions?"

The fear behind her question was real. She was afraid of me and what I'd bring on them. And she had good reason. I shouldn't be here.

"Two different occasions." I hesitated. "The world I lived in isn't like this. That's why I left." My stare went to Slade, as if to drive the point home. "I'm going to go get something to eat. Then I should probably be heading out."

"Eat, yes. But I can't let you leave. My sister would want you here. Think about that." He stepped back from Mary as I slowly slid on my shoes. Damn, I wasn't going to bounce back from this like I had the others. My ribs ached and I knew they'd cracked a few with the chest compressions. Not to mention, my arm was still sore from Lily catching the back of my elbow. Pain meds. That's what I needed. Whatever I was given in the hospital had long since worn off.

Slade walked me to the door, pushing my wallet into my hand. I didn't want to know how he'd gotten it. "Don't do anything stupid, Zain. Food, and then you come back. My sister doesn't need anything else to worry about. If she's able to call back, I want you here."

All I could do was nod. He was right in that regard. I needed to talk to Lily.

"I'll be right back." I opened the door, meeting Marcio head on. His narrowed expression eased and he reached into his jacket, pulling a gun out. My heart jumped and the memory of the explosion rang out in my ears, leaving my chest cramping.

"You might want this." His hand lifted and the anxieties lessoned the moment I gripped the handle.

"Thank you."

"Been there," he said, under his breath. "So, where are we going?"

Slade stepped out into the entrance with us, shutting the door behind him. "Deli on the corner and right back," he said, taking over. "Then, we come up with a plan to settle things with his family once and for all."

Our eyes met and the pull I felt toward him grew. Somehow, he understood me more than I could process, and I liked that. Tonight, I'd end things and find out if they had Lily. It was time to wipe my slate clean of everything bad from my past.

My hand gripped the gun tighter just before I lifted my shirt and placed it against my hip.

"Holy shit." Slade reached out, pulling the material up just past my belly button. It took everything I had not to reach out and crush his wrist. "What the fuck are all those scars from?"

I ripped the shirt down. Even all the tattoos I had covering my stomach, chest, and back, couldn't hide what my father had had done to me. The scars from the whip had been deep and covered from below my neck, down to my knees.

"Punishments throughout life, Slade. Most from before I turned fifteen. After that, no one would get near me if they valued their life. It was exactly what my father had intended when he started my training. The killer he created will soon be the executioner he'll face. And I look forward to it."

The room grew silent, only to be disrupted by the ding of the elevator. Brace stepped out, pausing as he looked at us.

"Great. Thanks, Brace." Slade strode forward, as if we hadn't just discussed the pain of my past. The powerful strides had him getting to his guard and taking the crackers in three steps. When he turned and met my eyes, understanding was there. And so was anger. Maybe we did share something I wasn't aware of. Had he gone through something similar with his father? Had he at least been on bad terms with him?

I walked forward, relaxing at the weight in my waistband. Marcio stepped in behind me as we nodded to Lily's brother and got on the elevator. The moment the doors closed, he looked over, shaking his head.

"I knew you were dangerous the first time I met you. You can't hide that sort of energy. It follows you around like an invisible mass. Only people similar to you can feel the threat. I felt it when we met as far back as that party."

My head nodded as he pressed the lobby button. "Like for like, I suppose. I felt it from you, too."

"So, you're gonna kill your dad? Is that plan?"

The way my skin crawled had me rotating my neck. I reached my palm up to run over it, easing the tension as my fingers gripped the side of my throat.

"He doesn't deserve to live after what he's done. If I don't stop him, a lot of girls are going to suffer and probably die. I made a vow to Lily and I have every intention of following through."

A deep exhale was followed by him clenching his jaw. "I know Boss is already going to put out the

order, but I'm with you, regardless. Nothing
would give me more pleasure than putting a stop to
operations like the one that took Lily. I…watched
her grow. She was such a sweet girl before she was
taken. When she came back…" his head shook. "It's
like I didn't even know her. I'm not sure the horrors
she lived through, but it left its mark on who she
was. No one should have the power to ruin a person
that way. If it hadn't of been for you, or Lily's spirit,
she'd have been worse. I'm glad you were there to
protect her."

My stomach turned and flashes of our lives
together nearly made me sick. Two people, confined
to a room almost all day and night to escape the
cruelty behind my door was almost suffocating. But
there were times I couldn't save her and those were
usually when I wasn't there. My Lily's heart was too
big. A girl in need had her facing her fears…and
ultimately paying a price she couldn't handle on the
inside…like our child's life. She was never the same
after that.

"When Lily is returned…" Not if, but when, I
made myself say, "I'll be heading back to my
father's home. I have uncles there who need to pay

just as much. I need you to make sure she's kept safe."

The doors opened, but neither of us moved. Our eyes locked and his head gave a quick jerk down. "On my life. I will make sure she never gets hurt again."

"Me, too," I said under my breath. And I would. Lily was never going to have to worry about another thing again. Once I eliminated the immediate threats, no one with ill intentions would ever dare think about coming near her again. I'd be there if they did.

Chapter 17
Lily

"Go on. Hold on to her arm, you know you want to."

A tear streamed down my face as I looked between the wooden arm of the chair where I was tied to Alec's pale face. He'd lost so much blood already. I couldn't stop my heart from breaking at seeing the torture he was going through before me. I wanted nothing more than to comfort him with words, but with my mouth gagged with cloth, all I could do was plead with my eyes for forgiveness. If he wouldn't have become involved with me, if he wouldn't have been nice to me, maybe this wouldn't have happened.

"Go ahead, scar her up a bit more. She doesn't mind, do you Lily?"

"Uh-uh," I tried to say. My head shook impatiently as I looked at Alec. Really, I didn't care. If he could use me to ease his suffering, I'd take whatever damage was caused. It would help the guilt I knew would follow.

"You have to stop this, Jonathon. You have to—"

A scream echoed through the room and blood rushed out at the slice across Alec's upper chest. I jerked against the rope restraining me, screaming. Not from fear, more a silent threat. Alec didn't deserve this.

"You're going to tell me what to do? After you turned your back on your family," he exploded. "You're a Brighton, Alec. This cunt ruined everything. She killed our father and brother, and you try to date her? To fuck her!" His eyes widened as he looked down at Alec's wound. It drove his hand up again, causing Alec's forearm to shoot off the table he was bound to. Only a few inches gave way before the hemp caught and his body jerked.

"Let her go. Lily didn't do anything wrong. She's paid for what she's done."

"Two months in a mental health facility for murder? That's a slap in the face and you know it."

Jonathon's eyes lifted to mine. It was like I was staring at Jordan all over again. Only…a younger version. They almost looked like twins. From their same perfect, thin noses, to their full lips.

Even Jonathon's hair was cut short like Jordan's had been.

"You took what was rightfully ours. Brighton Corp should have been left to us! We should have been taken care of, but were we? No," he said between clenched teeth. "Your brother bought out what my father worked his whole life building. All for what? To sell it off piece by fucking piece?"

Jonathon's large frame flew around the table and I moved back and forth against the chair, wishing I could run. I'd never been afraid to hold my own, but not being able to protect myself was the worst. Another beating was coming and there was nothing I could do about it.

"Do you know what you've done?" he roared. Pressure tightened around my throat as his fingers grasped onto my neck tightly. "You ruined our lives! You turned my mother into an alcoholic whore who's looking to marry herself off to anyone who will take care of her. My sister, her reputation is destroyed because of what you exposed. No one wants to date the daughter of a criminal."

A gargling sound came from deep within as I fought for air. Darkness edged in while I tried my best to thrash.

"You're going to die before this is over with, Lily. Both you, and my traitor brother. And you know what?" he asked, forcing my stare to meet his. "There's nothing you can do about it. If you think you'll be saved, you're wrong. No one will find you here. And they'll never know it was me. As for Alec, there's a chance the suspicion might lead back to him due to his disappearance. That'll depend on my big surprise, of course. I guess we'll find out soon enough."

The grip on my face loosened just in time for him to remove it and follow through with a hard slap to my cheek. The force sent my head spinning to the side. Blinding pain left me trying to curl into myself, no matter how hard I fought it. I'd been here before. Saul used to beat me every chance he got.

"Oh, how much fun it is watching you suffer. Now, grab her fucking arm," he yelled at Alec, turning away from me. With a quick movement, he reached toward his brother's fighting body, only to pull his hand toward mine. "Leave it here or else I'll cut it off."

My wrist tried to rotate and we somehow managed to clasp to each other's fingers. A sound was muffled through my gag as Jonathan walked around and picked the knife back up. His gaze stayed fixed on my and Alec's connection. In one swift downward motion, he buried the blade in what looked to be his brother's shoulder. An agonizing cry had my chest wracking with heavy sobs. Not just from seeing Alec suffer, but because of the crushing grip he had on my fingers. The combination left my walls crumbling.

"I said to grab her fucking arm, not to hold her hand. God dammit. Does she mean so much that even now, facing death, you'd try to comfort her? Let go." The last word was barely audible through his anger. The pure malice from what he was seeing between us was evident on his face. The hate he held left me pushing more into my chair, but for the life of me, I couldn't rip my hand from Alec's. He'd have to be the one to let go. I wasn't turning my back on him as he went through this pain. It was all because of me. I should have never gone on that date with him.

"I said!" His arms lifted over his head while he clutched the handle of the knife." Let go!" The blade disappeared in Alec's chest and I wasn't sure who screamed louder. Me, or Alec. Nothing registered as I fought against the ropes. The pressure on my hand was so tight, I couldn't feel my fingers anymore. The throbbing ache that was in tune with my pulse was the only reminder that they even existed anymore.

"Nnnnnn." My protest was blocked by the fabric, but it was still loud. Jonathan paused, the side of his mouth pulling up just seconds before he brought the weapon down again, in what looked to be dead center of his brother's chest. Bile burned my throat and I gagged, lowering my head so I could try to breathe. The pressure from Alec's grip loosened from mine and a gush of warmth surged to my fingertip where the circulation rushed in. Panicked, my fingers fumbled to hold his hand again. To try to elicit any response I could. Alec was facing away now. I wasn't sure when he'd turned his head. I'd been so fixated on Jonathan, I hadn't even noticed.

The knife remained in Alec's chest as his brother stepped away and grabbed a cloth, wiping the blood from his hands. Not once did he say anything to me as he continued to stare. Evil radiated between us and I could feel myself shaking almost violently in my chair. The door slamming had both of our heads turning toward the front. All of my fear extinguished as my stare connected with the one person who started it all.

"What the fuck are you doing here?" Jonathon walked over, grabbing Bethany by the bicep and dragging her to the wall while she fought to break his hold. Blonde hair swayed around her shoulders as she tried to look around him at me.

"I told you I wanted to watch."

"Stupid, stupid, fucking bitch," he said, slamming her even more into the wooden surface. "When I give you an order, you follow it. How do I know you weren't followed?"

The tall blonde jerked from his grasp, slapping him. "I don't think you know who you're talking to. Don't ever insult me like that." She started toward me, revenge written in her glare, when he grabbed her hair, pushing her back against the wall. The kiss he gave her was far from sweet. She fought against it only to submit halfway. My eyes widened as she pulled at his shirt, whispering in his ear.

Jonathan's head pulled back and he turned to look at me. What looked to be amusement had him smiling before he turned back to her. "Bedroom, huh? You want me?" he asked, pushing her legs apart with his knee. "Hmm? Say it, you fucking slut.

This turns you on?" He kissed her again. "Say you want my cock." His hand gripped tighter in her hair and he pulled her head back so he could nip at her neck.

"Please," she moaned. "Let's go to the back before we start this."

"Your husband? Where does he think you are?" He pulled harder.

"I kicked him out the night the detective left the house. He's gone for good this time."

Jonathan's fingers eased under her short white dress and I tore my gaze from them while I squeezed Alec's hand. *Nothing*. I didn't want to let go, but I couldn't continue this. I needed to try to escape. Days had gone by without any luck on getting free while they waited for Alec to take vacation. My time was running out, and fast.

Movement had my eyes darting up. Jonathan pushed his hands deeper between her legs while she moaned. It made me sick. If I could get out of these ropes, I'd grab that knife and slice them to pieces. As it was, my hand could barely move. Deep within, I knew I was in a losing battle. If they left me as I was, my life was as good as gone.

"Fuck me," she breathed out, pulling at his shoulders. "I know you want to. It's been so long."

One minute, they were all over each other, the next, Bethany was being thrown across the room, as if she were nothing. A grunt left her as she landed half on the sofa, half on the floor.

"Don't presume to know what I want. Fucking whore. I can't believe you're even here." He walked over, grabbing the knife out of his brother's chest. My stomach flipped and I breathed through the nausea.

"I ended things with my husband for you." She struggled to stand on her four inch heels as she began to stalk forward. "And you're going to treat me like this? I'm a Hagen," she screamed, advancing.

Jonathon laughed. "You're still a whore. And I never asked you to leave your husband. Why would I? It's not like I'd marry you."

Bethany slowed, her eyes going from narrow to wide and enraged in a mere second. Harder, I tugged at the ropes. Shit was about to get bad really fast. I could feel it.

"Is that all you see me as? Someone to screw while you plotted murder? What the fuck were those

I love yous you whispered in my ear? You…" her head shook. "You led me on! You…"

"Got you right where I wanted you," he said, laughing quietly. "Did you really think I didn't expect you to come, pumpkin? Why would I give you the address of where I was staying if I didn't? Sure, I made you beg for it, but don't I make you beg for everything?"

I grew still at his words, feeling my heart start to race.

"Think about it, Bethy. Let everything sink in. Why would I pretend not to want you here when all along, I really did?"

The determination on her face melted and her eyebrows drew in. She looked over to me, then back to him.

"Oh, come on. It's not that hard."

"This is one of your sick games. You wouldn't dare," she breathed out.

He glanced down at Alec and then turned back to her. "No? He was my brother and I think he's pretty much dead. You…you're no one, baby. Trash. A has-been who only wishes she was what she used to be in her prime. And let's face it, buttercup, we both know you're not even close to the Bethany

Hagen you used to be. Lack of money has left you a little…aged."

A yell tore from her throat as she rushed toward him. I could have cursed her stupidity had I not hated her so much. She never stood a chance.

"There we go," he said, wrapping his bicep around her neck and tightening his grip. Bethany's face turned red as she fought against him. 'Time to go to sleep for a while. When you awake, the real games will begin."

Chapter 18
Zain

"No, use the code with forty-one-eight-thirty-two at the end." My finger pointed to Brace's monitor, though I already knew he was on to what I was talking about.

"I've never heard of that code, what will it do?"

Brace's question had Slade's head turning in our direction. He put the coffee cup down and stood, walking over. My mouth wanted to purse at his sudden interest, but I tried to pretend it didn't affect me. Shit. Not good.

"Hey..." His head lowered closer to us. "What the hell? That's Mary's phone number. Those are my phone records. What are you two doing?"

Brace's jaw tightened as he looked over at me.

"I need Blake's number," I rushed in, grabbing Slade's phone from the counter. "And now I have it. Thank you, Brace."

The guard's eyes widened. "I swear, I didn't know what he was having me do, Boss." Brace turned back to me. "What was that code again?"

"I'll tell you in a minute." I punched in the number as Slade cursed.

"I could have told you the damn number if you would have asked. You didn't have to break into my personal records to get it."

My head shook as I entered the last digit. "Wrong. What you have isn't his real number. I mean, it is, but not his true one. You call that number and it won't cause his phone to ring if he has it rejecting calls or on silent. It's like…a spare, tied into his device. With *this* number and the ones I'll add to the end, it'll ring no matter what. He could have it off and it'll turn on and force my call through. That's the bad thing about these Smart phones. They're very easy to manipulate, if you know what you're doing." I looked up at Brace. "Go back into that main system and get into your tracking software. Then enter seventeen-one-one-four-nine-two. Now, if you'll excuse me," I said, standing and turning to the side for privacy.

Ring.

Ring.

"How the hell did you get this number?" I turned in time to see the screen turn into a map. It zoomed in and continued to do so until we were watching a moving dot. Slade waved his hand and I put it on speakerphone.

"Hello, Blake. This is Zain. Tell me what you have on Lily."

A large exhale rushed over the phone. "Zain. I should have guessed. I knew you weren't to be trusted."

I did purse my lips then. "Wrong. I'm one of the few people you can trust. Now, tell me about Lily."

Silence.

I looked down at the map, brushing Brace's hand aside as I punched in numbers to get his exact address.

"You're just outside of Portland, Oregon. What the fuck are you doing up there?"

"You're tracking me?"

The threat was there, but so was the surprise.

"You're not the only tracker, Blake. Now, I'm not going to ask you again. Please."

The one word that would have been like acid in my mouth concerning another man came easily. He was searching for Lily. That made him more than okay in my book.

"The cabin she was at before was empty, minus three dead bodies. I was under the impression from the recording that she only killed two. That means whoever took her killed off the man attacking her at the end of the tape. Unless it was the other way around, which wouldn't be very good in Lily's case."

I processed the information, letting it sink in. The anger swirled and I clenched my fist to stay in control. "So, one of them has her alone. Fuck," I said, beginning to pace. "What else have you learned? Do you have any suspects? Theories?"

A sigh came over the speaker. "I don't usually give a play by play on my investigations, Zain. I like to have evidence before I start saying anything."

My jaw tightened as reality carried in his tone. "You know nothing more on Lily's location and we both know it. At least, not yet. Instead of wasting time getting further away, come back and let all of us lay out your evidence and work together. We might have better luck that way."

"I like that idea," Slade said, interrupting.

Blake made an aggravated sound. "I work alone, dammit."

"Not all the time," I rushed in. "I know who you are. I mean, I've heard of you before. Everyone in the trafficking world has, Blake. You're a killer. And not in the sense of having to protect yourself. You enjoy killing. Look for reasons to do it, even. You're a serial killer, but you hide it well by what you do."

"You're walking on *very, very* thin ice, Mr. Cook."

"Collins," I corrected. "Zain Cook has been dead since he was a child. Listen, you have to come back. We'll go over the evidence and…I'll give you what you need. Help me kill my father and his men. They have a deal going down with a transaction of slaves either tonight or tomorrow. I've heard two different accounts of how they'll meet. My father probably regrets me hearing that now, but it's worth a try. And we have to act fast if we want to be ready. They know I killed two of my uncles and they had every intention of getting rid of me. I want to take them out first. Before those girls end up gone for good. I have locations of other traffickers, Mr.

Morgan. I can feed your deepest cravings for
months to come. I'm a wealth of information. You
help me and I will supply you with more names that
you'll know what to do with. But after that," I
looked over to Slade, "after we kill them tonight,
you're taking me with you to find Lily."

The line disconnected and I closed my eyes,
gripping the phone hard. He had to take me with
him. I couldn't just sit here and wait for any
information she might feed us. Lily belonged to me.
I needed to be there to find and protect her. Not to
mention, make whoever did this pay for what
they've done.

"If he doesn't have any leads, he'll come
back." Slade walked over, pouring himself another
Scotch.

Brace was still watching the map when I
moved in to sit down.

"Yep, he's turning around. Guess your deal
was too good to pass up. Don't you think your
information would be better with someone like
Gaige? The FBI might be able to bring the girls
home."

The thought was dismissed almost instantly.
"No. The FBI won't save them before the word gets

out. They'll move those girls so fast, they'll never be found again. Blake is the only one who can save them. Besides, those bastards deserve what's coming to them."

"I'm with you." Slade handed me a glass. "How are those pills working? You still hurting?"

My first instinct was to play the tough guy, but I shook my head. "I'm a lot better now, thank you. The pain is—"

Ring.

I glanced down, my eyes narrowing at the blocked call. "Does Blake's number show up when he calls?"

Slade slammed his glass on the counter. "We're not chancing it. Brace."

"One second, boss."

The guard's fingers pressed keys quickly and he nodded.

Ring

I swallowed hard and hit the button for speakerphone. "Hello?" Slade and I spoke at the same time and he twisted his mouth to me.

"Hello?" he repeated.

"Twenty million, wired into my account or she dies."

The woman's voice sounded monotone, but…shaky.

"Who is this?" Slade snapped. "Where's my sister?"

"Lily is fine," she said, annoyed. "Are you going to send me the money or not?"

Slade and I stared at each other and I motioned with my hand to keep going. As I turned, Brace's fingers were still working.

He's not picking up a location. Fuck!

I shoved the phone toward Slade and spun around, nearly knocking Brace out of the way. When it came to searching people out, I knew what I was doing. It was my life. My father wasn't only in the human trafficking business, he dealt in drugs and illegal weapons, too. People owed him more money than most could imagine. I was the one who searched them out and collected when they neglected to pay.

"Let me talk to Lily. I want to hear that she's okay before I agree to pay you anything."

Shuffling sounded and heavy panting broke through. I hit the last button just as I turned to face the phone.

"Slade?" A sob tore into my heart.

"Lily," I yelled. "Baby, we're going to get you back. I promise."

"Zain?" Another sob broke through and a scream immediately followed. I could hear the struggle of them trying to get her quiet again.

"Lily!"

"I'll be sending you the information on where to send the money." A sniffle. "You have two days."

The line went dead and I spun around to look at the computer.

"Amateurs," I said, shaking my head. "Let's get ready. We're leaving."

"Wait, wait…" Slade was already next to the screen. "That can't be right," he breathed out.

My head shook. "Why not? It says right there that they're in Washington. See," I said, pointing to the exact address. "Let's go."

"It can't be right," he exploded. "That's *my* fucking address and I know for a fact they're not at my estate. I would have been called if anyone even entered my road. It's private and almost impossible to get down. I fly in and out to the grounds directly because I keep it that way for a reason. I can say, almost for certain, no one flew in there. Something isn't right." He turned to Brace. "Get the exact coordinates of the estate and how close this location is to the actual house."

"Already on it, Boss."

"Slade tapped his finger against his thigh as he paced. "Play that recording back, too. I want to hear it again."

As it began, I closed my eyes, forcing myself to listen to every single sound I could hear.

"Twenty million, wired into my account or she dies." The woman's voice sounded devoid of emotion, but I could still detect shakiness. Was it because she was nervous?

"Who is this?" Slade rushed in. *"Where's my sister?"*

"Lily is fine." The annoyance was clear. She didn't like Lily. Her instant distaste was laced deep in each word. *"Are you going to send me the money or not?"*

As it played on, nothing about the woman changed that I could hear. She seemed very detached. My mind kept getting sucked in to every sound Lily was making. I strained to memorize each breath. Every sound I thought might be her.

"I'll be sending you the information on where to send the money." A sniffle. *"You have two days."*

Shattering glass had me spinning around. Mary was standing there paler than I had ever seen her. Slade was already rushing over.

"Hey, talk to me, baby, you okay?" His hand cupped her face as she clung to the front of his suit jacket. "Mary, honey, talk to me. Is it the baby?" I could see her legs giving out. If it weren't for Slade's arm wrapped around her lower back, I had no doubt she'd be on the floor. "Mary," he growled. "Talk to me."

"Play it again," she whispered. "Play back the tape."

Slade's head tilted as he peered down at her. Before he turned, Brace was already on it.

"Twenty million, wired into my account or she dies."

Mary's hand lifted to her mouth. The voice continued while tears rolled down her cheeks.

"I'll be sending you the information on where to send the money." A sniffle. *"You have two days."*

"Bethany, I'm positive," she said, breaking down even more. "Oh God, Slade, she's going to kill her. I know my sister. She's going to kill Lily.

He held her tighter to the side of his body as he walked her over to the sofa. "I had a feeling it was her."

"You have to call Gaige," she pleaded. "You have to report this right now. Lily is in serious danger. No more waiting."

Slade turned and looked at me, but brought his attention back to her. "I'll take care of it. You trust me, yes?"

"Of course."

He nodded, walking over and taking his phone from me. I could see the battle that played on his face. I wasn't sure what he was planning to do, but I knew the police getting involved wasn't going to be good for the revenge I had planned. For the life of me, I couldn't see letting them handle it turning out well. I could find her first. I could save her.

"Boss, the coordinates match up with your estate. Unless they're inside, I'm pretty sure this is fake."

"Routed," I repeated the word, walking over. "Let me see what I can do." I hadn't once been outsmarted on tracking a person. It wasn't about to start now.

Chapter 19

Lily

"I hate you," Bethany sobbed, jerking against the ropes. "I'll kill you. You watch, I'm going to—"

Jonathon stuffed the gag into her mouth, tying it tight behind her head. His palm pushed against her temple, making her head sway before he stepped back and laughed under his breath. God, they were all sick. Well, all but Alec. He seemed to be the only one I had met that came out of the Brighton family with good morals and a kind heart.

My eyes went back to the body that still lay on the table. I couldn't stare for long. The sight of Alec, dead, turned me weaker than I already was. It broke down my walls and left me on the verge of weeping. There was no room for that right now. Whatever game Jonathan had planned, I knew it was going to be bad. I had to stay strong. Fight to live. I'd come so far.

"Well, now that we've gotten the important part out of the way, I think we'll go over a few things while we wait for my friend." He paused, looking over at me and coming forward. The gag was pulled from my mouth. "Before we start…Zain." His face turned hard. "He wasn't supposed to live. There's going to be a lot of people who aren't going to be happy about that."

My heart raced as I stared up at him. "What do you know about Zain?" My jaw ached. I moved it open and closed a few times, trying to loosen the tightness.

Jonathon pulled my chair to face the sofa as he sat down. "I've been watching him off and on for the last few weeks. You see, my father was prepared for the worst when it came to his illegal activities. He may not have protected us against the loss of his company, but he didn't mind leaving his contacts my and Alec's information. They weren't stupid. They came to me. Knew I was the man for the job."

He pulled out his phone, checking the time, only to stuff it back into his pocket. "Mr. Amari was concerned over his son's loyalty when it came to our dealings. I didn't think he had a reason…until I noticed him following you in secret. It took me awhile to figure out why he kept a routine that didn't make sense. Then, when he went into Slade Industries..." a smile came to his face, "the pieces came together so clearly. Would have a lot sooner if his stupid father had mentioned you two being involved while you were there.

"I was so concerned over my brother and you, Zain was just an afterthought. But when I put everything together and he took you up to his penthouse, there was never a more perfect time to get rid of you both."

My head shook. "But why him?"

The door opened and I felt myself push back into the chair. Every inch of my skin crawled as my eyes connected with Zain's brother.

"Ah, perfect timing. Amir can answer that question." Jonathon stood. "Lily was just wondering why anyone would want Zain dead. Would you like to enlighten her, or should I?"

Dark eyes turned cold as he walked forward. Another man, who I recognized as one of their guards, followed, shutting the door.

"Slave, surely you don't have to ask that? I know he told you."

My teeth slammed into each other as my jaw clenched. I knew he called all of us women slaves, but I only allowed one to refer to me as such, and between us, it didn't hold the ugliness in which Amir meant it.

"I'm sorry, I don't know what you're talking about."

"Surely, you do," he said, plainly. "Maybe Jabir can refresh your memory."

My lips parted at what I knew was coming, but there was nothing I could do about it. I wouldn't betray anything Zain had told me."

Whack! The hit connected on the opposite cheek of where Jonathan had hit. A sound left my mouth while ringing in my ears had my head leaning to try to stop it.

"I do have you to thank for this. Your corruption of my brother led him to kill Samir and Bahr, which made it possible for me to take control. Now, here I am. And, you, right where you belong. In ropes." He reached forward, pushing back the hair that had fallen over my eye. I instantly jerked away before I could process what it would mean to him. The insult had him glaring.

"You think you're too good for me?" Fingers squeezed just above my jaw as he held my face to look at his. It made my anger surge.

"I *was* given to Zain," I said, lowly.

Whack!

Lights flashed behind my eyes and my heartbeat pulsed throughout my throbbing cheek.

"Someone forgets their place." His fingers locked back on, only making the pain worse. "I considered taking you back home. Making you my own slave. I'd do it right. You'd obey my every command." My head tried to shake at his words and it caused him to smile. "Thing is, someone else wants you more. Someone who's going to enjoy breaking you to pieces."

"No," I breathed out.

"Oh yes, slave. Saul is anxious for your arrival. It's almost time to go back home."

"No," I sobbed, dragging the word out. I couldn't go back there. Couldn't be given to Saul. He'd kill me and bask in it.

Heavy steps came up from behind us. "That wasn't the deal," Jonathan snapped. "Lily's supposed to die. At my hands, not anyone else's. You were just here to make sure she was dead."

Amir glanced over at him, but his hand never disconnected from my face.

"The plans have changed and you'll be compensated generously for it. If you have a problem with those terms, you can take it up with my father. Lily leaves with him tonight. But," he said, pausing and looking back at me, "as long as you keep her alive, have all the fun you want."

I was lost with his words. Internally, I was pleading, telling them not to do this. But the survivor knew groveling wouldn't work. I needed a plan.

A sniffle had my gaze shooting to Bethany. She'd been so quiet. Unfortunately for her, she caught Amir's attention, too.

"Who's this?"

Jonathan glanced over, immediately dismissing her, but slowly brought his eyes back. The evil didn't escape my notice and I felt myself lean more in my chair. "*This*," he smiled, "is Bethany. Pretty thing, isn't she?"

Her gaze jerked nervously between Amir and Jonathon.

"Why, yes, she is. What are your plans with her?"

"Death," Jonathon said. "She was my cover for Lily, but if you're taking my revenge back to Afghanistan with you, we can negotiate. What are you thinking?"

Amir's hand dropped and he turned toward her. "One hour. That's all she'll be good for. You get rid of the body."

A whimper left her and she began shaking her head, staring at Jonathan. Mascara trailed down her cheeks and I hated the twisting in my stomach. Amir might not snap her limbs like Saul would, but he wasn't much better. I wouldn't wish his sick sexual ways on my worst enemy. Not even Bethany.

"I was going to say a hundred grand, but she ain't worth it. Half and she's yours. I'll take care of whatever is left of her when you're finished."

"Done."

A muffled scream from Bethany filled the room and they both turned back to me, dismissing her.

"And I get her." Jonathon cocked his head, his eyes raking over my body. For the first time, I wasn't just revenge. I was revenge tainted with lust. It was a hell of a mixer I knew I couldn't mentally choke down. Not again.

"Remember, you're not to kill her. If you do, it'll cost you your life. I will not fail my uncle. She will be going back alive."

Jonathan licked his lips. "I won't kill her, but I guarantee she'll be begging for me to before it's over with." He pulled out a knife and clicked it opened. I knew I should have been scared, but I was more interested in separating us from Amir and his guard. If I could get Jonathon alone, I might stand a chance to escape. The windows surrounding us weren't boarded over like before. Dark curtains covered the glass, but it was still glass. I could break it if I needed to.

The ropes around my chest fell away and I watched as Amir's guard began cutting the restraints keeping Bethany secured. Our eyes met and she cried even harder. I wanted to believe an apology was written in her expression, but I knew it was wishful thinking. We were both going to die if it was up to these men and surely she'd be sorry for that.

"Up," Jonathan said, pulling my shirt to make me stand. The material burned my skin at the force and I commanded my legs to obey. Aside from restroom breaks, I'd been sitting down for days.

A loud, muffled scream had me bringing my attention back to Bethany. Free, I felt torn. If I tried to fight, they'd hurt me more than I could take. I'd be disabled from trying to escape. But my heart pleaded to help her. She might have done things to me that scarred me internally, but she was also going to die. I couldn't look past that.

"Don't fight him," I yelled. "He'll like that too much and it'll be worse. Just, don't—"

A hard shove had me sliding down the hallway, the air exploding from my lungs at the impact.

"She doesn't need your help." Jonathon stalked forward, landing a hard kick to my bicep before reaching down and grabbing a fistful of my hair. Pain tore into my scalp as he began dragging me to the back room. Bethany thrashed as the guard held on to her, dragging her in the same direction we were heading.

One room was passed. Two.

Jonathon pushed open a door directly in front of him and I held his wrists to ease the pain. My feet scrambled to find footing, sliding against the wood from lack of friction. The men's jeans I wore were so long, my feet were covered and they were barely hanging on my hips.

Light shone through curtains and I said a silent prayer as he stopped to toss me inside and shut the

door. I scrambled to my feet, pulling up my
pants, and searching the area wildly.

"Bed."

I stepped back, sidestepping as he took a step
toward me.

"Where you going, huh? I said *bed*."

The top part of my body leaned to the left and I
watched him mirror my actions. As I moved my
shoulders to the right, he was almost on cue with my
timing. The room didn't have anything but a full
sized bed in the middle. It was completely bare and
my hope sank at no sign of any weapon.

"You going to fight me? I like that, too, you
know."

"Fuck you," I spat. "You're not going to get
close enough to touch me."

A laugh filled the room and excitement shone
in his eyes. To him, this was a game. To me, I was
studying his every move. Rape would not find me
again. It couldn't.

"You ready?" He lunged forward, only to slide
to the side. His movements were so quick, it took
every ounce of concentration I had to follow his
actions. "Which way am I going? Left or right?" He
dipped left while I remained still, placing pressure

on my toes. I was ready, all he had to do was make his move.

"Your phone is in your pocket, yes?"

Another laugh, but this one sounded genuinely amused.

"You'll never get to it. Don't bother even wondering." He rushed forward and my hand shot out as I jumped to the side. I reached around and pushed down at the back of his head for balance. Jonathon caught himself before he hit the floor. Rage met me head on as he spun around.

Slowly, I eased back to the door as he wheeled around, ducking his shoulders lower. "Lucky," he said, lowly.

"Deadly," I countered, not sounding anywhere near as threatening as I wanted. "And I know you don't have your gun on you. You'll never make it out of this room alive."

"Bluff all you want. When I get you within my grasp, you're going to regret it."

I had no doubt he was right. But first, he'd have to catch me.

Chapter 20
Slade

"It doesn't make sense," Mary stressed as she looked at us. "Play it again."

A groan came from Blake as he tilted his head to me and raised his eyebrow.

"Do it," I ordered. "She may be right. It sounds like the sniffle is coming from Bethany, not Lily. If she was so hell-bent on the money, why would she be crying? It doesn't make sense."

The voice played back at full volume and the silence throughout the room ended when the recording did.

"That's my sister. I'm telling you, she's crying and she wouldn't do that unless there was a reason. Having Lily and her revenge would have been enough. Ransom? That just doesn't sound like Bethany. She's smarter than that. She just exposed her guilt when we were all clueless as to who it even was. It doesn't add up."

Zain nodded, bringing his head up from where it was resting on his fists. "She's right. I think it was

Bethany, too, and I don't believe she made that call willingly."

A knock on the door was followed by Marcio opening it and Gaige walking in. The power emanating from him couldn't be ignored. He wasn't the Gaige who'd told me about his wife and son. This Gaige was different. He was back to being the bad ass agent.

"You said you had news?"

His eyes scanned all of us before coming to settle on me.

"Play it," I said to Brace.

For what seemed like the millionth time, Bethany's voice echoed through the living area. Each time Lily screamed, Zain's fists clenched. I'd seen the reaction too many times and I wasn't sure how much more I could take.

"That's my sister," Mary stated. "And she's crying. Something isn't right with that call."

Silence reigned as everyone looked at Gaige. Had he picked up the crying, too? Did he think it was Bethany?

"Shit," he mumbled. "Alright, I have to make a few calls. I'll get one of my guys here, ready to trace any more calls that might come through. I'll make the rounds with my partner and see if we can locate Bethany. From what her husband told me earlier, they're no longer together. When I stopped by to ask about their supposed falling out, she was gone. I was trying to track her down when you called."

"I think she's in trouble," Mary said, lowly. "She's in over her head with someone, and now both her and Lily are going to pay for it. God." Mary stood, wiping the tears from her cheeks. I immediately followed her toward the kitchen area. When we were far enough away from the others, she turned and threw herself into my chest. "I'm so scared, Slade. I have such a bad feeling concerning all of this. I know I shouldn't care what happens to Bethany after all that she's done, but I can't help it. My heart is breaking. I just want them back. If my sister had any part, I want her to do her time. But...hurt or dead?"

"Shh," I said, wrapping my arms around her. "We'll get to the bottom of this."

The sobs grew heavier and I led her to the bedroom, hugging her tightly against my side. Mary didn't need any more stress. She couldn't afford it and neither could the baby.

"You're going to rest. I don't want you out of bed for the rest of the night." I led her to the dresser and opened the drawer, removing a white, silk nightgown. Slowly, I undressed her, easing to my knees to press my lips to her stomach. "Understand? Let's get you in bed so you can rest. I'll bring you dinner when it arrives."

With one more kiss and her nod, I stood, raising the gown to slide down her lifted arms.

"There. Now, let me tuck you in. I'll be back to check on you in a little while. Do you need anything? Crackers?" A bottled water was already resting by the bed and I took it, handing it over.

"I should be okay." She took a sip and placed it back down, grabbing a tissue. "Will you let me know if you learn anything?"

I nodded my head and pulled back the covers. "You know I will. Now, lay back and relax. Remember what the doctor said. You need rest, not worry. I'll do what I can."

Pressure gripped into the lapels of my jacket as she pushed to her toes and angled her face toward mine. Our lips met and I couldn't stop my hand from fisting the silk material at the small of her back. I pushed my fingers through the hair at the base of her neck, needing more. Mary was the only one who could calm me and make me forget everything but her. Even if it was only for a few seconds, my soul grounded and I felt myself calm.

"God, I love you." My deep breaths were met with hers and the green of her eyes pulled me under. I could get lost staring into their depths. Here, I was safe. Free from the dangers and pain of the real world.

"And I love you. Go help them find Lily. I'll be here."

I helped her into bed and leaned down for one last kiss. As she curled onto her side, I couldn't stop myself from placing my lips against her temple before I stood. Walking away was the hardest, but I knew she was right. I had to find my sister and bring her home safe. Maybe even Mary's sister. What in the hell was going on? There were too many questions and nothing for answers.

The door clicked as I pulled it closed. The men stopped talking as I walked toward them.

"What's the word? Any news in the last five minutes?" I'd meant it sarcastically, but from the looks on their faces, I'd obviously missed something. "What is it?" My heart raced while I stared between Blake, Gaige, and Zain. All three of them turned toward Brace, who was still sitting at his computer. My guard swallowed hard as he stood.

"Between Blake and Zain, we might be able to break through the shield blocking out the address where Bethany called from. Give me just a minute, boss."

I took a step back and turned, trying to remember where in the hell I put my gun. My mind was whirling in disbelief. Excitement and nervousness crashed, leaving me turning in a complete circle. Where the hell was my gun?

"Not going to happen," Blake said, deeply. "You're not going, Mr. Roberts."

I spun back, glaring.

"You have to stay with me," Gaige said, firmly. "I'm your alibi if this ever gets out. If we can pinpoint the location, Blake and Zain have to do this alone.

My jaw clenched. I couldn't stand it, but he was right. Together, they could bring Lily home. She wasn't mine anymore. Not really. My sister now belonged to Zain, and suddenly, I was okay with that. I trusted him, wounded and all. He'd almost died trying to save her before. He'd do the same again if it came down to it. And with Blake there, he'd be okay. The man was a professional killer. One who enjoyed it. Together, there was no fear for Lily's safety.

"Okay. Fine." I turned to Zain, my eyes glancing over to Brace as he worked to find us the address. "A word with you, first?" I could tell Zain didn't want to come, but I had to make something clear before he left.

"Sure."

The walk to my office led me straight to the Scotch. I poured two drinks and we both threw back our glasses, finishing the liquor in one drink.

"Bring her back," I said, placing the glass down. "Safely."

Slowly, Zain shook his head. "If we can pull this off, I won't be bringing her back here, Slade. Not immediately."

My gaze narrowed. "What the hell do you mean? Where do you plan on taking her?"

His mouth tightened, but he never broke eye contact. "Lily and I have some things we have to work out. If she's okay, I'm taking her to an undisclosed location and we're going to fix what's wrong. That could take days or weeks. I'm not sure yet. I do promise you this, your sister couldn't be in better hands. I love her with everything I am." He frowned and turned to stare back to the door. "When I return, I'll leave her in your care long enough to put an end to this once and for all. After that," he turned to face me, "I would like your permission to formally date your sister. I want it all with Lily and I won't hide my intentions. I want her as mine, always. When she's ready, I want to marry her."

My eyes widened and I blindly grabbed the decanter. "Marriage." I glanced over long enough to pour my drink. I had it finished before I could find my voice. "If Lily wants you that way, we'll go from there. I'm not sure I can give you a blessing until I see the two of you together for myself. But what I can give you is a job," I ground out. "You're going to need one of those. As for taking her…" I shook my head. "My sister isn't going to be dragged across the country to some place I'm unaware of. If you want to work things out, you'll stay in my place in Washington. That's final, or else I take back what I said. I want her safe and although I trust you, I want her protected to the max until your family is taken care of."

"Text me the address." He was already turning around when I stepped forward.

"No, bring her back here and once I see that she's okay, you can fly out. No easy access into the estate, remember?"

He paused. "That's right. Okay, I'll bring her back here first."

"Zain?"

"I got it!" Brace yelled from the living room.

Urgency raced through his features as he turned, looking over his shoulder.

"Get a damn vest from Brace. I don't need you back in the hospital."

"Blake already offered me one of his. I don't plan on going anywhere anytime soon." The door swung fully open and he dashed out, but I was left with uneasiness. What condition was he going to find Lily in? Was she okay? Was she even still there?

With the decanter in one hand and my glass in the other, I joined the rest of them in the living room. Zain and Blake were already rushing for the front door with Marcio following. I didn't question it. Didn't have to. He was like another brother to

Lily and she was in great hands. If only they could get there fast enough.

Chapter 21
Lily

A woman can be fast and strong, but compared to a man who is running at her full force, if she has nowhere to go, her power is limited. As Jonathon charged at me for the fifth time, I knew I was in trouble. More so than I wanted to accept. The anger he held at not being able to get me had long disappeared into frustration and rage. But now he had me cornered. There was nowhere for me to go.

Screams from the next room echoed around me, as if coming from a far off place. Time was slowing as my adrenaline peaked. It was all I had left. My body was already so exhausted and weak. If I didn't put an end to this soon, I was done for. I would be a victim of one of the worst crimes imaginable —again.

"No!' Bethany's long, drawn out scream penetrated my ears only a split second before Jonathan came crashing into me. The connection we made with the wooden wall behind me was enough to knock the air from my lungs completely. Stars danced around my vision, but muscle memory kicked in despite the pain and fear. My hands flew out and my thumbs pushed into his eyes as hard as I could. Only one was successful, but it was enough to have him jerking back and reaching for his face. The crunch under my palm as I smashed it into his nose was only a temporary victory. His arm locked around my waist and he used his shoulder to push both of mine harder into the wall. Had I had more room, I could have done worse damage with my blow, but it hadn't been enough.

"You fucking bitch. You'll be hanging on by a thread by the time I get done with you."

My knees drew up between his legs and I managed to add space, but not enough to do any damage or force him further away.

"You like getting your ass fucked?" His hand ripped at my pants, moving them to the very edge of my hips. Fear had me fighting harder. They were going to fall soon and there was nothing I could do to keep them up if my leg dropped. "I'm going to fuck you so hard, you'll be lucky to walk again. Dry, hardcore, ass fucking. And you're going to take it."

One minute, I was at the wall, the next, he was spinning me and slamming me on the hard floor. My head lifted on instinct, leaving my upper back taking the impact. All the air left me again and I clawed at him, trying to will oxygen back.

"What's the matter, baby? Do I leave you breathless? He laughed, tearing the shirt over my head in one swift motion. My swing was deflected only for him to catch it in his grasp. A small scream left my lips while I tried to pry my hand free. My only free one was quickly caught and pulled up with the other to be pinned above my head.

Bethany's screams continued and I tried to block them out, but Jonathon pulling my strapless bra down caused my own to mingle with hers. She and I were done for and it left me shaky and sick.

"Very nice." His fingers pinched my nipple and I couldn't stop the scream from escaping at the pain. I thrashed, trying to rock him off, but he didn't so much as budge.

"Stop," I cried. "Please. You…" Sobs broke through as he let go and his whole hand encompassed my breast. The slap over the sensitive skin had my head turning away. I couldn't be here anymore. Couldn't be in this room while it was happening.

Again, he slapped my breast. This time, harder. And harder. Tears blinded me, but I kept wiggling, twisting my body and arms back and forth until my muscles screamed from the stretching. The slaps burned down my chest, lighting a fire in their path all the way to the top of my panties. The pants were so low, they were barely on my hips anymore. I was almost bare. Exposed.

"In another life, I might have competed with Alec to have you. In this one, I think I'll just rip you apart and send you on your merry fucking way. You ready for me?"

His hand dipped below the waistband and I squeezed my thighs together as hard as I could. It wasn't good enough. A growl filled the room while he forced his fist through and cupped my pussy. Panicked, I fought harder, ignoring the barrier I was trying to make with my legs. Instead, I dropped my knee and kicked at him with everything I had. My heel caught the back of his calf twice, but it gave him the opportunity to slide between my legs.

"Bitch! You're so going to get it."

His hand shoved deeper and I tried repeatedly to turn to my side. My arms were released as he reared back.

"You hit her and I'll slice open your throat. Now, remove your hand from what belongs to me or

I'll cut it clean off." The deep tone left my breaths ragged and uneven. My eyes jerked up in time to meet Zain's. Although cold and distant, I could feel our connection. Seeing him again after I feared he was dead for so long was so emotional, I began crying even harder.

He stood behind Jonathan, one fist in his hair, the other holding a long knife blade under his throat. With a yank, he pulled back on his head and lowered to become even with Jonathan's ear. "I know you heard me. Do you think I'm playing with you?"

Slowly, the eased out. A small stream of blood ran down Jonathon's neck, but he didn't seem fazed as he continued to stare down at me.

"Stand."

A small sound left my lips at his knee pushing into my thigh. Zain pulled back Jonathan's hair even more, his eyes flickering in anger as he ripped him to his feet.

"You look familiar. Who the fuck are you and why do you have Lily?"

More blood trickled down, soaking his shirt even more.

Jonathan kept his attention on me, refusing to answer the question. God, he wanted to hurt me. To kill me. It was so clearly written in his murderous glare.

"He's Alec and Jordan's brother. His name is Jonathon." My voice was scratchy and more frail than I thought possible. Had that really been me? It spoke to how fragile I was on the inside, even if I wasn't feeling the actual effects of what was happening to me yet.

"Jonathan, it's so nice to meet you. The pleasure is about to be all mine. Did you think I wouldn't find you?"

Still, Jonathon stood quietly.

"Since he doesn't want to comply, let's just skip the introductions. Turn and look the other way, baby. Cover your ears. You're not going to want to witness this."

I knew better than to disobey when he used that tone. Death was coming. I'd been here before.

Robotically, I lifted enough to fix my pants. My arms ached as I turned on the floor and grabbed my shirt to pull over my head. Shuffling behind me had my knees drawing in and my head lowering to rest on them. I cuffed my ears, but didn't apply pressure as I tried to slow my breathing. I needed to hear that he was dead, regardless of whether I wanted to. The nightmares would be worse if I didn't live this.

A loud bump, as if they had gone to the ground, was followed by Jonathan's screams. It seemed like they went on forever.

"That's for touching what belongs to me. This might hurt a little more than the hands."

More screaming and rustling of fabric ended with gurgling that sent bile pushing against the back of my throat.

"How do you like choking on your own blood, motherfucker? Doesn't feel so good, does it? I think I'll let you fight for a few seconds before I kill you. See what it feels like to have your life ending while there's nothing you can do about it. I'll tell you, from personal experience, it's the worst. Only difference, I lived. You're going to die. Right now."

A deep internal grunt and a hiss of air had my hand shooting out at the lightheadedness. I swallowed, trying to force the facts into my reeling brain. Jonathon was dead. He was gone. He could never hurt me again.

"Lily?"

A hand clasping my shoulder had my whole body jerking defensively. Tears clouded my eyes as I turned and tried my hardest to stand. Blood was splattered along the stubble on his cheek and his eyes were so full of pain…yet, what looked to be relief. Before I could get to my feet entirely, Zain pulled me into his arms.

"Fuck. Oh, shit, baby. Let me see you. How bad are you hurt?"

"I think I'm okay." Still, I pulled him closer. "I wasn't sure you'd come fast enough. I was so scared. I thought he was going to…" Sobs took over while I held on tighter.

"Shh, I'm here. No one will ever hurt you again. I promise you that."

My head turned toward the door, fear once again surging to the forefront. "Your brother?"

"Is taken care of." Zain removed his jacket, placing it around my shoulders.

"Bethany?" I was almost afraid to meet his gaze. I hadn't heard her in a while.

"The screaming led me and Blake straight in there. We weren't fast enough. She's gone. She took a pretty bad beating."

My head buried into his chest as the tears flowed. I couldn't stop the part of me that cared.

She'd been scared, up to the point of death. It didn't sit right, regardless of what she'd done.

"Is Slade here?"

"No. He had to stay back so he'd have an alibi. I'd take you to him, but we're not going there yet. First, I want to get you to a hospital. Then, we'll talk about leaving.

My head shook. "Leave where?" I wasn't sure why, but panic once again took the lead. Although I loved Zain, I'd convinced myself for so long that things couldn't work. I was so confused.

"Your brother is letting us stay at his house in Washington. It's time we find ourselves again, Lilian. We need to start fresh. But let's focus on that later. First, the hospital. Did any of them…" his jaw tightened and I knew what he meant.

"No, just what almost happened. I'm fine, really. I don't want to go to the hospital." Slade's name came back into my mind and I let his words process. "Wait. My brother is allowing this?"

"He knows I love you. I've made it very clear to him."

I stayed quiet while he led me down the hall at a fast pace, holding onto me tighter. My eyes drifted over to where Alec's body was and I briefly squeezed them shut, hoping that would help erase what I'd just seen. The pale shade of his skin left me even sicker. The nightmares were going to be so much worse now and there was nothing I could do about it.

"How is she?" A blond man with huge shoulders and arms met us at the door. At how intimidating he was, I pushed more into Zain.

"I think she's okay. She doesn't want to go to the hospital. Let's take her back home and I'll check her better there."

I barely heard their words. At the sight of Marcio standing just outside, I broke from Zain and pushed through the door, rushing into his arms.

"You came," I said, crying even harder.

"Of course. You should have known I would."

My head tilted back and I couldn't fight the upturn of my lips. "Yes, I should have."

I gave Marcio one last squeeze and stepped back. Zain and the blond were coming through the front door. For the first time, I took in my surroundings. When we'd arrived, I had a cloth over my head. Large trees surrounded us and I turned in a complete circle, stopping back at Zain and the blond.

"Where are we? It felt like Jonathan had me in the car forever."

Zain was already leading me to the SUV. "Not far from home, sweetie. South of San Francisco."

"But…" my head shook, confused as I climbed in the back. Zain followed, closing the door behind him. "I don't understand. We were in the car so long after we left the first place."

"You were on the Oregon-California border the first time. They brought you back. I think it more had to do with my father. He's here and it doesn't look good. I think he knows what I've done, which may be why he played a part in taking you."

The SUV pulled out of the dirt drive and began heading down the winding mountain path.

"He knows," I confirmed. "I was supposed to fly back to Afghanistan with him tonight. They meant to kill you, Zain. They're going to keep trying until they're successful."

Zain cursed under his breath and my eyes came up to connect with Blake's in the rearview mirror. I had to suppress a shudder. He was unexplainably…off. I could feel it. Although there was no threatening expression present, it didn't stop the vibe he threw off.

"You don't have to worry, Lily. I'm going to take care of it," Blake said, as if reading my mind. "You focus on Zain and don't worry about anything anymore."

My Master's face snapped to the front. "I was only going to let you take out the dealers because I wasn't expecting my father to be present. I already told you he's mine. And I'll take care of him when I get back."

The admission had my hands subconsciously clutching Zain's shirt. Just imagining him returning to Afghanistan scared me more than anything. He wouldn't come back if he did. Not if it came down to him versus his two uncles, his father, and all of their guards.

"You can't go. I don't want you to."

"I'll be okay. Here, come sit closer to me." Zain's arms wrapped around my shoulders, but I pulled back.

Again, I looked between my Master and Blake. "There's no point in going to the deal. It's ruined now. Don't you see? The deal for the girls was between Jonathan and your family. He picked up where Julian Brighton left off. Now, they're dead, except for your father. He's going to know. He's going to have people looking for you. If you go, you'll be walking into a trap. You all will."

"The trap will always be there," Blake said, quietly. "He has to be taken out tonight. Just like I had planned to do anyway."

Zain shook his head, angrily. "Amir is mine. I can't just let you take care of my dirty work. I'll do it. We'll drop Lily off with Slade and head out."

Tighter, my fingers held onto him, but I knew there was nothing I could do. Zain would leave me to do what he had to once we arrived home. I just prayed he came back.

Chapter 22
Zain

The hood sat low and engulfed Lily's head, making it easy to hide her face as we headed for the elevator. If she'd just been the captive of a psychopath, no one would ever know. They'd never see the evidence of his abuse on her face. We'd made sure of that.

The elevator ride went too slow and too fast all at the same time. For the life of me, I couldn't let go of Lily. Imagining leaving her now made me sick, but my father would have to die tonight. If I let him return, the chance of him taking me out or dealing in more girls was too great.

Ding. The elevator stopped at the entrance of the penthouse and Brace was already standing there, waiting with the door open. I swept Lily in, noticing that she reached out and gave the guard's hand a squeeze before coming in. She'd always connected with people. It was one of the reasons I'd fallen so deeply in love with her.

Slade stopped pacing the moment he saw us.

"Lily." He rushed forward and she broke away, meeting him with her arms outstretched. Their hug was brief before Slade pulled back, pushing the dark hood from her head. "Son of a bitch. God, look at your face. They bruised you up badly."

"It's nothing," she breathed out. "I'm just glad to be home," she said, giving him another hug.

"I told her she needed to go to the hospital, but she says she's fine. I plan to do a check to make sure she's okay before I leave."

Gaige and Slade both stepped toward me. "Where are you going?" Slade asked, confused. "I thought you and Lily were headed to Washington."

If only it were that easy. I sighed, pushing my hands in my jean pockets. My stare went to Gaige. I knew I didn't have to hold back with him. He may have been an agent, but I knew his past. His wife had been a victim of human trafficking, tied to a huge drug cartel leader down in Mexico, before he came in and rescued her. The research hadn't been hard as I waited for word on Lily.

"I have to take out my father. Jonathon Brighton was working with my family. My brother, who was supposed to head up the deal, and Jonathon, who was on the other side of it, are now both dead. Amir will know I'm behind their murders when they don't show up. He'll come looking for me or send people who will. I can't chance it. He may already know if he's tried to contact my brother."

"Shit." Slade's hand came to rest on the back of Lily's head and he stroked down her knotted hair as he stared down at the floor. A few second passed before he began talking again. "What if I told you I wanted you to stay and let Blake and Gaige handle it?"

My head tilted and I could see something going on behind his blank stare. When his eyes rose to meet mine, I couldn't stop shaking my head.

"I have to do this," I said, lowly.

"More than you have to be here for my sister?"

Lily's eyes were filled with tears and I fought the emotions of what he was asking me to do. How could I just step back from something I'd spent the last twenty-two years planning?

"Lily needs you, Zain. Revenge doesn't. I want you to hand over your anger to the ones who specialize in this sort of thing. Let them take care of your father. Let Blake take care of your uncles. Walk away from that family into this one and don't look back. This could be a new beginning for you. It's right here with Lily. All you have to do is come get it. Take her and clean her up. Pack her clothes and leave to Washington. Your past could disappear just as fast as the two of you can. Take my offer...and you'll have my blessing."

There were no words for what he was asking me to do. I stood there in shock, yet anger.

"No." Lily broke away from Slade. "Don't you dare threaten him. Zain has to do this. No one else. The time to protect me is over, brother. You don't know how much I appreciate it, but this is beyond you now. I know his pain. I've lived it. Seen it," she stressed. "He'll never be able to get over this if you take the option away. And I won't be a part of that sort of sadness, not even by association." She turned to me, walking over. Her hands were shaking as she lifted them to cup my face. "Stay safe. I'll be here when you return."

Not once, not even through the beatings I'd suffered as a child, had I ever shed a tear, but hearing her stand up for me and knowing how scared she felt at seeing me go...tears burned my eyes until I was sure they'd escape.

"I love you," I whispered, pulling her into my arms. "I do, so much."

"And I love you. You promise to be safe?"

My lips pressed gently to hers. The roughness of them soaked into my memory. She was dehydrated and felt so tiny in my arms. How much weight had she lost? Too much. It only had my anger intensifying. This was what I needed—to feel the proof of my father's evil right here, under my hands.

"You know I will. I won't be long. Then, we'll start our lives together."

With one last kiss, I stepped back, meeting Slade's disapproving glare. He was afraid for Lily, I knew that, but he wasn't objecting. I had a feeling he also knew I had to do this, whether he liked it or not.

"Let's go," I said to Blake, quietly. Marcio began to accompany us when I shook my head. "Get everything ready for Washington. We'll be back shortly."

I didn't look back as I headed for the door. Truthfully, I couldn't. My heart ached. I just got Lily back and now I was leaving her. It tore me to pieces. The amount of time I'd had with her since I'd killed her kidnappers was almost nonexistent, and now I was going into a situation I wasn't sure the outcome of. My father was guarded by at least four men that I knew about. Were there more? Were some of Jonathon's men with him, too?

The elevator seemed to take forever, but the walk to Blake's SUV was even longer. It was as if no matter how fast I walked, gravity was pulling me back, urging me to stay. I pulled at the collar of my black shirt, tugging at the vest underneath as I climbed in.

"We headed to the location you gave me earlier?"

Blake's voice was deeper than usual. There was a killer next to me and not once since we'd been together had I forgotten that. I trusted the tracker, but I didn't let my guard down completely. If it ever came between me and him, it would be one hell of a fight to the death. Seeing him slice and dice my brother's guard while I took out my own blood was something to be admired…if one could praise such a task. Grace came with every slice of his blade. It was so fast and precise that I'd ended my brother's life quickly, just so I could watch Blake work.

"The address he gave me is the only one I know. Lily was right, it's probably a trap. Then again, he didn't expect me to leave the hospital without him."

"I'm sure he's there," Blake said, quietly. "It's one of the fanciest hotels in this city. But they have cameras. That poses a problem. We can't both just waltz on up there and knock on the door. There will be a trail."

I gazed out the window while Blake pulled out of the parking garage and turned onto the road. My mind raced and I knew I had to end this as soon as possible. But what was the best way? That was the question.

"I'll call him. Have him meet me."

"You're not that stupid. You'll be target practice, exposed to all his guards. Does it have to be up close and personal for you?" Blake's eyebrows drew in and he shook his head. "Stupid question. Of course it does. You're not going to settle for a shot through the head from a distance."

Hell, at this point, it was half tempting. I just wanted to get back to Lily. To hold her tight while we flew out on Slade's helicopter to Washington. But he was right. My father looking me in the eyes as I killed him was important. He deserved to die for the pain he caused. Not only to me, but the families of the girls he'd taken and helped sell off.

My hand reached into my pocket and I pulled out my phone, running my finger down the screen. Fuck, what was I doing? Was there a better way than setting myself up for a bloodbath? If there was, it wasn't coming to me. My heart raced and I let my slave's bruised and swollen face push to the forefront of my thoughts. Amir had planned to give her to Saul, damn well knowing what would happen. He wanted her dead for my crimes. I couldn't allow this to continue.

Angrily, I hit his number and brought the phone to my ear.

Ring.

Ring.

"Zain." One word, spoken with hate. He knew I had Lily. He knew I killed yet another member of my family, his only other surviving son. It was laced thick with the disgust in his tone.

"I need to speak with you."

"You know where I'm at."

My head shook. "No, I know a place."

"Where?"

I glanced at Blake, only to take in the surroundings of downtown. My father was roughly less than a mile away. We both needed time. Me, more so. Blake needed to get in position, prepare for what was to come.

"There's a lookout right past the Golden Gate Bridge on the left. This time of night, it should be somewhat private. We'll be able to talk there."

"You mean, you should be able to kill me there," he said in Arabic. "Don't play me for a fool, Zain. I know your intentions and you know mine. Let's cut the act and get down to it. You want to die? Is that it? Was this slave so important that you had to kill off your family? Did I teach you nothing?" he exploded. "Family is blood. You're my blood. They were all your blood. We look out for each other. I've done nothing but take care of you since I brought you into my home. I treated you better than everyone and this is what you do?"

Lava could have been boiling in my veins for as hot as I felt from my anger. "You killed my mother and Jeff. You beat me. Scarred me. You destroyed everything I was. How is that treating me better? Lily opened my eyes. She showed me what it was to feel again. Where you ruined, she healed. So do *not* try to preach to me about the definition of family. You don't understand the meaning."

"Understand this," he said, lowly. "Tonight, your slave will be the death of you. I hope she was worth it. I'll be there soon."

The line disconnected and I squeezed the cell in my hand as I lowered it to my lap.

"He believes I'll die tonight," I said, stuffing it into my pocket. "But he won't show at the location. It'll be his men who arrive. Head back toward his hotel. We'll catch him when he leaves for the airport."

Blake stayed quiet as he turned around. If I knew my father, he'd be leaving soon. After knowing what I'd done to Amir Junior, he'd want stability and he wouldn't find it here. Not so far away from his guarded palace. And he'd never make it back there if I had anything to say about it.

Chapter 23
Slade

The dirt and grime were gone and the knots brushed out of Lily's hair. She looked presentable and ready for work, dressed in a pair of black slacks, a black blouse, and heels. Aside from the swelling and bruises, it was as though my sister never left. The disconnect was back. The different Lily I had associated her with when she returned. Truthfully, she was only the old Lily when Zain was around. The composed business woman in front of me now was an imposter, a mask my sister donned to deal with being alone. Why hadn't I figured it out before? She was so collected, so strong looking, yet I knew that wasn't the case. It was all an act. My Lilian was scared and crying on the inside. She wanted Zain. She wanted to be happy. And she wasn't.

"I'm not sure I should go over the details of Bethany," she said, quietly. "Maybe I'll just tell Mary she…" Lily took a deep breath. "I'll just say…" Tears clouded her eyes and she looked toward the floor-length windows. The tears disappeared as she crossed her arms over her chest. "She didn't make it. That's what it boils down to. Not that she was raped and beaten to death." A pause had a ragged breath escaping. "For fuck's sakes," she said, bringing her hand up to her forehead. "God, I can't believe this happened again."

"Shh." There were no words I could offer for comfort. Sentiments were the last thing I was good at. All I could do was pull her into my arms while I held her. Still, she didn't break down like I expected. For minutes, I tried to comfort my sister, but she was so rigid and stiff. I couldn't help but feel like I was doing more harm than good. "Why don't we go wake up Mary? She'll be happy to see you. It'll be best to break the news to her before Gaige gets back."

Lily nodded, almost too happy to break away. My mouth twisted and I recalled how easily she molded into Zain's arms. She was like putty where he was concerned. It was a good sign. She needed to be with someone she trusted enough to let her walls down, but apparently they weren't where Zain wanted them. He said they had things to work on. What that was exactly, I wasn't sure I wanted to know.

"He's the FBI agent?"

"Yes. He's been working under the radar with us since you went missing, but he got called in shortly before you all arrived. I have a feeling it may have been related to where you all just left. If that's the case, I don't expect him here for another few hours."

Lily's head lowered and she didn't wait for me to head to Mary. I followed behind as she eased the door open and stood there, frozen.

"You okay?"

The moment my hand landed on her shoulder, she jumped.

"I've never really been afraid of the dark, but…I don't like not being able to see inside."

To me, I could clearly see the bed. It was further into the room that lay in pitch black. I nodded, walking past her and turning on the bathroom light. Mary immediately stirred. The action brought Lily forward, until she stood at the foot of the bed.

"Mary?"

Blonde hair flew over my wife's shoulders as she bolted into a sitting position. She looked lost, confused for a few seconds as she stared at my sister. Then, as if awoken from some dream state, she crawled on her knees across the bed to meet Lily on the side.

"Oh, God, I was so afraid they wouldn't find you." Mary hugged Lily tight and Lily seemed more at ease than she had been with me. "How are you? Are you hurt?" Their connection broke as Mary squinted. I turned on the bedside lamp and the color drained from her face. "Oh…Lily."

"It's not as bad as it looks. Just a few bruises."

Mary led her to sit on the edge of the bed, but I could see the horror in my wife's face. The way her eyes searched Lily's had me walking over to comfort her.

"Who did this to you? My sister called. Was…it her?"

Lily reached out, grabbing Mary's hand. "Not really. I mean, Bethany thought she was a part of it." Hesitation had my sister staring down at their connection. "Jonathon Brighton was the one behind it. He took over for Julian and began working with Zain's family, like his father had before I killed him. Your sister…she was seeing Jonathon."

Mary's back straightened. "That's why she left Charles? For Jonathon Brighton?"

"Yes. But he..." Lily shifted, "he had other plans for her. He was going to pin my murder on her. When he found out that Amir wasn't going to let him kill me, he..." Again, she stopped. "I'm sorry, Mary. Bethany didn't make it."

Lily's hand gripped Mary's tighter and I let mine rest on my wife's shoulder. The sniffling told me she was crying, but her head was angled to where I couldn't see.

"I'm sorry they took you, Lily. I knew from the beginning that Bethany probably had something to do with your disappearance. It just..." again, she sniffled, "it saddens me to know that my sister harbored so much anger that she ended up having to pay for it with her life. If she would have let it go, if she could have seen how evil they were instead of being blinded by her own hate and greed..."

"It happened," Lily said, hugging her. "We can't change how or why. We just have to keep moving forward. I'm truly sorry for your loss, Mary."

A sob left her while she shook her head. "I don't know how you could be. My sister was trying to kill you, yet you're the one sorry. You amaze me, Lily."

As they hugged, I could tell my sister was emotionally and physically drained. Not to mention, my wife. It made the exhaustion I was experiencing even more intense. The last two weeks had taken their toll. I quickly cut in.

"I just wanted you to know she was okay. You both need your rest. We can finish this discussion some other time."

"Yes," Lily said, standing. "Why don't you two get some sleep? I'm going to lay in my room and wait for Zain. I think I need to get some rest. Hopefully, he won't be much longer. We can leave tomorrow. I'm not sure I'm ready to fly anywhere tonight."

"Good idea," I said, nodding. "I'd like you here, just until everything calms down. I'll walk you out. I need to talk to Marcio real quick anyway." I turned to Mary as Lily headed for the door. "You okay while I go talk to the men real quick?"

"Yeah. Hurry and come back to bed."

The emotional pain was so deep that it made me not want to leave at all. Not in her condition. "Five minutes, tops. Then you have me for the rest of the night."

With her nod, I turned and headed for the front door, making sure to shut hers behind me. Lily was already gone. I took out my phone and checked the time as I approached the entrance. One hour and five minutes since they left. My jaw clenched as I opened the front door. Marcio and Brace stood a few feet away, next to the small table where they kept their drinks. Both turned as I closed the door behind me.

"I'm headed to bed. Mary is pretty upset. Let Zain in when he gets here, but tell him I said he sleeps on the couch. He can let Lily knows he's back, but in no way, shape, or form is he joining her in that bed with me under this roof. Clear?"

I could see Marcio trying to hold in his smile. "Got it, boss."

"Lily is too tired to leave tonight, so Washington won't be a go until the morning. Also, my phone will be on silent. Gaige might be coming back over. If I don't answer, inform him we have Lily. If he wants to see her, he can stop by in the morning before they leave. Unless, knowing him, he insists. Only then, are you to come get me. I'm tired, I'm hung over, and I want one night in bed with my wife without being interrupted by something. *Like, morning sickness.* Fuck, it was driving me crazy to see her body under so much stress. "Good night."

"Night, boss."

Even as they said the words and I walked toward my room, I knew sleep wouldn't find me. Not with Zain and Blake still out there. I talked a good fight, but Zain was quickly making himself apart of my family. And not just out of respect for Lily. I liked him. And I'd be restless until he walked through my door safely—or not.

Chapter 24

Zain

"Black car," I said, pointing to the luxury sedan pulling away from the parking garage of the expensive hotel my father was staying in. "He'll be in that one."

Blake's eyes cut over to me. "How do you know? That could be anyone."

My mouth opened, only to shut. "I just know. My father has one at home just like it."

"So do thousands of people in this country. This was a bad idea. It's like we're looking for a needle in a haystack. You should have just let me call and ask if he was still there, like I wanted. Maybe I could have gotten some information from the front desk clerk." Blake entered traffic, letting two cars separate us from whom I assumed was my father.

"Listen, I know Amir. He's a creature of habit. That's why he has guards. To protect him. He'll have had what he knows made available so he feels comfortable. That," I said, pointing again, "is my father."

"If you say so," Blake said, lowly. "If it's not?"

The challenging look had my head cocking to the side and my eyes narrowing. "Are you proposing we wager something? Like a bet?"

Blake shrugged. "Why not?"

My attention went back to the car. With the way the lights hit from oncoming traffic, I could see the silhouettes of three men in the back. It was perfect. It was him. "Fine. If I'm wrong, I'll—"

"Stand there and watch me kill your father."

"What?" I was aghast and my voice showed it. I looked at the tracker, shocked and angry. "You can't be serious? After how much you know I need this? That's the stupidest thing I think I've ever heard you say."

"This," he stressed, "is the stupidest *idea* I think I've ever heard from someone who claims they have experience in these sort of situations."

Anger intensified and I grabbed my coffee, taking a drink. "Do you do this sort of thing with Preston, the other guy you work with, too? Take his glory right out from under him?"

Blake's head snapped back toward me. "You leave Preston out of this." He waited few seconds and a smile eased to his face. "I actually got it from him. He started the whole bet thing, although ours are more on the humor side of things. With you, I just know where to push your buttons."

"Well, you should have stuck to humor and not tried to piss me off. That's not a good thing to do, just so you know."

"Hmm, well I happen to find humor in my bet. The look on your face was enough."

"You're such an asshole." I took another drink, trying not to smile. His had been glued to his face since the moment he started riling me up. Who was this man next to me, really? What kind of person was he around his wife? His friends? All I knew was he was true, honest in the way he carried himself. He came off hard and unfeeling, but that wasn't all he was.

The car turned and I put down my coffee. Pulling out my gun, I put a bullet in the chamber.

"Hold on." Blake's eyes scanned the area as we followed behind. A traffic light loomed ahead and he slammed his foot on the accelerator, jumping past the cars that separated us, until we were even with the sedan. "Do you recognize any of them?"

The windows were too dark to see inside. My head lowered, catching the driver's face from the glow of a passing car. The street was industrial and deserted. No businesses were close enough to catch anything, which only meant one thing—no cameras.

"Yep. The driver is a guard. Mohammed. Looks like I won."

Blake cursed under his breath and increased the speed even more while we both pulled down the masks sitting on the top of our heads. "I'll take out the driver and the passenger to buy time. You do what you need to do." He jerked the wheel, placing us in front of the car and slammed on the brakes. The force pulled me forward, but I managed to unbuckle fast enough. We both threw open the door at the same time and the cracking glass from the windshield was louder than the shots.

I raced for the back, my gun drawn as I approached. "Don't do it, Zain." My cousin's voice filled the street as the back door was thrown open. He raised the gun and time slowed as my heart slammed into my chest.

I weaved to the side and pulled the trigger as the sound of metal getting hit shrieked behind me. Though, it was only a distant thought as I watched my cousin drop to the ground. Such havoc and chaos reigned down around us and yet, I had no doubt people were peacefully sleeping not streets over. My breathing deepened as I saw Blake coming up on the other side.

"Out, now," I growled at my father. His eyes were wide, fearful, as he looked up at me. I'd never in my life seen anything but anger or emptiness cloud his vision. The sudden change of emotion had my hand reaching in and grabbing him out. The man sitting beside him was already dead. I'd never heard the shot coming from Blake's weapon.

"Make it fast," Blake said, quietly.

Arabic poured from my mouth as I grasped his throat, squeezing to make him kneel before me. He hit the ground hard and my fingers rose, clenching in his hair while I shoved the barrel of my gun into his mouth. "You spilled blood to bring me in. The blood of my mother and a man I considered more of a father than you ever were. Since then, you've done nothing but cause damage in the lives of others, doing the unthinkable to their children. I've been waiting for my time to finally make the bleeding stop. That day is today. You wanted a killer. Here I am, father," I said, pushing the barrel in even deeper. "It's time I take what is owed to me and everyone else you've ever hurt. Death to bring me in. Death to set me free. Say hello to your brothers. Expect two more shortly."

I thrust upward and pulled the trigger twice, letting him drop to the ground. Not once did I break eye contact. I needed to see his fear. See the life leave him. It didn't bring back the child he'd damaged, but there was a sense of peace within the man he created. A closure I hadn't expected.

"Let's go," Blake said, pulling on my arm. "I want to get the hell out of here."

I was already obeying before he could finish. The SUV took off at a fast speed and I ripped the mask free, tossing it into my lap.

"You okay?" Blake looked over, his mask also gone.

"Never been better."

My stare went to the urban setting outside and I let myself zone out. I'd been telling the truth. I hadn't felt this light since before I'd been taken. Lily was safe. Slade was on board with us being together.

My father and more of his men were dead. There were only two more people on my list, then I'd be completely released from my past.

"Can you give me some time with Lily before we head to Afghanistan? There are some things she and I need to take care of before I can leave." Asking Blake to wait didn't sit well. I had always been like him, solo, but he already had the address. If I didn't get him to comply, he'd go on his own and I knew it.

"Yeah, sure," he said, lowly.

I could tell there was something on his mind, but he kept his gaze straight ahead.

"Listen, I'm going to drop you off. Tell Slade I'll be in contact. My wife called earlier. I think I'll head home early and surprise her. Maybe spend a few days there before I head back this way to tie some things up with Gaige."

Blake turned down our road and I could tell whatever he was thinking about, it was deep. His eyes kept narrowing as if trying to calculate some impossible problem. I pushed it away as he pulled to the front of the building.

"I'll be back two weeks, to the day. Be ready."

I leaned back, putting the gun back in the big black bag. It wasn't mine or Marcio's, it was Blake's. Everything I was armed with was his.

"I'll be ready." I opened the door and slid out, nodding as I closed it and headed for the entrance. My mind slipped into thoughts and I let Lily take me over as I hit the button for the elevator. Was she waiting for me? Worried? Sleeping?

Stepping inside and hitting the button for the floor was a fog. Memories of how her body felt under mine had me leaning against the glass walls. So soon she'd be mine again. My slave would be kneeling and begging me for more. God, yes. I needed her submission. Needed her screaming as I made her come all over my cock.

The wealth of pent up emotions I held nearly suffocated me. I'd had a taste of what was mine. Felt her pussy around me for the first time in years. The beast inside had been teased and he was desperate for more. There was nothing else holding me back. No more barriers. The Master in me was about to be sated. I could feel him take over as the elevator opened and I was faced with Marcio and Brace. They immediately stood upon my entrance.

"All good?" Marcio took a step toward me.

"Done. Is Lily ready?"

I reached for the doorknob.

"Actually, she's too tired to leave tonight," he said, looking toward Brace. "She wants to go in the morning. Slade said you can tell her you're okay and here, but you're to sleep on the couch. That's final. Already put a blanket and pillow there for you."

I pushed the door open. "The couch. Of course." Had I been thinking Lily and I would be making love until dawn under some roof in Washington? I should have considered how exhausted she was. Shit, she'd been kidnapped and beaten for over two weeks. My priorities were out of line. It was time to get my head in the game. I was the Master of someone. That came with responsibilities. This wasn't about me or what I wanted. This was about what was best for my slave.

Silence met me as I crossed through the living room and turned left, down a hallway. I knew from watching her that her room was located at the end of the hall. I slowly eased the door opened and the glow of her closet light greeted me. Lily lay in bed awake, tears staining her face.

"I knew you'd be back." She threw the covers back and launched herself into my arms just as I made it to the edge of the bed. The scent of lavender from her body wash filled me and I let it intoxicate me.

"Of course I am," I whispered.

The black, silk nightgown she wore only came down mid-thigh and I held in a groan as my hand gripped the material. I could see her breasts pushed against my chest, but hated that I couldn't feel them from the bullet proof vest. It was probably for the best. I was seconds away from losing control and pushing her to the bed so I could have her the way I wanted, once and for all.

"Come to bed," she said, pressing her lips to mine. "Hold me."

Still, she continued to kneel on the mattress and kiss me. With each connection of our lips, her arms tightened around my neck. Torturously, I kissed her back, but extended my arms out so I couldn't touch her anymore. My cock ached. My heart, even more so.

"I can't, baby girl. Not here. I've got the couch tonight. Tomorrow, after you're rested up, we'll head out. Then, we'll focus on us."

"The couch? No," she breathed out against my lips. "The bed."

The order had me trying to pull back, but she held on tighter, trying to pull me closer to her.

"Bed. Please, Master."

My fingers twitched as I held them out. I did make a sound then. Fuck, her begging was going to kill me. Maybe even get me killed.

"Couch," Slade interjected behind me.

Lily's head shot up and I smiled as she turned her attention back to me.

"Couch," I repeated, a smile on my face.

"Shit." She let go of my neck and pouted before reaching down and grabbing her blanket and pillow. "If he has to sleep on the couch, I'll make a pallet on the floor. I want him near me. I can't sleep without him there."

Slade shrugged and yawned, waiting. I wrapped my arm around Lily and led her to the living room. The way he stopped and stood with his arms crossed over his chest as he let us settle made me feel like a kid being monitored. Respect was something I cherished, so I held to his rules, glad he was even allowing me under the same roof as his sister after everything that had happened.

Lily's pillow and blanket hit the floor and I immediately scooped them up and tossed them on the couch. I took mine, putting them in her place. She didn't question or disobey by taking them back off. The slave in her knew better. Instead, she climbed onto the leather and stretched out, snuggling in the covers pulled up to her neck.

"There are clothes in the hall bathroom for you to change into. We're close to the same size, so they should fit. I just want to make things clear before the two of you leave tomorrow. After this...*re-acquaintance* ends, things are going to..." He shifted. "Let me just put it this way. I want the two of you to date. No rushing into something and moving in together or eloping. Or..."

The stress he was under was evident. I could tell he was exhausted and worn out. I sighed, glancing at Lily, only to bring my attention back to him.

"Dating sounds like a good idea. After all, I'll see her at work. We can have dinners afterward. No worries."

"You're going to be working with me?" Lily asked.

"Not *with* you," Slade said, rushing in. "Just, there, at the office. I'm going to test him in a couple of different places first. See where he fits."

A slight smile came to her face, but she stayed quiet.

"Anyway, I'm just getting Mary more water. I heard you come in and thought I'd check on things. You two have fun on your trip. But…not too much fun." He turned and Lily smiled at me. I couldn't stop myself from returning it. To say Slade was taking his sister's sudden connection with me easily would have been the understatement of the century. He was lost and unsettled. If I wanted to put him at ease and get his overall blessing, I'd have to play by his rules. But only once we got back. These next two weeks were all me and Lily and I wouldn't take anything less. Master and slave were here to stay. Location wouldn't make a difference. Come morning, Lily was going to find that out.

Chapter 25
Lily

"They're perfect together, aren't they?"

The hum of a woman's voice flirted with my sleep and I tried to push it away so I could return to the darkness, back to where Master was whispering naughty things in my ear.

"I told her to stay on the damn couch," Slade bit out, quietly. "Did she listen? No. She never does. Women are the most stubborn creatures that ever existed."

Mary's laugh had me moving forward, trying to curl more into myself. When my head curled into Zain's neck, Slade's words suddenly made sense. I'd forgotten about sneaking off the couch in the middle of the night so Master could hold me from my bad dream. I'd fallen back to sleep immediately. Now, here I was, caught.

My eyes fluttered open, only to meet Zain's, mere inches away. The grin on his face didn't waver as my brother bitched in the background. His hand lifted, trailing down my face. No words had to be

spoken for me to know what he was thinking.
God, I loved him, too. I wanted to say it. Yearned to
throw myself into his arms and kiss him until we
couldn't breathe, but I knew my brother was still
watching.

"I'm going to go brush my teeth," I said,
forcing myself to sit. Pain in my shoulders and back
had me moving slowly. I wasn't sure if it was from
Jonathon's treatment or the floor. My guess was a
mixture of both.

"Bad dream," I mumbled to my brother as I
headed for the hall. The glare was only half there. It
was more annoyance as he sipped his coffee and I
fled. Damn, I hoped he didn't think anything
happened. I couldn't bear the thought of my brother
trying to imagine that. It was probably good we were
leaving. In Washington, all we'd have to worry
about was staff and they kept to themselves outside
of meal times.

My feet carried me faster at the thought. Me,
Master, together. Heat rolled from my body and I
couldn't stop my knees from turning weak. I gripped
the restroom door, pausing before finally walking in.
How long had I dreamed of this? It didn't seem real.
I'd spent so long convincing myself it could never

happen. That my brother would forbid the mere thought of it. He didn't. He was giving Zain a job for crying out loud. This could work. I could finally have the happily, albeit twisted, ever after I'd dreamed of since a child.

Visions of how Zain and I would be clouded my vision as I went through my morning routine. It didn't take me long from the excitement I felt. The getting dressed part was easy enough. A black, high-neckline dress that was form fitting, but not too tight, ending just above the knees, stockings, black stilettos, a pearl necklace, and earrings. My hair was already drying as I twisted it up and placed in the pins. As I walked into the living area, I froze.

A tall man with dark hair wearing a black suit stopped talking to look at me. Even the make-up I wore couldn't cover the train wreck of my face. His eyes narrowed with what looked to be anger, only to dissipate into something unreadable.

"Ms. Roberts," he said, walking forward. "My name is Agent Gaige Sullivan. It's a pleasure to meet you."

My hand extended to meet his as I looked toward Zain and my brother. Both appeared relaxed, not afraid of whom this man was. My sins, my guilt, had me shaking his hand rather stiffly.

"Pleasure's mine, Agent Sullivan."

Pieces of my brother's conversation while I was kidnapped filtered through and I could remember him saying something about working with a man from the FBI. If that was so, could I be truthful, or was there information I needed to withhold?

"How are you?" He seemed generally concerned as he stared at my face. I shrugged, trying to downplay what I knew had to look terrible.

"I'm okay. A little banged up, but I'll heal."

He frowned. "No, how are you? Here," he said, tapping against his head. "You okay? You've been through quite the ordeal. Twice. That can't be good for your state of mind."

Zain's eyes cut over to me and I could see his own concern. He was listening. Taking in my answers. My gaze lowered and I let the question sink in, considering his words.

"I'm...still not sure yet."

When I came back to look at Agent Sullivan, he was studying me. "Do you have someone to talk to? I know a therapist. She's very good. She helped my wife." He lowered his voice. "I trust her and you can, too, with whatever you might want to tell her."

Therapist hadn't always been on my side. I hadn't talked to mine for over a year and there was really no desire to see her again. But, should I find someone? The nightmares had been pretty frightening. They drove me into Zain's arms. But if things went like last night, he wouldn't always be there to comfort me. And I needed to be strong for myself.

"Your wife was kidnapped?"

Gaige gestured to a small circular table for two by the window. I led the way as he followed. Zain was still speaking to Slade, but his attention stayed on me as I sat down across the room.

"Elle, my wife, was kidnapped when she was in high school. I knew her back then, very well. She dated my brother." Gaige's hands interlaced on top of the table. "The man who took her, killed my brother. For over ten years, she was gone. Before I joined the FBI, I was a different sort of Agent. One who went really deep undercover. That's how I found her. Not intentionally. I was quite surprised to come across her supposedly married to the man I was investigating. She'd been taken to be sold as a sex slave. The man who abducted her decided to keep her instead, but he never stopped his crimes. He beat her regularly, amongst other things. I know what that sort of trauma can cause. I just want you to know that if you need anyone, someone who helps with your sort of experiences, I know a therapist. Or, if you'd prefer, my wife would love to help in any way she can. She's not a therapist, but her presence in the community to stop human trafficking is great."

My stare was pulled to the surrounding city, to the people in the distance walking along the sidewalks. They were living their lives so unaware of what was happening all around them. I suddenly felt rocked. The whole situation, this Agent's story, left me looking at the bigger picture. I knew I wasn't the only one this had happened to. I'd held the girls' hands who died in front of me…or in my lap. So, why hadn't I ever thought to reach out and actually try to do something about it? Even if it was volunteering or helping another woman in need who'd been in a situation similar to my own? I had means, money. I could contribute. Help with food or shelter. Maybe even by giving jobs to a selective few.

"May I have her number, Agent Sullivan? I think I'd like to speak to your wife."

A smile came to his face and he pulled out a business card, scribbling on the back. "You can call her anytime. She'd be happy to be of assistance." He stood. "Anyway, I should be going. There were some people found murdered not too far away. We have reason to believe they were tied to the cartel trafficking in this area, too. It was probably them." He winked at me and my lips separated in surprise. Holy shit. He was going to make sure we walked away from this without any problems. Tears came to my eyes and I stood as he did.

"Thank you so much. I won't forget this."

He smiled, leading me back to the men. "I have to get going. Keep in touch. If any of you ever need anything, you have my number."

Slade shook his hand and walked him to the door. The moment it closed, I took a deep breath. "He's covering for us. Dear God. I can't believe this. Why would he do that?"

Zain patted the chair and I didn't hesitate to step up to the barstool.

"Your brother has amazing connections," he said, pushing a plate of fruit in my direction. "We'll talk about that later, though. Time to eat. We have a helicopter to catch."

The bright color of his eyes darkened and my breath hitched in my throat. Even after everything we'd been through, me being taken, him killing his father...my Master was still present behind the exterior. And so composed. How was he, really?

"Are you packed?"

I bit into a strawberry, hesitating as his stare zeroed in on my mouth. Slowly, I brought the end down and placed it on the plate. It was almost impossible to swallow. "Yes, I took care of it last night. Marcio already has my bags. What about you? Can you get into your apartment yet?"

He nodded. "I actually called the police station earlier this morning. We're good concerning them, too. Now, you eat. I'll just head to my place and pack some things. It shouldn't take me long."

Slade came back through the front door and Zain kissed the top of my head as he walked in that direction. Though I knew he wanted to kiss my mouth before he left, the Master within him left my skin tingling. His behavior was in contrast to the way he was acting. The respect he had for my brother was evident.

"I'll be back. I'm going to grab some clothes from my place real quick."

"Take Marcio with you as a precaution."

Neither men paused in walking while they spoke.

"Got it." Zain disappeared out the front door and my brother pulled out the stool next to mine and sat down. I popped his hand as he reached toward my plate, taking a grape.

"You sure he's the one you want? You're still young. There's plenty of time and men out there."

I spun on the stool to face him. "Men that would die for me? Men who would kill for me?" My head shook. "I love him, Slade."

His eyebrows drew in. "Why did you never say anything to me? Why not tell me about him? Did you really think I wouldn't have understood?"

"No. If I would have confessed something to that magnitude, we both know you would have freaked out at the mere thought. Even now, I can see how uncomfortable you are around him. You like him, but there's something holding you back. So, what is it?"

The sound of a door opening had both of us turning toward Mary as she exited their room.

"I like Zain, don't get me wrong. I just want what's best for you. He loves you, that's clear as day to me. But he's not like most men, Lily. What if he can't hold a job? The guy is a killer, not an accountant. He might not adjust well to this life. What happens to the two of you then?"

My head lowered at his words. He had a point. "He'll do fine," I said, looking back up. "He'll excel at anything he gets handed. That's just who Zain is. If, for some reason, it doesn't work out at Slade Industries, he and I will take it from there. Don't worry yourself. We're both adults. Let us handle it."

Slade stayed silent and stood as Mary approached. He turned, wrapping his arms around her and leading her to the seat he just stood from. Dark circles were prominent below her eyes and I nearly gasped at how weak she appeared. He leaned down and whispered into her ear. Their nearly silent conversation seemed to last minutes as I picked at my food. When he straightened, I gave her my attention.

"Mary, you okay?"

Her fingers weaved through her hair while she forced a smile. It was so badly done that she let it fall and replaced it with a frown. "I'm not going to lie, I feel like shit. I was up sick again last night. I'm exhausted, but I'm so tired of trying to sleep. I'm calling the doctor today. I can't keep doing this."

For Mary to admit her true state, I knew it had to be bad. My eyes rose to Slade and I suddenly realized where the majority of his stress was coming from.

"Just keep the fluids going. Don't get dehydrated, it'll make things worse. Are you taking prenatal vitamins? Sometimes those can make the sickness worse at first. At least, that's what I…heard." I slowed, catching myself. My hand reached for the glass of orange juice and I took a big drink. I hadn't heard. It was my own personal experience. Zain had been so excited to bring me those prenatal vitamins, but when the sickness got worse, he cursed the day he got them. Fluid intake helped, but how sick I'd become made it hard to continue helping girls.

"You keep talking with so much knowledge. Who have you known that's pregnant? You stay in here most of the time." Slade said, confused.

I took another drink, slower this time. When I turned to him, I noticed Mary was staring at me inquisitively, too. My heart sank and pain filled my chest. How different our lives would be had I left Afghanistan pregnant. No…Zain would have never allowed that. He would have died trying to keep me.

"A slave. I helped deliver her baby."

"Deliver…?" My brother's eyes went wide as he stared at me.

Grapes rolled on the plate as I pushed it away. "Yes, she was lucky. Not many of them made it past the first trimester with the beatings they received. Most were intentional. I think they called it population control. Anyway, it's not important."

"Wait," my brother said, narrowing his eyes. "You mean, they beat the slaves to abort the babies?"

This was getting way too close to parts I didn't feel comfortable talking about. I stood, placing the back part of the barstool in front of my chest. Whether it was to guard myself from the pain I'd lived, I wasn't sure.

"Yes. They did that quite often. There were a decent number of girls there."

"How many?" Mary's hand shot up.

"Forgive me. I've never wanted to pry. It shouldn't start now. I'm sure you don't want to relive this. It's absolutely heartbreaking."

How many? Too many. "When I left there were nine amongst Zain's three uncles and his father. They had multiple slaves. But the girls were never allowed to be together. They almost always got into trouble and that wasn't good for anyone."

Mary's fingers pressed over her lips. "Nine girls. Between four men?"

"I thought Zain had four uncles and then there was the father?" Slade asked.

"That's right," I agreed. "But one didn't live there for long, and the other...well, he did, but Saul moved out. It's a long, complicated story."

The two of them got quiet, only for Slade to shift his feet. "Maybe someday you can tell me everything that happened. When you're ready. I've never asked, but I'd really like to know." I could tell he was holding something back.

"Maybe someday." Even as I said it, I'd already taken a step back.

"Lilian, I'm sorry, but I can't help but ask. With all this talk of babies and knowing that things were far from great there…"

Another step back.

"Obviously you didn't get pregnant or at least." He paused. "I mean, did you? Or I guess what I'm trying to ask is—"

"Slade," Mary hissed, "you can't ask her that."

"Well, if she was pregnant and one of the fuckers did something, I have a right to know. She just seems to know too much." He turned back to me. "Did they hurt you? Were you ever pregnant?"

The door clicking closed had my eyes jerking to the doorway. I couldn't contain my panic and it only grew as Zain walked forward with a surprised, yet hurt, expression on his face.

"You told them without me?"

My head shook and I wasn't sure what he'd heard, but my Master's presence and acknowledgement left my walls crumbling. It left the memories raw, real, as if I faced my loss all over again.

"So, it's true? Who?" Slade roared. "Start talking. This should have been something I knew when you returned. Lilian, I could have helped you. Or…Jesus."

My lips wouldn't move. All I could do was hug myself tighter to fight the emptiness I felt every time I remembered. Sorrow overtook me as I watched a tear fall to the floor. Frustration mixed with sadness as he spun toward Zain. "You got her pregnant? Yes?"

I looked up to see Zain press his lips together, his face turning hard as he came to my side. Instead of answering Slade immediately, he angled my face up and cupped my cheek. The strength I clung to within myself flickered and pain overtook the cold stature I wore like a life vest. More tears escaped while he lowered and placed his forehead against mine. "I'm here now. Shh. No more crying. Hold me."

As he spoke the words, I was already wrapping my arms around him. The barrier I'd made over my heart for protection against anymore hurt was gone, replaced with a wall of power I trusted more than my own. Zain pulled me directly in front of him and I let my chest merge with his. He wanted to protect me and I was upset enough to let him.

"That's right. I got Lily pregnant. It wasn't planned, but it happened. We were…happy when we found out."

"Continue."

Slade lost some of his anger as Mary's voice broke through. "You have no right," she said, quietly. "I know you're protective of your sister, but you're crossing the line. Can you not see it hurts her to relive this pain? Let it go. If she wants to tell you when she's ready, allow her that. She has Zain to protect her now. Look at them. Look at him. He's doing that."

"I want to know who was responsible." His tone was demanding, but a gentleness laced his words. "I have to know. Please. I feel like I don't even know you anymore. You're my sister, Lily. Your pain is mine. Just tell me what happened."

Zain's arms tightened and I turned to face Slade.

"I can't." I barely got the words out. That night had been the worst of all I could remember. The words that were spoken. The evil I'd seen come from behind his uncle's eyes as his rage was unleashed on me and my unborn child was something I was sure I'd never recover from. Even now, I was trembling so badly I could barely stand.

"My uncle, Saul. Lily was almost ten weeks when…" He paused. "I didn't think Lilian was going to make it. She was unconscious and barely breathing when I found her. I wasn't there when it happened or else he'd be dead right now. He was smart enough to be gone when I got home and stayed away until recently. Now he's back under my father's roof and I have every intention of making him pay for what he did. You don't have to worry about that. I don't forgive and I sure as hell don't forget. He'll pay with his life, you have my word."

Slade's head lowered to stare at the floor. His face was like stone, his frame stiff with anger. When his eyes rose to mine, the mask he wore so well slid into place.

"I'm sorry about your loss. Even more sorry that I couldn't comfort my sister when she needed it the most. That ends today. No more distance, Lilian. No more pulling away. We're a family and from here on out, we stick together." He turned his attention to Zain. "That goes for you, too. You're one of us now. Anything you need. *Anything.* All you have to do is ask. Family?" His hand extended and Zain walked us forward as he reached over and shook it.

"Brothers."

Chapter 26
Zain

The flight was mostly silent. Lily and I were both lost in our thoughts and the only comfort I got from the memories was the fact that she was curled into my side. As the scenes played out, I barely recalled how the mountains turned to hills and then became mountains again. The large estate brought me back to reality as we lowered to the helipad. Even the exit from the helicopter seemed surreal. It was as if I was still stuck in some dream state. The last few weeks had been more than what most people could take, and although I liked to think of myself as a strong person, the events had taken their toll. All I longed for was the one who I held close to my side as we entered the large mansion. Statues and large paintings decorated the space. My fingers pushed into her bicep as I led her past the entrance to greet the staff lined up before us.

"Ms. Roberts, it's good to see you again. Mr. Collins, it's a pleasure to meet you. I'm Harold and

I'm in charge of the staff. This is Mrs. Evans. She's the main housekeeper." He gestured to a short, older woman with gray hair. She reminded me of a grandmother, if I had ever had one. I liked her instantly. Her eyes sparkled as she smiled.

No one seemed to bat an eyelash at the fact that my slave's face was immensely bruised. It was odd, but I pushed it away as Harold went over meal times and excused the rest of the staff.

"Ms. Robert's last visit was to the East Wing, so we have everything already made up. There's a tray of refreshments waiting."

"Thank you, Harold. We'll be heading there now. I feel like I could use a nap before dinner."

Lily yawned as I led her up the grand staircase and I couldn't help but worry as we made it to the top. A door stood a good twenty feet ahead and two halls broke off to the left and right. As she turned us left, I weaved my fingers through her hair just above her ear and drew her head to rest on the side of my chest.

"Straight ahead?" I really didn't need to ask where her room was. My guess was it was bigger than the rest. That meant at the end.

"Yes," she said, quietly. "But I've only ever been here once, a few years back."

I turned the door knob and pushed open the barrier. An off-white comforter covered a massive bed centered in the middle of the room. There was a setup to the right with a black loveseat, facing a fireplace. My head shook while I tried to take it all in. The penthouse was one thing. The luxury I'd seen her in had grown on me. But this? My head tilted back to look at the large crystal chandelier above. When I brought my gaze down, I spotted French doors that led to a balcony.

"Your brother…"

"Is Slade," she finished. "He has quite the taste." Lilian broke from me, shrugged off the black, knee-length trench coat, and tossed it on the foot of the bed. When she turned to face me, my heart began to race. There was so much emotion playing on her face. I was smart to worry. Tears shown in her eyes and her lip quivered. For the first time, we were alone, safe, and not having to hide who we were. The impact was like a fist to my gut.

Lily rushed forward, collapsing to her knees at my feet. She hugged tightly around my legs, sobbing as if she were a child. She'd been so strong and I had known it would only be a matter of time before this happened. The girl who left me over three years ago had overcome odds few people in their right mind would have been able to handle. After three years of putting on a mask, it was falling, breaking, right at my very feet.

"Oh, slave." My fingers gripped her hair, holding her to me while she squeezed even harder. It was as if she was scared I'd disappear without the connection. Truth be told, I was almost weary myself. This seemed too good to be true.

"I was so afraid I'd lost you," she rushed out. "All that time with Jonathon, I didn't want to believe it, but I feared you were dead. Now this," she sobbed even harder. "Is this really happening?" Tears rolled down her cheeks as she looked up. "I can be with you? For good?"

"Forever," I said, sternly.

I wanted her to know I wasn't going anywhere. That she never had to worry about losing me again. But I still had to go back to Afghanistan. That thought had me reaching down for her and pulling her small frame into me. I couldn't think about that now. If I contemplated what might happen, I'd never be able to leave her, and I had to. Had to make my uncles pay for their crimes.

"I want you to look past these last few weeks and I want your head clear. I'll be asking you this question throughout the course of our stay." My hand stroked her face as I made her look at me. Before I spoke, I wiped away the tears. "I've told you once, and I'll say it again, with me, it's forever or never. You have my heart, Lilian. I want no one but you. Do you feel the same, as of right now?"

"Well…yes." She looked confused. "Of course I do. Right now? I don't like how you say that."

My tongue traced my lips while I tried to gather my thoughts in a way she'd grasp. "You love what you know of me. What we shared. But things are going to be different this time, slave. I'm still your Master, but you may not like what comes with that, here, in the real world. We had four months together before you were taken. The first couple of weeks, I took it easy on you, letting you adjust to your new life. Then, you were pregnant. You never experienced who I truly am."

Lilian's eyebrows drew in while she watched me speak. I could imagine how fast her mind was turning over my words.

"You're on birth control, correct?" I knew she was, but I wanted to hear her say it.

"The shot."

I nodded. "You'll stay on it for quite some time. A couple of years, at least. I want you strong and healthy when we decide to have another child. And we will, Lilian. At least two."

"Children." It wasn't a question, but something she appeared to have to say. As if testing the word out loud.

"That's right. You do want children, don't you?"

Her head shook. "I don't know. I haven't really thought about it. I suppose...someday."

"Good. It's nothing we need to go into now. As long as I know you're open to it, that's all that matters."

My fingers trailed up the back of her dress until I came to the top where the zipper rested. As I worked it down, Lily shivered and her breathing deepened.

"Until then, your body will belong to me. Completely. You have to grasp the definition of what I'm saying. When I want you, you will present yourself to me. Anytime. Anywhere. It doesn't

matter the location, slave. This," I said, pushing
her dress over her shoulders and letting it fall to the
floor, "belongs to me. Your body is no longer
yours."

Her mouth opened, only to close. The black
stockings were paired with black and white
patterned, lace panties, with a matching bra. Her
curves had my cock hardening instantly.

"You will take care of it. Treasure every inch
of yourself with the upmost value. Why? Because
you serve me. Seeing you flourish, makes me happy.
Tasting you," I said, nipping at her neck, "is what I
crave." My hands grasped both sides of her ribs and
I raked my nails down to her hips with just enough
pressure to make her gasp. "And fucking you is my
pleasure," I stressed. "That is the true way of a
Master and slave. I will protect you, love you, honor
and cherish who you are. But if you want me to be
your Master, you will obey my rules. Every single
one. Can you do that, Lilian?"

I pulled back enough to take in her expression.
There was one hell of an internal battle happening
inside her head. It showed by the way she bit her lip
as her eyes scanned the surroundings off to our side.
She'd been in control for so long. Could she just let

it go all of a sudden? It wasn't part of the new person she'd become.

"Work?"

Her high pitched tone dropped at the end and I couldn't stop my lips from setting.

"Definitely at work. Not noticeably so. I wouldn't jeopardize your status, slave. But there will be times when we're able to be alone. During those times, you drop being the boss and yield to the true one."

She got quiet. "My brother has cameras in the office, though."

"I know. You let me take care of that. No more worrying. No more questioning. That's what I'm here for. Just submit to me one hundred percent. Can you do that? Right now?"

"There you go again with that 'right now'. If I say yes, my mind is not going to change."

My hands moved to her breasts and I squeezed the generous amount with a steady pressure. "It might. I still haven't shown you who I am to the magnitude that you need to experience. You might not like who you see. Maybe you'll come to realize that the man you thought you loved isn't someone you want to spend your life with. Our time here will determine that for sure. Because once we leave this house, there's no turning back, slave. Ever."

"And if we don't work out?"

The fear that clouded her eyes had the gray almost turning silver. I paused, caught in the amazing color. My words formed in my head and I could have cursed with what I was about to say. I hated it and wasn't even sure I'd be able to comply with them.

"I'll always be here for you, Lily. I love you, regardless of how you end up feeling for me. That'll never go away. We've gone through so much. We've conceived a child together. Went through a loss, just the same. There's nothing I wouldn't do for you. If it's helping you move on." My jaw clenched. "To break from me once and for all and discover who you are, I'll do that, too. Anything to see you at your happiest."

Dark hair pooled around her shoulders as I took out each pin. The moment they were free, she lowered and rested her head against my chest. If I could have, I would have held her in that moment forever. It was our limbo — the moment before we started the testing, and the one place we were still in love with each other. Our illusion was real. But it was just that. An illusion. We weren't who we truly were in the moment and to see if we'd make it, we'd have to spend more than a few hours here and there together. We'd have to experience everything, and the moment Lilian was rested, we'd begin.

Chapter 27
Lily

Images blurred in a haze and I barely registered Jonathon's face when a light brush trailed between my breasts, pulling me from the nightmare trying to push itself though. Reality dawned and I felt my body relax as I remembered my Master was with me now.

My head turned toward where I knew he was laying just as the bed shifted. The soft caress moving toward my nipple was almost nonexistent. The nub tightened in anticipation, nearly making me moan. It had been almost impossible to go to sleep naked knowing Zain was beside me, but he'd refused to touch me. I hadn't understood it then, but now I was glad he'd let me get some rest. I would have never lasted in the state I'd been in before.

"Master." The last of the word was forced out as my eyes flew open from the suction that drew my nipple into his mouth. I reached for him, only to have my wrist captured.

"Go to the restroom and take care of everything you need to. There's a list of instructions for you to follow. I'll have the food brought up. You'll eat and then we'll begin."

Zain stood and I noticed his hair was still slightly damp. The all black suit had my heart exploding in rhythm. The black shirt was unbuttoned enough to expose the top of the tribal tattoo covering the entire expanse of his chest. I swallowed hard and eased from the bed, obeying his order.

Instructions? He'd never really given me anything but rules to follow and that mainly consisted of things for my own safety. This was different.

I shut the door and picked up the paper.

1.) Shower. There's a toy

waiting inside. Use it.

Do not come.

2.) Shave your pussy. Use the toy again. <u>Do not come.</u>

3.) Put on the clothes I placed out for you. If you need anything from your essentials bag, it's on the counter.

By the way, I love you,

slave.

-Master

I smiled only for it to fall as I remembered his words. Blindly, I fumbled with the knob on the shower, turning it on. My stare went straight to the toy. No, I'd think about that in a minute. I looked along the wall. Straight ahead was a long, lace dress. I lowered my hand, walking forward. The see-through material became apparent as I lifted the long sleeve. A large *V* was cut out of the back and there was a slit on one side. Hanging behind it were black silk panties and a bra. To wear them underneath would be a tease. My smile returned. Lying on the floor was a pair of black stilettos. All back. I didn't expect anything less from my Master.

Heat poured from my skin as I entered the shower and looked at the life-like dildo. While I washed my hair and my body, I didn't stop staring. A bottle of lube was sitting next to it and I felt myself blush even more. Water beat against my back and it was suddenly too much. I pushed the showerhead down and picked up the toy, holding it securely in my palm. The temptation was overwhelming. I'd thought about buying one during my plaguing fantasies of my Master, but couldn't bring myself to do it. Not with Brace always at my side. But he was only my excuse. I wouldn't even allow myself to come. I'd heard Zain say so many times, *don't come, slave*. It felt wrong without him allowing me. Even now, I was told not to. But he was here…and this was an order.

The click from the bottle opening could have been a cannon blast for as loud as it sounded. Guilt and embarrassment smothered me. What was wrong with me? This was okay. Natural. Most woman had toys and surely some of their husbands or lovers allowed or encouraged this.

I traced a line down the length and rubbed the clear liquor around. Biting my lip, I turned to lean against the cold wall. The shock from the temperature difference had my mouth opening. I pushed it away, lowering the dildo until the tip rubbed over the top of my slit. Harder, I bit, sliding it over my clit until it nudged into my opening just the smallest amount.

"Shit," I breathed out, looking down as I rotated my wrist to watch the cock slide deeper between my legs. More, I let it enter, only to bring the head back to tease the sensitive nub where I craved contact.

My free hand came up and so naturally, I squeezed my nipple. Pleasure exploded and a deep moan poured from my mouth. The sensations led me inching the toy into my pussy, suddenly needing more. Needing to fulfill a desire I'd neglected to give myself for so long.

Do not come.

I kept that in the shadows of my mind while I increased the speed of the thrusts and lowered my other hand to play with my clit. Tightening in my stomach only grew worse as I worked my fingers in a circular motion and pushed the toy's length in even more.

"I have to stop." My whisper was drowned out by the cascading water, but I knew I'd spoken the words. Meant them, even, as I continued to pleasure myself.

Heaviness pulled my lids down and I could so clearly see Master fucking me with the dildo. He'd grip behind my neck, holding steady, while his mouth ravaged mine. But he'd be better at controlling what I could take. He'd leave me edging for forever before he let me come. I'd be even more breathless than I was right now.

"Fuck," I groaned, pulling the dildo out, washing it off, and placing it to stand once again on the marble seat. I scooped up the razor and shaving gel, preparing to make it fast. Now that I'd sampled the toy, I wanted to go back. To continue using it while thinking of Master. I was even more of a hurry to get out there to the real him. Would he use it on me tonight?

In quick strokes, I took care of my legs. My swollen folds met my fingers as I began lathering my pussy. I was so wet. So fucking ready to be dominated by the one person who I knew would take care of my every need. He thought I wouldn't want to be with him after he showed me who he really was. Little did he know, I was more than prepared. With age, I felt I'd matured more than when I'd left him. I wasn't naïve enough to think I knew it all, but I was more mentally ready to take what he was willing to give. I also couldn't deny the tinge of fear that was still there. What was he going to do to me?

Steam clouded the doors and was thick in the air as I turned, washing the foam from my body. Once I finished, I spun around to face the toy again. My heart began to thud as I contemplated using it. The order was clear and it would be wrong for me to disobey already. But I'd been so close to coming. Would I stop this time?

I grabbed the toy and applied the lube once more. Stopping was critical. I'd just have to.

Cold encased my ass as I lowered and sat down on the seat, spreading my legs wide. I wanted this…too much. And not just the penetration. I wanted to come. Over and over. The need I'd held back was catching up with me and I felt obsessive in wanting more. Before I could process it, the cool toy was sliding back inside of me and my hand was already gripping my breast. I squeezed tightly, willing myself to slow not only my body, but my mind. Yes, I was ready for whatever my Master had planned.

I moaned, looking down while I pulled up on my slit. Halfway in, I withdrew, only to plunge it back inside of me. My pussy clenched around the width and I jerked, fighting the buildup that increased with every rub of my fingers. If I kept the contact over my clit, it would be a mistake. One I was half tempted to make, if Zain was going to punish me for it.

My legs inched together closer and my fingers spread open my folds. The slight sting from my shaved skin mixing with the lube hovered in the background while I watched toy enter me slowly. My clit pulsed and seeing it up close turned me on even more.

I have to stop.

The mantra repeated continuously as I grew closer to release. Just when I couldn't take the loss of contact anymore, I rubbed my fingers over the top of my slit and let the orgasm build to dangerous proportions. Deep breaths poured from my mouth and I pulled the dildo out, letting it rest on my legs as I closed them and tried to pull myself together. By the time I stood, I was still lightheaded.

In a fog, I grabbed a towel and dried myself off. Dressing was a chore. My fingers fumbled and my body shook from the arousal. By the time I had the dress on and my hair done, it had only gotten worse. My panties were wet from fantasies of Master being the one fucking me. As I applied the make-up from my essentials bag, I was so jittery from the anticipation I had to shift my feet against the tingling.

Red covered my lips and I pressed them together, leaning back to take in my appearance. My eyes widened and couldn't believe how sexy I looked, despite the bruises. My hair was piled high on my head, exposing my neck. Dark eye shadow gave off that smoky look and with the red lipstick and the see-through lace…I knew Zain was going to love it.

The clicks on the floor from the stilettos made my pulse spike and it went through the roof as I pushed the door open. My Master stood, leaning over the table, lighting candles. He froze, the light flickering out as his lips parted. I took two steps out when he rose and walked forward.

"Oh, slave. This," his hand locked on my side, drawing me close, "leaves me without words or thoughts. You look amazing." His lips pressed to mine and I grabbed at his lapels, pulling myself deeper into his body. The heat returned and I moaned, wanting nothing more than to strip everything off and pull him to the bed. I felt my fingers twitch and the urge to do just that taunted me.

Zain's tongue slid along mine and I could feel his grip tighten, rooting me into place as my foot took a step. He broke from my lips, shaking his head. "You don't lead, Lilian. Not here. Sit. We'll eat."

My eyebrows drew in while he pulled out the chair and I took my place. Baked chicken with rice and vegetables sat before me, but nothing about it was appealing. Not when I had other things on my mind. I knew what it was to be his slave. I'd lived it. Thrived in it when we were together. Could I do it again?

"You're going to have a lot of adjusting to do. I didn't expect this to be easy for you." Zain poured us wine and took his seat. I grabbed my glass, taking a sip while questions plagued me.

"I took a step. It's not a big deal. It was that…toy you insisted I use. I rushed."

Zain picked up his knife and fork, glancing up from his plate to give me a half smile. "You used to never rush. The problem is that you're used to being in control. You're going to have to learn to let it go with me. Completely."

A sigh escaped and I clamped my lips together. I couldn't blame the damn dildo. It was me. He was right and I couldn't deny that it scared me. What if I couldn't relinquish the power I now treasured? Not even to my Master?

Silence played out while Zain ate and I picked at the food. It wasn't until impatience had me looking up that I realized he was staring.

"You have to eat more than that, Lily. Remember what I said about taking care of yourself?"

"Yes." I stabbed my fork into the chicken, only for my eyes to go wide and shoot back up. "Yes, Master," I corrected.

He nodded, taking another bite and leaning back. How could I have forgotten the simplest rule of all? I knew who he was, but to forget to address him? My mistake baffled me. It had to be because of how unused to it I was. It had been years.

I took a bite, forcing down countless others afterward. By the time I was halfway finished, I knew I couldn't continue. Between nerves and excitement, I couldn't stomach anything else. My eyes rose and I laid the fork down. Relief flooded me when Zain stood, reaching his hand out for me to accept.

"You did well. I'm proud of you." He helped me stand and walked me to the foot of the bed. Watching him take off his jacket and letting it drop to the floor had me wet all over again.

"As much as I love what you've done with your hair, baby, I'm afraid what I have in store is best done with it down." Pins dropped to the ground as he worked his fingers through. Weight came crashing over my shoulders and the damp strands slightly curled. In upward movements, his fingertips loosened the tightness on the top where I'd brushed it back. When I thought he was done, his grip fisted at the sides of my head. Our eyes met and the lust he emitted pulled me under until I was sucking in air. I hadn't even realized I'd been holding my breath.

"You remember your safeword?"

"Red, Master."

"Yes. Although I doubt you'll need it just yet. Your body still has to heal. That will give you a few days to get back into the way of things before we truly start." He lowered, biting my bottom lip between his teeth and gently pulling. "I've missed you so much."

The words were whispered against my lips and I closed my lids, savoring the kiss that cut off my response. One of his hands moved to the small of my back while the other weaved into the hair at the back of my head. Zain pulled me into his body, holding me almost crushingly. I soaked it in, not caring about anything but our connection. Air, balance, nothing mattered or even registered as safety cloaked around me and I felt myself submit to him fully. Worries and questions disappeared and everything I knew of my Master came crashing back in a tidal wave of trust. My body went limp while I let him support my weight. Lilian was no more. I gave myself to Zain completely and I knew he felt the moment I had. Twist me, bend me, tie me up…I was his for the taking.

"Fuck," he growled. "You're the one for me. I could never want anyone more than I want you." His hands dropped and went to the slit of the dress. Both eased under the material and he brought it up slowly, caressing the outside of my thighs as he did. "Spread wide for me, baby girl."

I obeyed, raising my arms as his fingertips teased my ribs and pulled the dress over my head.

"Did you like your toy?"

My cheeks burned, remembering back. "Yes, Master."

"Let me see how much." Pressure pushed between my legs and he rubbed over the silk covering my pussy. "Hearing you moan was the best sound I've heard since you left. Do you have any idea how hard it was for me not to go in and fuck you right there in the shower?"

A gasp escaped as he pushed underneath the fabric and traced over my opening.

"No," I said, breathlessly.

"Damn near impossible." His finger slid inside and I jerked up to grasp his biceps for support.

"Did you come?"

I cried out louder as he added another digit and pushed in deep.

"No, Master. I promise. I wanted to, but I stopped."

Support from his grip locked around the back of my neck as he stepped forward and pounded his fingers into my pussy. I balanced on my toes, holding onto him even tighter.

"Very good. What about now? Do you think you can resist again?" The thrusts stopped as he withdrew to tease my clit. It took me a few seconds to respond.

"If you tell me not to come, I won't."

"You sound sure of yourself," he said, reaching up to remove my bra. "Let's see, shall we?"

Zain walked in closer, arching my back until the top half of my body was hovering over the bed. Leisurely, he eased me to the mattress, covering me with his large frame in the process. The material of his clothes had me wanting to pull them off in the impatience I felt. With a swirl of his tongue over my neck, he traveled down to my chest, erasing everything. Teeth grazed over the swell of my breast and I clutched to the comforter I was lying on.

"It's coming back to you." One of hands grasped my wrist while he sucked my nipple into his mouth. The plea that left me was gone before I even realized I was begging for it. My hips arched and I pressed my lips together at the desperation that left me on the edge. "Keep your hands down and don't move."

His teeth pulled at the tight nub while I watched him move on to give the other attention. God, I wasn't sure if I could continue to obey his orders. It had been too long.

Stubble down my stomach had me breathing deeply through my mouth. Lower, he went, until his mouth was level over the silk covering my pussy. He released my wrist and both of his hands pushed my thighs open wide.

"Master." I wasn't sure if I was urging him on or pleading for him to put me out of my misery. I was so aroused, it was almost painful. The heaviness in my stomach twisted and I ached for him.

"More."

The one word had me begging louder. Kisses interspersed with the occasional bite made their way over my thigh until he was running his tongue along the lining of my panties. My head shot up and I cried out, clutching the cover even tighter. His thumbs separated my folds and I could feel the material settle between. I couldn't stop my hand from shooting to the top of the fabric on my stomach.

"You're so wet, slave. And you taste amazing." Suction settled over the top of my covered slit as his eyes connected with mine. He held the contact while he sucked harder. Pain bit into my stomach while my nails clawed at the area where my skin and the silk met. With a rock of my hips, ecstasy shot to my core.

"Be. Still."

The lap of his tongue over my entire pussy left my head shaking back and forth. It returned to the sides of my folds, teasing, tasting. My head grew foggy and my lips tingled at my continuous sounds and deep breathing. I pulled at the lining of my panties, applying pressure to my clit. I knew I wasn't supposed to move, but I couldn't resist anymore. Zain was driving me crazy. The way his tongue was dipping beneath the material, so close to my entrance, was pure torture. I wasn't sure how much more I could take. The dominant part I'd developed wanted to rear its head and I wasn't sure what to do.

"It has been awhile. Maybe I was wrong. Maybe you did forget how to obey." His finger hooked into the silk between my legs and he pulled up hard. "If you're not going to listen, lay back and let me show you how it's done."

Chapter 28
Zain

My slave was at a breaking point. I knew she wasn't going to be able to take much more. As I pulled up the material of her panties and moved my hand back and forth, teasing her, I took in her flushed face. Her moans and cries hinted at the beckoning release.

"You want my cock, don't you? Tell me. Let me hear you say it."

"Oh, God! Please." Her hands reached for my shoulders, but I kept my distance. I didn't want her to have me until I was ready to grant her the gift. She had to learn, needed to know that *I* was in charge when it came to this part of our lives.

"Not good enough."

Lily's eyes welled with tears and her hands withdrew. "Please, Master. I want your cock. I want you to fuck me until I can't move. Then, I want you to do it again. I've waited so long. I can't take it anymore!" A sob escaped and a frustrated sound followed while she jerked beneath my hold.

"Are you throwing a fit? Have I taught you nothing?" I flipped her over, bringing my hand down on her ass.

Whack!

"More," she sobbed.

My connection grew harder. *Whack! Whack! Whack!* "You don't tell me what to do." Even with the cries, her ass lifted. She might have needed me, but I was dying here. If I didn't have Lilian soon, I was bound to lose control. Sure, I could make love to her and turn things slow and sensual, but those days would come. I already knew I was capable of that. If I didn't show her the darker part, the one that could possibly tear us apart, then I was just leading her on. I needed to be brutally honest with who I was, for both of us.

"I can't believe you, slave. Get on your knees, let me see what I own." My hand held her head down while I looped my arm under her hips and positioned her. My slap to her inner thigh had her spreading wider. "Don't you move. If you do, so help me, I'll stay in the room next door until you learn how not to act like a child. *Throwing a tantrum.* Jesus." I spanked her bottom again at the sheer disbelief. In other circumstances, I would have found it funny, even cute, but here and now…there was no room for mistakes. I was the Master and she was the slave and that's the way it had to be.

My fingers slid over her swollen folds and I massaged the wetness into the smooth skin. It didn't take Lily long to start moaning again. Her fingers fisted the comforter while I took my time, making her wait it out to learn her lesson.

"Master." Her voice quivered and I knew she had to have been reaching the cliff again.

"You used to edge so well. We're going to have to get you back to where you were." I slid a digit in halfway and her breath caught. Seeing her pussy so exposed, I barely noticed her sounds. It was as if I had tunnel vision. I told her, and myself, that she could decide whether she wanted to be my slave, but in truth, I couldn't let her go. There were no plans in my future of not making this work.

Pulsing in my cock had it twitching against the pants I wore. As I pulled at the buckle on my belt and the clasp on my pants, I slid another finger inside her and surged deep. The steady rhythm I kept had her body shaking within seconds. My pants dropped to the floor and I kicked off my shoes.

"Turn around."

Lily's head lifted and she opened her heavily lidded eyes. Her movements were slow as she pushed herself up and spun toward me. When her hand started to reach for my cock, she stopped and remained still.

"Good girl. Now, you can continue."

Dark hair swayed while she crawled even more forward and wrapped her palm around the base of my length. Her tongue came out and in one long stroke, she trailed over the tip, collecting the pre-cum beaded there. My jaw clenched and my fingers locked in her hair. Fuck, how I had missed this—missed her.

With a swirl of her tongue, she circled and encased the entire head into her mouth. The rotation encircled me again and I held her tighter.

"You always blew me away with this." The words were spoken quietly as she took more of me into her mouth. I drew myself in deeper, pulling her more toward me. I let my hand decide the speed and depth, and Lily didn't push away as I made her take me to the back of her throat. She held still, breathing in deeply through her nose. My eyes closed and I waited a few seconds before I withdrew, letting her get a good breath. Small sounds vibrated my cock and I leaned forward, spanking her ass and gripping the flesh. I pumped faster, feeling myself become taken over by her completely.

"You love me, yes?" I pulled out of her mouth, gripping my length and rubbing it over her lips as she spoke.

"Yes, Master."

I nodded. "And you want to make this work?"

There was a slight pause as her eyes narrowed. "Of course I do."

I took a step back, but remained facing her as I made my way to the drawer my stuff was in. The package of condoms was in the front and I picked up the box, taking one out just to show her.

"What are those for? I told you I was on the shot." Confusion had her eyebrows drawing in. I didn't answer as I walked back over.

"They're not for your pussy, baby."

Still, she seemed confused. "I don't understand."

"You will soon enough. We won't need to use one tonight, but soon. Now, why don't you go get the lube."

"Lube?" Lilian stood and took a step, only to spin back around. "Anal?" she whispered.

When I didn't answer, she continued to the restroom. I removed my belt from my pants as she walked back toward me slowly. Fear was so densely filling her expression, making me even hotter. This was what I had wanted. I liked her afraid, even if it did contradict every urge I had to protect her.

"Master, I don't think..."

"No, you don't. Nor will you when I'm in charge." I took her arm, pulled her in front of me, and gently placed my palm in the middle of her shoulder blades to ease the top of her body over the bed. "Lift your wrists up. I don't want you moving."

Slowly, they rose, and I pulled them up higher, wrapping my belt above her elbows instead of where she thought I'd be restraining.

"Do you trust me?"

"Yes." There wasn't a pause in her answer.

I stepped back and kneeled while I made a path down her pussy with my tongue. God, I was never going to get enough of her taste. I'd gone so long without it and once we returned to San Francisco, it was going to be a bitch to do anything if Slade had something to say about it.

Lily moaned and I covered her slit, pushing the tip of my tongue to trace the inside of her folds. When I reached her clit, I brushed across, barely making contact. Over and over, I teased the sensitive nub until she began to rock back against me. Wetness coated my lips and chin and the smell of her had *me* moaning. I stood, unable to take it anymore.

"Be still." I nudged my cock into her opening, closing my eyes at how hot her pussy was.

"Oh, God, yes." Lily's fingers drew in until she was close to making a fist. Inch by inch, I let my length slide into her, pausing so she could adjust to my size. The tightness made it almost impossible for me to hold back. The need to savagely pound into her clawed at my insides.

With my thumbs, I spread her folds apart even more. She was so wet that the sounds only enhanced my impatience. Her pussy clenched around me with every withdrawal and I plunged in all the way, causing her to cry out.

"Is this what you wanted, slave?"

I grabbed the belt just above her elbows, pulling back as I began to pound into her. Her moans grew louder and I reached forward, pressing my palm against her lips.

"You see," I said, pulling her even higher to hover over the bed, "if you are good, you get rewarded. I'm proud of you for getting the lube without arguing. Now, nod if you want to come all over my cock."

Frantically, Lilian's head moved up and down behind my grip. My hand holding the belt went around her waist while I gave her clit attention.

"Mmph." The muffled sound was no more than a moan and maybe a mix of some pleasure-spoken word. Hearing her try to speak and feeling the vibrations against my palm sent me into my own frantic state. I was here, having my way with the woman I loved, and doing it in ways that I enjoyed. How many times had I fantasized about this exact thing?

"Your pussy is getting so tight, baby." I let go of her mouth and eased the top part of her body back down. The lube sat on the bed and I grabbed it, pouring a generous amount over her back entrance. Lily jumped, but otherwise stayed still. "Try to relax, slave."

"Will this hurt?" Her voice was soft as she tried to peer back at me.

"Maybe a little at first, but if we continue to get you used to it, I think you might like how it feels."

I continued the movement of my fingers over her clit while I circled the one place I'd eventually have. It wouldn't be tonight, but a few weeks of breaking her ass in and we'd be good to go. Anal was something I wanted to experience with my slave. I enjoyed it and I knew I could make it to where Lily would, too.

Tight muscles encircled my finger as I placed the tip inside. I paused, letting her adjust and withdrew, gathering more lube from the area and using it to ease to my first knuckle. Lily tensed and I could feel her tighten even more.

"Calm," I said, soothingly. "I won't really hurt you. Trust me." While I teased and tried to get her to relax, my mind went over the ways that might help. There wasn't anything I wouldn't do for my slave. Right now, her comfort was my top priority. "Is it getting better?" More lube oozed over my finger and I stood, thrusting a little faster.

"Yeah, the burning isn't so bad as long as you move."

The motion had her body going lax again. Repeatedly, I thrust into her back entrance, pushing in further each time. When I had my finger halfway in, her moans grew louder.

"Time to come, slave."

I reached back to her clit and thrust my finger all the way in her ass, increasing the rhythm of my cock until it was pounding into her as fast as I could manage. It wasn't long before the double penetration matched up in perfect harmony.

"Oh, fuck!" Lily's hands fisted against my stomach and I leaned in closer, kissing her back. "Fuck my ass harder, Master."

A growl tore from my throat. Lilian screamed and jerked only seconds before spasms rocked her body. Feeling her grip around my cock and finger at the same time stripped every ounce of control I held onto. Cum shot from my cock and I couldn't grasp my thoughts as pure bliss left me dazed with each explosion of my release. What in the hell had happened? I'd never not been able to control my own orgasm. But here, she'd stolen it with her words. Her pleas for more repeated in my head long after she stopped saying them and I wanted to give it to her — again.

Chapter 29
Lily

"Rise."

Master's voice had me easing to my feet. My knees ached, but not once had I moved or shifted while I waited for permission to stop kneeling. For three days, Zain trained me. Nothing dark like I expected. Everything was more disciplinary. I kept waiting and trying to prepare myself, but the routine continued.

"Come, let me see you."

I walked forward and my Master lifted his hands, brushing the hair back to expose my shoulders. "I'm impressed. You did very well." He kissed my forehead and wrapped his arms around me, hugging tight. My forehead creased at the repeated closeness he'd displayed over the last few days. Zain had never been one for lots of contact or praise. It was enough to have me reevaluating how well I had thought I'd known him.

"Master?" I looked up, trying not to show my confusion.

"Yes, Lilian?" Still, he held onto me.

"Is something wrong?"

Only then did he glance down. "Of course not. Why would you think that?"

"I don't know. You just seem...different."

He led me to the sofa and sat us down. "Different, how? Because of this?" Pressure from his lips coaxed mine open and I was swept away at his taste. In a slow rhythm, he massaged his tongue against mine. My eyes stayed closed long after they broke away. A deep sigh of bliss left me and forced my lids open. For seconds, I blinked, staring at him.

"Yes. You're more affectionate now."

"I'm more *appreciative*. Love and the absence of it can change a man. I've waited three years to experience everything you are. Your touch, your taste, the way you feel...I never knew the little things like a hug or kiss could mean so much. They do, slave. I'd be content to just hold your hand if that's all we were allowed to do."

A laugh burst past my lips and I couldn't help it. "If my brother has his way, we'll be lucky to get that far once we get home."

Master smiled. "If that's what it takes to be with you, I'll take it. At least until..." He broke off, smiling even bigger.

"Until what?"

"You'll see." He turned more toward me. "Why don't we talk about the future? Do you see yourself staying at Slade Industries? Or are you eventually going to take another path?"

My lips pressed together at the questions. I'd asked myself the same ones a million times since starting there and although I was a natural and excelled, I wasn't quite sure. I had other plans. Bigger ones.

"You're thinking pretty hard."

I nodded. "I love working for Slade, but...I'm actually glad you asked. I've needed someone to talk to about this."

"I'm here for you, you know that. What is it?"

Zain's eyes narrowed and concern etched into his features. I clasped my hands together, wondering how I should go about stating my thoughts.

"Do you think my brother would be upset if in two to three years I decided to open my own business? One almost identical to his?" I rushed in. "It sounds really shady, I know, but it's not about overshadowing or stealing what he has. I just want something to create. To see it grow and thrive. Do you know what I mean? I feel like I've already reached as far as I can go with my brother's company and it's unfair to others. I see how they all look at me. Anyway, there's a combination of things that have kept the idea fresh in my mind."

Master's arm came to rest on the back of the sofa and he leaned his head against his fist. The muscle in his bicep flexed for the briefest moment and I took in the swirl of tribal just below his elbow. When he spoke, I had to make myself focus through the lust that roared. Damn, his arms were so much bigger than before.

"I think it's a great idea to start your own company, Lilian. But, I think it's best to stay for the two to three years that you mentioned. Maybe even five. The more experience you have, the better. And what if by then you don't want to take the risk? It's best to know for sure. And no, I don't think Slade would be the least bit upset. If anyone knows the need to create something and see it flourish, it's your brother. I think he'd be very proud of you."

"You're right. I'm only beginning in this field. Just because I'm good at it doesn't mean I'm anywhere near accomplished enough to take on such a task. Experience will be key."

His hand reached out and took mine. "And so will support. I'll back you no matter what decision you make. I may rule over certain things, but I will never stop you from accomplishing your goals. My job is to make sure you succeed. I'll do everything I can to see that it happens."

"Thank you." I drew his hand to my lips and placed a kiss on his knuckles. He had no idea what hearing him say that meant to me. Or maybe he did.

"You're very welcome."

Tenderness was mixed in the grin he gave. My pulse jumped and I felt like a schoolgirl all over again. There was something about my Master. Whether he was happy, disciplining me, or having moments like this one, my body reacted to every single one. A heavy heat whirled in my heart and butterflies fluttered in my stomach. It was rare that I saw this side of him and when I had, it seemed like forever ago.

"What about you? What does your future entail?"

Zain picked up a lock of my hair and twisted it around his finger. "You. Whatever your plans are, I'll change mine to fit them. If you want to stay at Slade Industries, so will I. If you want to own a business, you have me to lean on. Whether it's an accountant you need, an IT Manager, a partner, or a bodyguard, I'll be whatever you want. Just say the word and I'm yours."

My body trembled from adrenaline as I took him in. The dark T-shirt left his eyes practically glowing, and he was so serious, yet caring, as he looked at me. Love...yes, he loved me. "Will you say it again, Master?"

"Just say the word?"

I shook my head. "No, the end part."

"I'm yours?" His lips separated and he reached forward, pulling me onto his lap. "You know I'm yours, baby girl. I have been from the moment I laid eyes on you. I've said I love you probably a hundred times since I got you back. I'll say it a hundred-thousand times more if that's what you need."

"Will you hold me?"

To have his arms around me was something I craved. I wanted to feel safe. To forget about everything I'd been through the last few weeks. I couldn't deny I was still shaken. With the days that passed came the reality of what I'd undergone. It was all sinking in and leaving me an exhausted mess on the inside. And I knew my Master could see it. It was probably why he hadn't unleashed any of his secret desires.

"Keep talking to me. Tell me what else you want out of the future?" His arms pulled me in and locked around, holding extra tight. I felt my body relax and mold into his.

"I want what most people do. A home. A family. I want traditions of big Thanksgiving gatherings with friends and family. And a dog that can be raised with my children. I want to be happy."

His hand rubbed up my back slowly. "That sounds like the perfect life. It would be nice to have a home to come back to at the end of the day. A real home. Not a penthouse or an apartment building. I want a yard with a swing set. Maybe a barbeque pit." He paused for so long, I almost lifted. "My step father, Jeff, used to barbeque all the time. I remember waking up to the smell after I was taken. It was a phantom smell, but the memory left an impact. I missed my parents so much at the beginning. I never want our children to have to experience a single ounce of the pain we've been through."

My fingers gripped his shirt and I wasn't sure if it was because he used *our,* or the fact that we were talking about children after we'd already lost one. I hadn't been able to save our child then, and it wasn't from lack of trying. In my mind, I'd failed, in more ways than one. I put my unborn baby's life in danger to help a slave and we paid the ultimate price for my mistake.

"Lilian?" Zain's hands gripped my cheeks as he pulled me back to look at him. I couldn't stop the swell of tears. Would it ever get easier? "Don't," he whispered. "It wasn't your fault. You have to stop blaming yourself." I didn't have to ask how he knew what I was thinking. Zain knew me better than anyone.

"It was my fault. I should have known better. If I hadn't gone that time—" The sob cut off my words. I tried to hide my face in his chest, but he wouldn't let me."

"Listen to me. You didn't know Saul would hurt you. He'd been told not to. He had orders and he disobeyed them. Had I believed he would go against my father's wishes, I would have never allowed you to continue to help those girls. You are more important to me than anyone. We both learned a hard lesson that day, so no more blaming yourself. If anyone is at fault, it's me. I could have locked you in. I could have ordered you to stay put, but I didn't."

The pad of his thumb slid across my cheek, wiping the tears.

"Nothing will replace the loss of our first child, baby. Nothing. But I promise you this. My uncle *will* pay. And when he's gone and we decide to have more children, we will love and cherish what it means to create life. Every time we look into our child's eyes, we'll know how lucky we are to be blessed. Do you understand?"

"Yes," I said, sniffling.

"Good. Now, no more tears. Our past is full of pain, but our future won't be. Let's focus on that."

Master eased me back to his chest. The fast beating of his heart soothed me. I let it take over my consuming thoughts completely as I closed my eyes and tried to push away the hurt—a pain I knew would probably never go away. Minutes went by while my hair was stroked and soon, I found myself drifting between sleep and consciousness. With each breath he took, I disappeared from reality. Grotesque flashes of blood, mangled body parts of slaves, and evil men played before me like a slideshow. Even though I tried to ignore them, I couldn't shut out what had plagued me now for years, or the new horrors I saw. Jonathon. Alec dead on the table. Knives and guns aplenty. I tried reaching for something to protect me, but everything was too far away.

My nightmare opened up like a black hole, swallowing me until I couldn't breathe past the black masked men whose fingers raked against my skin, clawing to rip off my clothes.

"I'm going to make you pay, Lily. You're going to die just like I did. Just like my father and brothers. Alec wouldn't be dead now if it weren't for you."

I screamed, trying my best to fight off his weight. My eyes widened as his face morphed from Jonathon's to Alec's.

"You killed me, Lily. It was all your fault."

"No," I said, shaking my head. "I didn't mean to."

"But you did!" he yelled, grabbing my wrists harder. "Now, you'll pay. I want you. Come be with me. Stay with me forever. You owe me."

All I could do was plead no, repeatedly. My arms pushed against his, but I wasn't budging him. Something warm dripped onto my face and the blood starting to pour from his mouth had me screaming. Drip. Drip. The steady splashes made me go wild. My hips jerked while I tried to knock him off of me.

"Lilian!" Master's roar had me jumping awake. My fingers dug into his sides as I tried to get closer. "Shh. I'm here. I've got you."

Fingers through my hair became evident, and my nose running had my eyes blinking from the horrified wideness they were stuck in. With a swipe of my hand, I noticed how wet my face really was. Had I been crying? I lifted my head only to come within view of my Master's sad expression.

"You're getting worse as the days go by. Even I can't seem to break through your nightmares anymore."

I'd hoped that having Zain at my side would make them go away like they had at the beginning, but each night they returned. And they were only getting more graphic and stronger.

"It's only been a few days."

His eyes studied mine intently. "Perhaps we should go back and get you help. This was a bad idea. After being taken again, I should have known things weren't just going to change because I was in the picture. You need help, baby. Help that I can't provide."

"I don't want to go back yet. We came here for a reason. You—"

"Will do what's best for *you*," he said, interrupting. "If we continue down this road, I don't think it'll do any good. If anything, it will probably make matters worse. Tying you up, using my tools on you." He opened his mouth, only to stop. "Amongst a lot more fucked up things…it's too close to what you've been through. We may enjoy them in the moment, but this," he said, pointing at my head, "isn't ready to take something that significant yet. Let's go home, get you to your doctor, and we'll take things one day at a time."

Everything in me wanted to argue. We'd come so far with my training. I knew his kinks were right on the edge of being revealed...and now this? One nightmare during the day and I everything I'd waited for was getting ripped away? I felt like a piece of myself was missing out on discovering the foundation of who Zain was. I needed to see what he wanted for us. I also knew he was right. I wasn't sure I could truly handle how dark he wanted to go.

"So, we postpone the heavy stuff? What about when we go back? I won't get to be with you like I want. I *need* you there with me."

He sighed. "I won't go against your brother's wishes. To do that would ruin any chance of peace or happiness within your family. Plus, I'll only be a phone call away. When you have a bad dream or feel like you need me, let me know. I'll come over and put you back to sleep. I don't see Slade objecting to that."

"Do we have to leave right now? Can't we have one or two more nights? Maybe the nightmares will go away."

Skepticism weighed heavily in his features as he stared at me. I knew he was battling with what was right and what we both wanted.

Knocking on the door caused me to jump. I clutched him as we both looked to where the sound had come from. Fuck, I hadn't meant to show fear, but I'd been caught off guard by whoever decided to interrupt us. As Zain stood, placing me on the cushion, I could see he was unnerved.

"If you have a nightmare tonight, we leave first thing in the morning."

His back turned and he headed for the door. The tray of food that was wheeled in had me calming. I knew there wasn't anything to be afraid of anymore, but the jittery feeling just wouldn't pass. Is this what I had to look forward to now? Paranoia, dependency on guards and my Master? I'd come so fucking far from the first time. To the point where I was ready to drop my protection and live on my own. Now, this?

I had to get my strength back. Not only to deal with the life I had accomplished with my career, but for myself. I would be going back into my routine soon enough and I'd be damned if anyone saw me any differently. Saw me as…weak. I was Lilian Roberts, CEO of Slade Industries. It was time I started acting like it.

Chapter 30
Zain

How do you fix something that may be broken? By first impressions, one wouldn't see Lily as damaged goods. Even now, I didn't view her as such. But my slave wasn't okay. Not even close. She classified them as just *nightmares*, but she didn't see what I did. Didn't hear the blood curdling screams that broke the silence in the dead of night. Her pleas and the complete agony in her tone left my skin clammy. She didn't realize what hearing her most feared state did to me,. It was as if she was undergoing torture and there was no one for me to kill, to her from. It fucking destroyed me. How in the hell was I supposed to fight off the demons in her mind? By being here? Supporting her? Fuck, that wasn't enough.

"You're not eating."

My slave's voice pulled me from my thoughts and I looked up from the full plate of food, dazed. I couldn't get over the desperation I heard as she thrashed in my arms. To know how bad off her mind was…how truly afraid she was. God dammit. I felt helpless.

"Sorry, I was thinking."

"About going home." It wasn't a question. She knew what was on my mind. Although, there was something she didn't know. I didn't have a home anymore. Not the one that she assumed I'd be going back to. It wasn't safe. Not after everything that went down with my father. He had contacts, people who could possibly come looking for me. They'd have that address if my uncles had anything to do with it. Besides, I may have had a lot of money tucked away, but I wasn't naïve to the fact that I couldn't afford to live that life for long without having a job. Especially if I wanted to buy a home and still have a good amount in savings. Yes, Slade was going to provide one, but I didn't take handouts. I didn't want my salary to be any different than what everyone else in my department got paid.

I pushed the fork under the mashed potatoes and took a bite, nodding. When I swallowed, I looked back up. "Has to happen."

She remained quiet as we finished off our meal. The sun was beginning set and I dreaded the late hours. So far, she'd had these dreams every night. I had no doubt one would haunt her again.

I stood, walking over to help her up. The disappointment was there and I felt it within myself, too. It wasn't about feeling upset because I wasn't enough to help her. Lilian was a victim of two tragic kidnappings. One would have sent anyone over the edge to where they might never truly recover. But, two abductions? I was scared for the woman I loved.

"Go jump in the shower. We can cuddle in bed when you get out. Maybe we'll find a movie on."

"I like the sound of that." The grin that came to her face was forced. She walked to the drawer and pulled out clothes before shutting herself in the restroom. I immediately reached for my phone. The moment the water turned on, I hit Slade's number. Two rings sounded before he answered.

"Hello?"

My pulse thumped hard in my chest as I began to pace. "I think we're going to head back in the morning."

He hesitated and the sound of humming could be heard in the background, no doubt from Mary. "What's happened?"

"Nothing you need to be overly worried about. It's just…Lily's nightmares. They're getting out of control. I want her looked at."

"Shit." Slade breathed out deeply. "I was wondering how she was doing."

"During the day, she seems okay. I see little things that show me she's thinking not so pleasant thoughts. She's jumpy. Gets agitated rather quickly at times. Other than that, she holds herself together well. It's the night that worries me." I stopped. "No, it's when she sleeps that I know she's not okay. She fell asleep earlier and had a really bad one. Full blown fighting while she was out."

Footsteps sounded over the connection, and then clicking.

"I'm going to email her doctor now. I'll let her know that Lily will be coming to see her in the next day or so. They're probably going to want to put her back on meds. My sister isn't going to be too happy about that."

Subconsciously, I shook my head. "There's nothing she can do. If they help, she needs to take them."

"Agreed." Slade's typing filtered through, but he didn't stop talking. "Thank you for letting me know. And for doing what's best for her. I know you had plans to get reacquainted up there and you could have done the fucked up thing and kept her until your time ran out, but you didn't. That means a lot to me. It shows me that you're looking out for what's best for my sister. I respect that."

I headed for the balcony, pushing the door open to overlook the garden. The cold evening air cut right through the long-sleeved button up shirt I wore, but it was the least of my worries as I let the dilemma play out in my mind. "I love her. I'll do whatever I can to make sure she's at her best. Mentally, physically...whatever it is."

"I can see that. I'm glad I wasn't wrong about you." The clicking stopped and more footsteps returned. "Take care of Lily. I'll see the two of you tomorrow."

"Sounds good."

Just as I went to pull the phone back to disconnect, my name came back through.

"Zain?"

"Yes, Slade?"

"When are you planning to deal with your other family?"

The question turned my stomach. The reminder wasn't something I wanted to think about. "The sooner, the better. I want my focus to be solely on Lily. I think I'll stay until after her appointment so I know where she stands and then I'll leave her in your care until I return. I shouldn't be gone more than two to three days."

"You're taking Blake, correct?"

My hand rubbed against my rough cheek as I contemplated. It would be easier for me to get in and out without worrying about someone else. He had a wife. I'd feel responsible if something happened to him. He didn't know the layout of the house like I did. But I wasn't stupid to think I could do it alone either.

"Zain?"

"Yeah," I breathed out. "I'll take him. Only him, though. It's going to be dangerous. I can't risk putting anyone else's life in jeopardy."

"Understood. Blake's good. I've been looking over the information Gaige provided for me. Together, you're both in good hands. I know you'll look out for each other."

If only I was as confident as he was. What lay beneath that roof was a handful of killers who were almost as good as me. They'd be waiting. Ready for my attack. The odds weren't in our favor.

"Thanks. I'll see you soon."

As I disconnected, I hoped what Slade said was true. I knew Blake's reputation, I just prayed it lived up to the hype when shit really hit the fan.

I headed inside, shutting the door behind me. The shower was still running and I felt myself heading in that direction. My fingers were already working the buttons of my shirt as I got to the door. Steamed billowed out around me and Lily spun in my direction. Her hand shot up to her chest, startled. "You scared me," she rushed out, laughing. "I didn't think you'd be coming in here."

"We've never gotten to take a shower together." I didn't say anymore. She knew all too well the reasons behind that. It was too dangerous at my father's. I always kept a close eye on her. Always stayed ready to protect, if it came down to it. Here, we were safe. I could risk letting my guard down.

My shirt dropped to the floor and my pants followed. I kept my focus on her the entire time I undressed. Her eyes lowered to my hard cock and her feet shifted as I pulled open the door and stepped inside. The moment my hands came up, she threw herself into me, wrapping hers around my neck.

"You want me? Is that why you came in here?" Her arms tightened, trying to pull my mouth to hers. Instinct had my hand burying in her hair. I stopped myself from applying too much pressure or pulling back. I kept it there, steady. A warning for the slave I'd spent the last few days training. Immediately, her grip loosened and she stopped.

"I always want you. What about you?" Smooth skin met my fingertips as I made a path up her thigh and caressed down her pussy. "Are you wet for me?" The slickness from her arousal met my touch as I separated her folds, teasing her opening. "Oh yeah. You want my cock."

Lily held on tighter, but didn't pull. One of my digits slid in and I lowered my head, nuzzling my cheek against hers. Deep pants increased as I added another finger.

"I do want you," she moaned. "I've wanted you all day. But you never touch me when the sun is out."

A gasp met my mouth as I spun her back into the marble and surged in deep with my fingers.

"Training is for the day, slave. Making love is for the night. You can have both when you earn it."

Our tongues met and I removed my fingers. I couldn't stop myself from pulling up one of her legs from behind the knee and lowering enough to slide the underside of my cock over her slit. The heat she threw off burned so good, I didn't hesitate to push into her harder and deepen the kiss. Knowing her pussy was so ready for me left my brain sputtering to keep it together.

"I want you to fuck me with my toy." Lily's cheeks were slightly tinted pink as she pulled back and glanced over to the shower seat. Resting on top was her dildo and the lube, right where I made her keep it. It was part of the routine she was supposed to follow. "I was about to start before you came in."

Fuck. My hand slid higher up her thigh and I lifted her enough to move against me. Pre-cum oozed from my tip. Just imagining fucking her with it was going to do me in. How many times had I fantasized about just that? *Every fucking night.* It was the main reason I bought the damn thing. Sure, I wanted her to be desperate for me by the time she finished with her routine, but it was also because I liked to imagine her in here playing with herself while she was thinking about me. Why the hell hadn't I watched her before? I'd been in protective mode for so long, all I knew was to stand guard to make sure she was okay when she was at her most vulnerable. I didn't have to do that anymore. Not under Slade's roof.

"Sit on the seat."

I scooted the toy and lube to stand further down the bench-style slab, allowing her to get into position. Before she could even finish spreading her legs all the way, I was lowering my mouth to her pussy. My hands gripped her hips, tugging her closer to me while I sucked against one side of her folds, swirling my tongue up to brush against her clit. Her taste swept over me and I moaned at the same moment she did.

"I wanted you to come in here. I'd hoped..." The top of her back rested against the wall while she pressed her hands into the marble she was sitting on. I reached for one, positioning it at the top of her slit.

"And now I'm here. Play with your pussy. Show me what makes you feel good."

I returned, pushing my tongue into her entrance. A cry filled the space and her fingers worked over the sensitive bud, moving around her folds and pulling up to apply pressure. Continuously, she teased her clit, even spreading herself so I'd have a better view. I couldn't stop myself from watching in awe.

"I have to move. Please, Master." She rotated her hips at my nod and my tongue slid into her entrance deeper. The speed of her fingers increased while I held her hips tighter, allowing her the rocking motion she felt she needed.

"Fuck." Hair stuck to the side of her face as she turned toward the wall, moaning. I lifted, grabbing the toy. I didn't need lube for as wet as she was. I rubbed the tip around her opening and eased it in, watching her hand pause. Slightly, her lips separated and she bit the bottom one while she watched me inch the fake cock inside of her.

"Ah." Lily's fingers stretched straight out only to start working over the top of her pussy again.

"Holy shit," I mumbled. "Wider." The command had her legs spreading and her shifting on her bottom to allow me full access to both her pussy and her ass. The pulsing in my cock increased while I withdrew the toy, only to plunge it in deeper. "You like that, baby. Is this what you've been wanting?"

Lily nodded, but the only reply was more deep breaths and short sounds.

"Answer. Did you think of me doing this to you when you fucked yourself?"

"Yes. God, I did."

The edge of my mouth pulled back into a half smile and I increased the thrust until her legs were trembling. Only then did I grab the lube. A stream of liquid ran over the toy and I let it slide down until it was covering the entrance of her ass. With my index finger, I traced it around, pushing past the tight muscles until my finger was halfway in.

"Master." The uneasiness shook her voice and I knew it wasn't from pain or discomfort. I'd built her up so much that she was having a hard time controlling the urge to release.

"You're not allowed to come so soon. Fight it and enjoy what I want to give you."

In slow thrusts, I matched the rhythm of my finger with the cock, watching as Lily's heavy-lidded eyes stared at what I was doing. Her face was flushed and I knew the steam was getting to her. Fuck, I was burning up, too.

"Hold the toy steady but *do not* move it."

Her hand reached forward and the moment she took hold, I turned, moving the knob to cold. I never broke my finger from her back entrance. When I turned back, I thrust in all the way, grabbing the toy and fucking her hard with it until she was screaming.

"Now?" Her hand lifted from her clit, only hovering an inch above...waiting. Such a good slave. My teeth begged to sink into her skin, to show her the proof of my proud ownership.

"Come, baby. You deserve it."

Lily's fingers dove between her legs and seconds of teasing herself sent her body jerking with spasms. I continued the thrusts with both my finger and the toy while she moaned through her orgasm. My cock jerked repeatedly, begging to take her. Fuck, I wanted her worse than I could ever remember.

"So beautiful," I said, nipping her leg.

I stood, turning the water to as hot as it would go and washing the toy. The moment I laid it down, I adjusted the warmth and washed my hands before reaching down and pulling Lily into my arms. Her weight fell into me so trustingly and I gripped the hip I held to, along with the outside of her shoulder. The squeeze had her smiling up at me.

"I liked that."

"Me, too." I kissed her forehead, stepping us back into the water. I hated that we'd probably be leaving in the morning. All I wanted to do was spend every moment with my slave. But I had to do what was right. She wasn't okay. Not really. I could pretend all day that these were just dreams and they'd pass in time, but if I wanted Lilian at her best, she had to release and cope with what happened. Until she did, she'd continue to be unstable. I couldn't allow that to happen. I loved her too much not to give her the ultimate protection. Even if it was from her own mind.

Chapter 31
Lily

"Will you train again?" Zain glanced away from the TV to look at me.

My laughter died off from the stand-up comedian's joke and my smile faded as I took in his question. I knew what he was referring to when he said *train*. It was all the martial arts I'd learned. "I have to get better at self-defense. The confidence will help. It'll make me stronger. I need that right now."

He nodded. "I want to watch, if you don't mind."

Zain watch me get my ass beat and handed to me every day? My trainer didn't take it easy and he put everything into making me the best I could possibly be. I should have never quit when I did. I'd just felt so damn strong. I needed that back.

"You promise not to interfere?"

There was a slight tremble in my voice. He was my Master and I was basically telling him to butt out, but I couldn't go without this. I needed to learn more if I was going to get my nightmares to subside and the fear to fade.

"Maybe. Depends on if he teaches you well enough."

Zain turned over in bed toward me and I followed suit, facing him.

"And if he doesn't?" I asked, smiling.

"Then I take over and kick his beefy ass out the door. I've seen your trainer, Lilian. He's lucky he kept his hands to himself before. Let him slip once. I'll have him in a submission hold so fast, he'll pray I don't make the wrong move and snap his neck."

My lips separated. "Jesus. Well, you don't have to worry about that. He doesn't like women. You really think my brother would let someone that close to me if he had to worry about something happening?"

"No. But you never know."

"I do, and Chuck isn't interested. Trust me." I laughed at the teasing smile he cast. The happy sigh couldn't be held in as we kept each other's stare. Damn, I didn't want this to end. I was praying the nightmares held off for at least another few nights. I just doubted I was that lucky.

Zain licked his lips and reached forward, tracing his finger down my nose and across my lips. "I can't get over how lucky I am. You're so gorgeous, especially in moments like this."

"I'm not sure how you can say that. I'm still all bruised up. And they're at their ugliest now." The yellow outlines that were beginning to take over looked awful. Make-up did an okay job of hiding it, but it was only going to get worse before they were gone completely.

"You're beautiful to me, no matter what. I think I could stay like this, just as we are, for the rest of my life and never feel happier."

My mouth twisted and his eyebrow cocked at my expression.

"You'd be happier if you could be yourself. Will you please tell me more about your secrets? What are you hiding? What is it that you want to do to me that you feel would be so bad?"

A groan came from his mouth and he rolled to his back. "Slave, drop it. We have the rest of our lives to dabble with the dark. Maybe we'll never even experience it at full force. Let's just let it go for now, okay?"

"I don't want to," I whispered. "I feel like this is important to you. It's part of who you are. If I hadn't already seen what you're capable of, maybe I could have looked the other way, but you've gotten really…intense with me before. It's killing me knowing that you're ignoring what you want because of me."

"You want to know?" He sat back up. "What happens when I tell you? What if it pushes you further away from me? Disgusts you? Don't you feel like if I just did it, you'd get to experience it for yourself? Maybe do something you may have never done had I not told beforehand?"

He did have a point. What if hearing it was different than actually doing it? "I can't believe anything you'd tell me would make me not want to at least try. I love you. I think I'd do anything you found pleasure in."

A laugh came from his mouth and he fell back to the bed. I pushed up to a sitting position to look down at him. "What? I'm serious. I happen to think I'm pretty open-minded. Just tell me so I can let it sink in and we can build on this."

"Okay." Zain lifted, resting his back on the pillow he fixed to lean against the headboard. "You remember when I had you outside of my building? What I did to you?"

Lust exploded within, making my belly clench. I shifted on the bed. "I remember."

"And in my penthouse against the glass?"

"Yes." My body was humming just thinking about how he took what he wanted from me. I may have pretended to fight and sometimes it was genuine, but I'd wanted him all the same.

Zain's hand reached out, cupping my breast through the silk pajama set I wore. "That's a little of what I like, baby. Dirty, dark, I'll-take-you-wherever-and-whenever-I-want-whether-you-like-it-or-not, hardcore fucking. Things that are so wrong, they're right. Do you understand what I mean when I say that?"

My head shook, hoping he'd continue.

"You worry about work. About what I'll do when we're there together. And you should. There won't be a single desk in that building that won't be christened with our come by the time we're finally said and done at Slade Industries. Not a single one. It's wrong, but I want it."

No words came as I stared at him in shock.

"That's just the overall picture though. What you're neglecting to see is how you'll be while you're being forced to obey. There won't be enough tears left once I get done stripping you down and gagging you with my cock. When I feel you've earned some hardcore dick...well, I'll give it to you the way I like the best, brutally, and maybe even in your ass. You'll be lucky to walk. And no, I'm not saying that because I think it sounds hot. Baby, you really might not be able to take actual steps. You have yet to see my true colors. I long to rough you up, to bite and draw blood, bruise..." he trailed off. "Plus, more. We're not there yet and we may never be. You may think you can handle it, but those are just words. To say them is one thing. To experience them is quite another."

As I let his confession sink in, I stayed quiet, resting my head on his stomach while he played with my hair. Was this something he needed all the time?

Or just on occasion? I was pretty sure I could handle it. He'd turned me on before when he'd taken me. I'd tried my best to fight off my attraction to him, yet what he'd done had made it impossible. And I was confident he wouldn't seriously hurt me. I trusted him.

"I think I can do it." I turned, looking up at him. The suspicion was there. He wasn't so sure. I swallowed hard, willing the words that would help me try to convince him, to come. "I know I'm not necessarily okay. I won't deny that the nightmares scare me. But you don't. I don't feel anything we do will trigger my dreams to become worse."

A finger pressed against my lips, silencing me.

"I'm not risking it. You can try to convince me all you want, but as your Master and the man who loves you, I'm refusing to go ahead with this until I know you're better. I'll still train you, but I will not put your state of mind at risk. I won't."

There was no convincing him. I knew that in my soul. I'd have to not push and focus on getting better so he'd see I was ready. Zain would know how far to go and how hard to push the boundaries. My guess was that it wouldn't be much further than he already had.

"There's something else we need to talk about. It has to do with living arrangements."

I felt myself perk up, excitement nearly leaving my heart breaking through my chest. Living arrangements…I only wished he'd asked me to move in with him. I knew Slade wouldn't approve and Zain wasn't going to rush, but the hope of it happening was still there.

"Living arrangements?" I tried to keep my voice calm, but my eagerness slipped in.

Zain paused and his eyebrows furrowed. Any happiness over the situation faded away. This wasn't good, I could feel it.

"What?" I sat up, fisting the blanket.

"I'm going to need to start looking for a place when we get back. I can't stay in my old one. It might put me further away from you. Not too far, but not across the street."

Anxiety spiked and I tried to rein it in. I'd accepted him not being there because I figured he'd be close. But if he wasn't…*Stop this, Lilian. You're a damn grown woman. Independent, remember? You can do this.* So, why didn't I feel like I could?

"How far?" My voice rose in pitch and I lowered my head, trying to slow the shakiness taking over.

"A few blocks. Maybe a mile. Nothing too far. Hey," he pushed his finger under my chin, making me meet his stare. "You have nothing to worry about. I can run a mile in five minutes if I have to. Probably faster, concerning you. All it will take is a call and I'm there. Now, instead of looking at the negative, focus on the positive. I'm going to need

someone to help me choose a place they
wouldn't mind maybe staying at occasionally. And,
I'll need help fixing it up. You know, the whole
woman's touch and all."

I couldn't stop the smile from resurfacing.
"You'll let me decorate your place?"

"I'll even let you pick the bed sheets. I can
handle flowers, let's just avoid the bright neon
colors."

"No hot pink?" I pouted my lip, playfully, and
he laughed, cupping the back of my neck and
drawing me in close.

"Only if you beg. Then I might reconsider."

His lips pressed against mine. The tug against
my bottom one sent a moan slipping though. "Oh,
I'll beg," I breathed out. "I'll beg all night long."

"Better start now. I don't really care for hot
pink. It's going to take a lot of convincing."

I knew we were both playing. Truthfully, I
didn't care for a hot pink comforter set either, but it
would be funny to watch him come home to find his
bedroom done in nothing short of a teenage girl
who'd went neon-crazy with his least favorite color.
It would give us something to laugh about.
Something we could look back on and tease each
other over.

"Oh, please, Master. Let me have it. I'll do
anything."

"Anything?" His tone deepened and the vision of sheets and covers disappeared. I knew nothing but going into slave mode. In the place that made me happy. Submitting was something I wanted. No, *needed* to do for him. It was the only state of mind where I felt the happiest. Where I felt at home.

"Yes, Master."

"Good. You can prove it here shortly."

Zain's expression grew serious while both of his hands came up and held each side of my face. No words. Just staring into the depths of my eyes. It was almost impossible to meet his gaze for more than a few seconds. My pulse was racing, my breathing turned shallow. Sweat collected on my skin and the intimidation, the domination, was so thick, it had me desperate to lower out of respect. I knew my place and there was nothing more I wanted than to get there to please him. It had always been like that. Now, it was so naturally coming back and I didn't want to ever let it go.

"The next few months are going to very trying for you, slave. But they're also going to be full of change and surprises. Do you like surprises?"

There went that thing in my chest that only seemed to beat for him. The speed appeared to stop, only to slam harder, keeping a steady pace at all the things he could be insinuating. "I do."

"Good. One may be coming very soon.
Focus on that when your mind starts to wander.
Even when you sleep, think about all the things I
have planned for us. We may have come here so you
could make a decision, but there's not one to be
made. Is there, Lilian? You want to be with me, not
matter what. Am I right?"

I took his words seriously and knew my
answer immediately. "Yes, Master. No matter what."

A smile came to his face and he lifted my
hand, kissing my palm. "Then, come tomorrow, we
let the surprises begin."

Chapter 32
Zain

I couldn't remember the last time I sported a black eye. Maybe it was in my youth during all my training or possibly in my early teens, but I couldn't recall. Between Lily and me, we looked like quite the pair. And she wasn't half as amused as I was.

The nightmare we both knew would come, did. But not with the initial screams like I expected. The first cry I thought would wake me, didn't. Her punch did, though. The lights that exploded behind my lids caught me off-guard and I dove toward the one place my instincts told me it had come from. It took me all of a split second to place the soft cries of the woman I had pinned down. My attack had awoken her, leaving my startled slave fighting even more for her life in the pitch black. I was able to calm her down with my voice, but once I turned on the lights, she broke before me. Had it not been for the mirror within my view, I wouldn't have known why. The swelling was already becoming evident and it didn't take long for the dark bruising to set in. But it wasn't all bad. It was only in the corner of my eye, closest to my nose. I knew it wouldn't take long to fade, but even now, as we were about to land at her building, she still had that apologetic expression on her face.

"It's fine," I mouthed.

The tears welled in her eyes and she shook her head, looking out toward the roof. The moment we were out and heading for the door, I pulled her close, whispering in her ear. "It really is okay. You didn't mean to."

"I'm out of control. I can't stand this."

The door open and Brace's smile turned into a confused stare as we swept past. Lilian kept her head down, hugging her arms around her stomach as we came up on Marcio sitting at the entrance.

"What the hell happened to you?" He stood from the table, intercepting the door to get ready to hold it open. At the shake of my head, he glanced at Lily and turned the knob, allowing us in. Both Slade and Mary stopped eating at our arrival.

"Grab a...chair." Slade pressed his lips together, but picked up his fork and continued eating.

"Ugh, just say it. Or ask." Lily broke free and headed to the table, sitting on the other side of him. I took my seat, too, glancing at the food resting in the middle. The buffet style breakfast wasn't appealing after the sizeable one I'd eaten this morning. Lily had barely touched her food, she was so upset.

"You do that?" Slade asked, nodding toward me.

"Yes," she whispered. "But not on purpose. It was an accident."

Mary grabbed a biscuit, tearing off pieces as she stared between Slade and Lily. They seemed to have some unspoken conversation going on. Even I was getting curious about what they were thinking.

"Your appointment is at four. You know Dr. Klauson is probably going to put you back on your meds, right?"

"Yep. I figured as much." Lily stabbed her fork into some watermelon, placing it on her plate. "Did you get ahold of Chuck?"

Slade took a drink of orange juice. "Two o'clock."

A nearly silent laugh shook Lilian's chest. "Very strategic of you to put him before the doctor."

Slade smiled, looking down at his plate. "I figured if he wore you out enough you wouldn't argue with her orders."

"Very smart of you. I hate meds. They make me feel out of it. I don't like not having control over my own thoughts."

Slade peered up from his eggs. "But they helped with the dreams, didn't they?"

She shook her head. "Not always. Sometimes they just knocked me out so hard, I couldn't wake up from them. I'd almost prefer not to be stuck in my own personal hell."

The room got silent and I reached over, placing her hair over her shoulder so I could see her downcast face.

"Just try them out for a few weeks and see if it helps this time." My voice had her looking over and nodding. The heaviness in the room seemed to lift after that and Lily turned to Mary.

"You look like you're feeling better."

Blonde hair cascaded over her shoulder and she smiled as she drew in another bite of her breakfast. "My doctor put me on medication, too. But mine's for the nausea. It's working wonders."

"She hasn't stopped eating since she's taken it," Slade rushed in. "I had to order everything on the menu because she couldn't make up her mind." The teasing smile had her blushing, but it didn't stop him from nudging her small plate of fruit closer. The adoration he had on his face was as clear as day. And the dark circles were gone. Apparently, he'd finally gotten some sleep.

"Slade just knew you two would be here and he wanted to make sure you both ate before he started in with his plan." Mary raised an eyebrow at him before turning back to her plate. I felt my back stiffen as he shot his wife a look that almost said she'd spoiled some underlying secret.

Lily shifted in her chair, obviously picking up what I had. "What plan?"

"Not a plan," Slade ground out. "It's more…errands, if anything."

"Errands?" I asked. "What sort of errands?"

The impatience was there. He was hiding something.

"You know, just the regular stuff."

"Slade?" Lily cocked her head to the side. "You're up to no good. I know you."

"Bullshit." He shook his head. "Fine, if you want to know, Brace told me Zain mentioned he was ditching the place across the street. I figured I'd help him relocate, being the generous brother that I am."

She shook her head. "Now I'm calling bullshit. You never do anything without it benefitting you in some way. What are you up to?"

"Nothing. I have a friend in real estate. There are a few rentals I thought I'd take Zain to look at while you're preparing for your appointments." He walked over, picked up some papers, and handed them to me before returning to his seat. "Larry is meeting us in an hour, so we should probably be leaving soon."

My eyes scanned over the first paper, stopping at the price. I immediately shot my gaze up to him. The stare that met me was a hard one. One that I hadn't seen on his face before. I flipped to the second home. The third.

"Not going to work," I said, flatly.

"I think it does." Not once did he turn his attention away from me. Slowly, my head shook and I looked back down. Did he not hear what I said when I went into his office that day? If I wanted to be filthy rich, I would have taken my father's funds before I offed him. I didn't want dirty money. I hated that what I had in my account was tainted with bad deeds.

Again, I shook my head. "No. Unless you're telling me that an entry-level employee can afford a ten thousand a month rental payment, I can't go look at these homes."

Slade's jaw tightened and I let Lily take the papers from my hand.

"Petaluma!" Her head spun to her brother. "That's a good hour commute, at least." She flipped the paper. "Novato. Berkley. Freaking, Half Moon Bay? You can't seriously think he'd want to live that far away."

"It's a beautiful area. I doubt Zain would mind the drive."

A smile pulled at the corner of my mouth. I may have played into his rules concerning Lily, but I wasn't going to let him push me around. "No. I'll stay in the city and find something I can afford. That is, if you still want to hire me. If not, just let me know now. I can easily put in applications while I go house hunting."

"With your fake name, Mr. Collins? Or is it, Cook? Which one are you going to choose?"

My eyes narrowed and I held my clenched fists in my lap. Whatever the hell was going on, I didn't like it. What had happened to the sincere man I'd spoken to on the phone? The one that was grateful to me for bringing his sister back?

"I have a reason to know if you're going to want to be with my sister," he went on. "I mean, at least give me that if you won't take me up on the house listings."

Lily's fingertips were white as she pressed them into the table. My hand settled on her thigh and I leaned in closer toward him...and her. "Collins will do just fine. I appreciate you going out of your way to get me a place, but with Lily's nightmares, I'll be staying close."

"Very close," she stressed. "Besides, *I'm* helping Zain pick out a place. And I'm decorating." The smile she threw off had me mirroring it. "Now, if you'll excuse us, we'll be taking care of that now before Chuck arrives."

I stood and she followed. An array of expressions played across Slade's face before annoyance took the prominent role. Whatever he was up to, I wasn't sure I wanted to find out. It didn't look good and I didn't want things to go south now that we were almost to where we needed to be.

And I'd be damned if he tried to keep me away from her now.

The sound of Lily's heels clicked against the floor while we headed for the entrance. Slade's voice boomed from behind.

"Be careful and take Marcio with you. We don't know if it's safe yet."

Was that his problem? He didn't want Lily around me in public because he feared something bad was going to happen again? I calmed the earlier anger and nodded.

He had every right to worry. After all, I still hadn't taken care of my other family.

We shut the door behind us and found Marcio already waiting. Apparently, he'd heard Slade's yell.

"Where we going?"

All three of us loaded into the elevator car and Lily pushed the button to the garage. "We're going to find Zain a house. And we're taking my car."

Marcio cursed but stayed quiet until we came to a four door Jetta. And not a new one. My eyes cut over to Marcio, who was laughing under his breath.

"What in the world do we have here?"

Lilian climbed in, leaning over to unlock the passenger door. The smile she wore radiated and in that moment, I couldn't remember being happier. My slave was dressed to kill, sitting in a car worth less than the fancy half-trench that covered her.

"My first car. I couldn't bear getting rid of it. It's great, right?"

"Perfect." And I couldn't have been speaking more of the truth. This was what I had wanted when I dreamed of my future with Lily. Real. Simple. Happy.

She turned over the engine, and surprisingly, it started.

"The guards use it on occasion when they're...doing whatever they do," she said, as if reading my mind. Her eyes peered back at Marcio, but he kept quiet. "So, I have a few good ideas on where we could drive. Most of the owners stick signs in the windows. Maybe we'll get lucky."

"I like that idea."

We left the garage and headed away from downtown. I manually rolled down the window, letting the cool air fill my lungs. A few streets went by when she took a left, heading up a steep hill. Like a rollercoaster, we went through the motions, weaving through numerous tight knit streets until my hand shot up and I jerked forward, flying into the safety belt.

"There's one!" Lilian had already slammed on the brakes and I shook my head, trying to calm my rapidly beating pulse. Son of a bitch, she'd caught me off guard. A car honked behind us but she didn't pay it any mind as she pulled over and wedged between two parked cars. I turned to look at Marcio, whose eyes were wide. I was betting he was going to put on his seat belt the next time we started going.

Lilian pushed the car door open and climbed out. I was quickly behind her, barely making it out before she started walking around and heading toward the front door. All the homes were set up against each other, displaying the same black iron handrail going up the stairs in front of each one.

"I like it." She headed closer and I took out my phone, punching in the number.

"It's…bright orange."

Her giggle was swept away by the wind. "It'll go great with the new bedroom set." Dark hair swung over her shoulders as she spun in my direction. "Let's get it. Slade's penthouse is close enough."

"We haven't even seen the inside," I said, lowly. "It might already be leased." At the sad look, I hit the number. Jesus, this woman was going to be the death of me. *Bright ass orange house, a neon bedroom set, if she had her way, and beautiful eyes that could make me care less about any of that.*

A man's voice came though and I sighed, glancing over to Marcio, who was leaning against the car.

"Hi, I'm calling about the house you have for lease." I turned toward the intersecting road to see where we were when the phone disconnected. I pulled it back and looked at my screen to make sure I'd wasn't imagining it. "What the—"

The door to the next house over opened. "It's still available. You interested?"

Shit. That could be good and bad. My landlord living next door. Tough call, but it wasn't like I really had anything to hide. Not anymore. I was just a regular man who would have a regular job. Maybe it wasn't so bad. Orange was an okay color.

"Hi, yes. I'm very interested. Is there any way we could see inside?"

"It's two bedrooms. Are you the couple and he your roommate?"

The man nodded toward Marcio and Lily laughed. "Oh, no, sir. We're a couple, yes, but Marcio is just my cousin. We won't be living with Zain. I'll just be staying over on occasion."

A nod was thrown our way as the landlord hobbled down the stairs, favoring his left side heavily on the cane. Keys jingled as he pulled them out and walked up the stairs to the rental.

"Zain, you say?"

"Yes, sir," I held my arm out for Lilian to take as we followed.

"I once knew a Zain. It was back in eighty-three. Tulsa, Oklahoma, I believe." As he continued on, I let my smile surface, feeling better by the minute. It might be nice to hear his stories. I'd never had a grandpa, maybe this would be something like that. Or…not.

Chapter 33
Lily

Aching, sore, disappointed. So many emotions poured through me as I grabbed my pharmacy bag from Marcio and leaned back in the seat. He was driving now, leaving the local pharmacy while my Jetta stayed in Zain's care; sitting in front of his place like it was always meant to be there. Fuck, I hadn't wanted to leave. Training, pouring my feelings out to my cold therapist, none of that helped as much as being surrounded by those hideous bright blue walls and laughing with my Master about how much fun we were going to have painting them. It just went to show me that no matter where we were, he was my home. So, why wasn't I there? Why was I going back to my brother's?

Right. Because Zain said I had to. Men. They were so complicated. Where I saw no problem with acting based on my feelings, everything with them was so planned out and strategic. Love wasn't meant to be a game or puzzle. It was everything spontaneous. Everything brought on by the pull of one's heart. My gravity consisted of my Master. The further we were apart, the more I felt as though I were floating through a void without direction. I needed him close. Needed his attention and rules. It was just who I was. Needy? Only for him. In my everyday life, I could be the hard-ass, bitch boss. Fine. But when it came to the man I was meant for...God, he had me at his feet ready to please him any way I could. So, why the hell was I not staying and having dinner with him tonight? It pissed me off that I was even agreeing to this ridiculousness.

"You okay back there?"

I glanced up to see Marcio staring at me in the rearview mirror. Brace continued to look out the window, surveying the traffic to the side of us.

"Yep. Just tired."

"You can lie to your therapist all you want, but you're not fooling me. What's going on, Lily?"

A frown came to my face and I turned toward the blurring scenery, really not seeing any of it. "I just want to go home."

"We are going home."

My head shook, but I kept quiet. How long would this continue? When would Slade deem us ready to pursue more of an adult relationship? Like, staying over at my boyfriend's house for the night? I'd spent my whole life worrying about what Slade thought. I was starting to see that obeying his rules might not work out anymore. He was doing the brotherly, and even fatherly, thing. I knew that. But I was old enough to make my own decisions and what I wanted was to be with Zain. If he hadn't ordered me to step back and take things slow, I might have already been over there.

The closer we got into downtown, the heavier pedestrian traffic increased. What should have been a simple five minute drive turned into close to fifteen. My fingers twitched in my lap and I tapped one against my legs while we pulled into the parking garage. I was out the moment Marcio threw the Town Car in park.

"We made it."

Marcio's voice had me turning around to look at him as we approached the elevator. Without so much as a goodbye, he shoved the phone in his pocket.

"My brother?" I hit the button, stepping through the doors as they opened.

"Nope."

Silence. I clenched my teeth together, trying my best not to curse the stubbornness of all men. Today just wasn't my day. I was too amped up after my training. Where I should have been dead on my feet, I felt the need to fight it out again. It was showing in my attitude and I had to rein it back in before I came off as the bitch from hell.

"Your boy wanted to make sure you made it home alright. I told him I'd let him know."

"Oh. Thank you." My head lowered and I waited out the ride. It didn't take long before I was walking through the living room of the penthouse.

Slade was resting on the sofa, Mary already asleep with her head in his lap. With his index finger, he gestured for me to stop, so I did, watching as he eased out and propped a small pillow underneath her.

Quietly, we headed to my room and he shut the door behind us. Why did I feel like a child that was about to either get lectured or scolded for something I did wrong?

"How'd it go?"

I slid off my heels and sat on the edge of the bed. "Good. I told her the nightmares were coming back and they were worse than ever. She had me go over a few and then prescribed the same medication as before. She told me to let her know if she needs to increase the dose."

"Good," he said, nodding. "You're going to take them, right?"

I paused, not really sure why. "Of course."

"You need to if they'll help. I…" he crossed his arms over his chest and I could see the stress mounting in his stature. He was becoming stiff and his face more hard. "Lilian, I want to talk to you about Zain."

Preparing myself wasn't something I needed to do. I expected the worse, but prayed for the best.

"Okay, what do you want to talk about?"

"I know you love him. And he loves you, that's as clear as day. But I have a lot of things I'm worried about when it comes to the two of you being together. I mean, have you both talked about the future? Do you have a plan? You're set, personally, and I'll do my best to help him. He saved your life. His skills combined with Blake's led him to find you. Shit, the guy would easily lay his life down if it meant keeping you safe…but that says a lot, too. How do we know he's not going to mix with the wrong people again? What if he can't handle the real world? Think about this, Lily, because it's constantly on my mind. You can't turn a blind eye because of how you feel for him. You have to plan for anything to happen. Be prepared, here," he said, tapping against his chest. "And here." His hand lifted until he was pointing at his head.

"You're afraid of what will happen. I understand that and I love you for it. But you have to stop this," I stressed. "This is *my* life. Let me figure it out for myself. You worry and that's fine, but I know Zain. He loves me. All he wants is a normal life. You trying to spare me is only making things harder. Just, please, I'm begging you, let me do this on my own. Stop giving him a hard time. We don't need this added stress on top of everything else."

Slade's fingers weaved through his hair as he shifted. "It's easier said than done. Lily," he stopped and his eyes looked upward, only for him to shake his head.

"You want to say something, but you're not going to. What is it?"

"Nothing," he said, lowly. "You're right. I do need to back off. I'm just not sure how much I'll be able to."

I began taking out my earrings as I stared at the battle playing across his face. If Master had taught me anything, it was that sometimes being nice didn't drive the point home and it sure as hell didn't always get the job done. "Slade, I'm not going to ask you anymore. Back. Off. I appreciate what you've done for me, but I love him. If he told me he wanted me to move in with him right this very moment, I would. I did mention to him that I didn't want to leave, but his respect for you had him ordering me to stay here. *Ordering me*, Slade."

His jaw clenched but he let me continue.

"I know you want us to take things slow, and luckily, the man I found wants the same thing, but I'm telling you now, the moment he gives the okay, I'm gone. No more hiding for me. No more baby steps to see how I take to a situation. I belong to Zain now. I go by his rules, no one else's."

"Do you even really know him apart from living in some…place in Afghanistan?" The anger was sinking into my brother's voice and I glared as I stood from the bed.

"Do not go there with me, Slade."

His eyes widened. "Go there? Lilian, I'm being serious. You haven't seen him here. He hasn't even lived a real life yet. We don't know what is going on in his head because of what he's been through. All I'm saying is to give it a few months. Watch how he acts. Take it in and see if he's happy or downright miserable. Don't ignore any signs you may catch along the way. I want you to be happy. I do. But maybe you should be positive your future belongs with him before you leap off the cliff you're standing on."

A loud exhale sounded and Slade walked over, easing me down to sit on the edge of the bed. "Do you trust me?"

The pleading behind his stare made my anger fade. "Yes."

"Then I need you to allow me to continue with what I have planned. It's the only way we'll know for sure if Zain is the one for you."

"Plan?" My head shook in annoyance. "So, Mary was speaking the truth earlier. I knew you were up to something. Houses in Petaluma," I said, sarcastically. "What exactly is this plan?"

A smiled pulled at the edge of Slade's lips. "If you knew, it wouldn't work. Just go along with what I say and we'll both get to see just how much Zain loves you. To give you to him completely, I have to make sure. And before it's over with, you'll be thanking me for it."

"Or not," I said, under my breath. Flashes of Master having enough teased my mind and I tried to push them away. The insecurities were fictitious. I believed he wouldn't leave me, no matter what. I just had remember that. "I'll play your little game, but the moment I think it goes too far, I'm out."

"Deal. Just let me work my magic and trust in me. I'm doing this for your best interest. If Zain is the one for you, we'll know by the time this is over. You've both been through a lot and there's more to come. When he gets back from dealing with his family, we'll begin."

My eyes shot to the clock. "Does that mean I can go back to his place until then?

The slight amusement on Slade's face vanished at my words, only to be replaced with nothing short of distaste.

"He'll be leaving tomorrow or the next day. I need to be with him." I kept my tone firm. Although it appeared I was asking, we both knew I wasn't. I wanted to spent time with him before he left. What if he didn't come back?

"Blake called while you were at your appointment. He wanted to check up on you. He's already here, Lilian. I don't really think he ever left."

Panic surged while I fought the fear that told me Zain was already gone. Had he left without saying goodbye? No...he wouldn't do that. Would he? I stood, heading for my closet. In my heart, I knew my Master wouldn't just take off without saying goodbye. We knew the risks he was going up against.

"If I know Zain, he'll be leaving in the morning. I'll be back then." I walked over, grabbing my overnight bag. My hands grabbed clothes I wasn't even aware of. All I could think about was, come tomorrow, Zain would be in the presence of pure evil. Men who lived for only one thing—blood. They were trained to kill and protect, and the two men they guarded were going to be waiting. Waiting to put an end to the one person who held my world together.

"Lily?"

I glanced up from the adjoining bathroom door, but still pushed it open, grabbing my essentials bag.

"You're being careful, right? I mean..." Slade pushed from the bed and I could see how uncomfortable he was. "What you told me before you left..."

Sweat broke out over my skin just thinking about him knowing I had been pregnant. It was a part of myself I hadn't wanted to share. "We're careful."

I zipped up the backpack, going back and sliding on my shoes.

"I'm sorry about what happened to you. I think I was too shocked and angry before to come up with the right thing to say. But you have to know, had you come home pregnant, regardless of who by…I would have loved the child just as much as if it were my own. You mean everything to me, Lilian. I've tried to show you that over the years and I know I've failed, but—"

I crashed into Slade hard, hugging him with every ounce of strength I'd held back since returning. Maybe a part of me thought he would reject me and the life I carried if I had returned pregnant. The circumstances had been unconventional—a tragedy for those looking from the outside in. Growing up, I'd been preached to on how I needed to save myself for marriage. Save myself for a man worthy of my brother's approval. Deep down, I knew Zain was that man, but how things turned out for both of us didn't fit my brother's bill. Not from the lectures I'd been raised on. It was a scrambled situation and one I never thought my brother would begin to understand. He'd proven me wrong on every fear I'd harbored so far.

"You never failed," I whispered. "Never."

His arms hugged around me tight and he kissed the top of my head before easing up and stepping back. "If I haven't failed yet, I refuse to start now. If Zain is the one for you, he'll prove himself just as much. Enjoy your last night together, Lily. I'm afraid my plan doesn't call for any more of them. Not anytime soon."

Chapter 34
Zain

What a disaster.

I spun around, looking at the bright blue walls of the living room and stopping at the deep red of the kitchen. Who in their right mind would have thought that color combination was a good idea? My head shook and I let out a deep breath. This place was going to need so much work. Of all the rentals in San Francisco, never in my right mind would have I chosen this one. If my slave hadn't shone through with excitement over the location, I wouldn't have made it two steps past the front door. Hell, I wouldn't have even stopped. Bright orange outside, blue, red, and yellow inside.

"Yellow." I cringed at the word, remembering the bright sunshine paint that littered the upstairs master bedroom. Littered, because the bastard who'd done it hadn't even made it to the top. The four-inch gap to the ceiling still revealed the cream color that rested below. Fuck, I had a lot to do when I returned.

The air mattress shifted as I collapsed onto it. I couldn't bear to put it upstairs. Not when I wanted full access to the level someone would try to break into if they decided it was a good idea. Given the multiple guns and knives I had under the roof, it wouldn't be.

Music filtered through the walls and I turned toward the opposite side of where my landlord lived. I hadn't met the tenants yet, but given that I'd heard kids earlier, I was guessing they were a younger couple. Ones, who loved to yell. Damn, this was so different from the penthouse I'd been staying at. I wasn't even sure what to think at all the changes.

I pulled out my phone, checking the time. Blake had called not that long ago. Apparently, he was in town and heard I was back, too. There was no way he'd flown to Texas to spend time with his wife and came back in just four days. We were supposed to meet in two weeks. I wasn't sure why, but I was suspicious. Had he been waiting to see if I'd leave without him? Had he gone and just come back early? It just seemed odd to me. Too...convenient.

Knocking had me easing to a sitting position. Had he decided to come over? Probably. I didn't doubt he'd tracked my location when he called.

Groaning filled the room and I wasn't sure if it was me or the mattress.

Knock. Knock. Knock.

The quick succession had me looking out of the window instead of the peephole. I didn't trust them. Too many people assumed you'd use them. It was a great place to catch a bullet right through your eye.

"What the…" I reached over and turned the dead bolt, swinging open the door. Lilian flashed me a smile before she wedged herself in. At Marcio's wave, I lifted my own hand, confused. "What's this?" I asked, turning and locking the door behind me. "Did Slade change his mind?"

She dropped a backpack to the floor. "For the night, anyway. He said Blake called him earlier. That means you'll be leaving tomorrow. Am I right?"

The last of her question was almost nonexistent. Sadness and fear had me lifting my arms. She didn't hesitate to throw herself into them.

"I was going to come see you in the morning before I left."

Tighter, she clung around my neck, and I gave her a quick squeeze before letting go. With shaky fingers, she moved to the buttons of her jacket and only paused to wipe a tear from her cheek.

"Here, let me help you." I reached out, finishing down her stomach. Deep breaths left her and I pushed past the material to make a path up her hips and over her breasts before I eased the jacket from her shoulders. It fell to the floor while she kept her eyes on mine. "Why don't you tell me about your day?" It was almost impossible to remove my grip from her shoulders. I held to them, wanting nothing more than to use my touch to pull her close.

Before I could do that, I needed to hear how her appointments went.

Lily broke her stare and I led her to the edge of the air mattress where we sat down.

"I got the pills, but I think I need a new therapist. She's...I just don't feel like I can really talk to her. I don't know. Other than that, everything else went fine. I already feel sore from training, at least that means it's helping."

I took her hand, placing a kiss across her knuckles. "We'll find you someone you can confide in. When I return, we'll look into it."

"Actually, I was just thinking about calling Agent Sullivan's wife. She's...been where I have. At least, sort of. I think she might be able to help. I had plans of contacting her tomorrow after you left.

"Perfect. I think that would be a great idea." In slow movements, I traced my thumb over the length of her palm. A shiver had her licking her lips.

"So, what all did you get while I was out?"

A smile came to my lips. "The necessities. Bathroom stuff, food, drinks, amongst other things."

"Other things?" Her eyebrow cocked. "You say it in a tone that makes me suspicious."

"You're smart to be."

I lifted her hand and bit into the tip of her finger. Not hard, but enough to have her lips separating just the smallest amount.

"I'm happy your brother let you come." I glanced down at the bag. "And for the night, too. He doesn't know what he just allowed." I pulled off my long-sleeved shirt and tossed it to the floor. I didn't wait to have Lilian climb on my lap. My hands gripped her hips and I pulled her on top of me, lying down to watch her hover above. Dark hair fell in waves around me as she lowered and I let the vision burn into my memories. Our first night in my new place. Our new place if I had my way by the end.

A soft caress traced over the intricate lines tattooed in my chest and I closed my eyes, memorizing just how soft her skin was. Everything filtered through—the smell of her perfume, the heat from her thighs that were pressing against my sides.,the pressure from her pussy sitting on my hard cock.

"Kiss me, slave, and don't you stop until I tell you to."

Going back to the place I was raised held nothing but a twisted sense of hate and relief. I was ready to put an end to my past, but I couldn't stand the fact of facing it again. Knowing I'd be there so soon had me gripping Lily's neck as her mouth connected to mine. Harder, I held her, wrapping my other arm around her waist to spin her over. Desperation drove my hips forward and made me meet her tongue with an urgency I hadn't felt seconds before.

"Fuck, I don't want to leave you," I whispered against her lips. "I just got you back."

Lilian's arm tightened around my neck and I didn't deny her more. I couldn't. Master or not, I knew how much my slave needed me and I needed her just as much. If I didn't return—

I cut my thoughts off, refusing to believe my uncles would win in this war. They tortured me growing up. Saul had killed my unborn child and beat the woman I loved, not to mention all the slaves he'd killed over time. No, he wouldn't make it out alive. Even if I ended up dying in the end, he'd beat me to death's door. There was no way I'd go out without him paying for his crimes.

"Master, can I ask something of you?" Her words came out broken up as we continued to kiss.

"Don't. I know where your thoughts are." My hand fisted in her hair as I ground into her even more. Temptation was a hell of an invitation. Just hearing Lily's question opened the little dark box and I could feel the fight that raged on inside of me. It had my other hand coming up to lock onto the other side of her head.

"Show me," she moaned. "Don't leave without introducing me to the real you. Just this once."

A moan slipped through my clenched teeth and I pulled back on her hair until she made a small sound. "You can't take it, baby." I pulled even harder. "Don't you see that? You pushing this issue is only going to hurt you more."

"Wrong. You hiding it will. Do it," she said, angrily, jerking beneath me. "Show me what you're capable of or I flip the switch and introduce you to someone who will."

I didn't have to ask who she was referring to. The dominance she held behind her stare had me remembering her description of dominating Alec. I knew my slave possessed the will. She said she'd wanted to be me. Seeing her as she was now, I had no doubts she would try.

Angrily, I pushed the dress to her hips, hearing it split in the process. "You think you're going to order me around? Hmm?" The panties tearing from her hips had a smile edging to her face, but not for long. Something flashed behind her eyes and the next thing I knew, her arm was flying out and knocking mine further away.

"You want to be my Master? Prove you're worthy, or maybe I'll find someone else who will."

Lilian could have hit me with a bag of bricks for the force her words had. Rage flared even though I knew she didn't mean them. She was baiting me, and it was working.

"You'll never be rid of me, slave. Never. If you even think about trying to replace me, you'll regret the day. You're mine. *Mine*," I said, reaching back to pull her panties off completely. The struggle was there while she tried to wiggle further away. I let her feel the power in my hand as she pushed against my grip on the lace. Fuck. I could feel my darkness beginning to thrive with her fight. This wasn't good. Wasn't right.

The pressure against my wrist sent my hand flying back. My head shook and I lifted from the bed, turning to pace the living room.

"No going to happen. Not yet."

Mindlessly, I talked to myself, letting the calm try to snuff the need to completely overpower her. I could take what I wanted. *Whatever I wanted.*

"Don't you dare." Lily flew off the bed and undressed. It only made my urges even more intense. I could feel my shoulders cave in and my movements become more lithe. Faster, my heart raced, and I could see the Lily before me was no longer my slave. She was replaced by a woman who thought herself my equal and she glared back at me with every intent to pounce if I didn't first.

Slowly, we circled each other, testing, getting our feel for one other. I couldn't stop staring at the sway of her breasts. My fingers twitched while I tried to keep my distance and focus.

"You don't want to do this, slave. Your best bet is to go kneel and get in position. I'll let you apologize, you can get your punishment, and we'll pretend like this never happened."

Her head shook even as the unshed tears reflected in the light. "*I will not.* You owe me this after everything we've been through. Give it to me before you leave. Don't deny me a part of yourself that I might never get to experience again. I haven't once told you not to go. And I don't want you to," she sobbed. "Blake Morgan could handle it, but I know what you need. Now give me what *I* need."

My eyes closed, confliction clouding my mind, and my darkness easily winning in the process. And then...nothing. Gravity became nonexistent and I landed hard on my back. The air whooshed from my lungs and Lilian was on me before I could process that she'd even moved to begin with. My jeans tugged against my hips and she had them unfastened within a second.

I growled, kicking out my leg and easily pinning her underneath me. The waistline slid to my lower hips and my cock was so hard, it ached behind the material that kept it restrained.

"Your mistake was telling me you liked the fight. I'm about to give you one you'll never forget. Just don't say I didn't warn you."

A laugh bellowed out of me as I took in her small frame beneath me.

"I have you at my mercy, slave. What are you going to—?"

Both of her elbows came in and with a yank, her wrists somehow broke free from my grasp. I was barely able to deflect the heel of her palm thrusting toward my face.

"Nice," I breathed out. Damn if my adrenaline wasn't starting to shoot through the roof. This was my fantasy come true with added competition. It wouldn't be as easy. Lilian would make it hard for me. She'd make me work to have her where I wanted.

My hand shot out to grab one of hers and her body shrimped to the side. The fist that slammed into my ribs had my mouth parting in shock. What the fuck? I hadn't thought she'd get that physical.

"That's it." My fingers embedded in her hair and I tried to roll her onto her stomach, but her feet planted and she made it difficult to turn all the way. I added more of my weight and used my legs to separate hers to help with the maneuver. "Is this what you wanted?" I spanked her hard, causing her to yelp and fall onto her stomach. With one hand, I managed to grasp her wrists and with the other, I removed my pants completely. Lily's ass lifted, rubbing against my cock, but still she tried to break my hold. My hand came down on her ass again— hard. "You think this is so bad? That taking you is what sates my sick needs? Not even close," I said, growling in her ear. "You just fucked up, baby, because there's no going back now. You want it. You fucking got it."

Or so she thought.

The hand holding her wrists dropped and I wrapped my arm around her throat before she could block it. I didn't tighten, but kept her from being able to move. With my other, I forced my way to cup her mouth, easing from there to add enough pressure to make her think I was attempting to be rough.

Sounds filtered through, but nothing that alarmed me. I kept my entire attention on her behavior, waiting to see if anything triggered her past.

"Did you really think you could overpower me? Now you get to suffer through what I want from you. *Whatever* I want. I think right now that's for you to be my slut. Master's little fucking whore."

Lily's fight eased and her ass wiggled beneath me. The wetness that met my cock had my teeth pulling at her shoulder. I bit harder until she tried moving out of the way. Had I really wanted to unleash on her, I wouldn't have stopped. Wouldn't have held back like I did now.

"Oh, slave. There's no getting away for you. Take the pain I want to give and embrace it. I'm afraid you don't have much of a choice."

"Mmph." Lilian tossed her shoulders back and forth and I nipped at her earlobe, rubbing the length of my cock against her again.

"Let's do this right, once and forth all. You see that bag over there on the counter? It has your surprise in it. A for sure way that you lose all choice in movement. You ready?" I lifted, pulling her up and keeping the chokehold while I dragged her to my bag. Rope met my fingers and she gasped, going still.

Real fear flashed on her face for the briefest moment and I let go, feeling my stomach drop. I didn't want her to be afraid, but the rope did something to her in that moment.

"Red?" My eyes searched hers and she took a stuttering breath.

"No." With strength that amazed me, her arms came out in front of her and she waited. I could have gone on, wormed out why the rope triggered the anxiety, but I didn't want to. I had to see if I could help her overcome it. I wanted her trust and she was offering it so freely.

The hemp slid down my palms and I looped it around her arms, taking my time, adding the detail I wanted. For my slave, it had to be perfect. She may have appeared the captive, cloaked in rope, but her submission to my desires only had me working twice as hard to perfect the way I weaved in and out. Once I had her wrists bound, I brought them up to hover above her breasts. The rope went behind her neck and I brought it down, angled in an X over her chest. Over and over, I added more layers, until the fit was tight enough to leave marks, but not enough for her to be overly uncomfortable.

"This is beautiful," she whispered.

"You're beautiful."

My lips pressed into hers and her fingertips held to the bottom of my jaw. I couldn't stop my forehead from resting against hers as I broke away.

"Slave, about how far do you want to go?"

"Don't you dare pull back now. Please."

God, to really let go and give in...I'd kill to show her how good it could feel to experience that sort of pain and pleasure.

"Fine." I swept her into my arms and lowered her to the bed, positioning her so the side of her face was against the mattress and her ass was in the air. "You want to meet the real me? So be it. I'm done trying to fight what the fuck I want to do to you. I hope you're ready to burn, baby, because things are about to get really hot in here."

Chapter 35
Lily

Rustling had me trying to look back to see what Zain was getting out of his bag. My heart was racing and I was shaking at the fear of the unknown. What had he meant, burn? God, was he going to actually hurt me? Stupid question. Of course he wouldn't.

The sound of a lighter caused me to jump and I tried lifting my head more, but short of rolling onto my side and being caught disobeying, I was screwed. *Trust. Trust. Trust.* I continued to repeat it in my head, praying I hadn't just told the man I love to become some hidden monster that was best left in the shadows. He was scared I'd turn from him…was there really a reason for me to?

Footsteps approached and I tried to slow my breathing. Seconds went by while I waited. The shift of the air mattress caused my fists to draw in closer to my chest.

"We'll start out light. Just a small warmth. We'll go from there."

Fingers caressed down the length of my slit and I closed my eyes, letting myself relax. What felt like liquid dripped onto my ass and I jumped, but calmed immediately. *Wax.* Okay, I could do this. As long as he wasn't holding the lighter to my skin, I had nothing to worry about.

"You look so fucking hot lying there helpless in my rope. I should have tied you up long ago, baby girl."

The temperature increased as more wax drizzled over my ass, closer to my pussy. I bit my lip, moving against the finger rubbing circles around my opening. Fuck, I was so hot and wet for him. If this was a taste of his dark side, I was ready to get burned.

"Stay still or it will get worse a lot faster."

His finger inched inside of me and I gasped at the heat that made a line from one side of my lower back to the other.

"God, I love your body." Teeth sank into my skin not far from his fingers and I fought not to rock into him.

"Master." The high pitched tone showed nothing short of how hard it was for me. I realized I loved this feeling of helplessness when my Zain was in charge. The wax just helped intensify the experience. He could really burn me badly if he wanted, yet I knew he wouldn't go overboard.

"Shh, slave. Just feel. Fight whatever other tendencies that come and give in to what I do."

A single drip landed on the small of my back, followed by another that splashed a little higher.

More followed and I closed my eyes, trying to focus on the pattern he was making while his finger began a steady thrust into my pussy. Time blurred as it dragged on and the design got bigger and more widespread until I was sure there wasn't an inch of my back spared.

Another finger joined the first, pushing in deeper. A steady rhythm pushed in hard enough to allow me to rock with it.

"This will be more intense."

Fire raced from the bottom of my ass and down my thigh. I wasn't sure how close the flame had been, but the heat was enough to almost bring tears to my eyes. With the combination of pain and pleasure, I was pulled even further into the building ecstasy.

"You shouldn't have waited," I moaned.

Zain's fingers paused inside of me only to start again. "You like the burn?" Again, what felt like almost direct contact had me bracing for more. Just when I though I couldn't take it, the pain eased. A brush of his thumb over my clit had me nodding.

"God, yes. I love it all."

The tightening of my skin under the hardened areas had my nipples tingling. There were so many sensations that my mind was confused on what I needed more of. I took in each, letting them run electric throughout me. At Master continuing to tease my clit, I quickly felt all my focus go to the burning ache he was building deep within my core. I was sizzling on the inside and scorched outside.

"Be completely still," he said, lowly. "If you move, you're not going to like it."

I braced myself…waiting. The anticipation had my pussy clenching around his fingers. The teasing stopped and for the seconds that dragged out, I wasn't sure I even breathed. Then, in long succession, I felt the flame travel down my back only to return toward my neck. Repeatedly, my Zain walked the wire of pulling my pain tolerance to its peak. I took shallow breaths, too afraid to breathe in deeply and too aroused to deny what my body was enjoying.

A moan poured out of me and I pressed my lips together, dying for him to touch me again. I didn't have to wait long. I heard him take a deep breath and blow out the candle, then my Master was suddenly on me, molding his body to mine from behind.

"Fuck," he growled. "You're so God damn hot right now. I can feel it pouring from your skin. And you took it."

There was a certain awe in his voice that fed my submissive within. Pride within myself surged and I could almost feel myself blush.

"I told you I liked it. Will you do it again when you get back?"

"Oh, baby, I'll do it all the time. Whenever you want. Jesus, I have to have you."

His cock pushed into my opening while his hand reached underneath, grasping onto my tied wrists.

"You're going to be marked up so beautifully by the time I release you. I can't wait to run my fingers over each one while I hold you."

Tighter, his grip became, and I cried out as his cock plunged into my pussy. Where I expected slow and gentle from his words, I got the opposite. Hard, brutal thrusts sent me right into trying to stop my orgasm from coming too soon. His fingers raked over the hemp until he was scratching down my stomach.

"Tonight you come as many times as you can. No holding back." The brush over my clit combined with his words sent me into spasms almost immediately. Faster, he pounded, relentlessly slamming into me until I was screaming through the intensity of the euphoria he evoked. The room spun from the power of my orgasm and I let it while I tried to catch my breath.

"This might not be your favorite part, but you'll take it."

I couldn't process the words before I felt him begin peeling the wax from my back. At the pull, I clawed at the sheet.

"Jesus," I barely finished before he moved on to the next piece. The stinging was brief and I felt myself temporarily relax. The higher he got, the less painful it became. With each section he removed, the more I began to savor the attention. But I knew he was headed back down and I didn't worry until he got to the small of my back. I bit my lip while he dragged it out, taking his time. His cock slowed and I focused on how each inch filled me up before he withdrew, only to do it again. By the time he got to the wax on my ass and thighs, I was tingling all over. I could feel where the thin hair had been pulled and I couldn't get over how alive I felt.

"Time to flip over."

Zain pulled out and spun me over, pushing back between my legs. My fingers were almost numb from the weight. I flexed them, already feeling the blood rushing back. His gave them a good rub, teasing me even more with the long strokes. The half-smile he displayed caused me to move my hips down so I could get closer.

"Oh no. You stay right there. Let me look at you." My Master reached forward, caressing down my face as he stared into my eyes. "Tu ai-je jamais dit combien vous dire vraiment pour moi? Bientôt, je vais vous montrer. Tu ne aurez plus être mon esclave, mais ma femme. Mes toujours."

My world nearly stopped as I took in what he had said in French. I'd never heard him speak anything but Arabic and I'd been lost then, but this…this I could understand. *Have I ever told you how much you truly mean to me? Soon, I'll show you. No longer will you be my slave, but my wife. My always.*

Something flared behind his eyes as his head cocked to the side. "You know what I said."

I swallowed hard, nodding. "I speak French fluently."

The smile returned and he lowered, grasping my bound hands. "Then it's no secret. I want you, Lilian. Always. I mean to make that happen. Not too soon, but within the next year or two. If you agree, I want us to get married."

Married. "In a year or two?"

His cock pushed into my entrance and I moaned while he inched in deeper. "Seems like a good enough amount of time. You can adjust and get better while we get to know each other even more."

I opened my mouth to speak when he plunged all the way in, leaving me in a frozen state. Remembering what I'd wanted to say became difficult. His thrusts increased, but stayed relatively slow. Muscles flexed in his arms and shoulders while he worked his hips, sending me into even more of a blissful fog.

"Tell me what you think. Is the thought even appealing to you?" His voice was deep and rich with pleasure. I forced my mind to clear enough to answer.

"Two years is too long. A year even seems like forever."

"So, you like the idea of it then?"

I met his kiss, sucking his bottom lip into my mouth. A growl had him pushing his cock in even deeper.

"It more than appeals. I want it. I want you."

"You have me. God, slave, I'm fucking yours. Right here," he said, tapping his chest, "this belongs to you. When I died on that table, they may as well have taken it out and given it to you. You're all I saw. All I knew."

The deep, red scar that covered his chest was something I could hardly take in. He'd almost died because of me. Had…died. If he hadn't come back. If he didn't come back this time…

"Marry me sooner. Marry me now. Before you leave."

The thrusts stopped and the seriousness on his face made the room sound eerily quiet. Seconds went by while he stared.

"Lilian…"

"Please. What if something happens? What if—"

His hand covered my mouth. "Don't say it. I'll be back. And we'll talk more about this then."

The moment his hand lifted, I couldn't stop from arguing. "Marry me now. Tonight."

A groan had him slamming his cock into me. "I can't."

"Why not? You can. We'll go to Vegas. We'll get married the moment we get there and you can still leave by tomorrow."

Zain's hand came back down to silence me and still, he pounded harder. "You're making this impossible," he groaned out. "Do you think I don't want you as my wife right now? Fuck, I do, slave, but I can't. I gave your brother my word that we wouldn't rush. You know I can't break that."

A sound of frustration pushed against my throat and I tossed my head back and forth, sinking my teeth into my Master's hand. His eyes narrowed, but he stayed silent as I let go.

"Damn you for doing that. This is our lives, not Slade's. Between the two of you, you're going to drive me insane. Now, just…"

"What? Fuck you? Oh, honey, I'm going to. No one is more pissed about this than me. If I had any idea you would have even teased the idea of marriage, I would have never promised."

I could have screamed for as angry as I was, but I let the slamming thrusts take over, erasing how my brother seemed to be manipulating us all. But I knew his reasons. He wanted to make sure Zain was the one and I had to admit, he was a lot smarter than

I gave him credit for. He was right to force us both in the corner. Unless we defied Slade, we were at his mercy.

"Hey, right here." His fingers clasped onto my jaw as he brought my attention back to him. My face jerked, challenging him, trying to drag out whatever else he was hiding. At the tighter squeezing, he dove down, crushing his mouth to mine. The hold eased and he moved further down until he had my neck in his hold. Air faded, drawing me back to the moments where he held, but never stole, my oxygen. Now, I knew just how much he wanted to. There were times he'd applied pressure but never like he did now.

I tried to move, tempting his darkness. His other hand rose and locked in my hair, making me immobile. Oxygen was almost nonexistent and my sudden rush of fear had me fighting harder. His hand rose, slapping against my cheek in a steady tap.

"You fucking do it for me," he said, going back to holding my face and kissing me. I felt my arousal shoot through the roof as his finger pushed into my mouth and his tongue traced over it, circling around my lips. "I want your pussy tightening around my cock again."

The rotation of his hips had the friction against my clit, sending me right to the brink. Over and over, he pushed up against me until I was almost screaming from pleasure.

"Come, baby girl. Give me what I want."

With one last thrust, I arched and felt myself jerking from the sensitivity. My orgasm sent me rocking with his increased speed and I did scream as wave after wave, he drew out my release. The swelling of his cock had me moaning and I met his tongue as he kissed me, then shot his cum deep within my pussy.

"God," he growled, slamming into me harder as he finished. For seconds, he didn't move. Sweat dripped onto my breast and his finger traced it over my skin. "Ropes off. Then, we go again. I'm not wasting a moment of the time we have together.

Chapter 36
Zain

Leaving my slave was the one of the hardest things I'd ever done. The tears, the fear in her eyes as she held and looked up at me, were forever going to haunt my memories. I didn't want to do this. Not really. I wanted my uncles dead, but I didn't want to leave Lily to do it. Life was never going to be easy. I had to just suck it up and get this over with. The faster I killed off my uncles, the sooner I'd be back to my new life.

God, had she really tried to convince me to marry her last night? As I stared up at Slade, I felt the top of my lip pull back in distaste. Yeah, she sure as hell had, and here we were...*not* married. Not honeymooning in Vegas. All because of the man before me.

I brought my attention back to my slave and pressed my lips against her again. "Give me a minute?"

She nodded and I looked back at Slade. The way his eyes narrowed told me he was cautious. He was probably plotting his next move to get me further away from his sister.

"Can I have a word with you?"

Slade glanced at Blake, who stood behind me, and turned, heading toward his office. I followed, shutting the door behind me.

"You're in a very pissy mood, Zain. It may be my imagination, but I don't think so. If I didn't know better, I'd say it was aimed toward me."

My arms crossed over my chest as I stared at him. "No, you have it right. I'm pretty upset and it revolves around you."

"Why is that?" Slade sat on the edge of his desk, holding the overhanging. The longer I let it linger in my mind, the worse it got.

"Lily wanted me to go to Vegas with her last night. She wanted to get married before I left. I had to tell her no." The last word had my tone deepening. Slade stiffened and I could tell he was trying to act like my news didn't affect him, but I knew true fear when I saw it.

"No one in their right mind tells the person they love no when it comes to something that big. I would have married her in a heartbeat, had I not given you my word. If something happens and I missed my chance to ever call her my wife, so help me, I'm coming back to haunt your ass."

He glanced to the floor, only to bring his attention back up. When he did, he was fully composed. "Rushing into marriage after such a short amount of time isn't going to benefit either one of you. Trust me when I say you'll be glad you waited."

My head shook and I moved my hands to rest on my hips. "You haven't given me a reason to trust you yet. I thought I might be able to, but your ploy to get me further away from Lilian had that disappearing. You're up to something and I don't like it. If you're trying to push me away, I'm telling you now, it won't work. Lily is mine and nothing or no one will change that."

I went to spin around to leave, when I halted and walked closer instead. "Just so you know, I'm buying her a ring when I get back. *When* I propose isn't decided yet, but I'll be ready. I suggest you get ready, too, because I'll be asking her soon. That doesn't mean we'll rush to get married, but she will be my fiancée, if she chooses to be."

Slade sat quietly as I headed out the door and made my way back to my slave. It was so hard watching her try to hold herself together. Knowing how she tried to act tough, when I knew she was breaking inside, was the worst. "I have to get going. I'm going to miss you."

Her arms flew around my neck and I hugged her tightly. As my eyes closed, I took in her smell and the feel of her body against mine. Three days tops. That's all I'd allow myself. I couldn't be separated from her longer than that.

"Be careful," she whispered. "I love you."

"I love you, too." I pulled back, kissing her one last time before I forced myself to let go and leave. The door shutting behind Blake had me going straight to the elevator and pushing the button. I didn't want to remember her cries. The feel of the sobs shaking her body this morning almost had me changing my mind.

I turned to Blake as I waited. So clearly, I could see his knowledge of where I was at. He knew I didn't want to go. From the thin, set lips, to the slightly narrowed eyes, he was reading me like an open book and I hated being that exposed.

At the ding, I walked to the car robotically and held the metal rail as an anchor to keep myself from rushing back in and taking Lily home. My head lowered and I waited for the doors to close.

"We haven't left yet. You can still stay. I'm more than capable of taking care of this, you know. I *do* have a partner. All it will take is a phone call. He'll be ready in no time."

My head shook while I held on tighter. "No. This has to be me. When Saul dies, it'll be by my hand and my hand only. He took a life that belonged to me. That I created. Now he owes me his. There can be no other way."

"So be it." Blake hit the button to the parking garage and I made myself get into my killer mindset. Lily would be waiting for me. If I was going to get back to her, I needed to focus on the task at hand. It was who I was. What I'd been raised for. Death would be coming for those who deserved it and I couldn't wait to deliver.

A slight jolt had the door opening and we headed to his SUV. Lights flashed from him unlocking it and I didn't hesitate to climb inside. Before I realized what was happening, fingers laced into my hair, jerking back, and there was a knife at my throat. I didn't think. Instincts kicked in and he wasn't even finished adjusting the blade against my skin before I grabbed his wrist and twisted. I spun, drawing my gun from my waistband and pulling his arm forward, using it to bring myself closer so I could press the barrel against his temple. Voices sounded distorted and nothing was making sense. All I knew was the pretty-boy who stared back at me only inches away. He was stuck next to the headrest, trapped by my grip and he was all I could see. My finger was already tightening on the trigger and I had to calm myself past the defenses I'd naturally thrown up.

"Chill, he was just testing you." Blake's voice broke through my wall and I threw a glance at him before moving back to the one who didn't look the least bit afraid. There was a lack of emotion in his eyes. The void drew me in until I had to blink past it. For someone who was extremely attractive, he was practically gone on the inside. The realization had my finger not quite wanting to move from its ready state.

"He's good. Better than you let on." The stranger tried looking at Blake, but settled back on me. "I'm Preston, Blake's partner."

"Partner?" Of course. Blake wouldn't bring anyone close he didn't trust. And with what he did for a living, he'd have to find someone almost just like him. I let go, watching him move back on the seat. "This was supposed to be just me and you. It's bad enough taking one person in, but two? You don't know what you're getting yourselves into and I'm the one who'll be responsible when one of you dies."

A snort came from the back and I glared at Preston.

"No one's going to die," he said, shaking his head.

"You don't know that. I've been raised with these people. I've trained with them. They're deadly and to dismiss that will be your biggest mistake."

Blake turned over the engine and pulled out of the parking space. "No one is going to die, Zain. Just buckle up and listen to Preston."

The dimness of the garage gave way as we pulled onto the road. I kept myself turned in my seat, watching as Preston pulled a laptop from the floor and opened it. The clicking had me curious. What had they found that made them think we'd get in and out without a problem? I knew my father. Knew the security system he'd had installed inside and out. After all, I'd helped build the thing.

"Saul, that's one of your uncles, correct?"

My adrenaline spiked at hearing his name and rage left my hands flexing into fists. "Yeah."

Preston peered up from the monitor. "He's pretty much taken over for, I'm assuming, your father. He just left a meeting with a man we've been watching for a while. Reynaldo Pena. Ever heard of him?"

The name had my stomach turning. "He's in charge of shipping the girls out of Cuba. It's one of many stops and he's one of the men I know in the business."

"Men you'll be handing over to me," Blake said, glancing over. "You already provided a few names, but I want them all. Every single one."

"You and Gaige, both," I breathed out. The information was a ticket to a new life. To a no strings attached free pass and I planned on taking it.

Blake glanced over. "Feel free to give them to him, too, but I won't be waiting around until they get their evidence to make any arrests. Preston and I will do just fine taking care of these shitbags and making sure they get what they deserve."

I had no doubt he meant that. Preston turned the screen and I watched a slideshow of pictures begin. All of Saul standing outside of Reynaldo's home. One I'd only been to at my father's request. The man may have made a lot of money selling off girls, but he had a hell of a hard time paying his debts.

"Saul won't be there for you to kill, Zain. Figuring out if or when he plans to return just might be impossible."

Frustration had me almost slamming my fist into the dashboard. Somehow, Saul always seemed to slip under my radar and I couldn't stand knowing I was headed there when he might not be going back anytime soon. He'd disappeared a handful of times over my life and sometimes it lasted months, even years.

"What about Adul?"

Preston glanced down at the screen "Your other uncle is there, but I can't say we've really picked up on him doing anything. Hell, we really can't find a damn thing on him."

"Nor will you. He's guilty of shit, though. Just nothing in the trafficking world except keeping and killing slaves. He dies. Eye for an eye."

I left it at that and it didn't take long for us to near the airport. We all kept quiet until we loaded onto Blake's private jet. The luxurious set up of leather coaches and screens were hard to appreciate once my attention was stolen by the multiple pictures and corkboards covering the walls. My mouth separated as I walked forward, taking them all in. Some had a red mark over the faces and I could only imagine that those were the ones they'd already killed off.

"Holy shit," I breathed out.

"Indeed." Blake took a seat on one of the recliners, staring at me instead of around the room. While Preston sat closer to the door, I relaxed on the sofa. But I didn't stay so for long. The double-take I did had my heart dropping. Each face on the wall represented a wanted man. A dead man, either now or in the future. So, why, resting above Blake, was my picture on the wall?

Chapter 37
Lily

I held my purse close to my side while I sat and waited for my brother's rant to end. For an hour, he'd vented his frustration over me trying to convince Zain to run away and get married. I knew he was just about finished. The rage was dissipating and true concern had him shaking his head at me.

"What did we talk about not hours before you asked him, Lilian? I told you to trust me. To let me prove to you that Zain was the one. You agreed. Why go out and try to get him to elope after our talk?"

My gaze lifted to his. "I told you, I love him. Maybe we *should* wait. Maybe it was stupid to try to get him to marry me, but I didn't think so in the moment. I still don't. What are you planning to prove? Whether he's stable? He is. He'll adjust to society. Everything between us will work out just fine and if we have problems, we'll handle them like adults. There's nothing either of us are going to do to jeopardize each other's future."

"That's what you may think now. But you don't know that, Lily. No one does."

"Exactly. Including you." I pushed up from the chair. "What does it matter anyway? We didn't get married, nor will be probably for quite some time. My Master—" Nausea swept over me at my mistake and I took a step back from my brother as his eyes flared, only to narrow. If I'd ever seen Slade's temper spark, apparently I hadn't witnessed it to this degree.

"Your...*what*?"

My head shook and no matter how much I wanted to cower, I forced myself to stand taller. "Nothing."

One step. Two. The closer Slade got, the faster my heart raced.

"You...will *never* refer to him as that again. Ever," he roared. "You may have been a slave once before, Lily, but you are far from that now. To think that that's where your mind goes when you think of him, I'm not so sure I want this for you, despite what he proves to me."

Words...nothing came as I felt the train wreck of my life come to an explosive end. Why had I done that? Where had it even come from?

"What I need for my mind does not warrant your approval, nor what I need in my life. Remember that."

"Are you threatening me?" Slade only grew angrier and I was at a loss on how to mend this. Was it even fixable?

I eased my purse to the ground and took off the white blazer I wore. The black shirt underneath was sleeveless and I glanced down at my arms before lifting them in Slade's direction. The scars stood out in contrast to my skin, but he didn't see them. Not when he was forcing himself to look at my face.

"I'm going to tell you a story. The story of a slave who was saved by her Master."

"Lilian," he growled. The threat was there, but I continued.

"It all began from darkness. You see, I was drugged when they brought me to Afghanistan. Drugged and raped by four men. My virginity was gone, brutally and viciously. I awoke long before I opened my eyes. The foreign language that was spoken around me had me praying for death. As I laid there and let what had happened to me sink in, I never wanted to breathe another breath. I was terrified, yet dead already, at least on the inside. Or so I thought."

Slade stayed quiet, a mix of emotions of his face that I couldn't even read. Sadness, pain...yet nothingness. I made myself continue.

"When we arrived at Amir's palace, I was even more confused than when I was trying to figure out what was going to become of my life. After all, why would someone that rich need me? I was ruined. Soiled from what had happened. I truly believed that if I survived and somehow escaped, no one would ever want me after the rapes. Hell, I didn't even want myself." My hand moved, as if to shove away the memory of how gone I was in those moments. "While two other girls and I were led inside, I tried to study everything. My brain was fuzzy and I can remember my tongue feeling thick in my mouth. I could barely swallow. Barely walk.

"I was taken to a man I remember being terrified of. I feared he'd be the one I was meant for, but he wasn't. That was when he took me to Zain. I was told that he was my Master and I was his slave. I was a gift for everything he'd done and although I didn't view myself as belonging to him at the time, I quickly realized that the only reason he'd accepted me was to spare my life. He didn't want me, Slade. Not like that. He saved me. Where girls were constantly dying because of their beatings, he tried to protect me from anyone who got too close. He made me wear a wrap around my face so I wouldn't attract attention. Whenever I had to go to the restroom or take a shower, he stood outside the door and guarded me."

Memories took over my vision and I let them. "Even though he was...harsh, at first, I could see that he was so sad. So...broken, just like I was. Our lives there were nothing short of being prisoners. Even though he was Amir's son, he was still a captive. His back and legs bear so many more scars

than I will *ever* carry. If you could only see what
I have, live through what we were made to, you'd
understand why I have so much faith and trust in
Zain. The whole time we were together, we clung to
one another. I was his light where all he'd known for
so long was dark. We fell in love, fast and hard."

Slade came back into view as the images
subsided. He was staring at my arms, a blank look
on his face.

"It happened, Slade, whether you want to
believe it or not. I was a slave. *His* slave, and I will
not shy away from that. It saved my life. All of these
claw marks you see were someone's sister or
daughter. Maybe even someone's wife. I could still
be gone right now. Dead, even. So when you get
mad at me for slipping and speaking the words of
my past, that should just show you how comfortable
I am around you. Enough so that I let the mistake
fall through my cracks. I try to hide what happened
to me from everyone. The last person I want to know
what I experienced is you. But I am who I am now
because of being taken and if I had to change it and
forget I ever met Zain, I'd choose to go through hell
all over again. Listen to me when I tell you, for the
millionth time...*I love him*. Keep that in mind when
you're conducting this plan you've convinced me to
go through."

A sniffle had me turning. Mary wiped the tears
from her cheek and I slid my blazer back on and

reached down for my purse. I didn't want this to be some hug-fest or for them to tell me they were sorry for what I'd gone through. My brother just needed to know where I stood. I wouldn't be letting Zain go and no one or nothing was going to stop me from being with him.

"I have to go. I'm meeting Gaige's wife, Elle, at the coffee shop down the road. I shouldn't be gone more than an hour. Brace will be going with me."

Silence followed me to the door and I was thankful for it, but I didn't miss Mary's voice echo through the moment I shut it.

"Slade, what did you do?"

The sadness was still in her voice and I tried to push it from my head as I met Brace halfway and we got on the elevator. Soft classical music filled the space and I looked over to him, raising one of my eyebrows. Trying anything to erase what had just happened. The slight smile had me mirroring his. If there was one thing I could count on, it was my silent giant. He had always been there for me. Just like Marcio.

"You up for some shopping later? There are some things I need to pick up and I could use your help."

He shrugged and nodded. "Fresh air would do me some good. What sort of shopping?"

"Furniture shopping, amongst other things. I have a house to decorate and I want to keep it feminine, yet manly. I'm sure you can help me with that."

"Zain's? Or are you thinking about leasing your own place? Doesn't seem like you've been getting along so well with your brother since he's been back."

The elevator doors opened and we walked through the busy lobby. Cool air rushed into my face and I hugged my arms to my chest, cursing the fact that I didn't grab a jacket. I looked over at Brace while I let his question tempt me. "Zain's. There's no point in me getting a place when I'm just going to eventually move in with him anyway."

Brace stayed at my side while we walked at a fast pace. The jacket he put on my shoulders had me hugging to it tightly, even if it did swallow me.

As we waited for the crosswalk light to change, I couldn't help but wonder how my brother's and Mary's conversation was going. What did Slade think about what I'd told him? I knew he was aware that I'd been raped, but the number of how many times had never been revealed. I kept the numbers out the courts, along with being drugged. They'd only gotten the necessities out of me and even that had been hard for them to do.

"Brace, do you think—"

Squealing tires had my words freezing in my mouth. My hand instinctively reached out to my guard as I prepared for…what, I wasn't sure. Being taken again? In that moment, all I knew was fear like I'd never felt before. The buildings swayed, warping around me in a wave, and sound disappeared as my pulse took over every inch of my body. The thumping became a life of its own, rocking me with the steady rhythm.

"Just a red light. You okay?" Brace's arm was around my shoulder, yet I never felt him step closer. My skin tingled and I attempted to slow down my breathing.

"Fine. I don't know what happened. I just…"

"You're pale. I think we should head back."

The crosswalk light came on and I took a step forward. "No, let's go." With each foot of distance I covered toward the coffee shop, I felt myself grow even more aware of my surroundings. The buzz of voices was almost nonexistent. Car engines decreased and then revved as they zoomed by. Sweat was starting to cover my skin and I handed back over the jacket, not able to bear the weight any longer. The faster I got this over with, the quicker I could get back home. I suddenly needed the security of my walls. They'd help this episode pass.

A soft bell sounded as I pushed open the door and glanced around the small space, almost wanting to rush back out. People sat with their laptops or tablets in front of them. Some were in line. A blonde with long, wavy hair motioned with her hand and the smile she gave me was genuinely nice. She was beautiful and tall. Inches taller than me and Mary.

"I'll order your latte."

"Thank, Brace." Had I still been holding onto him? My hand disconnected with his wrist and he pretended not to notice while I tried to decipher what was happening. My goal had been to become strong. I'd started training again. Taken the pills as prescribed to sleep at night, which were working, but were they? It was as if my nightmares were now creeping into my everyday life. Would it go away?

"You must be Elle." I met her halfway, shaking her hand, and following her back to the table. Again, I scanned the area before coming back to her happy face. Her eyes immediately drew me in. The color was almost teal. So bright and grabbing that it took me a moment to process her words.

"Oh, yes, I'm Lily. Sorry. I was...thinking."

A soft laugh filled the space as her hands gripped around the coffee's Styrofoam cup. "It's okay. I do that a lot. So, Gaige tells me you've been trafficked before." Her words were slow, quiet, and very careful. Hearing the correct term left me even more anxious.

"Yes. Once, a few years back. I was taken again not that long ago, but that was under different circumstances. But it was by the same people that were linked to my situation before." How messed up did that sound? I repeated what I'd said through my head, trying not to dwell on how it made me feel.

"I'm sorry." Elle glanced toward Brace, but brought her gaze back to me. "You're lucky they found you. Usually, the second time a woman is taken, she doesn't fare that well. How are you?"

Everything in me screamed to say that I was perfectly okay and bouncing back, but I knew that was a lie. I was here for a reason.

"Not good." My head lowered. "The nightmares are better now that I've been put on sleeping pills, but I'm...scared." As I rose to meet her eyes, I felt as though I could tell her anything. That didn't happen often with the people that usually surrounded me. I had a hard enough time talking to my therapist. I sighed, pushing myself to continue. "I heard someone braking just before we made it in here and the sound set me off. That's never happened before. Not like that."

Her gaze lowered and the cup turned from the push of her fingers. "I think we're all triggered by certain things. Brakes get me, too. Vans or SUVs stopping next to me, even more so. Years may ease the fear we feel, but I don't think it'll ever quite go away. We'll always be more aware of the little things most people don't even give second thought to. My best method of coping comes from the work I do at the organization. It helps."

"I looked at the website earlier. I'd like to contribute in some way. Whatever I can do."

Elle glanced up as Brace neared the table. I took the latte and watched as he went a few tables over, sipping on his coffee.

"We're always taking on volunteers. Why don't you come by in a few days and check things out? See what you think. If you find it to be too stressing, there's always other ways to help, too."

A pamphlet was pulled from her purse and I took it, glancing through the pages as she continued.

"There are several forms of trafficking we associate ourselves with, but I focus mainly on the cases more…severe. Ones like ours. International. But you'd be surprised how rare that's becoming. The US has seen a major increase over the years on the number of women who are made to become slaves right here in the United States. It's a frightening epidemic. One that I'm afraid is going to get a lot worse before we can make it better."

My lips separated and I grabbed the table for some form of stability. "Here? I don't understand. How is that possible?"

"Well, most of the boys and girls are young. Junior High age and up. Some even younger. They're taken and fear is instilled to the point of them being too afraid to reach out for help.

Sometimes drugs are administered for dependency. They're made to prostitute to numerous men on a daily basis. In hotels, truck stops…there are things I've heard that would turn your stomach. We try to do everything we can, but like I said, the numbers are growing at a very alarming rate."

"I had no idea."

Elle took a drink, keeping her focus on me. "Not very many people do. And when they hear about it, most think they'll never be affected by trafficking. I just wish they would see how bad this situation really is."

"Yeah," I said, lowly. My mind was going while I tried to figure out a way to cause awareness. There had to be something I could do. Something that went beyond the norm. A billboard? Was there already one? Maybe if I had ten posted up. One hundred? Maybe a commercial?

A horn blasted outside and I jumped, my vision distorting. Elle faded out as the honking increased in volume. God, I was swaying. I felt sick. Over and over, I could feel my restrained self rock back and forth. Arabic yelling broke through and repeatedly the horn blew. I tried curling more into myself, but the ropes were too tight, restricting most of my movement. The smell of sweat and blood assaulted me and I gagged. My mouth was already full of something. Cloth.

"Lily? Lily." The voice grew louder and my gasps were the first thing that came to light. Elle's eyes were wide. She was standing before me and Brace was kneeling on my other side. Pain flared at my scorched hand and the Styrofoam cup I'd been drinking from was crushed in my palm. Instinct had me pushing to my feet at the agony that had taken over my skin. "Let's get her to ER."

I nearly tripped over the chair behind me at Elle's words. "No, I'm fine now. I want to go home." My response sounded slurred. Loud. God, was my tongue swollen like before when I'd been drugged? Suddenly, I couldn't breathe at the realization that I had relived my first moments awake in Afghanistan. "Thank you for meeting me." I spun, already heading for the door. Brace's arm went around me and he led me to the left. I almost fought, but his voice had the urge easing.

"Let's wash your hand first. It'll stop some of the pain."

He pushed the men's door open and pulled me through at a fast pace. The cold water had it soothing on impact, but what followed had me wincing. It wasn't too bad. Reddened, but the skin wasn't missing.

"Fuck, get me home." A sob escaped and I tried my best to hold it in.

"We're going, sweetie. Come on." His arm held on tight as he pushed open the door and the cold air rushed to meet us. "Put this on." The jacket was already being placed around me and I accepted it gladly. With the temperature difference, the shakes turned into full-blown trembling. My jaw chattered and my legs felt weighted down. Each step was harder than the last.

Traffic zoomed through the light and I closed my eyes, trying to make myself disappear from the hectic everyday bustle of the city. A hand pressed over my ear and Brace pushed my head into his side. When we started walking again, I kept myself closed off, trusting his direction. Forever seemed to go by and yet, only seconds. We came to a stop and his hand removed. My eyes opened and I unlocked my fingers from his shirt. The elevator was before me and I stood straighter, catching my reflection as the door opened. Shit, I was so pale. I looked so rattled.

"He'll know."

"Slade needs to," Brace weighed in. "And you'll tell him."

Chapter 38
Zain

"So, let's go over this one more time." Blake paced in front of the sofa, the notepad full of names I gave him, smacking against his palm. "You're one hundred percent positive that you have never dealt in the trafficking of humans, male or female?"

My gaze had him coming to a stop. "I've said no three times. The only deal I was supposed to be a part of was the one I botched. Do you seriously think I'd participate in something I was so openly against? I told you, I dealt on the money side of things. Collected debt, so forth."

"For *slaves*. And you accepted one to begin with." Preston had been quiet the majority of the time. I looked over to where he sat, throwing him a look that had a warning written all over it.

"Slaves were a very rare debt I had to collect on, but yes, amongst other things. And you watch how the hell you speak about Lily. I saved her life. To understand what it would have meant to decline is something beyond you. You were not raised in the same household, nor in the same culture."

Blake glanced down at the names. "If you hadn't been taken yourself at such a young age, I'd kill you so much as look at you. That's the only thing keeping you alive. That, and the fact that you didn't willingly, per se, carry on with the life you led. I believe you didn't have a lot of choices. I, for one, would have found a way out a lot sooner, but you're not me, and I didn't live your life. Perhaps I'm wrong on that account, too."

"You're right. You *haven't* lived my life. Every return to my father's could have been my last. I'm not afraid to die. What I am afraid of is leaving Lilian in a state of mind or place where she might not be safe. I couldn't have protected her dead. And I needed to know she was okay before I returned in her life. Buying my time to make sure I didn't fuck her up worse was the hardest fucking thing I've ever had to do. Do not, for a second, try to put yourself in my shoes. You don't deserve to be there! You'll never know what distancing myself did to either one of us."

My gaze cut over to Preston again. I couldn't stop the anger I had for both of them. I understood their dislike toward me, but it didn't mean I had to put up with it.

"Can we get off the damn plane now? We landed over an hour ago and we still have a long way to travel to even get there. I want this over with. I'll kill Adul and take care of Saul at the first opportunity that presents itself."

"I don't think so," Blake said, placing down the notepad. "You see, I didn't bring you for your help. I've got it covered. What I needed were those names. You being here," he said, gesturing around the interior, "was a great cover in case I didn't want you to return."

I stood, pulling my gun free from my waistband. "Well, you got what you wanted, but I didn't come all this way to chill out in your jet while you took care of my dirty work. This is *my* family. My responsibility. Not yours."

"Unfortunately for you, this is no longer a choice you get to make. My ass is covered if something happens. Yours isn't."

I moved my head in quick shake, signifying that I didn't care. "I'm going, that's final."

"I'm government protected. You're not."

Blake pushed a button on the coffee table and the lid lifted, exposing a mass of weapons. He put something small in his hand and stepped closer. I lifted the barrel, aiming it at his chest. "You take more step, I'll pull this trigger. I won't be hitting that vest either."

Preston moved to the side and I jerked the gun in his direction just in time to feel pain shoot through my thigh. The small dart was unmistakable. My eyes widened in surprise.

"Sleep well, my friend. Someday maybe you'll understand why it has to be this way."

The room flickered and time slowed. Darkness swept over me almost immediately and I could feel myself falling. I was out before I ever hit the floor.

****

"What's your name?"

Crying had me trying to force my eyes open, but for the life of me, I couldn't find the strength. Throbbing pounded against my temples and the need to gag was on the verge of pushing itself out.

"It hurts," a girl sobbed.

"I know, but we're going to get you all better soon. Drink this."

Preston's voice was calm, soothing. I groaned, finally seeing light flicker though as my eyes obeyed the commands in my mind. Lifting my head felt like the hardest thing in the world, but I somehow managed to hold it up long enough to see Blake sitting across from me, staring. A large scratch rested on one of his cheeks and there was blood soaked at the hem of his neckline.

"Wake up," Blake growled, lowly. "I have some questions and you're going to answer them."

Turbulence had me forcing my eyes back open. His threatening tone didn't.

"Just ask."

I heard him get closer before I processed the action. My fist clenched. If I would have had the power to swing, I would have clocked him good for what he'd done. Drugging me. Denying me what was so rightfully mine. It pissed me off to no end.

"I know what room was yours. You care to explain the chains mounted to your ceiling?"

My eyes closed at the pain and I rested my head back again. "That's none of your business and has nothing to do what you probably think it does. Since when is kink a crime?"

Silence.

"You don't believe me, ask Lilian," I continued. "Not that she should have to answer or be interrogated."

"Did you have those before she came to you?"

"Like I said, kink isn't a crime. It's just who I am. Are you going to call your government friends and get permission to off me, too?"

I lifted to catch his reaction but all I got was a hard stare. "I need no one's permission when it comes to who I take care of. I wasn't always government, Zain. They came to me not long ago and I still go by my rules. No one else's. All they want is names and I have no problem providing those. Luckily for you, I believe what you're telling me."

"I have nothing to hide." A groan left my mouth. "Did you kill my uncle?"

Blake glanced toward the three girls Preston was speaking with. "I did. Not nearly the way I would have liked. He killed one of them in front of us to prove that he'd do it again if we got any closer. Fucking coward. I've never lost a girl. Ever. God, I would have loved to just…" His jaw tightened and he looked toward the floor. "Anyway, they're all dead."

"All but one," I said, trying to force myself to sit up straighter. "And he *is* mine. If you take that from me, Blake…" My head shook as we stared into each other's eyes. "Don't."

"I gave you your revenge or did you forget? You killed the man who took you. This one—"

"Killed my child!" I yelled. "He's mine." My hands went to my head to try to balance the room. I was beginning to spin. To feel sick from not only whatever was in my system, but from the mere thought of not being able to finishing this.

Blake's face turned hard and he looked down, becoming quite. My stomach knotted at having to bare my painful past and a ragged breath left me. I felt drained and exhausted. All I wanted was to spill blood from my enemies or be with my slave. Not be in the presence of Blake and Preston.

Crying had me groaning and glancing over. I knew all three girls. Two, barely at all, but one for years. It immediately had my heart racing. She could help me. I switched to Arabic, knowing that was her primary language now. Russian was now part of her past. I wondered if she even knew how to speak it anymore.

"What is your name?"

There was a hesitancy, but she came closer. "Alina."

"Alina. That's a nice name. You knew my Lily. You remember?"

She took another step. "Your slave. Yes. She helped me."

"Yes," I said, smiling. "Lily always tried to take care of all of you." I swallowed back the bile as I moved to the edge of my seat. "It's time for me to help her. I need to find Saul and put a stop to him once and for all. Have you heard anything that could possibly help me?"

One look at the other girls and they all exuded the same fear.

"He can't hurt any of you anymore. Please. If you know something, you have to tell me."

The newest one began crying again and Preston threw me a look that clearly said to back off.

"I don't know where he is." Alina pulled at the wrap around her head and eased it off, revealing long brown hair. "When he learned of your father's death, he planned to make you pay. He said he wouldn't be back until it was done. But you're alive." Her voice quivered and I knew it must have been hard for her to defy the man she'd spent years fearing.

"Thank you, Alina."

I took the bottled water Blake held out and swallowed a big drink. "She doesn't know anything."

"You sure about that?"

"I just said it, didn't I? He left and vowed I would pay. She didn't expect him to return until the threat was carried out." Another groan had me collapsing to the sofa. All I wanted to do was go back to sleep, but I couldn't. Not yet. "How long have I been out?"

Blake sat down beside me. "For a while. Listen, I need you to read something for me. I could call it in, get someone to do it, but I don't want the hassle. I found it at your father's. Maybe it'll be of some help."

My head rolled in his direction and I reached out, taking the paper. The Arabic writing was so poorly scribbled, it took me a minute to decipher.

"Tell me why I should help you anymore than I already have. You tricked me. Lied to me. Stole part of my revenge. Shot me with a dart and drugged me. I feel like shit because of you."

His mouth twisted and he shrugged. "You're alive. Does that count for something?"

"No."

"I called your woman for you while you were out. How about that?"

A big thump in my chest had me sitting up "Now that might count. Tell me what she said and I'll decide if it's worth telling you over."

He sighed, dropping his hand in his lap. "She was asleep. I talked to Slade. Apparently, she had some sort of episode yesterday when she met Gaige's wife, who I happened to call and question for you, too, by the way."

I jumped to my feet, feeling nothing but panic set in. "Episode? What sort of episode?"

"He didn't say and apparently neither did she. From what Elle told me, I'm guessing some sort of flashback or something. Said Lily mentioned it happening on her way there. Something about the sound of brakes setting her off. Then a car honked and she froze up. Busted her coffee cup in her hand and didn't feel the burn until she snapped back to. If you ask me, I'd say she has PTSD, but I'm thinking you already know that."

Any form of sickness I felt didn't compare to the rage that overwhelmed me. "Get me the fuck home. Now," I roared. "It was pointless for me to leave to begin with. Now Lilian has to do this alone. No. I could have easily given you the names without your interrogation type settings. I could have done that while still being there with her." I paced, shaking my head, wanting nothing more than to rush back to San Francisco. Being trapped in a small ass room, I was losing my mind.

"The paper, what does it say?"

I turned on Blake, having to stop myself from ripping him off the sofa and pounding my fist into his face. My slave was alone. Probably scared out of her mind. She wouldn't open up to Slade or anyone else. She needed me and once again, I was unavailable.

I reached over, grabbing the water, but never breaking our eye contact. "It's an address. But you'll never know what it is from me if you don't promise me something right now."

Blake raised an eyebrow, not the least bit fazed. "And what's that?"

"When we get off this plane, you're finished with me. I know nothing more. My uncle will be handled, so you have nothing to worry about that. Just drop me off and go track down everyone else on that list. If you can give me your word, I'll tell you right now."

A bored expression faded and he shrugged. "Sure. Doesn't mean you'll never see me again, but I'll stop hassling you."

I wasn't sure how I felt about that, but if it bought me enough time, I'd take it. "It's the penthouse I was shot at. He'll be looking there to see if I stayed or not. When he does, I'll finish him off." It was the truth, but a lie concerning my uncle. He wouldn't go. He'd send someone to see if I still resided there. Regardless, any inquiry would lead me back to him.

"I'll have it verified. If you're telling the truth, you're off the hook. For now."

Chapter 39
Lily

The city lights blurred in a spinning motion, getting faster and faster as I stared up at the tall buildings. Laughter echoed around me and I knew it was Bethany's without even seeing her. Fear embedded deep within and I could feel tugging on my hand.

"Come on, Lily. We're going to be late."

A dark SUV was suddenly before me and I jerked back, turning to try to run. Suddenly, I felt so young. So naïve and stupid. What was I doing here, again? Bethany was trying to take me and I was going?

"Lily, hurry, you're going to make your Master upset. He's waiting."

More tugging had me pulling with everything I was capable of.

"Get away from me. I don't want to go."

Long blonde hair billowed out around me and I knew I was falling back. Falling with Bethany on top of me. Hitting the sidewalk never registered. All I could feel was her weight as she wrestled with me. Hands grabbed my feet and I screamed. They had

*me. I knew in my heart they were going to take
me again and this time, I'd never be saved. I was as
good as dead. She'd kill me. Saul would kill me.*

*His deep voice was suddenly filling my ears
and my mind told me he was the one holding my
ankles. I cried, clawing with my hands to try to get
Bethany off of me so I could run, but with every
movement I made, she grasped me tighter. And I was
moving down. Closer to the SUV.*

"Baby, wake up. Lily."

"No." My arms flew out, finally free from the
restraint. Blindly, I fought, throwing myself to the
side.

"Lilian." The tone registered and I felt myself
still. Light broke through and I blinked past the
dimness.

Zain was sitting on the side of the bed, worry
filling his face as he stared at me. His hands reached
out and I didn't hesitate to throw myself into them.
Sobs left me and the events from the café had me
breaking down even more.

"Shh, baby girl. I'm back now."

"Something is wrong with me. I can't stop
them no matter how hard I try." My broken voice
only made my anxiety worse. Something deep
within was shattered and I wasn't sure I'd ever get
myself together this time. "I'm so scared. Don't
leave me tonight. Please? I can't do this."

One minute, I was holding on to Zain. The next, he was pulling me into his lap. The cradling was a relief...until I saw my brother standing at the door. My head lifted and I wiped away the tears, unsure of how I should act. Who the fuck was I that I was looking for everyone else's direction but my own? My therapist, my brother, my Master. Where was Lily? *Who was Lily?*

Slade stepped back, giving me a look I couldn't comprehend, only to turn and walk away. I curled into Zain's chest, trying not to think too much about anything but feeling safe.

"I missed you." His kiss to my forehead only put me more at ease.

"I missed you, too."

He pulled back to look down at me. "What happened when I was gone? I heard you hurt your hand."

My hand flexed and I pulled it closer toward me. "I was suddenly there again, on my way to your father's. I could hear the men honking and speaking in a language I couldn't understand. It was real. I could have sworn I was there."

A sigh left him and he brought me in closer.

"Why is this happening? Why now?" I said, trying to stop the tears. I was over being weak. Each episode that brought me down was making me internally worse.

"I don't know. Probably because it's almost happening all over again. Maybe because I'm back in the picture. My family. I don't know," he repeated, under his breath. "We're going to get you better though, I promise."

Zain placed me on the bed, covering me up. As he moved in beside me, on top of the covers, we held on to each other. I got lost in my thoughts, barely noticing that the sun was already starting to rise.

"I wanted to go back to work today. I thought it would help."

"After what you just woke from?"

The nightmare had been one of many I'd always had. It was a repeat and although I wasn't too afraid of it after I woke, during was a different story.

"This is routine, believe it or not. At least, to an extent. I'll be fine."

My body was pulled deeper into his and I smiled as he snuggled against me. "Maybe you're right. Going back might help. Then again, it might make it worse."

"I'm going to leave early. I see my therapist at one. After she heard of my episode, she wanted to see me at my earliest convenience. It'll have to do until I find another I like better."

"Yes, I want you to go. I'll get the address from your brother and meet you there. I can wait in the lobby until you're finished."

My head drew back. "You'd do that? Just come to wait outside?"

"Of course." His eyebrows drew in. "Why wouldn't I? I told you I was going to take care of you. Even if I can't be in the room, I can be there to support you when you're finished."

Warmth rushed through my chest and I reached up, sliding my palm over his rough cheek. "Thank you. You don't know much that means to me."

"That's what people do when they love each other. And I love you." His lips brushed against mine and it was amazing how fast I could feel myself bounce back. His presence made me stronger. Made me believe that I could overcome anything.

"How did the trip go? Did you..." I trailed off, waiting for the good news. If he was here and well, that meant something. The way his features hardened had me lifting my head. "What happened?"

"Blake is what happened," he said, deeply. "But Adul is taken care of and so are the guards that were in that house. Saul wasn't there." He paused. "They did manage to get three of the girls out, though."

"Oh, thank God." A sigh of relief left me, but my head shook, thinking about Saul. Zain's hand reached up, rubbing the length of mine. "No worrying, slave, he's not going to hurt you. You're well protected. We'll just be sure to keep an open eye out. You trust me?"

"Yes," I breathed out.

"Good. Then why don't you get up and start getting ready for work? I'll go make you breakfast."

At the final kiss, he stood and I followed suit, watching him leave the room. I wasn't sure what he had planned for Saul, but if I knew my Master, he was keeping information to himself to protect me. It only meant that I needed to focus on getting better and step up my game. I would not be afraid. People with PTSD overcame their obstacles every day. I just had to stay positive and forge ahead. I'd done it once. I could do it again.

I opened my closet, pulling out a pair of black slacks, a white and gold button up shirt, and a gold belt to match. The boots I removed from the bottom were stilettos and I threw my black half trench on the bed for when I was ready. Showering didn't take long and after I blow dried, fixed my hair, and put make-up on, I was rushing into the kitchen. The smell of coffee nearly had me moaning.

"You look better." Slade's voice had me peering over to the dining room area where he sat, sipping on coffee. The paper was resting in one hand and he was already dressed in his suit.

"Thank you. So do you. Are you going in today?"

The paper rustled as he set it down on the table. "Yeah, there are a few things I need to take care of. I hear Volstin is ripe for the picking and I want them."

A smile came to my face. "Then you'll have them. I'll get together with Willard and we'll look over the numbers, see what we're working with. Alec..." My stomach dropped and I pressed my hand against it, trying to stop the flip-flopping. "Whoever has taken over for him will try to beat us to it. We'll have to act fast."

Zain walked over, handing me a glass of juice. "You okay?"

"Yeah, I think so. I forgot. God, how did I forget that?"

"It happens." He led me to the table. "Sit while I grab your plate."

I took a deep breath, meeting Slade's blank expression. Something was there just behind his eyes, but I couldn't read it.

"We'll get it. Money talks and so do you. You may be new to this and less experienced when it comes to the dealings, but you're the best. I wouldn't have let you move up as fast as I did if that weren't the case. You've got this, Lily. You're a Roberts. We get what we want."

A small laughed escaped and I took a drink. "What I want is normalcy. I don't see that happening for quite some time."

"But it'll happen. Just give it time. That'll be your worst enemy right now," Slade said.

Zain placed a plate in front of me with fruit and a bowl of oatmeal. I threw him a smile while he sat down next to me with his own breakfast.

"What do I do? I can't just sit around doing nothing. You still going to hire me?"

The men looked at each other and Slade took a drink of his coffee, continuing to stare. When he placed it down, he sat up taller. "Come in at nine. You can follow me around for the day. I'll show you the different departments and let Richard introduce you to your new desk and what you'll be doing.

Zain nodded and I went back to trying to eat. The meal went by in mostly silence and I pushed from the table, only for my Master to take my plate before I could stand completely.

"I'm going to go ahead and take off to work." I turned from my brother's acknowledgement and walked Zain into the kitchen. "I guess I'll be seeing you in the office then. What are you going to do in the mean time?"

I grabbed my purse from the bar, looking down at my watch. It was still early, barely past seven.

"My clothes are at the house. I'll swing by there and get dressed. I'll meet Slade there. That way I'll have the car. You want to ride with me to the appointment?"

I smiled, nodding. "I'd like that."

"Then it's done. I'll see you soon."

Zain opened the door for me and Brace was already waiting. I eased out, giving him a small wave before he closed it. From what I thought was going to be a horrible start to the morning had turned out better than I could have hoped. The ride down the elevator and to work went by in a haze as I relaxed into what I was hoping would be routine. Maybe Zain could come by and pick me up for work every day. Now that my car was actually being put to good use, it would be nice to ride in it. I hated driving and didn't mind him stepping up. It could work. At least, I liked to think it could.

The car pulled in front of Slade Industries and it took me a second to realize we'd already arrived. My door was opened and I took a deep breath as I stepped out and straightened my shoulders. There was no room for my submissive nature here. Not with the role I played. I had to remember that. Too many people looked to me for direction. To show weakness would get me eaten alive.

"Morning, Ms. Roberts."

"Morning, Chan." I kept walking, passing the metal detectors, and heading to the elevator being held open for me. Brace was already by my side, Caleb opposite of him, flanking the back. I knew this routine. Thrived in it now that I wasn't looking for a reason to drop my guard. "Zain and I will leave for my appointment at one. Follow and stay close behind. Watch everything," I said to Brace, lowly. "We're not out of the woods yet. I'm sure you already know that, though."

He nodded and I forced a smile for him as I stepped onto the elevator car. The moment the doors shut, I let my shoulders sag, even if for the briefest moment. I trusted Zain to protect me, but I also knew I could be a distraction. He had a lot on his mind and his uncle wanted him dead. I wasn't going to risk anything. Not concerning him.

Ding.

An empty room full of cubicles met me and I headed to the lounge to start the coffee. As I waited for it to be done, I could hear people beginning to file in. Some placed food in the fridge, keeping their heads down or gave a quiet hello, while others knew to avoid me altogether. Taking my time, I made a cup and headed to my office. The blinds were shut and I suddenly didn't like it. I wanted to see Zain arrive. Watch him in an environment he'd never been in before. Slade's questions had crept in and although I didn't doubt that my Master would do more than excel, I felt fascinated to watch.

Heads spun in my direction as everyone watched my room become nothing more than a window to view them out of. I could see the whispers, but I ignored them as I sipped my coffee. Patrice, my secretary, stepped off the elevator, a big smile on her face…until she saw me. The fast paced walk had her hurrying to my door. The knock was a quick succession of three raps.

"Come in."

"Ms. Roberts, I was told you weren't going to be back in for another few days."

I shrugged, placing my cup down on the desk and standing from the edge where I'd been sitting. "It was time I came back. What did I miss?"

"Oh." The word sounded overwhelmed. I held up my hand, having her pause in rushing from the office to her desk.

"You know what, just bring me the messages. I'll read through them, it's not a big deal."

Her mouth shut and his eyes blinked a few times, as if she were lost. "Yes, Ms. Roberts." She headed for her desk and I went back to watching the elevators. People came, some left. The room calmed while the constant hum of voices took over. Minutes ticked by while I took my time reading through the thick stack of notes Patrice had made. I knew the second my brother walked in. An eerie silence had me looking up in time to see Slade and Zain halfway to my office. The dark suit Zain wore sent my pulse skittering all over the place. The power he emanated couldn't be mistaken. God, just seeing the way his eyes were intensely staring into mine made me melt. He looked ready to eat me alive and fuck if I didn't want him to.

Slade glanced at Patrice before opening my door. He stayed in the doorway, leaving Zain just outside. "If you need me, call. I'll be giving the tour. Find out what you can on Volstin."

"I already have Rebecca's number pulled up. I'll give you a report here shortly."

"Great." He stepped back, shutting the door behind him. As they headed down the hall toward Slade's office, Zain's eyes raked over my body and back up to mine. If I didn't know better, I'd think me being in the position I was in turned him on. Not to mention what he'd told me about the desks...

They disappeared and I started scanning the room. Damn, there were a lot of them. Did my Master see us sprawled out on each one? Him pounding his cock into my pussy, while he imagined the person unknowingly coming back to do their mundane work the next day? I shifted just thinking about it. The fantasy was so wrong, it should have put me off. Instead, I could feel myself getting wet.

"Volstin," I said, under my breath.

It was time to get back to work. I knew nothing would happen today, but we had a long road at Slade Industries ahead of us. I had no doubt he'd prove to me just how serious he was over time.

Chapter 40
Zain

What was a somewhat silent room turned into a frenzy of activity. Although people sat quietly in their cubicles, a handful of men and women from surrounding offices began swarming Lily's room, only to rush out. Some held paperwork in their hands while others skimmed through their handheld devices. She pointed, she spoke, and they either hurried off or their fingers frantically moved to produce whatever she wanted.

Fascinated, I tried to listen to Richard as he went over what I'd have to do.

"You can find 'input page' here," he said, hitting the icon. "Just add the figures in the boxes below. Make sure the numbers match up, that way you know you're entering the right amount."

"Got it," I said, under my breath.

"I think that's it. Pretty simple. Just let me know if you need any help."

I nodded, reaching out and shaking his hand. "You bet."

He walked to the next cubicle over and I lowered to the chair, thanking my lucky stars that mine gave me a view of Lily. She appeared calm and all of the others probably thought so, but the slight tension in her brow told me she was stressed. Her head shook and she let out a deep breath as she began to pace. It only caused the older man next to her to begin altering his tie.

The light hum of her voice floated through and I grabbed the mouse, focusing in on it as best as I could.

"That's not right. Volstin was talking to Cal Corp." Her head shook. "Get Aaron on the phone. I want dates. I want to know exactly when this happened." The deepening tone at the end told me she was getting angry. Something wasn't right with the account she and Slade had been talking about and it made it almost impossible to sit still. I wanted to help her figure it out, but I knew my place. Here, behind this desk, for probably the next few years. I didn't have Lily's schooling or experience. She'd been raised in this environment from Slade. She knew what she was doing.

"His wife said he's sick and can't come to the phone right now." The man looked downright terrified and I narrowed my eyes, not sure exactly why.

"Sick? He's sick?" Her voice was clipped. "He's not sick, Willard, he's quitting and taking over for Alec. Son of bitch. I was sure they'd give it to Winston. Okay, let me think." Her hands came to her hips while she stalked the length of the room. "Give me the number from Cal Corp again. What are they offering?"

As he spouted off some obscene amount, Lilian clenched her jaw. "We can't do it. Fuck." She paused mid-step. "Get Mr. Volstin on the phone."

"The owner?" he asked, quietly.

"That's right. You're going to call and get him on the line for me."

"One minute. I'll have to see if he can be contacted."

Lily's eyebrow raised. "Oh, he can, and you're going to make it happen."

The man rushed from the room and the moment he did, Lily reached up, holding her head and closing her eyes. The Master in me was desperate to do anything he could to relax her. She didn't fare well under stress. Not with these new episodes. If she pushed too hard, it might put her right back into the past.

"She'll be fine," Slade said, peering over the top of the cubicle. "Believe it or not, she needs this. Her being at home or anywhere else would only have her perseverating over what has happened. You being in her familiar environment will be the perfect solution. Just let Lily do her thing and you do yours. Do not, under any circumstance, leave this desk unless it's time for you to. Understood?"

"I know my place here," I said, spinning back to the computer, but looking up at him. "Say, you want to go ring shopping with me later? I could use your advice."

His arm came up to rest over the top and he cocked his head. Anger flashed behind his eyes, but so did something else. Something I'd seen before. He wanted to like me. Wanted this to work. It was going to be up to me to show him it would.

"You want me to go ring shopping with you? Does that mean I get to pick the date when you'll be getting married, too?"

"No, it just means that you get to help me wow her. I already know the date."

That had him standing taller. There was something about poking at Slade that I found all too fun, which was probably a stupid thing since he'd accepted me this much. "Do you, now? When?" The question was almost growled and I had to rein in my smile.

"You'll approve. I won't rush this. Lily is more than worth waiting for. I've done it this long, what's a little longer?"

"Exactly. Keep that mindset. Now, back to work. We'll talk ring shopping later." Slade walked off and I let the smile I'd been holding in appear as I faced the screen. I'd win him over completely before it was over with. Taking our time seemed to be the watchword lately. It sure needed to get on our side.

Numbers filled the screen and I looked down at the large stack of papers before me. Comfort

settled within and I let my fingers move as I went
down the page, entering them in. For something so
simple, the amount of pleasure I received at knowing
I'd be able to provide for my future wife left me
happy. I was working a real job, or at least a legal
one, for the first time in my life and it felt amazing.

"Uh-oh. You ready? I give her five seconds."
A man's voice had me breaking my stare from the
monitor and turning to look at the white wall
separating us.

"Ten," a woman said, laughing quietly.

"Fifteen," another man chimed in.

The wheels on my chair let me slide back to
the edge quietly and I was met with a row of heads
looking my way. Or...Lily's.

"What are we betting on?" I asked, curiously.

A red haired woman glanced at me and
pointed to the left. Willard was leaning against the
wall at the other side of the room, just inside the
hallway. Sweat was beginning to show through
under his arms on the long-sleeved shirt as he
scrolled through his phone almost nervously. My
attention went to Lily, who was pacing and looking
at whatever paperwork she had in her hand.

"What happens when the time is up?" I was
almost afraid to find out. Was there a side of Lily I
didn't know? Surely not. I'd seen her in every
mindset she held.

The back of Willard's hand brushed over his forehead and he straightened his tie, walking toward her door at a fast pace. When I looked back at the men and women from the cubicles, they were gone. I rolled to my desk and watched as Lily stopped in her tracks, looking up at him.

"I'm sorry, Ms. Roberts, I wasn't able to get ahold of him either. His secretary told me he's not taking calls right now."

"He's not taking calls?"

Willard's head shook quickly and he swallowed hard, once again reaching for his tie.

"Did you tell them you were calling for Ms. Roberts from Slade Industries?"

Willard's mouth opened only to close. "Well...no. I..."

One step. Two. Lily's eyes narrowed and standing tall, she was level with his face. Her expression was one I couldn't mistake. I knew that dominance. Her brother held the same air about him. She was intimidating as hell and my cock hardened as I ached to put her in her place.

"Willard, who do you work for?"

"You, Ms. Roberts."

"How long have you worked for me?"

His head dropped and he looked back up, as if he'd been trying to think. "Almost a year."

"And you still haven't learned? How many times do we have to have this conversation? When you make important calls at my request, you tell them who you are and who you work for. Me," she snapped. "Do you understand how under the wire we are here? I don't have time to go over this again. It's every single time." Each word was enunciated and she took a deep breath, walking to the phone.

Willard's fists flexed and I turned more in my chair. My pulse jumped as I kept all of my instincts ready. He was mad. That was clear. But I didn't expect him to do much of anything. Then again, I wasn't sure.

"You know, maybe if you would have given us some time to prepare instead of taking vacation at the last second, we could have had everything ready for you. You always just come and go when you please."

Lily's hand paused in reaching for the receiver and she slowly turned toward the man who had his chest puffed out. The room grew eerily silent around me. I had no doubt everyone was listening. Willard hadn't shut the door and they weren't necessarily talking quietly.

"I beg your pardon?"

"You didn't even put in for vacation. You just disappeared. If one of us did that, we'd be fired."

"Well, he's toast," someone whispered a few spaces over.

Lily crossed her arms over her chest, advancing at a leisurely pace. "I think it's time we part ways. I've given you a year and even the smallest things are becoming a chore for you to remember."

"You can't fire me."

"I think I just did."

"For telling the truth?" he said, his voice rising.

I stood, but stayed firm, allowing her to take the lead. It was a hell of a thing when everything in me said I needed to protect what was mine.

"No, you're right on that account. I should have put in notice. Emergency situations are a little hard to plan for, so I apologize for that. As for you being fired, that has everything to do with your job performance. I understand you try very hard to be a good worker, I just think that maybe this position isn't for you. I've given you more than enough time to learn and you still forget the basics. With what we have at stake, I can't afford to allow this to go on anymore. I'm sorry, Willard, but I have to let you go."

"You...*bitch.* I have a family. You can't fire me."

The hardness stayed on her face and she turned to the window, looking right at me. Still, she didn't soften.

"Don't make me call security. You need to leave my office and get your stuff together."

Willard stormed from the room and one minute, I was looking at Lily, the next, blinds slammed closed, disrupting my view. I sat, hating that she was in there dealing with this alone. Lily wasn't cold like that, no matter how much she projected it. There was no way she enjoyed what she'd just gone through. Which only meant one thing—she was in her office now, probably in tears, and I was supposed to sit here like I hadn't just witnessed any of it.

Fuck. My hand clamped to the desk and I tried stopping the anger as it grew by the second. Slade strolled casually from the office at the end of the hall, stopping at Willard's door. I couldn't see inside, but from the silence and Slade moving on, apparently there wasn't much more of a threat. He checked his watch before knocking and walking in. I could hear her voice, soft, sweet. She was on the phone, probably with the owner of that company. I didn't get to hear much as the door closed behind Slade.

Silence continued and seemed to turn into a living thing as Willard walked through with a box and waited for the elevator. I couldn't see from my angle, but I knew when he disappeared inside. The buzz throughout the room grew and I twisted my mouth as I let it all sink in.

"The Ice Queen strikes again. I wondered how long it would be before the next. At least he lasted longer than the others."

"He was her personal assistant, though," the woman said. "He doesn't count. It's the team members that she goes through like candy."

Two men came to her door, knocking. When Slade called out, they headed inside. A woman pushed through at the last minute and I turned away from it all, going back to my numbers. More laughter rang out from one of the cubicles and I couldn't wrap my head around it. Was this what everyone looked forward to? Lily and who she would fire next? Did she terminate a lot of people? What sort of drama went on in this office building? Did it always revolve around her? There were too many questions and I wasn't sure of the answers, but I knew in a few hours, I'd find out.

Chapter 41
Lily

The smile on my face couldn't have got any bigger. I kept my back to Slade and the team on purpose, trying my best not to show my excitement through my posture. When I delivered the news, I wanted it to hit them as a shock. I damn sure deserved at least some satisfaction. To get ahold of the owner was usually impossible, but my name and reputation were taking me far. I used it to my advantage every chance I got. I was a damn hard worker and the news I was about to deliver was proof.

"Thank you, Mr. Volstin. It was a pleasure talking to you." I turned around, placing the receiver down. Slade's eyes widened while he shook his head.

"Well?"

I shrugged, collapsing into my chair to stare at my team. They fidgeted and looked nervous, trapped in the same room as my brother and me. It was bad enough watching them when it was just me, but Slade's appearance had them squirming. They knew he wanted Volstin and they also knew how he'd react if he didn't get it.

"Well..." I hit my mouse, making my screen come alive. I pulled up the calendar and typed in the time of the appointment. "You, Mr. Roberts, have a meeting with Mr. Volstin tomorrow at ten a.m.. He'll have his lawyer present. If he likes what he hears, he's willing to sell."

A smile lit up my brother's face. "Excellent job, everyone. I knew you wouldn't let me down. Be ready by nine, Lily, you're coming with. Also," he spun, looking over the team, "you, you, and you," he said, picking out Patrick, Charlie, and Vanessa, the leaders. "Team up and discuss who's moving to Atlanta. We'll have Volstin by tomorrow and that's where I'm building the headquarters to the new Slade Industries." His smile grew bigger and he turned, strolling from the room. The team was right behind him, shutting my door and leaving me in silence. For the first time since I'd arrived, I felt myself completely relax. The break between accounts was my down time and come tomorrow when Slade bought out Volstin, I'd finally be able to get the breather I'd been hoping for. At least, until my brother set his sights on something new.

The darkness that surrounded me felt so comforting that it didn't take long before I could feel the floating sensation of almost being asleep. I held to the feeling, not letting myself go to the one place I didn't want to. Instead, my mind replayed firing Willard. I hated having to let him go, but truth be told, I never should have kept him on for as long as I had. He didn't have the drive it took to keep up and he wasn't willing to learn. He did enough to half ass it and I knew at times he cared, but a majority of the time he didn't, which was putting more stress where it didn't need to be.

Knock. Knock.

I opened my eyes, sitting up. "Come in."

Zain stepped through, giving me a smile. My stomach fluttered as I returned it. I had to rub my eyes to make everything focus. I still felt so tired.

"Everyon is already gone for lunch. Well, minus the people eating in the lounge, and a few still at their desks." Shit, had I fallen asleep and not known it? He shut the door and I stood. My pulse skyrocketed as he locked it and came forward. The look in his eyes darkened the closer he approached. "How are you? You doing okay? Pretty ugly argument earlier."

My hands held the edge of the desk and I nodded. "I'm good. It had to be done. Should have been done a long time ago but I wanted to give Willard the benefit of the doubt."

He paused, as if he were thinking something over. "I figured as much. You get Volstin?" His hand cupped my hip and he pulled me forward. My palm settled on his chest as I tried to stop the trembling from my arousal and fear of being caught.

"I think so. Slade and I are meeting the owner tomorrow morning. It's pretty much in the bag."

"I knew you'd do it."

Tighter, my hand buried into his suit jacket as he leaned down and nipped at my bottom lip.

"My brother has cameras in here," I rushed out. "He's probably watching."

Zain shook his head slowly. "He left about fifteen minutes ago. Besides, he doesn't have it recording. No one is watching. Would it matter anyway? I already told you my terms, slave. If I want to tie you to your desk and eat your pussy until you come all in my mouth, I will. Do you think you're going to try to stop me?"

My body swayed as he jerked at the clasp and zipper of my slacks. I could barely open my mouth before his hand was pushing into my panties and his finger was rubbing over my entrance.

"Fuck, I've been so hot watching you all day. I'm half tempted to bend you over this desk and pound your pussy right now. I've missed hearing you scream."

I gasped as his hand latched in my hair and he pulled back hard. It lined up perfectly with his finger surging into my pussy. A small cry escaped me as he began a hard and steady thrust.

"Master, I..."

"Are going to come before we go to lunch. Better stop worrying about all of these people outside of your door if you want to hurry things along. Otherwise, when my hand gets tired, I'm going to strip these pants completely off of you and sit your sweet little ass on your desk while I suck all over what's mine. I bet you'll come so fast that way, won't you, baby girl?"

Imaging Zain's head buried between my legs had me moaning out. "Yes, but..."

"I already explained this, but let me do it once more. You are the slave. I am the Master. Period. It's too late to go back on your decision now. You've already made it. Now, you don't have a choice." I nearly pushed down on his finger and begged him to fuck me. It was so hot, him leaving the decision out of my hands. It was something I needed. "I'm tempted to make you prove it." I pulled at the buttons on his shirt, pushing the material back on his chest so I could place my lips against the tattoos covering his skin. Pressure pulled me back until I had to look into his face.

"That's a very dangerous thing for you, Lily. Don't trigger my dark side. Right now is not the time. You get better first and then you'll get more than you can handle."

"Did you ever think that maybe your dark is something that might help me, versus make things worse?"

Zain's lips pressed into my mouth, as if to silence me. "There's no guarantee. Now unless you're moaning, no talking." His hand left my hair to move to my ass. I was pulled in close as his finger rubbed against my channel. At the pressure of his palm over my clit, I held him tighter.

"Move, slave. Fuck my fingers and make yourself come."

The command sent my hips moving in a rocking motion. I didn't hold back or worry about anything outside of my door. All I knew was my Master and how he was touching me on the inside. The push and constant attention to my G-spot left me rotating my hips even more.

"Can I touch you?" My voice was thick and deeper as I stared up at him.

Slowly, he shook his head, applying more pressure to the top of my slit. "Not this time. Right now, it's just for you."

He pushed in deep and I could barely control not releasing. Faster, he thrust, until I was biting my lip not to scream out.

"You're so fucking tight around my fingers. I know you want to come, but you're fighting it." A smile pulled at the edge of his mouth." Maybe you need some help." The arm around my waist tightened and he lifted me higher, until I could barely reach with my toes. My face shot to bury in his neck while his fingers pounded into me. The slapping against my clit had my hand clawing at his suit. There was no way I could hold off any longer.

"Do it. Come, baby girl, but you better fucking leave your mark as you do."

Even as he said it, I was already reaching up and pulling at the buttons and tie. With his neck before me, I aimed low and sucked as hard as I could. The spasms hit me in waves, causing me to moan while my body jerked against him. French poured from his mouth and it was something I noticed he did a lot when he was in his element.

"God, I love you." He left my pussy and brought his arm up, sucking my juices from his fingers, only to pull me in to kiss over them. My tongue traced up his digit, pushing into his mouth. "Fuck," he growled. "I'm going to enjoy ravaging you tonight."

"Yeah?"

"Oh, you have no idea." Blindly, he buttoned up his shirt and tightened his tie. "I have the day all planned out. We'll eat lunch. Your brother explained I would only be working the first part of the day, so Richard already knows I won't be coming back until tomorrow. After your appointment, I'll drop you off at home and pick you up for dinner. Seven sound okay?"

"Perfect."

As I fixed my pants and put on my coat, I couldn't stop from smiling. I felt lighter. So much more relaxed now that he'd made me release.

Zain led me out and only a few people looked over as we got onto the elevator. The ride down was a blur, as I stayed trapped in his gaze. There was such intensity that I was shifting to have more of him. The moment the doors opened, Brace met my gaze and I smiled, nodding my head just the slightest bit.

We turned to the right and I didn't glance back to see if my guards were following. I had no doubt they were. When we made it to my car, Zain got in and started it, looking over. He was truly happy. The big smile he wore was nothing like I'd seen in our past. Even at our happiest moments, his face had never lit up as much as it was now.

"This is great, right? You, me, work. And here I am, taking you to lunch and a doctor's appointment, like I should have always been doing. It really couldn't get better than this."

"I suppose not." I smiled, a million things bombarding me. I might have been happy that this was the way our lives were turning out, but there was still a lot on my mind. Like Saul, for one. And then there was the whole Slade thing. How long was he going to put restraints on our relationship? It aggravated me. I felt so…out of my control. I'd had it for so long and now I didn't. And Zain had no part in that. I loved submitting to him, but…there were things that just weren't right.

We left the parking garage and headed onto the main street. Warm air engulfed me from the heater and I tried to let myself relax. The problems would be there until they were addressed. In the meantime, there was no use in worrying over them. My guards would be keeping an eye out for any threats and time was the only thing that was going to assure my brother. I just had to take it day by day and with Zain by my side, I knew everything would be okay.

Chapter 42
Zain

One hour? Two? How long did Lily's appointments usually last? I'd assumed an hour, that was the standard amount, but she'd been in there for over two and at the moment, I could hardly think. There was only one thing on my mind and it took me over completely.

I scrolled through the display of rings on my phone, not really seeing anything that felt right. My slave would need the best, but not the usual style most women wore. She was special, therefore needed something just as much so. If I could get an idea of what I wanted so I could show the jeweler, I'd be better off.

A groan poured from my mouth and I glanced back at the door that sat between us. What in the world was going on in there? If I didn't know she was perfectly safe on the fourth floor, I'd have been knocking to check on her already.

"Sometimes it takes a while." Brace entered the lobby area, sitting down next to me. His hand came up to rub over his shaved head and I lowered the phone.

"Define a while."

He shrugged. "Longest it's been was a little over three hours. Lily doesn't have a set time. When she's finished, she's finished."

"Ah." I lifted the phone, beginning to scroll again. My eyes cut back over to Brace. "You've been following us all day. Is that a precaution on your part, or a lack of trust on hers?"

The confused expression melted from his face into something of annoyance. "How the hell did you see us? We stayed as far out of view as possible. Any more and we would have missed everything."

"You didn't answer my question."

"I look out for Lily, regardless of what she may or may not order."

My forehead drew in. "Did she order you to or not?"

"That's between me and her. I like you, Zain, but one hundred perfect of my loyalty is with Lily. You have to understand that."

"Are you going to sit outside of my house when she stays over in the future? Or when she moves in with me?" It had been made as a joke but from the look on his face, I sat up straighter. "You're not going to still be there, are you?"

Brace sat back in the chair, crossing his arms over his chest. "If Slade wants me, or even Lily, all she has to do is say the word and I'll be there. I have to admit, I don't think I'll back off until this uncle of yours is taken care of. I don't like Lily under that sort of danger."

"That makes both of us, but you have to know that I'm always on the lookout. I won't let anything happen to her again."

"Oh, I know you won't mean to. It doesn't mean to say that something won't happen that's beyond your control."

A sigh left my mouth and I looked back down at the phone, moving to the next page. "Lily will be safe. I'm putting all the precautions out to protect her from all angles. If you want to follow us around, that's fine, too. It will just mean she's safer."

"Exactly," he agreed. Movement from the corner of my eyes caught my attention and he leaned in closer. "Rings, huh?"

"Yep. I'm trying to find the right one and it's proving to be harder than I thought."

"Does Slade know you're going to ask?"

Muffled voices had me clicking off the phone. "Yeah, he knows it's coming. Not really sure what he thinks about it, but I'm not waiting. Lily's belongs with me. If I can't marry her, my ring will be on her finger until the day comes, however long that may be."

The door opened and Brace and I stood as Lilian walked out. Her eyes were puffy and I immediately headed in her direction.

"Remember to call me if you need anything." The blonde woman's eyes narrowed at seeing me, but she stayed quiet.

"I will, thank you."

My arm went around Lily's shoulders as we headed for the exit. Brace followed behind and I stayed quiet until we made it to the car. "You okay?" I pulled the strap over her chest, buckled her in, and kneeled down, staring deep into her eyes.

"Yeah, I think so. Reliving all of that just wears me down. I feel better, though."

"As long as you're okay." I gave her a light kiss on the lips and stood, shutting her door. Brace was walking in the opposite direction of the parking lot and I waited until he got closer to the SUV before I moved. Lily watched me warily and I wasn't sure why. Did she know I suspected that she was having Brace follow us? Did she not trust me or was Brace truly just being safe? I got in, buckled my seatbelt, and started the car.

"You feel like telling me how things went in there?"

A sniffle had her wiping her nose. "Eight to nine months. That's the average of how long I'll have to go through this. That's why I'm upset. My doctor said it could become manageable before then, but there's no telling. I just can't imagine having these flashbacks for that long. And, yes, they might not happen every day or even every week, but it just seems like a long time. Especially when you throw that number out of the window and face facts that this could continue forever."

"Or never again," I assured.

"I just want to be normal."

Where I thought she'd burst into tears, she didn't. Lilian's face turned hard, but a tear still escaped.

"What is normal other than someone else's view of the way things are supposed to be? It's bullshit." My hand cupped her cheek. "I'll be here for you, no matter what happens. If it continues forever, then so be it. You have nothing to fear with me by your side. When you return from whatever scares you, I'll be there to hold you and remind you that there's no reason to be afraid. I'll take care of you, Lilian. Forever."

Her hand reached out and grasped my wrist, holding it while I kissed her again. When she pulled back, she gave me a grin.

"There, I like that. Keep smiling, baby girl. That's what I love to see on your face the most."

I started the car and took off toward Lily's building. The drive was hindered by traffic but we made it to the parking garage just in time to see Slade walking toward his car with Mary and his guards in tow. He waited until we parked and got out.

"I was just about to head out to do a little shopping. How'd the appointment go?" His attention went to Lily and she stepped in closer to me. My arm automatically pulled her to my side.

"It went good. I still have quite a ways to go before things get back to the way they were, but I feel better now that I've talked about it."

Slade nodded. "Good. I'm glad to know you were able to open up to your doctor. It'll do you well." He paused. "Listen, I was going to call a little later, but I should just tell you now. I talked to Mr. Volstin. He changed his mind about the meeting in the morning. He wants to discuss things over dinner. Be ready by six. You can ride with me. It may take a few hours to negotiate what I have in mind, but it has to be done."

Lily's head lowered, only for her to look up at me confused. I could tell she was torn on what to do. This was her job, but I knew she was worried about our plans.

"Go. We'll have dinner tomorrow night." I gave her a reassuring squeeze and I could feel the tension in her shoulders ease almost immediately.

"Thanks," she whispered to me. When she turned to her brother, her confidence was back. I could so clearly see it by the way her face became serious as she took on her business expression. "I'll be ready at six."

"Good. See you then." Slade turned and headed toward his car where Mary was waiting. She gave a wave that Lily returned. Brace and Caleb were getting out of the SUV and they trailed behind as we made our way to the elevator.

"I'm going to leave you here," I said, turning Lily to face me. "I have a few errands to run. Are you going to be okay?"

There was surprise on her face while she peered up at me. "Yeah, I mean, I'll just be getting ready in an hour or two."

"Rest before then. You need all that you can get after what you just went through. If for some reason you need me, don't hesitate to call. I'll come right back."

"I will." There was strength in her voice as she stood tall. I couldn't help but feel a sense of pride in my slave. She'd been through so much, but if I knew anything about Lily, she was a fighter. She'd come back from this and the setback would only make her stronger in the end.

Brace and Caleb led her inside and my stomach dropped as the doors shut. I knew what I was about to do had nothing to do with rings or visions of fancy romantic engagements. It was time I found out if Saul was trying to locate me, and I didn't even have to go back to my car to find out. If anyone had talked to the front desk of my old building, they'd tell me. What I discovered would set the path on what I needed to do. Or…who I needed to deal with.

Chapter 43
Lily

First the multiple dinners, now this?

I stared up from my desk, glaring at Slade. I knew what he was up to and I wasn't so sure I liked it. Four days of nonstop distractions for both me and Zain. I was quickly discovering the motive of my brother's plan was to keep us apart.

"Lunch with the team?" My voice was sarcastic as I stood and crossed my arms over my chest. "What's next, a business trip to the Cayman Islands? A business meeting in Tokyo?"

Slade's lips parted and his finger pointed at me, bouncing just the slightest bit.

"Don't even think about it," I snapped. "That's going too far. I'm not ready to be out of this state, let alone the country."

"Damn. Would you consider going to Tahoe?"

"No!" I walked around the desk, trying to compose myself. Zain was bent over paperwork, his fingers working the keys on the keyboard. The pile next to the one he was working on was so high, I knew it would take him weeks to reach the bottom of it.

"Come on, Lily. Work with me here. It's barely been any time at all. If I can just get you to draw this out for just a little longer, we'll have our answer."

My head shook. "I'll give you a few weeks, but not every single day. I've barely gotten to even hold a conversation with Zain. I miss him and I know he misses me."

"That's the point," he ground out. "He needs to be distanced and put under the ultimate pressure while doing so. It'll show me everything I need to know."

I couldn't help the small laugh that escaped. "You piss him off too much and he'll stop playing by your rules. You can't seriously think he's going to let you keep us apart for too long. Have you not learned anything about him the last few weeks?"

"The guy is…" Slade's mouth twisted. "I know how far to push him before he snaps. He'll be fine. Hell, I bet he'll thank me in the end."

"I doubt that. You'll be lucky if he doesn't cut you out of his life completely. Zain doesn't play games, Slade."

A defensive looked darkened his features. "This isn't a game, Lilian. This is your future we're trying to secure. Let's make sure that you're not going to get hurt anymore, okay? Just a few more weeks and if your boyfriend is still around and proving himself, you have my word. I will back off completely and let things fall as they may."

"Fine. A few more weeks and that's it. But you're not keeping me away completely. If your plan isn't work related, I keep my dates with Zain. Period." I grabbed my purse from behind the desk, preparing to have lunch with Slade and the team. "By the way, I'm spending the night with him tonight. Don't try to stop me either. It won't work."

A low growl filled the space between us and I raised my eyebrow in challenge. When he stayed quiet, I headed for the door. It was as if whatever world Zain was in disappeared at the slight squeak of the hinge. He turned around, checking his watch. I frowned as I headed over to tell him the bad news.

"Let me guess. You can't go to lunch."

I glanced back at the team meeting up next to Slade. "No, I'm sorry. We have a business plan to discuss. Slade wants to go over a few companies and get an insight into what we're dealing with." I lowered, moving in closer to his face. At his lips parting, everything in me wanting to kiss him. From the deepening of his breaths, I could tell he wanted to, too. "I'll probably catch a ride home with Slade, but will you pick me up afterward? I'll bring my overnight bag."

The smile that had pulled at my lips disappeared at the pained expression Zain held.

"What is it?" I lifted back, getting a better view of his face.

"I won't be home tonight. Or for the next few days. I was going to talk to you about it over lunch, but…" He swallowed and his jaw tightened in anger. "Your brother is having me and two other men go down to the LA office to review some accounts. We won't be back until Friday."

Heat poured from my skin and I turned, glaring at Slade. He only held my stare for a few seconds before turning back to the conversation they were having. He gave me nothing. Not an apologetic look or a *please understand* expression. He was stoic, just like he always was.

"LA." I repeated the word, letting the venom in my voice underline it. So far, I'd done okay with the nightmares and I hadn't had another flashback, but what if Zain wasn't there for the next one? I knew I needed to be strong and learn to depend on myself, but it was comforting to know my Master could come over if I needed him. Now, he'd be hours away.

"Do you want me to tell him no?"

I looked down, only then realizing I was still giving my brother a death stare.

"Oh, no. You go ahead. This is your job. We're both having to make sacrifices. It comes with the territory."

"So I've noticed." Zain picked up my hand, only to let it go. The frustration was evident. I knew he wanted to kiss my palm or knuckles. It was something I loved for him to do. But here, we couldn't be too obvious in what we shared. I really shouldn't have even come to him in such a public place. I'd have to remember to be more private. "You have a good lunch," he continued. "I'll stop by and see you before I take off."

"Okay, sounds good. I look forward to it." I forced a smile and stepped back, heading toward the elevator. By the time I got there, Slade and the team were already walking my way. I hit the button, crossing my arms and trying not to look at my brother as I waited. He'd known the whole time and he never said anything.

The door opened and I walked in, moving to the very back. Slade moved in beside me, staying quiet, but he didn't have to say anything for me to feel his presence. It pressed against my skin like a living thing. Just like Zain's did. The dominance was undeniable, but there was a difference. I bowed to my Master and followed his direction. I was willing to bend to Slade, but not for everything. Not for this.

At the ding, everyone walked out and we followed, but just past the opening, I cupped Slade's arm, pulling him to a stop.

"Don't hide anything like that from me again. If you're planning to send him off, you better tell me. I don't like surprises. Not concerning him. You know I need him right now."

His eyebrow cocked and he exhaled loudly. "Fine, I'll tell you, but you're wrong. You need no one. You're stronger than that."

My fingers pushed into his arm as anger swelled. "I choose to need him. I want to have that sort of connection and if you can't understand that…" I was so upset that words evaded me. "*I choose this.* Respect my wishes and I will respect your game."

I let go and stormed ahead. The limo was already waiting in the front and the team was piling in. Slade's long strides had him making it to my side before I could get halfway.

"Lily, wait."

I glanced over, coming to a stop.

"I should have told you or warned you beforehand. You have a right to be angry." At my silence, he continued. "We've been butting heads since I've been back. A lot."

"Yes," I agreed. My shoulders went lax and I studied his worried face. "We've seen each other in passing, but we haven't really had to spend this much time together. I'm afraid we're a lot more alike than we knew."

He nodded and shrugged. "Not a bad thing. Just something we're going to have to work on, that's all. Communication is key. I should be grateful you're allowing me to test him. I'm sorry if I'm coming off as an asshole. I'll be sure to talk with you more about what I want to happen."

"I'd like that. Although, I have faith in Zain and believe what we have will last. I respect your opinion and choices, but don't forget that I'm allowing this. You have to keep me informed. No more surprises."

"You have my word," he said. "Let's go brainstorm. The team is waiting."

We started heading that way again with Marcio and Terrance following. Trust was an issue I had a problem with and I felt myself accept what my brother told me. He wouldn't just give his word to anyone. When he said it, he meant it.

We climbed in the limo, the guards taking their place in the front. Although the members were usually on edge, there was a happiness about them that lifted my spirits even more. My job as CEO was so broad and covered such a vast amount of things that I'd neglected the most important part—morale. My team feared me, and although I liked it in a way, they also needed to see the other side. The one that not only took care of her people, but lifted everyone's spirits and showed her appreciation of their hard work.

"Charlie, how's the wife taking to the idea of Atlanta?"

The blond looked up at me, the corner of his brown eyes crinkling as he smiled. "She's excited, Mrs. Roberts. She's already looking for apartments."

I looked to Slade. He was typing something on his phone. Slowly, my head shook. "Not necessary, Charlie. Slade Industries will set you up with a very nice place. I was sure that was already disclosed. After all, you're going to have a lot of responsibilities as it is. A place to live shouldn't have to be one of them. We'll take care of everything."

Slade's head came up, but lowered, even as he nodded his approval. I knew he didn't mind. He'd made it clear from the beginning that I should run things as I felt appropriate. He trusted me...trust...yes, he did trust me. Even with his own livelihood. His company was everything to him and he'd put me in charge. The most obvious truth suddenly became apparent and all my thoughts jumbled together, throwing me off for a few seconds.

"Thank you, Ms. Roberts. Mr. Roberts," Charlie said, excitedly. "Georgette will be happy to hear that."

"You're welcome." My voice sounded winded, weak as I tried to collect myself. "Vanessa and Patrick, you're both running the team. Tell me what you've decided on direction?"

As they began talking, I tried my best to listen. It was almost impossible to stop my racing mind. I knew it was in part because of the medication I was on. Sometimes it clouded my thoughts, but I made sure the dose was low enough not to hinder my judgment. Right now, it was really leaving me grasping to understand how things were playing out. Patrick's voice broke through and I squinted as he described a new company we hadn't heard much about. The excitement in his tone was matched by the other team members' smiles.

"Lafel? Why hadn't I heard of that one?" Slade slid his phone in his pocket, his interested apparently piqued.

"You could call them a diamond in the rough. They're numbers are amazing." Patrick scooted to the edge of his seat and his hands lifted as he gestured with his words. "Vanessa was the one who actually discovered them. It was an amazing fi—"

The impact that crashed into us from behind, along with the brakes being slammed, sent me flying into Harris, one of the newest members who was sitting along the side, in front of me. The impact knocked the air out of me and I grabbed his shirt as I fell to the floor. Slade's eyes went wide as he pushed up from Patrick's side. The smell of rubber was so thick, my nose wrinkled.

"What the hell?" Slade turned to where we'd been sitting, just as glass exploded all around.

Deafening screams pierced my ears and weight crashed into me, pinning me to the floor. Someone's foot stepped on my arm and the limo rocked with the frantic movements of everyone inside. I could hear Marcio yelling in the distance, but it faded out as a series of loud pops followed. Fear ran so thick within me, I couldn't scream or move. Slade's cologne was my only comfort and I held to him as I felt us jerk forward again. The turn that was taken had my brother rolling off of me, but pulling me in close.

"Boss!" Marcio's voice rang out over the cries surrounding us and I turned, taking in the damage. Wind whipped at my hair that had fallen loose from the pins and blood on a few of the team members had nausea taking over.

"Oh, shit." I struggled against Slade's hold, trying to break loose, but he wouldn't let go.

"Lily and I are okay. What the hell is going on?" Shaken, my brother held a fear in his tone I'd never heard before. "Terrance was hit. He's back there. I think he's…" Marcio paused. "I think it got him in the head."

A sob broke free as I let the news sink in. Tears blinded me at the loss of one our guards. He possibly died trying to protect us. My heart ached and I pushed my palm into my chest, stopping midway as my eyes lifted. I thrashed against my brother who was holding onto me even tighter.

Vanessa's throat was covered in blood and Patrick was holding her in his arms, applying pressure with his free hand.

"Let me go," I screamed. "I have to help her."

Only then did Slade seem to see what was going on around him. His arms immediately eased. He sat up, letting me crawl the three feet that separated us. I stripped off my blazer, pulling the scarf free from my neck. My scars stood out brightly on my arms as I reached forward. I didn't miss Patrick's gaze jerking toward them, but they didn't stay focused on me for long. His hand moved and I pressed the black and white silk into the side of her neck, applying a heavy amount of pressure.

"Hospital, Marcio!" How I sounded so calm, I didn't know, but I focused on the woman gasping below me. Blood sprayed out at her cough and I tried my hardest to think of something more to do. Aside from trying to stop the bleeding, I was helpless.

"Brace, Terrance has been shot. I'm guessing about four blocks from the building. Find him, get him help, and get your ass to the hospital now. We have a few wounded and I want you here." Slade hung up and moved further toward the front where Charlie lay. "Jesus," my brother groaned, "he's dead."

Chapter 44
Zain

The buzzing of voices went on and on, coming in and out as I tried to focus on the numbers. No matter how hard I tried to block them out completely, it just wasn't happening today. All I could think about was my slave and how I kept telling her I'd be there for her, when in truth, I kept getting pushed further away. I couldn't stand it.

I pushed back from the desk and spun to the other side, grabbing my bottled water. As I began unscrewing the cap, I paused, taking in what the hell everyone was going on about.

"No, I just heard about ten minutes ago. Pete, from downstairs, said Mr. Robert's guard tore out of here in a rush. Said he heard something about a shooting."

I jerked to face the cubicle, but didn't get as far as letting it come into focus before I was already standing.

"Who said that?" I broke around the wall, scanning the surrounding cubbies. "What happened with Mr. Roberts's guards?" Silence had my heart racing even faster. "You," I growled, "who said that?"

The man who sat directly across from me pointed to the side of him.

"You," I stormed toward the heavyset man in his mid-fifties, "what happened?"

His mouth opened and closed in shock and what looked to be fear. "The guards. They raced out of here. Something about Mr. Roberts's limo getting shot up. Pete said he heard a call come in over the scanner about a few people being injured. Even dead. It fit the description of the rumors floating around."

My skin turned cold as I raced for the elevator. The longer it took, the more I slammed my palm against the button. I reached in my pocket, grabbing my phone and hitting Lily's number. It went immediately to voicemail.

"God dammit!" I took a step back, charging forward the moment the doors opened. The ride down was the slowest in my life. When I broke into the lobby, Brace, Marcio, and Terrance were nowhere to be seen. I headed for the entrance, dialing Slade. Before I could finish, my phone rang.

"Hello? Hello?" My greeting came rushed and panicked. I jogged through until I broke to the entrance of the parking garage. I hit a dead sprint to the car as I waited for someone to talk. "Hello?"

"Lily is fine. She's talking to the police now. She wanted me to call you in case you'd heard anything."

My legs almost gave out at the sound of Slade's voice.

"Fuck. What the hell happened? Some guy in the cubicle across from mine broke the news."

Slade took a deep breath and I could hear his shoes against some type of flooring. "Terrance is dead. Vanessa and Charlie, two of my team leaders, are also dead. Another was shot in the arm. Marcio says it was white SUV that hit us from behind. When he stopped and they both got out to check the damage, three men exited the vehicle and began firing. The accent they had would have this pointing toward you." The blame was clear as he ground out the words. "What have you discovered on your uncle, Zain? I thought you had this taken care of."

I pulled open the door and froze. I had locked that door, now it was unlocked. The realization had me slowly lowering down to look under the dash and the underbelly of the car. I left the door open, reaching under the seat where I had my gun and knife hidden under the flooring. Once I pushed them into the waistband of my slacks, I turned to head out of the garage. "I suspected he might be here, but he's staying under the radar. *We're* not, though. Call the bomb squad and get them to remove that bomb strapped to Lily's car. You might want to have your building evacuated too. Fuck," I breathed out, stopping at the ground level entrance. "You have to leave. Take Lily and Mary and head to your estate. San Francisco isn't safe."

Slade's voice sounded distant as he told Brace to call his building, then the volume increased as he came back to me. "You know Lily won't leave without you."

My free hand fisted. "She doesn't have a choice. You tell her I said to. End of story. Now, I have to go. I'm ending this once and for all."

"How are you going to do that?" There was a slight edge to Slade's voice that had me questioning my sanity. My slave's brother was too close of a connection to her. He represented what I could so easily lose. My brain told me to me to get home. To face the men who were waiting and finally get my revenge. My heart told me to think smart and call the only backup I trusted.

"Let's just say Saul may be stealthy, but he's a lot like my father. He's a creature of habit. I know his next move and I plan to turn the tables on him. He might think he has me where he wants. He may even suspect that I know what it is. What he fails to see is that I think outside of the box. I cover every possibility and I calculate the best outcome. I know what I have to do."

The footsteps returned and I assumed Slade began pacing again. "Just make sure you wear the damn vest. I swear, you should just leave it on with the rate you're going."

"You don't know Saul. He's not going to be aiming for the chest, brother. He's going for the head if he or his men take a shot. It's the kill factor. They don't chance survivors. If they're pulling the trigger, they want you dead."

"Wear the damn vest anyway," Slade snapped.

Cars thickened as I stared at the traffic. Was one of Saul's men out here waiting for me? Or did they assume I had been in the limo? It was hard to say when I didn't know whether they'd witnessed the group crowding to get inside. If I knew one thing, it was that Saul was already in my home, waiting to see if I came back. He'd know my new residence. I was betting my life on it.

"I have to go. Tell Lily I love her."

"You should get your ass here and just tell her yourself. I can't stand her always being in the middle of this. You should let Blake or Gaige take care of it."

My jaw tightened and I hung up the phone. Slade would never understand why I had to do this. He didn't live my life or see the things I had. Saul's death deserved to be painstakingly slow. I wanted him to suffer. Just like his slaves had. Just like he hurt Lily. Bloody...brutal...

Sirens echoed in the distance and my arm shot out, hailing a cab. As I spouted off a road a few streets over from my house, I let my plan work out in my head. This had to work. It would. If it didn't, I was fucked. And if something happened to me, they'd come for my slave. I couldn't allow that to happen.

The blur of colors helped my mind race. So clearly, I could see what was going to happen. I wasn't naïve. I knew things rarely played out like in one's thoughts, but as different scenarios flashed, I embraced each one, letting them feed and burn into my mind so I'd be prepared for anything.

I closed my eyes, focusing on the pressure at my hip. My fingers pushed into my thigh and I could feel a smile pull at my mouth. This would be the last time I had to kill and I'd enjoy every moment of it.

The pull of the brakes had my eyes opening, I took out my wallet, paying the fare. The sound of the door closing had the new Zain retreating. The old one surged through me and my ears adjusted to my surroundings. Cars passed. Pedestrians talked and laughed as they went in and out of homes. I walked two blocks, letting myself just…feel. For what was about to happen, a calm sensation cloaked around me. Death had been my forte. I'd spent my life living it, and all I had to do was commit the act once more. There was a sadness mixed with my blood lust. The finalization to my past hit me hard and I pushed away the sense of grief I felt. This was for the best. For Lily.

I stepped onto my block and looked down at all the stairs aligning the connected homes. Potted plants rested by some doors. Others had welcome signs. When I got to my landlord's, I peered up at his closed door. Was he alive inside? Dead?

My feet bounded up the concrete steps and I pulled out my keys, sliding one into the lock. From slow to fast, my pulse increased. I turned my wrist, unlocking it, and pushed the door open. In a quick turn, I put my back to the outside of my home and waited. The soft muffled sound of shots going off were almost undetectable. Just like my own—silent. I pulled my gun, crouched, and turned into the entrance. *Bang.*

A man fell at my shot and I moved back out of range. Two total and the other wasn't my uncle. Shit.

"It's him!" was shouted in Arabic. From the sound of the voice, I could tell he'd moved further toward the stairs where the bedroom rested. I spun back to the entrance and rushed inside, yanking the door closed behind me. Multiple shots rang out as I sprinted toward the kitchen. I only had to pull my trigger once to drop the last visible guard. Warmth coated my side and I cursed myself for not wearing the fucking vest. I hadn't even considered taking it from the trunk of Lily's car. I knew it wasn't bad. More of a scratch than anything, but I'd been damn lucky.

"Saul!"

I flipped the table onto its side as I slid to a stop. Scraping sounded on the floor while I angled it to the front door and the stairs. If he came down, I'd have perfect view of his feet before he could even see me. But the big question was, if...

I switched to Arabic, hoping to at least get a response. The man had been yelling at someone. There was a chance my uncle wasn't even here, but I wasn't betting on that. Saul wanted me dead. He wanted my slave. This had to have been his plan.

"Saul, come down. I know you're up there."

The echo was loud in the silence of my home. If the guard wouldn't have made it obvious, I would have assumed no one else was here. But...there had to be. I rose the slightest amount, peering at the open space around me.

"Saul!" A growl poured from my lips and I stayed low, running deeper into the kitchen. Weapons were spread around my house at random locations, but that wasn't what I was after. I stood, swinging the cabinet open and grabbing the gauze. As I made my way back to the table, I took off my jacket and pulled my shirt open, not caring about taking the time to unbutton it. Button's spun around the floor and in fast wraps, I circled my stomach. The scratch from the bullet was deep, but nothing I'd need stitches for.

Annoyance mingled with impatience and I looked back up at the stairs while I finished fastening the bandage. "You better be praying," I yelled out. "By the time I get up there, you're going to wish you would have."

"Always so sure of yourself. Not this time, Zain."

My hands dropped and I grabbed my gun, aiming it for the stairs. From my angle, I couldn't see the top, but I kept it trained to where he'd first come into view. *If* he decided to do so.

"Really? Are you sure, because I think it is. Listen to your gut, Uncle. What does it tell you?"

A laugh was followed by footsteps from above. I glanced up, but stayed focused on the stairs. There was no telling whether he was up there alone.

"Zain, Zain..." Again he laughed. "You know, I have to admit, this is going to be rather fun. Had I known how much, I think I would have done this a lot sooner."

What sounded like a soft voice had me tilting my head to get a better angle. Whispering buzzed and I couldn't make out what was said. The sob that followed had me standing. It was feminine, making my heart drop. Slade had said Lily was at the hospital. She was supposed to be safe. If this wasn't Lily...then who?"

I took a step, my feet seeming to weigh more with each inch I grew closer.

"No?" Saul laughed quietly. "You know, I've done this before. You'll thank me, I promise." The sobbing increased.

"Saul!" I placed my foot on the first step and gripped my gun tighter while I keeping it aimed above. All he had to do was peek his head over the side and I'd blow his brains out. But from what I could see, he wasn't by the edge.

"Did you finally decide to join us?"

My jaw tightened and I hated that he knew I was approaching. I walked faster, my finger remaining on the trigger.

"Come on. Come say hello." There was a drawl in his tone. Almost as if he were coaxing a young child. My head came to the top of the opening and I counted to three before I took a quick look. Time stopped as I pushed my hand to the wall for balance. So, that's what he'd meant. *He'd done it before*. Rage had me seeing red and I felt almost disconnected as I took a step higher. My hand slid into my pocket and I pulled out my phone, hitting Slade's number. I didn't even raise the phone to my ear. I placed it on the top step, out of view, and walked the remaining distance until I was standing in the room.

Rope was strewn over the rafter above and Mary's arms were bound high enough to where she had to stand on her tiptoes to stay balanced. Tears stained her face and blood was smeared along her mouth and chin. The swelling on her cheek had me circling the room for a clear shot. Saul was standing behind her, holding the knife to her throat, one hand on her slightly rounding stomach.

"Mary, it's going to be okay. Just don't move, okay."

"Za-in." My name came out broken as her eyes closed and more tears spilled out.

Saul's finger splayed and his fingertips pushed in, gripping the fabric of her loose, light blue dress. Mary began noticeably shaking as she let out an angry groan. It was followed by more sobs.

"Let her go. This is between me and you. No one else."

"Wrong," Saul snapped in English. "When one becomes the enemy, everyone they're connected to is fair game. I believe *this* would be sorely missed if it were taken away. What do you think?" His hand rubbed over her stomach again and Mary tried to move to the side. The shift had her gasping. Blood ran down her neck and I stepped in closer, moving my barrel up and down, trying to find a shot that would work. Where he stood, there was no way I could take him out without risking Mary's life. One wrong move and she could be dead.

I answered back, speaking loud in case Slade was listening. "You hurt that baby and so help me, I won't be the only one gutting you alive. You taking her might have been your biggest mistake. You won't make it out of this room. You have to know that."

"They killed Caleb," Mary said, crying harder. "They—" Her voice diminished at my uncle angling the knife to where she had to lift her neck. More blood escaped, soaking down into the high collar of the dress. Saul spun them slightly, dropping the knife from her throat and pulling out a gun. I moved with their direction, keeping my aim and watching where he had his.

"You're wrong. You're the one who's going to die. As for her," his hand gripped into her stomach making her cry out, "she's going to send a message to your new friend that you don't mess with Saul Amari and get away with it."

Chapter 45
Lily

"That's all you saw?"

The detective's deep voice was drowned out by my worry for my brother. He held his phone, pale, completely still. I nodded. "Yes. I know nothing. Please, excuse me." I was already walking away as my words flowed from my mouth mindlessly. Slade's arm shot out to Marcio, fisting his coat.

"Get Gaige on the phone now. I need to talk to him." Panic laced his words and he broke from Marcio, rushing toward the exit of the Emergency Room. I followed behind, staying silent as Brace moved in close.

"Mr. Roberts, you need to stay here while I get the car. It's safer that way."

Slade's gray eyes darkened as they snapped our way. "Safer? Fuck, safer. That son of a bitch has Mary and I'm going to kill him."

I didn't need to ask who. We all knew who was responsible for the events that had gone down. Air would barely come as I thought of Mary being in Saul's clutches. I jogged behind Slade as he ran for the car. He seemed oblivious to everything but what he was hearing on the phone. The power locks clicked and I followed Slade as he climbed in the back.

"No, you stay." His hand came out to stop me from getting in and I slapped it away.

"Don't you tell me to stay. I know Zain is the one who called you and I'm going."

"Boss." Marcio got in the driver's seat, reaching back to hand Slade his phone. I climbed in at the distraction and Slade gestured to Brace, who was already pulling out his laptop from the passenger seat.

"Hurry up with that fucking address." My brother lifted the phone to his other ear and squinted before he began talking. "Gaige, I need you."

There was a moment of silence and my brother lowered his head. His shoulders sagged and I froze as I prepared myself for him to break down completely. So many emotions filtered across his profile while he stared down at the floor. All I could think about was how I was invading what should have been a private moment between him and this agent.

"Saul Amari has my wife and Zain is the only one there to help her. I can hear what's going on and...he's threatening to kill Zain and my child to send a message."

Bile burned my throat and I gripped the handle of the door with everything I had. Saul would do it. I knew he would. Something told me if Zain could have killed him, he would have already. There was something holding him back, but what?

Slade's head flew up. "Address, now!"

"Working on it, boss."

Deep breaths were coming from my brother and he shifted. "I think I just heard a shot. I'm not sure. There was something. Maybe a bang on the wall? Fuck, I don't know! The connection keeps breaking up." He went to say something but hesitated. "How long?"

Brace's head turned in our direction. "They're at Zain's."

"Address," my brother bit out.

As Brace told him and my brother repeated it to Gaige, I went over the layout of Zain's place. Were they downstairs? Upstairs? Were they going to see us pulling up? Had someone been shot or were they fighting? So many question spun wildly in my mind.

Tire's squealed as Marcio left the parking lot and floored it in the direction of Zain's. Like my brother, I couldn't sit still. If something happened to Zain or Mary, neither of us would ever be the same.

"See you there." Slade hung up and dropped Marcio's phone at his feet. He pulled back the other, hitting the speakerphone button. Silence.

Seconds flew by and I glanced over at my brother nervously. The loud sound of a horn had me jumping. A traffic jam rested before us and my lips parted in panic. Slade's head came up at us coming to a stop and he looked around, as if he were lost.

"Come on," Marcio growled. We all seemed to scan the surroundings, but there were no other options. We were stuck unless we got out and walked the ten miles it would take to get us to Zain's.

"I told you I wasn't going to be the one dying."

Time stopped at Saul's voice. My nails subconsciously clawed into the seat. It couldn't be true. It couldn't.

"Fuck!" My brother's hand reached for the door and he seemed to battle with the same thing I did. What was faster? He was in dress shoes, me in heels, and it was a good thirty degrees outside. Neither of us had our jackets and we were now on the freeway. Barriers from construction prevented us from driving into the grass to move around the cars. What did we do?

Static filled the interior and a light noise in the background grew into a loud scream.

"Mary!" Slade's yell sent chills throughout my body. Loud sobbing and her calling out Zain's name had the phone Slade held turning blurry as tears filled my eyes.

"Now...it's your turn." Saul's words were broken up and almost impossible to understand due to the heavy accent, but I knew what he said. Silence suddenly filled the car and Slade pushed the button on the phone, displaying the home screen. The call had dropped.

"No." His head shook. "No!" The door on his side flew open and he jumped out, racing ahead, in between cars. I didn't wait, couldn't, knowing that Zain was supposedly dead and Mary could be next.

I kicked off my heels and pushed myself as hard as I could to try to keep up with Slade. Cold air filled my lungs and cut right through the blazer I wore, but I barely felt it as I focused on running as fast as I could. The further I went, the faster Slade seemed to run. He quickly became so far ahead of me that I knew I didn't stand a chance in keeping up.

Cars moved at a slow creep along my side and cramping eventually took over my side, but still, I forged ahead. The exit that lay ahead was backed up as well. Slade took it, racing right for the light at the congested intersection.

I cut between two cars, merging to the far lane, following. My legs were growing heavy and my feet throbbed from the pounding against the road, but if I didn't hurry, I was going to lose Slade completely. And I didn't know this route to Zain's. Or even this part of town. I may have grown up in the city, but there were still parts I wasn't familiar with.

Horns blasted from all around and colors rippled before me. Fear took over, causing me to stumble. No, this couldn't happen right now. I refused to let this happen! The noise grew louder as I grew closer to the intersection. Slade was already weaving through the cars and making it to the other side of the road. Someone yelling out their window to the people in front of me had my body shaking worse than it already was. Anger swelled and I let the facts cloud everything out. Zain and Mary needed help. Lord only knew what they were going through or what happened. Discomfort or subconsciously harbored fears were not going to stop me from getting there. I had the control. Me.

Brace made it to my side and a sense of calm took over. Traffic began to move at the change of the light and Brace suddenly had his gun withdrawn. His eyes scanned the cars as we stayed even with their flow. One minute, he was next to me, the next, he was throwing open the door of a sedan and was halfway inside. The car jerked to a stop and the man climbed out, running away.

"Get in," he yelled. My legs were practically numb, but I rushed around and climbed in. My heavy breaths filled the interior and we shot forward. He got in the far lane and turned right at the light, immediately crossing through traffic to take a left at the first road. Slade was so far ahead that I couldn't believe the progress he'd made.

"How much further away?" I looked at
Brace who increased the speed toward the hill ahead.

"A ways. We'll get your brother and make it
there within a few minutes. It all depends on traffic.
We're going to have to go the long way now that
we're off the freeway."

Slade was suddenly before us and Brace's yell
barely even broke through the zone he was in. A
wild look was in his eyes as he turned, looking at us.

"Get in, Boss. Let's go get Mary."

The decision shouldn't have been hard, but
Slade was gone. He stared ahead, only to turn back
to us.

"Get in," I said, calmly. "Mary and Zain are
waiting."

He blinked and reached for the door with
zombie like movements, climbing in the back. His
phone was still clutched in his fist and his cheeks
were red from the cold. Dark strands fell over his
forehead and he breathed in deeply as he blinked a
few times. With a slow look down, he brought the
phone up, hitting one of the buttons. A few seconds
went by and he brought it down. The car jumped at
hitting a dip at the high speed, but neither Slade nor I
seemed to really notice as we held each other's stare.

"If Mary is…" he licked his lips. "I'll make
that motherfucker pay, Lily. I promise you with
everything I have, he won't live another day when I
get my hands on him. He's a dead man."

"They're going to be okay." I forced the words out, regardless of whether I believed them or not. "But, if..." I didn't break eye contract, "if Zain or Mary are hurt, I'm helping. They're ours and no one messes with what belongs to us. That's the way you raised me and that's the way we finish it. Now promise me."

A twitch pulled at my brother's cheek, but he nodded. "You have my word. We won't stop until this is done, once and for all."

Chapter 46
Zain

My uncle had never been a good shot, but this time, he hadn't missed. Fire engulfed the top of my shoulder and I stayed perfectly still as I listened for his footsteps on my wooden floor. My gun still rested in my hand and I was taking a chance by being a sitting duck, but if I wanted not to risk injury to Mary, I'd have to continue to play dead until he at least got far enough away from her for me to do anything.

His voice filled my ears and I tried making my breathing as light as possible.

"Your husband has been nothing but a nuisance since he came into our lives all those years ago. Things were never the same after he took Lily. Her actions when she returned ruined everything. You have no idea the pleasure I'm going to get out of this."

Footsteps had one of my eyes opening the slightest amount. Saul was still behind Mary, even more out of my sight. He moved in on the side of her, his fingers gripping her hip from behind. "And we'll get there very soon. But first..." He moved around, his face coming into view. My eye lowered, closing, and I knew he'd probably missed it. One footstep. Another. On the third, I opened my eye the smallest amount again and let them fly open as I caught his gun trained on me only a few feet away. I rolled more toward the wall closest to Mary and pointed away from her as my hand flew up and I pulled the trigger. Blood oozed from the wound in the front of his thigh and he buckled, falling to his knees. I shot at the gun, watching it fly from his hand and slide a few feet away on the floor.

"You were always pathetic when it came to anything but beating slaves. Now, *I'm* going to be the one to enjoy this."

I stood, keeping my weapon aimed at him as I grabbed his gun and put it at the small of my back. I walked over, untying the rope that restrained Mary. Her arms dropped and I caught her as her legs gave out. Grunts of pain left my uncle, but I ignored them as I steadied Mary.

"Are you okay?"

"I think so," she said, sniffling.

"Good. I need you to listen to me and follow my orders. Do you understand?"

Blonde hair swayed as she nodded and I untied her hands. She cried out as she tried to lift her hand to wipe away the tears.

"I need you to go sit down against the wall and not move until I come back out and get you. Do you think you can do that?"

Her eyes went to the back wall and then to my uncle. At her glare toward him, she nodded, confidently. "I'll be waiting. Take your time."

I almost smiled, but instead, I handed her the gun. "If anyone you don't know comes up, feel free to shoot them."

"Gladly."

I left her side and grabbed the rope. At me stalking forward, removing my shirt, Saul tried to crawl away. I placed my gun in the lining of my pants and weaved my fingers through his hair, jerking him up.

"No, don't do this. Zain, we're family. Zain."

I stuffed the bloody part of my shirt into his mouth, more punching my fingers into his mouth than anything. Saul gagged while I tied the cloth around his head.

"Yeah, we're family. Can you taste it, Uncle? They say blood is thicker than water, but I'll take water over bad blood any day." My palm flattened on his back and I pushed him toward the restroom with everything I had. The door exploded open at his force and he fell to the ground, catching his head on the sink on the way down. I stormed forward, grabbing for his shirt as I tossed him in the bathtub.

"Speaking of blood, I do believe you owe me some. Did you really think you could take my child away from me and live? Did you think I wouldn't find you and make you pay?"

I pulled out the knob, cranking the water to as hot as it would go. With his head toward the drain, I waited for the temperature to increase.

"The pain you're about to experience is nothing compared to what you've done to me or Lily, but I'm sure as hell going to try to make it as even as possible."

His shoulder-length hair floated in the pooling water, mixing with the blood that seeped from the deep laceration on the side of his head. I reached into my waistband and pulled out my knife, clicking it open. As I rose higher on my knees, my other hand grabbed at the shirt he was wearing. The blade slid easily through the material until his chest and stomach were exposed. His eyes went wide and I could tell he was still somewhat out of it from the fall. Muffled sounds filled the room and he began to thrash.

"Why don't we start where you caused the most pain for my slave." I slammed my hand over his mouth and plunged the tip of the blade into his lower stomach, slicing toward his navel. He screamed and I pushed harder on his mouth. "Do you think that's the sensation she felt when you repeatedly kicked and punched your fist into her stomach?" I narrowed my eyes. "No? How about this?"

Before I had only used maybe a half inch of the blade, but this time, I pushed in deeper, dragging up the other side. Scorching water burned my fingertips and I lifted my lip in disgust as I stared down at his struggling body.

"Perhaps I'm getting a little closer. If I remember correctly, which, trust me, I haven't forgotten a single bruise you placed on her body, I do believe you made sure to get her entire midsection. Let's take care of that area, too."

The constantly low-pitched screams surrounded me and I didn't take my eyes off of his while I lightly cut my way higher up his stomach. The blood made my hands slippery and I gripped tighter, using his body as resistance to get better grip.

"Oh, yes. This is definitely making me feel better. How do you feel, Uncle? Are you beginning to regret hurting Lily and all those poor girls? I hope what I'm doing to you isn't shit compared to what you're going to experience in hell."

"Whoa! Whoa! Whoa!" Hands were suddenly gripping my arms and pulling me to stand. I jerked against the restraint from behind, not ready to be finished. Gaige's voice barely filtered through, but all I saw was my knife floating in the water. Slowly, I lifted my gaze and watched Saul's eyes roll. He wasn't fighting anymore. Crimson soaked his stomach and chest. Spray littered the side of the tub. He'd bled so much that the little amount of water surrounding him was a mixture of light and dark red.

"Fuck," Gaige breathed out. "How the hell am I going to explain this?"

"You're not going to have to." Blake walked around the edge of the door, a smile pulling at the edge of his mouth as he stared down into the tub. "Nice work. I'm impressed. Although, I'd say you got a little carried away and made him bleed out a little too fast." He tilted his head and followed the steam up to the ceiling. "But the hot water was a nice touch."

Gaige let go, shaking his head. "Okay, we can compare later. Blake, call who you need to and...do your thing. Me, I'm getting Zain and Mary out of here."

Pounding footsteps had all of us looking over. Slade broke up the stairs, barely looking at us as he turned and rushed deeper in the room. Crying told me he made it to Mary and I was about to turn away when I saw Lily rush through the opening. Dark hair hung loosely from the pins and she wasn't wearing shoes. I could barely process what I was seeing before she was throwing herself into my arms.

"I thought you were hurt or..." She held me tighter and I wrapped my arms around her, wincing at the pain at the top of my shoulder and my side. Both were just nicks, but the stinging was hard to ignore.

"Wait." She pulled back, looking at my body. "You are hurt. Jesus."

"Shh." I pulled her back to me, but she looked up and into the tub.

"Oh…my God." A strangled sound left her and my stomach flipped. My hands spun her back to face me and I pulled her from the restroom as fast as I could.

"You don't need to see that. Come here, let me hold you. I was so scared when I heard about the shootings."

Lilian melted into my arms and I glanced up to see Slade holding Mary, but looking at me. I couldn't read his face. Couldn't even begin to decipher what he was thinking. In that moment, he could have hated me or been grateful and I wouldn't have been able to distinguish the emotion he was so good at hiding.

"Let's go home," Mary said, pulling back to glance up. It was enough to break Slade's stare.

"Of course. We'll get you home and have the doctor come over to check you out. Are you sure you're okay?" His finger traced her face and she nodded.

"I'm fine. I just want to go."

"The moment Marcio arrives, we will. Brace had to ditch the car we came in."

Gaige emerged from the restroom. "Come on, I'll take you. Blake needs to take care of things here and we shouldn't be in his way."

"It's okay. I'm responsible. I can stay." I held Lily tighter, giving her a squeeze before I stepped back.

"No," Slade ground out. "You're going. The doctor needs to check you out, too. Apparently, someone doesn't listen very well when they're told to wear their damn vest." At that moment, I knew. Slade didn't hate me. His expression softened and he shook his head, breaking his gaze and wrapping his arms around Mary as he buried his face in her hair.

As I looked down, Lily's eyebrows drew in and I could have cursed Slade for ratting me out. He'd probably done it on purpose.

"We'll talk about that later. Let's get you home." I looked over, nodding to Blake, a silent *thank you* I knew he caught. He returned the gesture and I grabbed a shirt, sliding it on. Gaige led the way down the stairs and I knew it was probably the last time I'd ever go down them. Lily wouldn't want to live here. She wouldn't want to take a shower in the only tub I had, where my uncle had been killed. I was going to have to start over again, but this time would be the last. No more rentals. No more prolonging what I knew I wanted. The next house would be purchased and it would be the one Lilian and I would come home to after our marriage. It would be the one we raised our children in. It would be the one we'd build the foundation of our new relationship on. My past was history now. It was time to start a new beginning. One with the woman I loved.

Chapter 47
Lily

Three months later.

Air burned my lungs as I raced through the crowded streets in my heels, dodging couples emerging from the packed Italian restaurant. No more guards. No more protection. In this moment, I was free. Unafraid of being hurt or alone. I'd come so far in the months that followed Saul's death. I felt unstoppable when it came to my confidence, but that barely registered in my impatience to make inside.

I slowed enough to weave around a man exiting and broke into the entrance, nearly sliding on the tile floors as I came to a stop. Stands of hair fell from my bun and I reached up, trying to pat it back.

"Robert's party, please." My breathless request was greeted with a smile from the hostess. I followed while she began to lead me through the tables, toward the back. Work...I'd been so caught up in the details of closing this newest deal, I'd completely forgotten to check the time.

We stepped through a door and a table of women looked up. Zain sat in the corner with Slade, Blake, and Gaige. My brother and boyfriend both smiled as I gave an apologetic expression. They had an all too knowing look on their face and I couldn't stop the guilt from making me rush forward. Mary stood from the table, her rounding stomach visible as the dress fell loose.

"I'm sorry I'm late. I tried to hurry."

She laughed while I came around to sit beside her. "You're only a few minutes late. It's okay. We were keeping ourselves occupied with stories. Elle was just telling us about her adventures with Connor when he was a toddler."

My smile grew as our eyes connected. Elle and I had become very close while working together at the foundation. Even Kaitlyn was present for the baby shower, although we were only just getting to know her. Our pain had brought us all together and it hadn't taken long for Mary or Blake's wife to want to help in any way they could. A chapter was being opened in Texas and we were determined to bring in more awareness in whatever way we could to what we all knew needed to be stopped.

"So, where do we begin?" I asked, grabbing a strawberry from the platter of fruit on middle of the table. "I'm dying to know if I'm having a niece or a nephew. The anticipation is killing me."

Mary glanced over to Slade, but turned back to all of us. "I was told we had to play a few games before we cut the cake. Don't worry, though, it's been driving me crazy, too. Slade and I have had to wait a week already. I can't believe we decided not to know until we saw the color inside of the cake. Whose idea was that again?"

"Mine," Kaitlyn said, laughing. "And it's a great thing to do. The torture will be well worth it when you learn what you're having."

"Agreed," Elle said, standing. "So, let's get started. I can't wait to find out either." She reached into a small bag and pulled out a clothespin, opening and closing it. "This, will be our first game. She grabbed what looked to be an old milk bottle from the table and walked over, setting it on the ground. "What you're going to do is hold the clothespin against the middle of your stomach, like so," she said, demonstrating. "And then, see if you can make it in the bottle. The one with the most wins a prize. Mary," she said, gesturing, "you're first."

Slade laughed as Mary walked around, took a handful of clothespins, and began letting them drop. One bounced off the rim and she closed one eye, trying to aim.

I grabbed another slice of fruit and leaned over the table to see better. One by one, she let them fall and everyone cheered when she dropped the fourth one inside.

"Great job!" Elle took out the clothespins and we all waited as the other nine women went. When it became my turn, I couldn't stop staring at Zain. The hunger in his eyes was undeniable. The last few weeks consisted of nothing but hello and goodbye as we both stayed extremely busy. But not by Slade's choice. By mine.

Something happened to me the day I saw Saul's stomach shredded. Zain's brutality hadn't scared me, but my curiosity regarding my brother's concerns did. I'd been in denial for so long about what Zain really did, I'd shut myself off to the possibility that he'd possibly need that sort of lifestyle. I knew I could accept it if he did. It was just who he was, but not knowing for sure was what held me back. Was he done with the darker side of his life or was killing something he had to do? So far, he'd buried himself in work at Slade Industries, and deep down, I knew it was going to last. The more I saw him learn and grow from the corporate world, the more I believed he'd found his passion. His determination was quickly moving him up the ladder, but no faster than anyone else putting in just as much work. He fought for everything. Stayed the long hours right beside me, volunteered for assignments...he was quickly making a name for himself.

"Three! Good job, Lily."

I laughed, glancing back up at my Master, who never broke his stare. It sent my heart thudding and my body burning for whatever he wished to do.

Elle pulled out a box and I tried to focus as the next game began, but I couldn't stop taking quick looks over to the table where Zain sat. He was leaned back in the chair, his dark suit accentuating his light eyes. The intensity had me blinking and glancing up at Elle as she had me draw a number from the box she held. I glanced down, repeating it as she moved on to the next person.

I grabbed a glass of water, sitting before me and took a big drink. The coolness traveled all the way down my stomach and I shivered. More from the sensitivity within me than anything. Even when I wasn't looking, I could feel my Master's eyes on me. My hand came down, pulling at the black, knee-length dress and I paused, gripping at the hem. Flashbacks of Zain cornering me in the kitchen had me shifting in my chair as I remembered back.

"You're avoiding me." The top half of my body was pushed over the top of the counter from the flat of his palm. I had immediately moaned as his fingers traced up the back of my thigh, pushing under my dress until he teased over the lace covering my pussy. "You keep doing that, by the time I get my hands on you, you might come to regret it. Fuck, slave, I want you so bad."

Talking through the hallway had cut our episode short, and that was four days ago.

"Is it almost time?" Mary glanced over at the cake and Elle handed Kaitlyn a length of string.

"Almost. Last game. Now," Elle stretched out the length in her hand. "I'm going to walk around and everyone needs to cut the string where you think it'll wrap around Mary's stomach. The closest to the actual fit will win."

I grabbed the scissors as she came to me first and stretched the string out, looking over at Mary and trying to imagine the perfect size. I moved closer in, seeing that she wasn't that big. Not yet.

"There." I smiled placing the rope on the table while everyone else had their turn. Squeals and heavy laughter had me feeling lighter. I watched while everyone came to wrap their piece around her. There were a few that came close, but when I moved in to check mine, my jaw dropped and I raised my eyebrows.

"Winner," Elle said, handing me a baby rattle. "Great job, Lily." She handed me a lighter. Would you like to do the honors? I think we're all ready to see the big surprise."

I took the lighter as Slade came over with Mary to stand beside me. The flame flickered and I watched the wax melt from the wick, sliding down toward the icing. My stare became trapped for the slightest moment as memories of Zain and I with the wax exploded in my mind. Just as I glanced up, he stood, coming forward. Slowly, I lifted, stepping back so my brother and Mary could take their place.

"Again," Zain whispered, coming in behind me and pulling back against him. "Tonight."

Swallowing was almost impossible as I nodded and stared ahead. Slade and Mary both lowered, blowing out the candle. Their hands connected over the knife and I smiled while they eased it down. Laughter shot out and Mary giggled as her excitement shone through. They drew the handle back and wedged the slice. Silence filled the room and Mary let go, letting Slade lift the piece.

Cheers erupted and my hand shot to my mouth as I laughed. "Pink!" More than one person yelled it and Mary began clapping as Slade's eyes widened in shock.

"Congrats," I said, stepping forward and throwing my arms around Mary and then my brother.

"Oh shit," he breathed out. "We're having a girl?"

"A girl," I assured. My tone rose in pitch and I couldn't withhold my excitement. "I'm going to have a niece!" I hugged him again and stepped back as Gaige slapped his shoulder, laughing. A million expressions crossed his face while I settled back against Zain. I watched, soaking it all in as my Master wrapped his arms around me from behind. The smell of his cologne brought me to a blissful state of mind and I couldn't imagine the moment being anymore perfect. Aside from keeping things slow, the last three months had been heaven. I hadn't had any more flashbacks. The foundation I volunteered at left me with a sense of purpose and each moment with Zain was full of passion and want. And it didn't even have to do with the sex. The smallest gesture of his hand down my face as he smiled lovingly was enough. I knew my future was set with him. Our love was stronger than ever and it was time for me to let things play out without holding back.

Mary took turns hugging the girls that came up and Slade was beginning to have a smile on his face. I knew my brother. It would take time to sink in. He was afraid of having a girl from what he went through with Mary and me, but that little girl was going to have a wonderful father and she'd have Slade wrapped around her finger from the moment she was born. From the way he stretched out his hand to fit over Mary's stomach as she conversed, maybe she already did.

"What a beautiful moment," Zain said against my ear. "I'm so glad I get to be a part of all this."

I turned in his arms, outstretching mine to fit around his neck. "Slade told you long ago that you were part of this family. Do you feel it?"

"More than you know." Zain's forehead came to rest against mine and I closed my eyes, savoring our moment.

"I miss you. Stay with me tonight, and not just for dinner. I want to show you something."

My eyes fluttered open and I pulled back to meet his gaze. "Show me something?"

A smile pulled at the edge of his lips. "If you think you can handle it."

Immediately, my fingers clutched his suit jacket. Arousal swept through me and I felt myself get wet.

"Anything for you. I mean that." I studied the way his eyes narrowed. "Anything. I can handle it."

"I know." He turned me around before we could say any more. His arm went back around my chest and his face lowered next to mine as we watched everyone celebrate. With all the cheers and conversation happening, I barely heard a thing. All I could see and hear was what my imagination was supplying me with. Hot, passionate, *dark* fantasies. Ones I hoped came to life tonight.

Chapter 48
Zain

Shadows followed Lily and me along the brick building as we turned from the restaurant and faced the alleyway that led to the parking lot. She paused and slowed in her steps, glancing back at me as I came to a stop. My hands went into my pockets and I motioned my head, not saying a word. She looked back at the darkness and slowly advanced forward, alone. A smile pulled at my lips and I watched her disappear from view.

Leather was smooth against my fingertips as I pulled out the gloves and slid them on. I cut to the side, closest along the wall. It took a few seconds for her to come into focus, but she stayed in the middle, holding her arms as she walked faster toward the dim light that rested further ahead.

I kept my footsteps quiet and my breathing light as I advanced. Something rattled to her left and she jumped, moving even faster. The thin rope sitting in my inside pocket called to me and I came up closer on her side, knowing she wouldn't be expecting what I had planned. My gloved hand clamped over her mouth while my arm hooked around her waist, pulling her ass back to press against my hard cock. A muffled cry was followed by a moan as her surprise turned into lust. I grinded hard against her, lowering to breathe against her ear.

"Tonight, you're going to be tested more than you ever have. Keep that safeword ready because you just might need it."

My hand lowered and I fingered the material of her dress that rested just where her thighs connected. Heavy breaths left her nose and I pushed between her legs, bringing the length of my fingers to rub the distance of her slit. Harder, I pushed, applying more pressure to her clit as I turned to cup her pussy.

"You don't know badly I've missed touching you." I moved up, dipping past the lining of her panties. Moans vibrated my hand and I lowered the top part of my body more into her back, having her bend over. My finger plunged inside of her entrance and the slickness from her juices was so abundant, I heard myself moan along with her. Tightness hugged my gloved finger and I added another, letting her stretch around me as I teased her channel. "You like this, baby girl?"

A swift nod of her head had me thrusting faster. Her hand flew up to my arm that covered her mouth and she clung to me as I pounded into her.

"This is just the beginning."

Continuous sounds grew louder until she was spasming beneath me. My teeth sank into her shoulder with enough pressure to cause her to jerk. "I don't think I gave you permission to come, slave. You're going to have to pay for that." I withdrew my fingers, twisted her panties in my fist, and jerked to the side. The lining broke free and I did the other side, pulling them off and stuffing them in my pocket.

Silk slid between my concealed fingers and I pulled out the two pieces I had brought with me. I dropped my hand from her mouth and stood long enough to bring it around her face.

"Open."

The pause was followed by her lips separating. I pushed the silk through and tied the length behind her head.

"Close your eyes. We're going for a little ride."

Lily tried to say something, but failed with the gag. I didn't wait. I placed the other piece over her eyes and fastened it.

"I'm going to pick you up. Stay quiet and don't move." I swept her into my arms and walked swiftly toward the car. Lily's weight curled into me and my pulse spiked at how trusting she was. Nervousness surfaced and I tried to push it away. I knew she was okay now, but I had never gone as far as I was about to. And that wasn't even my biggest concern of the night. She might be able to take my dark side, but would she want everything I had to give when she learned what we'd all conspired while she was busy working?

I reached into my pocket, pulling out the keys. As I approached, I scanned the area, making sure no one was watching. I placed Lily down next to the passenger side door. The moment I opened it, I pulled out the rope and crouched down. The black stockings drew me in and I pressed my lips just above her knee. Once I started, I couldn't dare break myself away without getting to taste her first. My gloved hands pushed under the sides of her dress, lifting the fabric up as I advanced toward her bare pussy. The shaking of her body didn't stop her from spreading her legs for me.

"Good girl," I whispered, swirling my tongue over the skin just above the lace lining. Juices met my tongue the higher I went and I nearly growled at how my control was slipping. In that moment, I knew nothing but my slave. Her taste was an addiction of its own and it fed my need for her with each stroke of my tongue. I used the tip to separate her folds and my fingers gripped the outside of her thighs tightly. I couldn't help but suck her into my mouth. I was desperate for as much of her as I could get. If I missed any of her essence, I'd become a lost man. It had been too fucking long, but here wasn't the place. I wanted her home. To our home. Lilian had no idea and I couldn't wait to surprise her.

"You're in so much trouble, baby. God dammit." I pulled down her dress and unknotted the rope, looping it around her legs. When I finished, I rose, grasping her wrists and doing the same. When she was secured, I placed her in the seat and buckled her in.

Lilian's scent was all I could smell as I climbed in. It was taunting me to take her right there and now. With her defenseless in my ropes, I couldn't remember wanting anything so much. My eyes closed and I couldn't help myself. I reached under my seat and grabbed my knife. The flick of my wrist had Lily's head turning toward me, but knowing she couldn't see what was coming drove me on even more.

"Don't. Move."

I licked my lips, lowering the tip of the blade to snag at her stockings. The material gave way and a sound left her. It had my eyes lifting for the briefest moment, but I couldn't resist lowering back to what I was doing. The higher I got, the faster she breathed. My cock ached at the restraint of my pants and I groaned, lifting the hem of her dress. The sharpness caused the thick cotton to split and I kept moving higher until a good three inches exposed what I wanted to see.

"Jesus…fuck." I made circles over her skin with the tip and she moaned loudly as I went to the other leg. The stocking there snagged and I pulled upward, bringing the material further from her limb. The small hole tore and I brought the edge up. I shut the knife and returned it, reaching for the stocking and shredding it with my hands. As I kneaded the skin just above her knee, my eyes went back to her pussy. Dammit, I couldn't wait to return to taste what was about to truly belong to me. My hand came out and I angled her more toward me. She didn't move as I started the car and pulled out of the parking lot. Focusing on traffic was almost impossible. Red lights had me forgetting to check when it turned to green. The way the city lights played across her face was hypnotizing. I was a gone man. A man in love so deep, he was drowning in the sensation.

I exited the freeway, turning into an upscale suburban neighborhood. My heart hammered in my chest while I took in the two story homes. It had taken me weeks to find the perfect place. Not just one I could bring my future wife to, but a home where I could raise a family. When I found this one, I just knew. Just like I had known Lily was the one for me from the beginning. The voice inside said Lily would adore it and for a large house, it spoke of a place we could grow into. One with new beginnings. One built on love and memories.

I hit the garage door open and pulled inside, closing it behind me. My BMW I'd kept hidden away was parked next to us and I turned off the car, walking around and lifting her out. When I opened the door and walked us inside, the smell of lavender had me smiling. It smelled like Lily, one of the first memories I had of her. Even then, the small trace left an unforgettable impression. My hand reached up and I flipped on the light, lowering her to the ground.

"I'm going to take this off now." I removed the gag and edged my fingers under the silk covering her eyes, pushing up. Lily squinted and blinked a few times before she began to scan the open kitchen and living room area.

"It's beautiful. Where are we?" she asked, lowly.

I smiled. "Home. Our home. It's time."

Her eyes widened and her lips separated as her head spun back to take in the surroundings. "Ours?"

"If you want it." I lowered, untying the rope at her feet. As I removed her heels, she stepped down, only to kneel, becoming level with me. Her head bowed and she leaned forward, resting her head against my chest. Her fingers pulled at my jacket, brining me in closer.

"I want it. I would...love to live here with you."

I took off the gloves and cupped her face, making her look at me. "Good, because I've already had your stuff moved in. Slade helped, of course."

A broken sob had her turning more into me and I drew her face toward mine, letting our lips connect and massage into each other's until I couldn't stop the hunger from breaking through the tenderness. "From here on out, it's me and you, baby girl. Our life begins now. Whatever we want. First, I think there's something we need to get out of the way."

Gray eyes rose to mine. "Yes," she whispered. "I'm ready. Show me *everything*."

Chapter 49
Lily

"Kneel."

The dim light that surrounded us gave way to only three main things — cuffs mounted next to the back wall, a large X that rested to the right, and a black leather table with three red straps over the top of it, to the left. Tools aligned the wall next to the X, and toys and candles rested on a shelf just to the side of the table. At the sight, I couldn't stop the excitement that slammed into me. This was my Master's deepest desires, what he loved above all else when it came to sex. and he was finally going to share it with me.

As I lowered to my knees in the center of the room, I bowed my head and waited for his instruction. Would he put me in the cuffs, something I knew to be his favorite thing? Or would he take a new route tonight?

"I'm not going to start off slow or try to break you into what I want. I think you're already. Our trust in each other is going to be what we'll use. You know what to do if it becomes too much. Let me hear you agree before we start."

I blinked past what I knew was about to come. This wasn't going to be easy missionary style stuff. The taste in the alley, the night with the wax when he told me he liked when I fought, it was all meant to prepare me for what was to come. And I knew it wasn't going to be tame, like some of the other stuff he'd done with me. I had to be completely sure. And I was.

"I agree."

Without acknowledgement, the lights suddenly went out, leaving me in absolute darkness. My head shot up and I felt my eyes go wide. Movement ceased to exist. Table, toys…nothing remained of the once room that hinted of sex. The only thing I knew was me—my deep breathing, brought on by fear, the hair that tickled my face from the strands that continued to escape, and…God, the rope that kept my hands from being able to defend myself. I swallowed hard, pulling at the hemp, knowing it was pointless to try to break free. The knots were too tight and he wanted me to have a reason to fight. I saw the way he stared at the training I continued to do. What wicked thoughts he must have harbored while seeing me try to protect myself, fantasizing on what he could be doing to me if he had been on the other side.

I nearly moaned at the thought, but instincts had me pushing to my feet. Staying low was critical. As I moved across the room, I tried to stay as quiet as possible. It didn't take long for my senses to heighten and the thrill of the situation to make me grow wet. Although I knew pain would come at some point, I thrived under the new pressure. We both may have never have to use our skills again against anyone else, but here, we had our release. Him, for the skilled killer that lived within. Me, the survivor. I suddenly realized that he'd feared me experiencing this…but he was so wrong. I needed this as much as he did. Here, I was safe. With him, I could be the real me. The one I hid from the world.

My bound hands came out in front of me and I pointed my fingers out, feeling for the wall I knew lay ahead somewhere. Clinking had me jerking them back as I recalled the cuffs hanging from the large X on the right side of the room. I cursed myself for not being as low as I had assumed. I turned, heading in the other direction. Out of nowhere, arms locked around me from behind and I stomped my foot down, turning and using my bound arms to aim for where I assumed his stomach was. A hand grabbed my wrists and fingers locked in my hair, pulling me forward. Lips crushed into mine and I yelped at the hard pull.

"Good, but not good enough, slave." He let go of my hand and I cried out at the fire that raced over my spanked ass. "I could fucking have you right here. Is that what you want?" Fingers gripped my flesh and he used it to bring me more into his cock. I didn't answer as I pushed hard against his chest and tucked back. The air left my lungs as I hit the ground, but I immediately began rolling away. The moment I got back to my feet, I brought my hands back out and walked at a faster pace. It felt like forever before I came into contact with a wall. I slid down, twisting my arms inside of the rope. I almost gasped as it gave way and more space became available. I wiggled faster and knew I was making too much noise, but I was too close to being free. Hands hit the wall above me and my surge forward had the ropes falling to my fingers. I did the only thing I knew. I wrapped it around both of my palms, leaving enough in the middle to use as a weapon.

"My safeword also applies to you, right?" I spoke, but continued to move around the room as I said it.

"Oh, I won't be needing a safeword, slave. But if it makes you feel better, sure."

I tried not to smile. Maybe I shouldn't have been enjoying myself so much, but for once, I was truly free and I loved it.

My shoulder connected with the wall and I stepped back, right into another. I spun, shooting my hands up, but it wasn't where I had intended. Zain grabbed the rope and with one pull and the hemp burned my palms. Before I knew it, my plan was being reversed. I reached for the pressure that shot around my neck and moved with him as he led me forward. The wetness of his tongue traced over my lips, even as the rope tightened. Rules ceased to exist in that moment. My hands came up to his neck and I pulled him in harder, adding my own pressure, but not to his throat…to the pressure point that had him jerking back from pain.

I broke free, only to be tackled to the ground. We hit hard and he pulled the rope free, covering my body with his. Fabric from the split in my dress tore under his hands. The sound of his buckle was like music to my ears, and I grabbed his face, kissing him as he began to tear at his own clothes. Just when I thought we were about to start something even hotter, he disappeared. I pushed to my knees and my hand flew up as the light came back on. By the time I adjusted, I barely caught his nude, powerful body stalking toward me. His hand shot out and he pulled me up, spinning me around to unzip my dress. My bra was unfastened with a snap of his fingers, leaving me even more impatient for us to continue.

"Take it off and go to the cross."

With a whoosh, my dress and bra fell to the ground. I didn't have to be told what the cross was. But with each step, I felt the fear coming back. Not from what he'd do, but from the unknown. I pushed it away and came to stand before it. I was only able to stare for a few seconds before his hand pressed on the middle of my back, leading me forward.

"Hands up, feet apart."

I obeyed and stood still as he placed the cuffs around each of my limbs. I reached up, gripping the length of chain that would come to hold me captive to his darkness.

Leather traced up the back of my thigh and I closed my eyes, waiting for whatever it was my Master needed. The path led over my ass and up the small of my back, only to double down and head back to my other thigh. Over and over, he let me get used to the tool he'd chosen. When I completely relaxed, I felt it disappear and then come down over my ass with a bite I hadn't expected. I tensed and let the sting register. Another followed. And another, right next to the first two. I gasped as the fourth connected.

"Oh, slave. Only in my dreams have I ever gotten this far." A hand trailed down my side and I felt him lower, placing his lips against the dull throb. At the swirl of his tongue, I gripped tighter to the chains.

"Arch your hips for me, baby girl."

I didn't have to hear the command twice. The moment I gave him full access to my pussy, his mouth sucked onto my folds. I cried out, moving the slightest bit as his tongue flicked over my clit, repeatedly. Deep breaths left me and the burn that took over was one I needed more of, but was quickly denied.

Zain stood and the pleasure turned to an even more intense set of strikes. *Whack! Whack! Whack!*

Scorching heat poured from my thighs and I sobbed past the shock.

"Are you supposed to move?"

"No, Master."

"But you did. And you came in the ally when I didn't give you permission. Didn't you?"

My head moved before I could even speak. "Yes, Master."

"And now you're getting your punishment." He moved in closer. "But you know I love you. And you'll take this, because you love me."

"Yes," I moaned, as his finger slid inside me. The thrusts were slow and deep. They explored without any sense of urgency. I could feel myself being brought back up and I didn't care that he was about to knock me back down. The caressing of my G-spot had me not worrying about anything but the ecstasy I was experiencing.

The hand holding the crop came to the front of me and his other left my channel. As he gripped the handle on one side, he reached up, taking the other end and placing the length under my chin, angling my head back.

"Acting tough when things are past your threshold is a true sign of weakness. You are *not* weak. You call red if you need it. If you don't, you will ruin what we have here before we even get a chance to enjoy it. I can say I know your threshold all day long, but in truth, I can only push you to what I think you can take. You hold the control now, Lilian. Use it wisely."

He stepped back and I gripped tightly as the first set of strikes landed along the top of my back. I noticed he avoided certain areas. Ones I was sure weren't supposed to be hit. His knowledge gave me strength. With each slap of the leather, more tears fell, but never because I couldn't take it. He wasn't hitting anywhere near as hard as I knew he could. What he released with each blow was something I didn't even know I needed freeing. I could feel myself become lighter. Better within myself.

The stinging moved down to my thighs, only heightening the previous strikes to my ass and back. They eased the further down he got and suddenly, I felt more alive than ever. My whole body tingled and burned. In that moment, everything changed. I wanted more. I knew the punishment had ended and what he was giving me now was the good that could come out of his passion.

"You did so well." Fingers moved in circles over my pussy and I held still as he teased over my opening. I licked my lips and turned my face toward him. His eyes met mine and I held his stare.

"Master, maybe it's time we moved on to something I know you want."

His eyes narrowed the smallest amount. "What's that?"

"I've had plenty of time to work myself in for you."

He paused and his eyebrows rose. "Your ass?"

Slowly, I nodded. "I think I can take you. I've been...preparing."

Fingers gripped my cheek as he stepped in and held my face still. With gentle bites, he nipped at my bottom lip, moaning as he pushed his hard cock into my lower back. His fingers teased my clit and I couldn't stop from pulling at my hands. "You make me so happy," he whispered against my cheek. "I'm going to be gentle and fuck your ass so good. You're going to love it, slave. I'm going to make you want it all the time."

"Prove it to me," I moaned. "Master."

"Oh, I'm going to prove it to you alright." He left me, moving to the back of the room. When he returned, his hand was already covered with lube. He sat the bottle on the shelf by the tools and circled over my back entrance.

"Relax, baby."

My lids lowered and I let the darkness consume me. I felt the tension leave and my Master's finger eased inside at a leisurely pace. The sensation was one I'd gotten used to. Even enjoyed. I breathed out as he withdrew to the tip and eased another in. I tightened for the briefest moment before I went lax again.

"There we go." He got to the first knuckle and let me adjust, moving even deeper when I didn't resist. "Oh…fuck." His fingers buried inside of me and moved out, only to thrust in again. The rhythm quickly had me building. Especially with the attention he continued to give the front of my slit. The pressure teasing my clit left me damn near sobbing.

"Please."

"Please, what? God, say it. Let me hear you speak the words I've longed to hear."

My eyes opened and I met his stare. "Fuck my ass. Let me feel your cock this time. Not some toy. I want the real thing. I want you."

Zain's eyes closed and he leaned forward, kissing my shoulder. With that, he withdrew his fingers, disappearing. He was back an instant later and I heard a condom package tear. The kissing continued across my back like he'd never left at all. My body flared back to life. The pads of his fingers began rubbing over my pussy again and I took slow breaths as pressure pushed against the opening of my ass. His width was more than I had taken, but he was being careful, taking his time to inch his way in.

"Almost there. You have no idea how amazing you feel." He withdrew, taking away some of the burning and at his advance, I held my orgasm at bay.

The impossible wave that tried to force its way out left me trembling.

"Hold on, tight, baby girl, this may hurt a little."

I barely could process his words before he broke into uncharted territory. I gasped and a sound broke free of my lips. Zain held me tightly through the moan he let out against my neck.

"Fuck, I love you." His teeth bit into arm and I gasped. "Now, the pleasure really begins."

He didn't have to tell me. At his thrusts, I quickly found myself become louder by the second. My legs twitched and at the suction over the junction of my neck and shoulder, I quickly began begging.

"Let me come. Master, I have to come." My body was pushing down to take him in faster, even against the resistance of his grip.

"Hold that orgasm off a little longer." His hand rose and he pinched my nipple until I was crying out. The lack of attention to my clit had me sobbing. Twisting in my stomach left it aching to be built up to where I needed to be once again. The thrusts became harder. Faster. Coolness drizzled over my ass and I knew he was applying more lube. The slickness and ease had me screaming as he went even harder.

"Please," I sobbed. "I need…"

"What I give you. Nothing more."

Zain collected my hair in a ponytail and pulled back until I was arched and his mouth kissed mine. "You're my slave. Say it."

"I'm yours," I rushed out.

"That's right. Only *now* can you come. Never again without me hearing you speak those words."

He continued to hold my head back while he began teasing my clit. Within seconds, my orgasm had my legs going out from under me. If it weren't for Zain holding me up and continuing to pound into me, I would have dropped to the floor. Teeth pulled at my bottom lip, only breaking away when his language changed. I couldn't understand what he said through the pounding of my pulse, but his cock swelling left me not caring.

"Slave." A deep sound vibrated my body and he squeezed as his release left him holding to me tighter. I could barely move by the time he pulled out. Shortly thereafter, he unbuckled the cuffs and when I attempted to take a step, my legs wouldn't work. He swept me into his arms, holding me close. "I told you this might happen."

"You did. And it was worth it."

My words almost slurred as the home blurred by. I curled into his sweaty body, basking in knowing that this was where we'd live. My dreams were coming true and it almost felt surreal. From the steps, I knew we were going upstairs, but nothing else registered aside from the happiness giving me butterflies. I forced my eyes open as we came to a stop in a dim, large master bathroom.

A large round tub sat in the back, next to a glass shower. Deep red rugs lay throughout, but I could barely focus on the details as I winced from the pain of him sitting me on the edge of the tub. He looked over uneasily, but I nodded that I was okay. The water began feeling the tub and he stared while he tested the temperature. As it began to fill, he reached over, lighting candles that sat along the side. When only the glow surrounded us, he helped me in, lowering me to sit in front of him as he moved me up to cradle into his lap.

"How bad do you hurt?"

I knew not to lie. The pain was there, but not more than my happiness. "How much do you love me?"

A smile pulled at his mouth. "More than I think you'll ever truly know. There's not a cap on the way I feel for you. It's too deep to put into words. But know that it's great." His wet hand came up, brushing back the hair from my face. "How much do you love me?"

My mouth twisted and I searched for the right thing to say. "You're right. There's no words to describe it. I love you enough to know that what I feel will never fade. You're the one for me, Master. You always have been."

"And I always *will be*," he said, kissing my forehead. "But what do you say we make it official?" His arm outstretched toward one of the candles and I raised my head, watching as he pulled a ring out from behind one of them. My eyes snapped to his and I could feel my lips part from the shock.

"You planned this? Even up to this part?"

The smile grew. "We all did, in a way. Your brother helped me pick out the ring. Mary said I should do it with candlelight. But now the rest is up to you." He brought the ring level with my face. I could feel his heart pounding underneath me and blindly reached up, tracing over the scar on his chest. He'd died for me, and now he was wanting to spend the rest of his second chance by my side.

"There's no one else for me, Lilian." He licked his lips and the emotion in his eyes had tears coming to mine. "Marry me. Be mine for real this time. No longer just my slave, but my wife. I'd do anything for you. Let me do that as your husband."

My head was nodding and I held my hand toward him, trying my hardest not to break down. "Yes." The answer barely got out before his mouth crushed into mine. The weight of the ring slid onto my finger and I immediately brought my hand over to cup his face. I pulled back, looking at the light and shadows flicker over his face. The diamond sparkled and I almost couldn't stop the sobs that wanted to escape. "Is this happening?"

"Oh yeah," he said, pulling me in to straddle his hips and meet his lips. "You're mine now, for the world to see. Forever."

From years of pain came love and pleasure. The strength behind our emotions had stayed true, only building over time. Trials and tribulation had tried to break both of us, but we didn't give up or stop fighting to survive. And most importantly, we never forgot our love of one another, even when we were made to believe it was wrong. We may have met under unfortunate circumstances, but I wouldn't have traded what I suffered if it meant I didn't have my Master. He was mine, and I…was his. Officially.

The End.

About the Author

Alaska is an erotic BDSM author who also goes by the pen names Jennifer Salaiz and Jenny May. She lives in the SF Bay area...for now. She's a dreamer, and longs for the day when her husband and kids can load up in the car and drive until their hearts' content. Adventure and discovering new places play a huge role in Alaska's life. It drives her, and feeds the creativity of coming up with new locations for her stories.

Within the last two years, Alaska and her family have drove across the country twice, and also drove the distance from Texas to California three times. Asked, if she could choose one place to permanently settle down, where it would be, Alaska laughed. "Montana, today. Tomorrow, it may be Alaska, again. I go back and forth."

When Alaska's not dreaming of spontaneously hitting the road to find a new place to write about, she's being a mother and wife. If you're looking to connect with her to learn more, feel free to email her at alaska_angelini@yahoo.com, or find her on Facebook. You can also stop by her website jennymayauthor.com.

Are you a Dark
Paranormal fan?
Coming Soon!

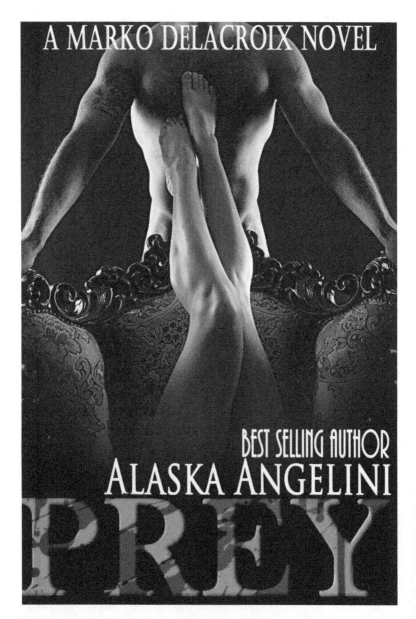

A MARKO DELACROIX NOVEL

BEST SELLING AUTHOR
ALASKA ANGELINI

PREY

Also look out for…

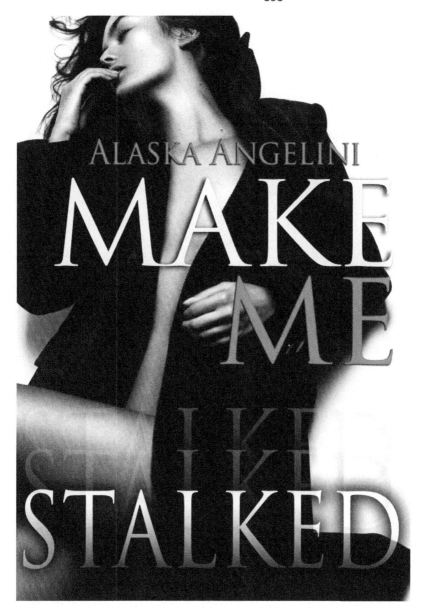

ALASKA ANGELINI

MAKE
ME
LIKE
STALKED

Made in the USA
Middletown, DE
11 September 2024

60649157R00335